THE PRINCE'S SONG

LAURA VANARENDONK BAUGH

ÆCLIPSE PRESS

THE PRINCE'S SONG

THE EYES OF MANDORAL
BOOK 2

LAURA VANARENDONK BAUGH

NEGOTIATIONS

CHAPTER 69

LISVETH LIFTED THE AMULET to look it in the golden eye. "I hope this thing works as well as we think."

Galen shifted his weight restlessly, realized what he was doing, and crossed his arms to try to keep himself still. "I'm not really comfortable with you doing this."

"Are you going to try to stop me?"

"No, because we both know that would be a waste of time. But I'm going to tell you I'm worried about it."

She lowered the amulet and faced him. "The whole point of this is that I'm not supposed to get into a fight. If it goes well, they won't even know that I'm there."

"And if it doesn't go as well as you hope?"

"Then I will have to fight my way out. Using my magic with which I somehow kept myself safe before I ever met you." She lifted her chin and pushed her blonde hair over her shoulder.

Galen gave her a skeptical look. "The magic you admit is not up to this Kayvin's level?"

She looked a little less confident. "Then I'll need to avoid a fight. Which is my first plan."

Galen raised his hands in surrender. "Fine. I can't argue with that brilliant rhetoric. You've got it all covered." He tried to keep his tone light, but irritated worry bled through.

Lisveth sighed. "I appreciate your concern, but this is the best way. If we can determine their goals, learn what is driving them over the mountains, we can shorten the fighting, or maybe even avoid it altogether. That's hundreds or thousands of people saved. That's worth risking a single night of espionage."

"Why you?"

"Because I'm the best at illusions, so I'll be the least visible even before we add this—whatever it's called." She lifted the amulet again. "And if this really does make the wearer less noticeable, then I should be all but invisible to Kayvin." She settled the amulet about her neck.

A squawking made Galen look at the window, but it was only a bird. Maybe it was establishing territory. Odd, it wasn't the right season. Sometimes birds could just squawk, he supposed. But—

Something touched his arm. Oh! He'd nearly forgotten Lisveth. Right; she'd put on the amulet and his attention had slid from her. He blinked at her, trying to focus.

Lisveth came back into clear view, the amulet chain in her hand. "There has to be a more convenient way to activate these. We should do some experimenting. Anyway, besides all that, we're being paid. It took a cartload of haggling, but in the end the general agreed to twenty taler."

At the price, Galen nearly lost his stern expression, but he managed to hold it. "And do we know the amulet will work even against him? The Rideis have different magic than we do, right?"

Lisveth poked him in the chest. "You are just a delightful comfort to me, dear partner. Such a comfort." She shrugged into a jacket and buckled it, pulling up the hood against the autumn cold. "I don't know when I'll be back. It will depend on what he's saying and whether it's interesting."

"Don't take any unnecessary risks," Galen cautioned.

"You know me. I never gamble unless the odds are overwhelmingly in my favor, and then preferably if I've cheated." She smiled and headed for the door. "Good night."

Galen watched the door close behind her and heard her feet upon the stairs. He counted to fifty before following her.

She was still visible as she exited the front door, and that was the only reason Galen could catch up with her. He had just stuck his head outside, hoping to spot her without her spotting him, when she stepped into the shadow of an overhanging roof and her outline faded in the dark. Galen drew his own cloak about himself and set off in the same direction, repeating his destination in a tight whisper in case the amulet's effect stretched to him over the distance.

Traffic dropped off in the twilight, but not so much that she would be suspicious of anyone on the road behind her. He squinted in the dusk, catching glimpses of her on the road but losing her again almost immediately. Whether due to her natural illusion ability or the amulet's aid, she was difficult to notice even with his certain knowledge of her. An unsuspecting bystander would never note her passing.

The tavern at the end of the stock market was The Selk's Head, and Galen could not quite decide if that should be ominous or amusing. He did not see Lisveth enter, but he assumed she slipped inside as others were entering or leaving, since there was a steady stream of patrons through the door. He caught the door as a tradeswoman left and went inside.

The Selk's Head was lit with candles, lamps, and an open fire at one end, but not extravagantly so, and Galen judged it a good place for Rideis and human spies to hide their features. He'd planned to station himself in some out-of-the-way corner and wait, just in case she was discovered, but the inconsistent light would make Lisveth's stealth even easier than they had anticipated. He wondered for a moment if he should give up his surveillance and leave her alone. But a group closed in front of the door, talking and hugging and enthusing about some common joy, and he slipped to one side to wait for the exit to clear.

The table to his right was mostly available, just one man slouched with three empties on the table before him. Galen decided at least two of them belonged to the reclining patron, or possibly all three, and took the empty place on the bench beside him. He gave a friendly smile to the slouching man, who nodded back, and the two of them leaned back against the wall.

Galen let his half-closed eyes skim the public room, searching for signs of Lisveth. He did not see her, but his heart jumped when he realized Kayvin was sitting just a few paces to his right. A woman—the same who had pulled him away from their fight, Galen supposed, though he did not want to look again to be sure—was sitting across from him.

His palms and neck began to sweat. He would never have chosen a seat so close to their targets.

Galen turned his face to the left and leaned his head back, so he was looking away from them. He realized he could hear their words below the general buzz, reflected by the wall behind him. He adjusted his ear to catch them better.

"I don't like this," the woman said.

"I know you don't," Kayvin answered her. "But it's necessary."

"It's dangerous. What if they see you?"

"They won't see me."

Galen fought a smile at the familiar debate. *Know your enemy as yourself, they say.*

"Let me go with you," she urged. "It's no more of a risk. They know your face better than mine."

She had a point.

Kayvin must have nodded in agreement or permission, for she continued, "If it goes poorly, and if there's any killing to be done, let me do it."

Galen stopped smiling.

"I can handle it better than you, my lord. You're a good prince, but you're a bad murderer. Your heart's too kind. You'll hesitate, and that could lose everything."

"I won't hesitate," Kayvin protested, sounding like a small boy insisting he could use an outhouse by himself.

"Like you did not hold back when I dragged you away from those bandit-chasers?"

"I told you, I hit him. He might have had one of the protecting amulets."

"And that makes sense, yes, that a bounty hunter in bedraggled clothes would carry one of the seven great artifacts of the previous age. Far more probable than you not wanting to kill a man you admit you liked."

Kayvin's voice dropped a few notes. "Yovela, you speak with great privilege. Don't endanger that."

"I speak only so that you will not endanger yourself, my lord."

"Heh. What are you now, my bodyguard?"

"Someone must be. The prince should not be wandering in hostile territory unprotected."

"Bodyguards are for those who need to be preserved," Kayvin said, his voice freshly bitter. "Pasiphae Jade does not care if I come back alive, only that the amulets come to her. If she could acquire them without me, she would."

Galen closed his eyes and tried frantically to sort these facts in his mind. Kayvin, though a prince, served someone called Pasiphae Jade, who had the power to command the prince and who wanted the amulets. This woman Yovela served the Rideis prince.

There was a pause, long enough to make Galen first wonder if they had noticed him and then to suspect that when Yovela finally spoke, it was to broach a topic she knew they would argue over. "You know she's lying to you."

"Don't," Kayvin warned.

"You can't lie to yourself, too. She knows she is alive only because she holds your mother's life as collateral. She cannot afford to release her and let you both live."

"Enough!" snapped Kayvin. "I have to do this. Do you understand? I have to."

"You are a prince. You have to do what is best for your kingdom."

"And right now, that seems to be to follow Pasiphae Jade's orders, as she is the only one who claims to know how to counter the spawning. Can you argue against that?"

Yovela was silent.

Galen's mind spun. Pasiphae Jade had Kayvin's mother as hostage. What might this mean for stopping the Rideis? And what was the spawning?

A man stopped at Galen's table and collected the empty cups. "Anything for you?" he asked amiably.

Galen flinched, afraid he'd draw the eyes of the nearby Rideis. He needed a quick order to end conversation with the serving man. "An ale," he said quietly, keeping his face turned away from the other table. "Thanks."

The serving man left, and Galen had missed some of their exchange. "In, amulet, out," Yovela was saying. "I understand. Simple. Right up until they realize you're trying to steal one of the most valuable objects in their country."

"It's the only one we know," he said. "Pasiphae Jade's plan to flush the others into the open hasn't been so successful. If they're gathering the amulets, they're not talking about it."

"There's a knot of soldiers to the southwest." That would be General Artextra's camp. "I'll bet the amulets are there, or are being taken there."

"So you think we should try to steal them from their concentrated military?"

"Of course not, or at least not without some of those bandits making trouble all around to pull their forces away."

"Then we start with the temple."

The serving man brought Galen's ale, and he nodded his thanks.

"I wonder what Dielo's doing," Kayvin said, with a tone of attempting to change the subject.

"Probably he's in Pasiphae Jade's sleeping pit," Yovela said with thick disdain.

"That's not funny."

"It's not intended to be. I don't trust him."

"Still? You have a hard shell."

"He's a whore."

"He is a member of my sera qadra, the same as you."

"He's sweet and kind and supportive, or well-trained to play that role," Yovela said, "but there's no denying that Pasiphae Jade blatantly placed him close to you, and after you turned out those who might have been agents for her."

"She forced my hand, yes, but in a manner that could not have fostered much loyalty to her. And anyway, what could he report that she does not already know? He can't tell her anything of my efforts here in the human lands, and I'm sure she does not care whether I've added a fourth line of harmony to my latest composition."

"Still. I don't trust him. He makes me feel...watched. I just don't trust him."

"Then don't trust him. It doesn't matter, as he's still in Saragu."

The serving man walked by again with an inquiry in his expression, and Galen shook his head, indicating his cup was sufficient. The slouching man beside him settled onto the table and began to snore quietly despite the noisy chatter.

But Kayvin and Yovela fell silent, and Galen turned further away on his bench in case their attention wandered as the conversation lapsed. A few minutes passed, and he began to think about leaving. But then they muttered agreement and stood, and he lifted his cup to his down-turned face as they passed.

Galen remained still for another moment, letting them get safely to the stairs before he moved. They had just disappeared above the level of the public room's ceiling when a sharp pain bit through his shin. "Ow!"

"Stupid farm boy! You cow-handed chicken choker! Great red stumblebum!" Lisveth came into view beside him, fierce with frustration. "What was the point of me coming quietly, or at all, if you were going to walk right in and sit next to them with a bell around your neck?"

"They didn't see me," Galen said, raising his hands. "I didn't mean to sit next to them. I didn't see them until I was sitting."

She rolled her eyes. "And none of you saw me. Which was the entire point. I could have done it all without you risking the whole venture, while also distracting me from what I came to hear."

"I'm sorry. I was worried for you. I came to see that you—in case you needed backup."

She dropped to the bench beside him. "You'll notice I didn't"

"I know. I'm sorry." He swallowed. "Don't call me that."

"Cow-handed chicken choker?"

"Red," he said, and his throat tightened as he said it. "I don't mind the other bits. But don't call me red."

She turned toward him. "It's the only part that's true."

"Don't."

Her expression softened. "It doesn't mean—"

"I don't care what it means or doesn't mean," he said more sharply than he intended. "I've been called a lot of names. Sometimes I deserved them. But that one I can't help."

She quieted. "I'm sorry. I didn't—sorry."

The room's noisy chatter bustled about them and did not penetrate the silence that hung between them.

Galen took a breath and searched for a way to relieve the awkwardness. "You're just upset that you used a magical artifact and your spells to accomplish what I also achieved by buying a single mug of ale. Jealous."

She elbowed him, and everything was fine.

"Did you hear?" Galen asked.

"All of it. I was an arm's length from our Prince Kayvin, sitting still as a mouse. You?"

"Most of it. I think they're going to rob a temple for the amulet."

She nodded. "Tomorrow, I'd bet. We should be there."

CHAPTER 70

KAYVIN KEPT HIS HOOD up over his red hair as he and Yovela left their room. The humans had never liked red hair, but it was even more important to conceal it now that the streets were full of rumors of Selk bandits, and now that the mercenary team might have spread word of his own presence and appearance.

He had tried to disguise his hair, with help from Yovela and a sack of black walnuts from the market. The stain had clung to the landlord's basin, the floor, and Yovela's skirts, but not Kayvin's hair. So he relied upon his hood and the encroaching autumn chill, which made it more natural to keep his head covered.

They entered the temple gate, and Kayvin kissed the palm of his hand and placed it against the inner gate pillar as he had seen the faithful humans do. It was mostly a gesture of disguise, blending with the others visiting the temple, but he also felt a measure of guilt for what they were about to do, and he offered the ritual kiss as a gesture of apology. They were not here for war, not yet, and he was violating all laws of hospitality.

As they entered the temple courtyard they stepped into a wide circle, demarcated by colored stones set into the paving and a few plants, sagging and brown in the late season. Kayvin hesitated, surreptitiously watching the adherents so that he did not accidentally commit some travesty and draw attention.

But the circles could be trod upon and across. Two or three people were walking the labyrinthine lines of the circles, possibly praying or meditating, but the rest went directly to the temple door at the far end of the courtyard. Kayvin started forward again, Yovela staying beside him.

Love was written in the first circle, set in worn tiles along the stone edge. The second was *Joy*. They crossed next over *Peace* and *Patience*, and then Kayvin stopped watching the ground and concentrated on the building they were approaching.

The architecture looked eerily familiar to him. Here in the human lands, the mountains did not shelter the cities from winds and weather, and most of the buildings were closed and dark to Kayvin's mind. But the temple, while not the open palace of home, at least nodded to a more temperate construction, with a wide colonnaded porch and a tall entrance that should have been impractical to heat in the local winter.

"It is as if a forgetful old man described your palace to a child, who drew a plan for an architect," Yovela muttered. "Do they worship your family, my prince?"

Kayvin suppressed a chuckle. "Hardly." But the visual similarity was curious, and he put it aside to wonder at when he had the leisure.

They crossed the last of the courtyard circles and entered the temple itself.

There was no statue of a deity, as Kayvin had expected, but only a large golden symbol of interlinking triangles at the far end of the hypostyle hall. A few rooms opened to either side, but it was clear this was the main worship hall.

Which meant it was not where they would find what they'd come for. "Look for a treasure room," he murmured to Yovela.

"Perhaps we could follow that priest," she suggested, nodding to the side of the hall where a man in temple robes carried a gold-covered coffer.

"Well, that is convenient," he agreed.

The priest went into a side hall, and they hung back to watch from the arched door. He glanced over his shoulder, but only perfunctorily, and crouched to unlock a round door set into the floor. He pulled back the door and descended what must have been a spiral stair. A moment later, he reappeared without the coffer. He replaced the door, locked it, and turned toward the arch.

Kayvin and Yovela spun away from the door, moving a few paces down the wall and pretending to be absorbed in studying a painted mural of a vineyard in which two human figures appeared to be murdering a third. Curious religion, thought Kayvin.

When the priest had passed, they turned back and went into the empty side hall. "Keep watch," Kayvin ordered as he crouched to the lock.

It was a good bolt, with a unique key, but it could not withstand the concentrated magic Kayvin set on it. He sheared the block of iron that held the door in place and pulled the door out of the way, revealing stairs curving down into darkness. "Here," he said. "Let's go."

The treasure room was dark and unoccupied, so Kayvin went first, letting Yovela watch above them as they descended. She had insisted on coming to guard him, but Kayvin intended to be done and gone from this temple without encountering anyone, much less fighting. Still, it was nice to know someone thought of his safety.

Filtered sunlight came through the high, narrow windows of the secondary hall and down through the round door, barely illuminating the room below. There was just enough light to make out tables and cases all around them, ringing the stairs, and one pedestal with an upright stand and a clear display of honor. On it, suspended on a chain from a wooden stand, gleamed a red-gold eye within a twisted nest of golden wire.

"Good," breathed Yovela. "Get it and let's go."

Kayvin reached for the amulet when the empty lamp above the pedestal sparked to life. Light flared, and in quick succession each lamp about the treasure room lit and filled the room. Kayvin wheeled to stare at the ring of armed soldiers, all leveling weapons. Yovela spun, raising her hands, and the door above was darkened with soldiers leaning close over it.

Kayvin withdrew his hands from the amulet.

"Now, perhaps we can talk," the blonde mercenary—Lisveth, he recalled—said. She stepped forward, enough to make herself visible but not enough to interfere with the archers' view of Kayvin and Yovela.

"You knew we were coming," Kayvin said unnecessarily. "You knew what we wanted."

"Obviously," Lisveth said. "But we don't know why, and we're curious about that."

Panic rose in Kayvin's throat, and it was not for himself. If they were captured, Yovela would be harmed, and his mother would die when he did not bring the amulet to Pasiphae Jade. "I will fight free," he warned.

"We were sure you would mean to, naturally," Lisveth answered. "We have made a study of the Rideis wars, and we feel confident this troop could at least hold you and trap you here long enough to render you harmless."

He glanced at the door above, and then back at her. "But sealing us in would trap you as well."

She shrugged. "Most people would consider the sacrifice of a pawn to gain a prince a wise move by a skilled gamer. Certainly the state mages wouldn't mind losing a freelancer."

"And all these soldiers?"

"Naturally, we would all much prefer to leave alive," she said, nodding. "Which is why we hope you will accept an invitation to discuss our situation in a more civilized manner. Preferably someplace with fewer weapons and more supper."

Yovela, still turning slowly in place in case a soldier approached from behind, caught Kayvin's eye. She did not believe they could fight their way out before the door was sealed, and in a manner more permanent than the simple trap they had sprung.

And if they went with Lisveth, he might learn if her companion carried an amulet of protection.

He held up his hands, palms out, fingers wide, displaying to the sorceress that he did not conceal any spell-working. "We will talk with you," he said. "Yovela and I pledge our good faith for a conversation and our amiable parting."

"You speak for her?"

Kayvin frowned. "I am a prince, and she is a woman in my *sera qadra.*"

Lisveth's brow furrowed. "That's not a term with which I'm familiar, but I can accept that a prince may speak for his entourage. I'm Lisveth, as you may recall, and this is Galen." She gestured to the red-headed man Kayvin remembered, standing among the waiting soldiers.

"And how do we know your invitation is genuine and of good faith?" Kayvin asked.

"We might ask the same of you," Lisveth said, "but I'll go first." She raised her hand and made a short gesture, and the soldiers vanished.

Kayvin spun, looking into the darkness, and then looked at the round door above. It was also empty.

Yovela sputtered something, probably a curse. Kayvin turned back to Lisveth. "Very nicely done," he said honestly. "But I suppose now I could just take this." He plucked the amulet from its stand.

Lisveth tipped her head to one side with a disappointed expression. "Really?"

Kayvin looked down again at the amulet in his hand, and it was a half-eaten chicken wing. He sighed and flung it across the floor. "I should have expected that."

Lisveth gave him a flat, professional smile. "And for your good faith?"

Kayvin raised his hands. "I am the Amethyst Prince of the Rideis, and my word is law, even to myself. I swear I—and my woman Yovela—will do you no harm during our reasonable conversation and our departure, and we will respect all the laws of hospitality until they should be broken by our hosts."

Lisveth frowned. "Neither Galen nor I are princes, but our word has always been good enough for our employment. Laws of hospitality until broken, or however you said it. I'm sorry, my words are not as pretty as yours, my lord, but they are sound."

Kayvin inclined his head. "Good enough. Shall we speak here?"

"In this dark pit? Let's go somewhere more sociable, if that's acceptable to you. The Selk's Head, perhaps?"

So they had been spotted. Kayvin accepted this fresh defeat with the best grace he could manage. "Of course."

CHAPTER 71

THE SELK'S HEAD WAS busy, but they were given a roomy table in the corner, and the four of them looked at each other stiffly.

Galen fought the urge to repeatedly check the satchel at his belt, where the second amulet was stashed. Lisveth had flicked an indicating finger as she followed Kayvin and Yovela up the stairs, and then she'd dropped the torches, leaving Galen a moment to dart into the darkness and feel around for the amulet Kayvin had flung away when he thought it a piece of chicken.

He wondered absently if the new amulet's effect would work if he were not wearing it, only carrying it. But Lisveth was still carrying the golden-eyed amulet somewhere, and she was perfectly noticeable as usual, so it seemed they had to be deliberately worn.

Lisveth could identify an amulet if she cast magic at it. He hoped Kayvin could not somehow sense their presence in a more passive way.

A woman came to serve the table, someone Galen did not recognize, for which he was grateful. He didn't want the serving man commenting on his return. "Good evening, folks! I'm Juliet, and this is my place. What will you have tonight?"

"Ales all around, I think?" Galen suggested.

Kayvin nodded. "Yes, and what's in the kitchen?"

"We've got root vegetable stew tonight, or half a chicken with lentils, or a rabbit pie."

"I'll take all three," Lisveth said. She marked a wide space on the table between her hands. "From here to here."

Galen chuckled. "Glutton."

"That was a lot of magic," she protested, "and anyway General Artextra is paying tonight." She looked at Kayvin and Yovela. "Are you having anything?"

"Er, the rabbit pie," he said. "Yovela?"

"The stew, thank you."

"And I'll have the stew and the chicken," Galen said. It would be a shame to waste the general's coin.

And if this meeting went poorly, at least he wouldn't die hungry.

When Juliet had gone, Lisveth turned to the Rideis. "We have some questions, which we hope might prevent a great deal of bloodshed on both sides."

Kayvin looked uncomfortable. Yovela said nothing.

Lisveth looked expectantly at Galen. He was surprised; usually she did the negotiating. "We know you want the amulets," he said, which was a stupid opening, as they had just caught them in the temple treasure room with an amulet. "Why? Do you plan to use them against us?"

"No," said Kayvin simply.

They waited, but he did not offer further explanation.

"But you plan to use them."

"Yes."

Again, they waited.

At last Lisveth crossed her arms on the table. "Let us save each other time and frustration," she said. "What does Pasiphae Jade want with them?"

Kayvin's eyes whipped to hers, the whites flashing with his surprise. Yovela's fists tightened on the tabletop. Kayvin opened his mouth, spoke with difficulty. "You know of her already?"

"Some," said Galen. "Not everything."

Kayvin looked at Yovela, who said simply, "Dielo."

"What?"

"If he followed me here—he might have betrayed you."

"Dielo has no reason to do so," Kayvin said to her. "He could not serve Pasiphae Jade by betraying me to the humans so that I could not retrieve the amulets she wants." He looked at Galen and Lisveth. "What do you know?"

"Enough to know you have little reason to like her." Galen hoped vague suggestions would be enough to prompt more.

"Then you know enough to understand I have no choice but to take her the amulets," Kayvin said. "If you help me to acquire them all, then I can recall those bandits currently plaguing you. If you do not, then I must continue to search for them myself.'

They looked at one another, caught in the impossible impasse.

"Food for you!" came a cheery voice, and Juliet began handing out an impressive number of platters. The serving man who had brought Galen his ale on his previous visit was carrying additional plates and bowls for her, but he did not comment on Galen's return.

Lisveth set into the stew as if Kayvin might try to snatch it from her. Yovela kept her eyes on her own meal.

Kayvin set his eyes on Galen. "You have one, don't you?"

Galen froze, not wanting to lie but not wanting to admit the truth. "I didn't know what it was," he said slowly, letting his true embarrassment show. "I thought it was a stupid charm."

Kayvin stared at him. "You have let them fall to common thieves who don't even know their value," he said in soft outrage. "You don't deserve to have them."

"I'm certainly glad I had that one when I did," Galen said dryly, and Kayvin had the grace to look ashamed.

"They're protected," Lisveth said through a mouthful of stew. "The others were already in treasuries. That one had been lost, now it's found. We are protecting them."

Kayvin's lips thinned and he said nothing.

"Could you placate her another way?" prompted Galen, hoping for more information about this Pasiphae Jade person.

"No," said Kayvin firmly.

But Yovela looked at him as if she wanted to speak, and Galen remembered their disagreement. Yovela had insisted Pasiphae Jade was lying. "Do you think she's trustworthy?" Galen ventured.

His barb struck home. Kayvin's pie folded in his hand, and the muscles in his jaw flexed visibly though he had not yet taken a bite.

Yovela raised her eyebrows as if Galen's question was self-evident proof of her own assertion, but she said nothing.

There was information to be gained here, crucial information that could shift Prince Kayvin's actions and bring or prevent war, but Galen did not know how to pry it free. He looked at Lisveth, who was halfway through her stew. She continued to eat.

Kayvin took a bite of his pie, which broke and steamed into the air. He winced as the filling burned him.

"Will you be bringing your Rideis army as well?" Galen asked. "Raiding our villages and farms, taking children for prisoners, carrying them back over the mountains?"

"If we do, it's only fair," Kayvin muttered to his pie. "When an ally ceases to be an ally, he becomes an enemy."

"An enemy?" repeated Galen. "When have we crossed the mountains for your villages and farms?"

Kayvin turned a baleful glare on Galen. "Exactly," he snapped.

Galen had no response, confused speechless.

Lisveth had rarely been speechless. "You say we were allies," she said, setting aside the scraped bowl and starting on the roasted chicken. "But you also say you are here to steal the amulets we have used for protection for centuries. It seems you are no ally to us, either."

"It was your people who betrayed mine," Kayvin said. "After that, it is no shame to take what was ours."

"Yours?" repeated Galen. "It was our sorcerers who created the amulets."

Kayvin snorted. "Your sorcerers are children. They draw adorable sketches, but they do not create works of art. We made the amulets, for our protection."

Galen raised a hand. "There are stories, very old stories, with little detail, which say we once fought alongside the Selks against a common enemy. Are you saying that's history? Do you know the rest of it?"

Kayvin stared at him. "I knew your promises are short, but I had not expected your memories to be shorter," he said with a bitter tone. "Have you no histories?"

"Histories can be lost," Galen said. "Tell me."

Kayvin hesitated, considered, and then shook his head. "You are two bandit hunters," he said. "Even if I told you, and even if you believed it, you would still be two bandit hunters. You cannot pledge me an army to save my people and to retake my throne. And unless you can do that, you cannot help me."

"You might be surprised at what we can bring," Lisveth said over her lentils.

"I will not treat with someone without power," Kayvin said.

"By that logic, we shouldn't be bothering to talk with you." Lisveth licked a finger. "After all, it's Pasiphae Jade who rules the Rideis."

It was a guess, possibly literal or possibly metaphorical and based on the barest of evidence, but it struck the quick.

"She is a venomous usurper!" snapped Kayvin. "She is a murderer who has killed the Arch Potentate. She was a courtesan to my father—a cheap, untrained girl in his sera qadra."

That explained his hatred for her. Galen glanced toward Yovela. Given Yovela's introduction and her disgusted expression, Galen wondered if she too was a cheap, untrained girl in a sera qadra.

But now they knew more of the woman who threatened Prince Kayvin into hunting for amulets. "And what does she offer you for your service?"

Kayvin's face went rigid. He looked at his broken pie.

It was Yovela who answered. "His mother's life."

Galen's stomach twisted.

Kayvin shot Yovela a murderous look, but she did not stop. "But she lies. She will kill both when she has what she wants."

"What she wants is to save our people," Kayvin retorted. "And that is what I must want, too." He stood, leaving his half-eaten pie on the table. "We're going. Our peaceable departure marks the end of our agreed truce."

"I'm sorry to hear that," Galen said, and he meant it.

Kayvin looked surprised for an instant, but he departed without speaking.

Yovela stood, picking up her stew and reaching for his discarded pie. "He'll be hungry later," she said. "Thank you for supper." Then she followed her prince across the public room and up the stairs, presumably to their let room.

Lisveth started on her own pie. "Well," she said through a mouthful, "that was interesting."

CHAPTER 72

"I KNOW I'VE HEARD that before," Galen said. "It's far back, it's vague, but I know I've heard the Selks were our allies against a common enemy."

Lisveth pulled off her second boot, back in their own room. "Do you know what this enemy was?"

He shook his head.

"Nor I," she said. "I was hoping to hook him into telling us more, but it seems we weren't big enough fish to bait him. Or whatever that metaphor should be."

Galen sat on the floor before the fire, letting it warm his back. "So let's put this together: A courtesan named Pasiphae Jade killed the Arch Potentate of the Rideis and took his place as ruler? Displacing the prince and heir?"

"Because she has the queen," Lisveth added, "and the prince doesn't want to risk her life. But Yovela, who is likely also a courtesan, thinks Pasiphae Jade will kill the queen anyway. And maybe Prince Kayvin, too. And this Pasiphae Jade—fair night, what a name—wants Kayvin to collect the amulets for her, and she's using his mother as leverage."

"And she will use the amulets to do—what?" Galen stretched his arms overhead. "He said something at the end about her saving their people. That doesn't make any sense if it's just a war of succession."

"They want our amulets at least, if they can't have a human army." She sat down beside him, facing the fire. "So who are they fighting?"

"And why wouldn't Prince Kayvin just ask for our help?"

"Well, I can grant him that lapse, since we've been at war far more recently than we may have been allies, if ever we were allies." Lisveth wriggled and spread her toes, stretching her feet in the warmth. "She must be a formidable woman, to kill the Rideis ruler and hold his throne against his grown son."

"Maybe she's a sorceress, too."

"The Rideis are all sorcerers, aren't they? So either she's very powerful in magic, or she's very powerful politically, or both."

"He didn't speak of her as if she were a respected political figure."

"The woman killed his father and is threatening his mother," Lisveth pointed out. "I doubt he'd speak highly of her no matter what her position or abilities."

Galen acknowledged this with a nod. "So what will we tell General Artextra?"

Lisveth sighed. "We tell her what we know. The bandits and Prince Kayvin are here for the amulets, which means we should gather and protect them. We don't know if they're planning a full invasion as in the past, as this seems to be a succession battle, but we can't rule it out."

"And it wouldn't be a bad idea to ask some scholars to determine if we did betray the Rideis, or if there might be something they construed as a betrayal, which could explain their continued hostility." Galen tried to scratch an itch in the center of his back, but his shoulder pulled tight. He tried another angle. "I don't know what we'd do about it—it's not like we can apologize ourselves for something that happened hundreds of years ago—but it might at least give us some insight as to what they want now."

Lisveth extended an arm and casually scratched the place on his back. "I don't know that Kayvin cares about an apology as much as he cares about saving his mother. He didn't have much of a rebuttal when Yovela said Pasiphae Jade will kill her anyway."

Galen shook his head. "No, but sometimes you have to believe you can do something to help, even if it won't, just so you can do something."

"In this case, we need him to have something to do that isn't bringing bandits over the mountains and stealing our amulets." Lisveth leaned forward to grasp her feet, stretching the muscles all along her legs.

"I'm sure Kayvin would welcome any suggestions you have for removing the usurper who threatens his mother and sends him off like an errand boy," Galen said, folding forward to stretch his own legs and back. He could lie flat on his legs, unlike Lisveth. His fighting required more stretching than her magic.

"I'll think on it," Lisveth promised. She yawned. "Ready for bed?"

They set aside their jackets with their cloaks, warm enough with the fire to wear only their summer layers, and wrapped themselves in blankets before settling back to back as usual. The fire settled to a steady glow, and they slept.

They set out early the next morning and arrived at General Artextra's camp shortly after noon. Lisveth went directly to the central building, commandeered as the general's headquarters. "Hello, Anela! We're back, with news for the general."

Anela nodded, pushing back a loose strand of chestnut hair, and pulled out the notebook in which she kept the general's schedule. "She can see you in an hour or so."

"That'll just give us time to get lunch first," said Galen. "Is the kitchen open?"

Anela nodded. "I could take a break myself in a few minutes." She smiled and glanced up.

"Maybe we'll see you there," Galen replied.

Lisveth made a strained face. "Come on, farm boy. Let's get there before the good bread is gone."

He followed her. "What was that about?"

"If you have to ask..." Lisveth rolled her eyes. "Anela would have liked to have been asked to join you."

"Didn't I say that, more or less?"

"No, you said she could join us and everyone else in the kitchen. That's different."

"Oh." Realization came slowly. He felt himself flush, red on red again. "I didn't do anything wrong."

"You don't always have to. But no, you didn't do anything—at all." She took a bowl from the counter and put it into his hand. "You haven't done anything with anyone, not that I can recall. You all right there, farm boy?"

He scowled at her. "I don't remember you picking up many lovers along the road."

"I'm not as fine a catch as you." She grinned. "Those shoulders, and those eyes, and that jaw." She flicked a fingertip across his chin. "It's a wonder you aren't swarmed over with interested parties."

"Stop." His face was burning, and surely his ears had blended color with his hair by now.

She mercifully put the jokes away, but she did not drop the subject. "Did it never occur to you to ask Anela, or anyone else? I'm not complaining, but..."

He shook his head stiffly. "There's nothing wrong with me."

"I didn't think so." She grinned. "That's how Anela got us into this conversation."

He turned away, more irritated than he could justify. And what would it hurt if he did ask Anela to join him for a meal? Lisveth clearly wouldn't think anything of it, and anyway he didn't care what Lisveth thought.

Lunch was filling, but unimpressive after the feast of the night before. Afterward, they went to apprise General Artextra of what they had learned, without being specific about the Painter's Eye, and of how they'd foiled the burglary of the temple, and of what they knew so far of Pasiphae Jade and the struggle for the throne. "And here," Galen added, placing the Singer's Eye on the desktop. "This is the one he was stealing. We thought it better to bring it to you than to return it to a place we'd already seen him enter."

The red eye stared dully at the ceiling. It did not look like a hinge pin between nations.

The general frowned as she tried to work through the implications, just as they had. "So, does that mean they aren't invading?"

"At least, not at the moment. But they might in the future. They do want the amulets, at least."

"Well, they can't have them," General Artextra said flatly. "There, that's settled. Now what's left to negotiate?"

"Perhaps plenty," Galen suggested. "He was willing enough to sit down with us to talk, but he said he could not treat with us, as we had no authority. He might be willing to sit with you, as a general, and talk much more."

Lisveth held up a finger. "Or perhaps you could grant us an honorary rank while we're working on this?"

Artextra snorted. "Nice try. But that's not a bad idea about extending a truce to find out what's going on. We don't have much intelligence on the Rideis, and any information, even their own, would only help." She called through the door to Anela. "Did you hear enough of that? Send a messenger. Offer safe conduct, hospitality, and safe departure for the prince."

"He has Yovela with him," Lisveth added. "A concubine or something."

"He may bring her along, of course, but he'll have to come himself to negotiate. We won't treat with a concubine," General Artextra said. "We have protocols and rank to observe."

Galen shrugged. "If what the prince says is true, we'll be treating with a concubine if we come to war with the Rideis."

CHAPTER 73

YOVELA DID NOT ATTEND the council. Neither she nor Prince Kayvin seemed surprised or distressed by this. Yovela only gave him an intense look when they parted at the camp's entrance. "Be careful, my lord." She turned her eyes on Galen and Lisveth. "You will watch for his safety." It was not a question.

Galen was flattered that she seemed to trust them more than the general's word, even though they had been the ones fighting Kayvin when she pulled him away on the road that night. "Of course. This is just a talk. Our end is to prevent war, not to start it."

They would meet in General Artextra's borrowed house, in a room that boasted several framed windows and a solid door compromised by a gaping frame. Chairs were set around a long table, and it was surprisingly crowded. Anela counted out the seats: General Artextra, Anela herself, Major Etak, Lord Bryuki, several nobles and military figures Galen hadn't had the courage to ask about lest he reveal his depth of ignorance, and then of course Prince Kayvin, who would be given a sturdy chair set a little apart from the others. Galen and Lisveth were not given chairs at the table, but they would have seats near the door, as Kayvin had apparently agreed to this meeting only on the condition that they were present. "I have dealt with them as private citizens and as representatives of the Sayinian Octovirate, and I trust them to honor their promise of safe passage."

Again, Galen was flattered by the Rideis trust in him, and he resolved to prove it well-founded. Also, it was amusingly pleasant to be called a representative of the Octovirate.

So when it came time for the meeting to commence, Galen and Lisveth escorted Prince Kayvin to the exterior door of the meeting room, flanking him as if they were an honor guard. General Artextra and Major Etak stood beside the door, with the rest of the impromptu council arrayed nearby or behind them. "Welcome, Your Highness," General Artextra said with a gentle bow.

"Thank you," the prince answered, making a bow in return. "I am sorry, but you have the advantage of me, while I know no one but my escorts. I have come to meet with General Artextra."

"I am she," the general answered. She gestured at her field uniform. "It's not court uniform, I admit, but I try to look the part."

Prince Kayvin suppressed his surprise within a few heartbeats, but not before the general and their observers had noted it. Galen glanced at Lisveth, whose mouth had flattened into an irritated line.

"I see," Prince Kayvin said, making a second bow. "I apologize for my ignorance. It is pleasant to meet you, General Artextra."

She smiled tightly. "Please, come inside."

They filed into the narrow room and closed the door against curious eyes.

Major Etak opened the meeting with a frank statement of purpose. "We are of course very pleased to have for the first time a prince of the Rideis visiting our land," he began.

Kayvin's smile grew cynical. "Not the first. But the first in a long time, that is true."

"Alas, we have no record of the Rideis throne represented here before. But," Major Etak continued, not waiting for Kayvin to answer, "if we had received word of your coming and intent to discourse, we should have preferred to welcome you here in a more proper setting, an honored guest of this Octovirate and welcome in the court." He paused just long enough to emphasize that Kayvin's current appearance was in fact the opposite. "Our purpose here today outshines even the notability of this gathering, and that is to prevent war between our nations if possible. Prince Kayvin, we understand that wars occur because of conflicts of interest, but we cannot guess what conflict lies between us. We look forward to your enlightenment of this council."

Beside Galen, Lisveth muttered, "Pompous windbag. He sounds like he's bartering with an obstreperous merchant over some aged shellfish."

Kayvin set his hands flat upon the table. "I am not familiar with the customs of your court," he said, "but I have spent many weeks now in your society."

Ah, Prince Kayvin could also deliver two meanings at once. His unsubtle reminder of his successful incursions made the officials' smiles flicker.

"In your markets and public houses, I have heard many stories of demons and magic and even cursed children. I did not recognize my people in those stories, though I was meant to. Yet how could a red-headed child be the result of a demon's curse, when your own emissary and I both grow red hair?" He gestured toward Galen near the door.

"He is not our emissary," Major Etak muttered.

"No? Then did you send a man of no consequence to me?"

"It is our understanding that you do not presently represent the Bull Throne," Major Etak said with a smiling dagger's edge to his voice.

Kayvin's throat worked, but his voice remained steady. "I am the Amethyst Prince, the heir. Just as I was a year ago. Where will you be this time next year, your lordship? Oh, I'm sorry, I've confused your proper address, and of course you are not an aristocrat. Major?"

Galen leaned to whisper to Lisveth, "I think a measuring stick would speed this meeting along. It might settle all this more quickly."

Lisveth shook her head. "The only one in camp is marked in handspans, and anyone making this much noise is surely going to need one in half-inches. Or maybe stitch-lengths, if they keep going like this." She snorted. "Besides, no one would know how to document General Artextra's clear victory."

At the table, Prince Kayvin continued, "Perhaps you could explain more clearly to me the purpose of this meeting, if I was not invited as an honored representative of state."

"Then let us be simple," General Artextra said, leaning forward. "Tell us why the Rideis would invade our sovereign land."

Prince Kayvin's face hardened. "It is not your land that we want."

"No, perhaps not. You invade our borders, you raid our food supplies, you take both adults and children as prisoners. And then, without explanation, you retire to your own lands and disappear again for a generation or four. We have no explanation for your actions but hostility and malice." She frowned, deepening the lines framing her mouth. "We would like to know if we can come to some sort of arrangement that might avoid the repetition of centuries past."

Kayvin met her eyes coldly. "Perhaps you should have thought of that before you severed our nations' more cordial relationship."

"With respect, we have only your word that there was ever a more cordial relationship, or that we severed it."

"Children," Lisveth muttered, "play nice." But only Galen heard her.

"With respect," returned Kayvin tersely, "I have only your word that you are a general, and not an impostor set to mock me. I have to wonder at your assessment of my credulity."

There was a subtle intake of breath around the table. General Artextra's face went stiffly expressionless. "Prince Kayvin, I am indeed General Artextra. I now point out we did not plainly accuse you of lying as to your identity as a prince of the Rideis, though you have furnished no proof."

That was because he had never intended them to know, Galen thought, and they were meeting with him only because he had failed to keep his princely identity secret.

Kayvin set his jaw. "An honorable man would not prevaricate in the same way as a woman." His eyes widened slightly, but he pressed on, "Nor would a woman be trusted to command an army."

The air was growing very awkward now, with council attendees shifting on their chairs and exchanging outraged or suspicious glances.

General Artextra face had gone flat. "As we're dispensing with the polite language, I'll share this suggestion: Next time, send word ahead with an official envoy and come for an official state visit, and you may meet someone who outranks me. But sneak across with a troop of bandits to murder our civilians, and you get a general." She leaned on the table, arms folded. "Prince Kayvin, if you suggest this meeting cannot progress because you are expected to negotiate with a woman, then I'm afraid we must assume our conversation is at an end."

Kayvin raised his hand, palm out, and shook his head. "If you can assure me of your credential, then I mean no offense. I only have never heard of a woman entrusted to lead an army."

Major Etak countered with a contending finger. "Being a qualified leader is less about personal conquest and more about logistics and looking after the greater good." He frowned and arched an eyebrow. "If your nation does not understand that, that might be why you're suffering a coup."

Kayvin's mouth thinned and his throat worked. "That coup illustrates my point. Women are skilled at espionage, perhaps—you sent one to spy me out—but not at negotiation."

Galen blinked and looked for Lisveth's reaction. She looked almost more surprised than indignant.

"What do you mean?" a lord with a patchy beard asked. "Please explain."

"Women are ideal for spying, but not for official business. They plot, they connive, they work in secret, and a straightforward man cannot fathom what they intend. Rulers are generally men, so they may treat with each other in good faith. I do not speak in malice, but in observed fact. A study of women at court will show quite the opposite behavior to that of open men, all whispers and innuendo and treachery." Kayvin turned up a palm, as if stating the sky was blue. "Women scheme."

General Artextra raised an eyebrow, and Galen thought for a moment she would reach across the table and casually seize

Kayvin's throat. But Lisveth lifted a hand, and the general looked at her expectantly, apparently willing to share the task of evisceration.

Lisveth looked at the ceiling, at the walls, around the table of faces. "Curious, isn't it, how none of us are fighting at this moment?"

"What?"

"Every single one of us in this room requires air to breathe. We will quite literally die without it. It is the most precious thing, the greatest priority, to each and every one of us. And yet not a one of us has considered killing for it."

"We don't need to," said the major in a tone of exasperation.

"Exactly. There is plenty of air, and none of us have questioned if there will be enough. So why would we waste time and blood in fighting for a resource that isn't scarce?" Lisveth gestured about the room, encompassing the door and the several windows. "And yet, if there were a shortage of air, we might feel very differently."

"What does this have to do with anything?" The major shook his head and turned away from Lisveth.

But Kayvin scowled at Lisveth. "You suggest they have no prestige and so grasp for it. But you know I have great regard for Yovela."

Lisveth nodded. "And yet she is absent from this meeting. If Yovela came here now, and if she was announced by her court position, what would she be called?"

Kayvin hesitated and then said firmly, "She is a member of my sera qadra."

"And what would her role be here? What exactly would she do?"

"She would..." Kayvin hesitated. "She would sit... Look, in our land, a sera qadra is a thing of status. It's expected a man of influence will display his sera qadra, just as your nobles here are displaying their own jewelry. You do not think less of them for wearing their gems and gold chains."

"No," Lisveth agreed amiably. "But it is not the gems and gold chains who are respected by their possession and display."

The general grunted.

Kayvin clenched his jaw. "For all your talk, I see more men than women among your soldiers. Even in this room." He gave a pointed look at General Artextra.

"That's true," she agreed. "More men than women volunteer to fight, and we allow each to serve as their skills and desires bend. It is not a matter of roles and rules, but of preference and proficiency. Are you certain no one is pressed against their inclination in your court?"

Kayvin's neck stiffened, and then his words tumbled out in a rapid rebuttal. "Our culture honors strength because fighting was what preserved us. We fought not only to unite Rideis under a single banner and a single throne, but we fought to preserve those Rideis from devastation. Without our warriors, we would have been overrun by dragons—and so would your Sayinia." He jabbed the tabletop. "Trade keeps a country healthy, and song has its place at times, but above all, survival depends on fighting and strategy. Men are better at these things."

"Forgive me for bringing up a painful subject," Lisveth interrupted in a lazy tone, "but aren't we gathered for this conversation only because a fourth-level concubine toppled your government in a single night?"

Kayvin's jaw flexed and bulged, and Galen thought he might explode with some magical burst of fury. But with an effort he exhaled and pressed his arched fingers into the table's surface. "You have made your point," he bit out, "from your perfectly arranged society."

"Far from it," Lisveth growled. "It is still full of people." She propped an elbow on the knee she drew to her chest. "Keep talking, though, so we can clear up any lingering doubts on how you might have lost influence in your own court."

"This is all very interesting to some, I'm sure, but there is a large square stone in the town plaza for anyone who wishes to lecture or discourse," said Lord Bryuki dryly. "Surely we have more pragmatic matters to discuss here."

"We certainly do," General Artextra snapped. "We need to know why the Rideis would send their prince to crawl about our land without announcing himself, and why he would want to steal from a temple treasury."

Kayvin turned his head slightly. "It is rude to accuse a visiting dignitary of theft."

"It is rude to burglarize a temple treasury."

"I took nothing."

"Not for lack of trying," Lisveth interjected pointedly.

Kayvin kept his face neutral. "I was indeed trying to learn if you still had the amulets, and where they might be. Now I hope we can come to some agreement regarding them. I should very much like to borrow one or more of them."

"Borrow?" repeated Major Etak in a tone one did not normally use with foreign princes.

"Pasiphae Jade, the present Arch Potentate, has charged me with bringing these amulets to her," Kayvin explained, his voice strained. "She wants them to serve the purpose for which they were first made."

"To defend against you and your Selks?" Major Etak interjected.

General Artextra gave him an irritated glance.

Kayvin's lips thinned, but he spoke on. "Before they were wielded against us, they were forged by us. I ask that you return them, if only for a time, so we may protect our people."

"We need them to protect our people," Lord Bryuki said flatly.

"From raiders," Etak added, pointedly avoiding Artextra's gaze.

Kayvin's veneer of dignified calm was wearing thin. "Those amulets were made to fight dragons that preyed upon our people and yours. If you do not honor us today, will you at least honor that shared history? Will you not return the tools that can save my people from another spawning—"

One of the lords, a man whose name Galen did not know, began laughing aloud. "You want to take our greatest artifacts, the tools that have defended our people from yours, to fight dragons?" He looked back and forth, inviting others into the joke. "Has anyone seen a dragon? Has anyone's grandfather seen a dragon?"

"It is not dragons we face now," Kayvin said quickly. "And they were never as prevalent on this side of the mountains. The Rideis bore the brunt of their predations—"

"Did dragons ever really descend on villages and plow through their fairest youth?" the nobleman asked. "Like a bard's tale or a puppet show?"

Kayvin's eyes were beginning to look slightly frantic. "Did you ask me here only to mock me?" he demanded. "Do you not remember anything of this history?"

"Who says it is history?"

Kayvin stood. "I think this conversation has continued far past its end. I bid you all good day."

General Artextra stood. "Your Highness, wait—"

But Kayvin was already striding to the door. He did not look toward Lisveth or Galen. He barely slowed as he shoved back the door, ignoring the guards on either side who turned, startled, as he swept past.

General Artextra turned on the laughing nobleman, who sobered. "What have you done?"

"Come, general, you know he only sought an excuse to flee. He never came here to treat honestly, not with stories like that. He came to distract and mislead us—if he's a prince at all, which seems unlikely."

"He's a con man," agreed someone else. "And not a very good one."

Galen's chest tightened. Kayvin had come here in desperation, and he had not only not found the aid he wanted, he had been disbelieved and mocked. It could not sit well.

Lisveth squeezed her fingers on the edge of her chair's seat. "How do you think this will end?" she asked quietly, her words nearly lost beneath the table's terse conversations.

Galen shook his head, unsure of how to describe his thoughts. He had not expected to bear sympathy for the foreign prince who had once attempted to kill him.

"I feel much the same," Lisveth said obliquely. "Let's wait outside."

The nobles left in a flock, and then Major Etak, and then Lord Bryuki. Artextra and Anela came last, the aide scribbling notes as they walked. Lisveth stepped partly onto the path. "General Artextra, what will happen now?"

The general was not pleased with the interruption, or that it came from Lisveth. "Nothing. Nothing happens now."

"But the prince..."

"If he is a prince—and I don't pretend to know, I'm only leaving all possibilities open for the moment—if he is a prince, he is by his own admission a prince in name only, struggling for the throne."

General Artextra folded her arms. "That choice is simple. We will not involve ourselves in a Rideis war of succession."

"But it's Pasiphae Jade who is pushing Prince Kayvin to come here. He explained that he did not come of his own accord."

"According to what we've been told, neither of them means to move against the state of Sayinia, and we have no standing to interfere in their state business. We would resent their interference in our government's processes, and so we accord them the same courtesy."

"And what about the amulets?"

"We protect the amulets, of course. It is not a choice of either assisting the prince to reclaim his throne or surrendering the amulets. We may guard them even if we do not offer military aid to the prince—we should guard them, in fact, given what we know. Anela, get someone to track down where the rest of them are stored." She huffed a dismissive sigh. "And then we wait for the two factions to weaken each other, so the survivor presents less of a threat to Sayinia."

Galen did not like her cavalier attitude, but he could not argue the validity of what she said. Kayvin could offer little enticement for the army to support him in his own claim to the Rideis throne, and they owed him nothing, despite his claims of a long-forgotten alliance. General Artextra's position was calculating, but logical.

Lisveth seemed to agree. "As long as the amulets are safe," she repeated.

General Artextra gave her a narrow look beneath her thick eyebrows. "May I remind you that you are neither military advisers nor nobles of the king, but bandit hunters who happened to luck upon this news?"

"Bandit hunters who are the only reason you knew of the Rideis and of the threat to the amulets, and who have kept at least one out of Rideis hands," Lisveth answered, unimpressed by the glare. "Yes, thank you for acknowledging our efforts."

Artextra shook her head. "If you don't have anything else useful to offer, kindly stay out of the way. Or consider moving on to hunt other bandits, maybe with a more ordinary pedigree."

The general and her aide walked on, leaving Lisveth watching. "Do you think Kayvin is still around?" she asked.

Galen shook his head. He'd recognized that state of fighting humiliation and anger and outrage, and needing to escape before it overwhelmed and led to more humiliation. "He's gone, I'm sure of it. I doubt he even slowed between the meeting and the gates."

Lisveth nodded in slow agreement. "Well," she said after a moment, "let's go to the kitchens before the rush."

CHAPTER 74

THEY HAD MOCKED HIM.

They had denied responsibility for their history, they had refused to give up the amulets—which were not theirs to hold—and they had set him to negotiate with a woman just as if Pasiphae Jade waited even here for him as well. It was not his fault. Like Pasiphae Jade's court, this had never been a place he could have succeeded.

Yovela stood when she saw him, her mouth dropping open. "What happened?" she gasped, taking a step forward. "Are you hurt?"

"What? Of course I'm not hurt."

"Did you fight?"

"No, it was a negotiation."

"You looked—I thought maybe things had gone poorly."

"Things did go poorly."

She led him to the bench where she'd waited, and she sat facing him. He sat forward, his eyes on the dusty road beyond. Town traffic passed without bothering about them.

"What happened?" Yovela asked again. "In the negotiations?"

Kayvin considered all that he wanted to answer. *They sent a woman to hear me. They resent our flights across the mountains. They said I was not a ruler to negotiate.*

Yovela's eyes sat heavy on him, and he wanted to snap at her.

"What did you tell them?" she pressed.

I told them women were untrustworthy and not fit for negotiations. I told them women were treacherous. But now, sitting on this plain bench beside the woman who had followed him into a hostile country to help him, who had initially stayed with him for the moderate safety his rank provided in a horrific world, he could not say such things.

He had, pressured and desperate, parroted all the things he had learned. In the moment where it mattered most, he had tried to emulate the power he knew, and he had done so in the face of Yovela's quiet devotion and General Artextra's rank and even Lisveth's frustratingly competent magic and wit.

"Kayvin? What happened?"

"I don't want to talk about it." That, at least, was true.

She drew back. "Are we at war? Are they hunting you? Tell me that much, at least."

He shook his head heavily. "No, no. If I don't represent Mandoral, it's hard to declare war on Mandoral through me. There's one happy accident."

Yovela looked at him and waited, wanting more but saying nothing.

Kayvin blew out his breath sharply. He tried to make his next words light. "None of the philosophers I've read dared to suggest the simplest and most obvious truth: that self-awareness is the greatest danger to blind contentment."

She folded her hands in her lap. "Oh, to be a child screaming until he is given a sweet so his mother can weep uninterrupted in a corner?"

"Please don't agree with me just now." Kayvin shook his head. "Don't argue with me either. I just failed in one of the most critical discussions of my life and proved they were right not to treat me as a prince."

Yovela put a hand on his shoulder. "No matter what else, you are—"

"I have a title. A title without power, and no sense to use power if I had it. Let me come to grips with this."

He could insist that he had been right; he had Pasiphae Jade to point to for evidence, and the humans' ancient treachery in keeping the amulets and abandoning the Rideis in their hour of need. But now he'd peered from beneath his insulating hood and had seen more.

Yovela withdrew her hand and stood. "I'm going to buy something to eat. I'll bring two."

"I don't want anything."

"Then I'll eat both, if you're going to sulk."

He glared after her. Then she was gone, and he sat alone on the bench, his elbows on his spread knees, his stomach churning.

After a few minutes, Yovela returned and extended a roll of soft dough and goat cheese. It smelled heavenly. "Is this yours or mine?"

"Empty void, you put that scent under my nose and then ask?" His unsettled stomach would calm for this.

She smiled and sat down again beside him, taking a bite of her own roll. "Do you want to talk about it yet?"

"No." Never, not with her. He had made lies of his words to her, when he had told her he was sorry for her losses, and he would make up for that somehow. He pushed bread and cheese into his mouth so that he would not have to answer further.

"Did it go too poorly to try again?"

Empty void, he had not considered going back. But he could not imagine what he would say, now that he had offended General Artextra and the officials and nobles around her. And he could not appeal to a history they did not seem to remember.

After a few moments, Yovela asked, "Can you at least tell me what we'll do next?"

He swallowed the last of his roll. "We go the same way, and we find an amulet."

CHAPTER 75

THE NEXT DAY, GALEN stopped by the commissary to see whether any of the savory vegetable pies were left—it didn't hurt to look—and saw Anela at the end of a long table, a little separate from a chatting threesome. He hesitated, not wanting to give the wrong impression, but he felt awkward about what Lisveth had interpreted for him the other day, and it wouldn't be wrong to be friendly, would it? So he went by the end of the table. "Is this open?"

She gestured. "Go ahead." She was partly through a vegetable pie of her own. "Where's your partner?"

"On a walk, or shopping, or something. She's likely browsing in a market, but she probably won't come back with anything. She doesn't do well sitting still."

"You don't look like siblings."

"What? We're not."

"But you're not..."

"We're partners, as you said. For jobs."

She nodded.

"What about you? Are you the general's daughter?"

"What?" She sounded offended.

"I don't know much about the military, but you seem younger than you should be. Artextra must have been a general for a while, and she seems the type to keep her people."

"Feora died two years ago."

"Oh." Galen looked down at his pie, but it offered no recovery. "I'm sorry."

"I was working under Feora, so I knew some, and I'm a quick learner." She turned her wooden hand slightly. "And I wasn't coming up through the ranks another way."

Galen nodded. "Again, I'm sorry."

"Oh, that's all right. It's not something for you to be sorry about. Mostly this gives people the idea that I was a great warrior before I became an aide."

Galen raised an eyebrow. "Are you suggesting that isn't the case?"

"Traffic accident. I fell, and a cart rolled over my hand. But I got out, which is more than some."

He winced. "Oh, I'm sorry. Got out?"

"This was in Atalasu City, in the fire. I fell in the crowd. It was a stampede, really. But we were ahead of the fire."

News of a fire in Atalasu City had not made its way to the Heel, but she spoke as if it were common knowledge, and he didn't want to admit he'd never heard of what had clearly been a devastating event for others. "It must have been terrifying."

She nodded briefly. "But, I got away better than many, and I'm always grateful for that. Mostly." She gave him a self-deprecating smile, and it looked good on her.

"Do you like working as an aide?"

"I'm very good at it."

"I've seen that." Galen tipped his head. "But that's not exactly an answer, so... I'm sorry, I suppose I'm asking personal questions."

"It's a bit late for that worry, after we've talked about the hand." She looked flustered. "I...I think we don't have much time, maybe, so I'll be blunt. I'd like to settle down, as they say. Find a husband, have a family, live in one home. I'm a very good aide, and the general knows it and treats me well, but...a girl can wish, too."

"Wouldn't being an aide be a good way to meet a lot of soldiers?"

She laughed. "First, there's the general. Most enlisted men don't have the courage to step out with someone in her office."

Galen grinned. "I suppose you're right."

"Secondly, it is a good way to meet a lot of soldiers. But the problem is, I know a lot about soldiers." She chuckled to undercut the words.

Galen laughed.

"And then..." She sobered, and she wiggled her hand again. "There's this."

Galen frowned. "But...but that's not..."

"It is, for some. For a lot." She shrugged. "Maybe you could understand that."

Because...because of his hair? Galen's pie went tasteless.

"So I like to say what happened early on. Get it over with, so to speak." She spoke casually, but there were tight lines in her face.

Had she looked at Galen because he also had an impediment to a good match? But that was a cruel assumption, and even if she had, it meant only that she knew some might not like red hair, and it clearly wasn't an issue for her. Still... "I hope you find someone who sees past such a small thing," he said, unsure if it was the right thing to say.

She nodded. "That's clear enough, and kindly meant. Thank you."

He felt guilty for no reason he could define. "I'm sorry."

"No need. I got that answer back in the office. I only thought maybe, when you stopped here, you'd reconsidered."

"I'm sorry," he repeated. "To be clear, it isn't...your hand."

"I didn't think it was." She smiled. "I think you're waiting for something else."

"Maybe."

"There was someone I would have waited for," she said wistfully. "Oh—I'm sorry, but if things are clear, we can talk about it, right?"

"I suppose so," he agreed uncertainly. "Even if you say anything you regret, I'll be out soon and you can forget it was ever said."

She laughed. "I like a practical sort. Anyway, there was a caravan guard—sort of like a soldier, I suppose, but different in the better ways."

"I was a caravan guard once," Galen said. "So I think they're probably better than soldiers, yes."

She laughed. "Were you?"

"Only a very short time. So you liked this one?"

"I liked him. Pretty well. But when we talked, I kept my hand under the desk or behind the basket I was carrying or, you know, because I was still a bit ashamed of it then."

Galen nodded, and then he hoped she would think him interested in her story and not agreeing with her shame.

"At last he asked me to go out for a drink, before he rolled out of town again. I wanted to, but I couldn't that night—the general had an important meeting—and when I was trying to explain, I forgot to keep the hand down... Anyway, I think that's what happened. He said he was sorry I couldn't make it, nice enough, and then the next day he was gone. Never came back through that town." She shrugged. "Now I make sure things are clear, so I don't waste my time getting dreamy over someone who won't want it."

A rush of irritation ran through Galen. "If he didn't come back because of that, then he was never worth your dreams."

She tipped her head to the side to look at him. "See, I thought you were a good one." She smiled. "Just not a good one for me."

"I'm sorry."

"No, I think I am. But I wish you the best." She laughed. "And that was probably too near something I shouldn't have said, and now I'll have to hope you finish your business here soon so I can forget it was said."

His ears and neck burned, and he knew he was blushing, and he wished he could hide his hair and his flush under the table or behind a basket.

She had mercy on him. "Well, my pie is done, and I should get back to my desk. It was good to talk with you, and thanks for sharing a table." She stood.

He nodded. "It was good to talk with you. I wish you all the best fortune I can muster."

"I'll take it, thanks."

When she had gone, Galen sat still, trying to decide how he felt. It had been...nice, to be seen. She had been both straightforward and fair, even if she had hinted at his hair. And she... Well, he almost wished he'd understood her lunch invitation, back in the general's office. No, he wasn't interested in settling down with her, but someone would be fortunate to do so.

For now, though, there was only more waiting and wondering. Chafing. Perhaps Lisveth had the right idea with wandering the market instead of sitting still.

CHAPTER 76

GALEN AND LISVETH, AFTER picking up fresh rolls from the kitchen, went to the clerks' office to watch the morning processing of reports. Galen found the process reassuringly dull. Two clerks skimmed the daily or weekly reports for notable news that should be forwarded to officers or nobles. Another took rapid notes if something significant was found, summarizing it aloud to crosscheck details with the first reader, and then dispatched the update. Generally, reports were not urgent.

After about forty minutes, however, a clerk indicated for others to listen. "There's a strange report out of Barkerton."

"Strange? In what way?"

"I mean, it's a small town that shouldn't have anything beyond the occasional chicken theft, but they say their temple was burgled."

Lisveth nudged Galen, but he was already listening more closely.

"Well, that was only a matter of time. Even small temples have a bit of gold in them, and people get greedy, especially when there's uncertainty in the air. A few rumors of bandits or demons, and it's a wonder we have only one temple treasury lost."

"But that's the strange thing of it. The gold wasn't touched. Only one item was taken. No accounting for idiots, I suppose."

Galen's own amulet brushed the skin of his chest, and he almost imagined it must be visible through the shirt.

Lisveth slid off her bench and followed the clerks' delivery girl to the general's office. Anela received the box with a nod of thanks and then looked over the departing delivery girl to Lisveth and Galen. "Yes?"

"One of those reports," Galen said, nodding toward the box. "We think General Artextra will be interested."

Anela did not roll her eyes, but she managed to convey her wish to do so. "Of course she'll be interested. That's why it's in her report box."

"Amulet's been stolen," Lisveth said bluntly. "Like we said."

Anela gave her a look that wavered between incredulous and worried. Then she opened the box.

"Fourth one down, I think," Lisveth supplied in a neutral tone.

Anela took out the sheet in question and ran her eyes over the summary. Then she rose and, carrying the box with her, knocked at the general's door.

The general was indeed interested. She snatched the sheet from Anela and scanned it, her eyes leaping from line to line as she swore under her breath.

"Was anyone hurt?" Galen asked.

She shook her head tightly. "Not according to this early report. It sounds like it was a break-in overnight." She blew out her breath in one more angry epithet. "Not two days after that Selk prince told us he wanted the amulets for his own rebellion. Not two days."

"There will be less panic if no one was hurt," Anela said. "But I'll get some eyes on that area."

General Artextra shook her head again. "It's a small temple in an out-of-the-way town. I don't think anyone was convinced it was a real amulet, one of the old ones."

"I can't imagine that he would have taken it if he got to it and discovered it was a fraud," Lisveth said practically.

Galen nodded. "I think he knows exactly what he's looking for."

Artextra made a broad gesture. "It doesn't matter if this one is real or not. He's willing to thieve them, and that's enough to get people stirred up. And the next one might be real. Or it might be in a major temple in a city with enough guards to make trouble when a Selk prince tries to raid it. Things could get messy."

Lisveth's face tightened. "You mean, one of the major temples?"

"Why not? The Vernal House, or the Three Wings—or, I don't know, does the Three Wings claim to have an amulet? I need the notes."

"How many guards can you put on a temple?"

Artextra scowled. "Not enough, unless the priests are sufficient."

Galen gaped. "You're not sending any guards to the temples?"

General Artextra held up a hand to stave off his incredulity. "Look, it's not as simple as my decision."

"But you're a general," Galen replied before he could stop himself. "Who else would decide?"

She gave him a sour look and crossed her arms. "One advantage to an octovirate instead of a king is that with a king, you need only one panicky, stupid, or disinterested individual to enact a bad decision, and with an octovirate, you need at least four." She retreated to her desk and dropped into the chair, which creaked.

"The unfortunate fact, however, is that there is no shortage of panicky, stupid, or disinterested individuals in the world. And in fairness, you have the luxury of focusing only on this one concern, instead of all the myriad issues of governing a nation, especially one facing an increase in highway bandit activity. Protecting trade must come before heeding a single madman who claims he can use lost artifacts to reclaim another throne that, frankly, we don't mind seeing weakened." She waved a hand vaguely. "After considering submitted opinions—and weighing some more heavily than others—the Octovirate does not think setting guards on temples, many in smaller towns or rural places, or trying to track down rumors of amulets, some real and some local legends, is a better use of resources than setting those soldiers on the roads to deal with the bandits directly."

"But he's said plainly that he's here for the amulets," Galen repeated. "He's already stolen one."

"A man who has said he is a foreign prince, without any credentials or state regalia or even a proper escort, has said he wants a handful of quasi-legendary relics currently scattered across the countryside. Even if he finds them, what would he do with them? They're a story, and like all good stories, maybe there was something true about it once. But maybe this one has become something else in the telling."

"The amulets are real." Galen shut his mouth too late, after the words had escaped like goats.

But General Artextra did not ask why he had said so or why he believed as he did. She leaned back in the chair and threw a glance at the door. "Anela, when is Lord Carbor due?"

"Not for another few minutes." Anela stepped to the door and stood against it.

Artextra nodded and looked back toward Galen and Lisveth. "I've seen an amulet before, one we know to be real and one of the originals. The Sculptor's Eye, it's called, and it's part of the state collection in the palace. It's supposed to increase the strength of the wearer, make him or her capable of profound feats." She smiled, a little fondly. "The stories they tell... Once a captain leaped from one ship to another, it's said. Once a man threw a spear that pierced a tree. And who knows? Maybe those tales were true. It's not so impossible to leap from one ship to another, after all, if one has little fear of water and if the two ships are lashed nearly together." She shrugged and chuckled.

Galen wanted to protest that the stories were real, that the amulets worked and the magic was real—but there was no way to say so without betraying more information than they were prepared to give. If she did not believe in the value of the relics, he did not want to identify them and be asked to relinquish them to her.

"But whatever the case in the past, it's useless now. It's a piece of jewelry, that's all, and not a particularly precious one. No diamonds, no gold, just a creepy staring eye." General Artextra sat forward, resting her elbows on the desk. "The amulets burn out, the stories say, and nothing our mages have done have restored them. If they were powerful once—and for the sake of argument, let's say they were—then their power does not last. This Prince Kayvin may exhaust himself trying to find the pieces to his puzzle, and then eventually he'll see that he's gathered, not a phenomenal weapon to use against us or his interloper, but only some trinkets."

Galen's frustration colored his tone. "So you'll just let him have them, then? Because they're not worth anything?"

"They have historical value, of course. And some are undoubtedly culturally important to their local temples or communities, regardless of whether they're authentic. But they are not worth leaving the roads unprotected and our citizens at risk, and that's the decision of the Octovirate. And a good general cannot disregard the feeling of the Octovirate, or at least of the four who prefer to squeeze their eyes shut and hum."

"This Sculptor's Eye," Lisveth prompted, thoughtful. "When the state mages tried to revive it—when was that?"

"What? Oh, I don't know. It's been a project of interest intermittently for a hundred years or more. I remember hearing about it back when I was climbing ranks in the capital. But you can see it, you know. Every year, when the state treasures are open to public viewing, it's one of the items on display." She laughed. "If Prince Kayvin wants to wait for the founder's birthday and then take on all the capital guard and the state mages guarding the crown jewels, just to steal an amulet no one has been able to coax any magic from in generations, well, that's his choice, I suppose. But I wouldn't put money on his success. He'd do far better with the others, don't you think?"

"I suppose the mages documented their efforts," Lisveth said slowly.

"I'm sure," General Artextra said with the mildest of interest. "Such attempts, with that amulet and any known others, would be well documented. That's all in the mages' library."

"In Atalasu City."

The general nodded. "In Atalasu City."

Lisveth stared at the desk.

"So there's no profit for someone stealing them. Thank you for bringing the one you did, but it's all the same in the end. We'll return it, eventually, when the discussion has died down."

"If we could prove," Galen blurted in sudden effort, "if we could prove the amulets had power, would it make a difference?"

General Artextra looked at him. "If you could prove the state mages wrong and restore one? Or if you could find one that had not yet lost the final dregs of its power? Well, I suppose that one would be worth protecting, obviously. But I don't know how you'd know where to look." She looked down and pulled a drawer from the desk. "This drawer sticks. Annoying. Oh, by the way, I believe you still have that letter you talked Lord Bryuki into giving you?"

"That's right," Galen said. "But..."

General Artextra nodded. "Yes, I'm afraid you'll have to return that, so that you cannot use it again to gain entrance to see the temple priests and ask about the amulets. We can't have bandit hunters going around in a march lord's name. Please be sure you leave that with Anela."

Lisveth nodded. "We'll be certain to return it," she said, enunciating each word carefully. She did not look at the aide behind her. "I'll hand it directly to Anela when next I see her."

"It's a sensitive document now," the general agreed, "so make sure you put it directly into her hands. If she happens to be out when you stop by, you can bring it back later."

"Of course," Lisveth answered.

Behind them, Anela put her hand on the door and pushed it open. "Lord Carbor will be here soon."

"Then I suppose you'd better get going," General Artextra said to Galen and Lisveth. "Oh, and Anela will pay you for your services—those you've rendered already, I mean. There should be enough to take you along the road for a bit." She reached for the report box. "I need to at least skim the rest of these. Fare well."

Anela stepped behind the door as she held it for them. Lisveth went straight out, looking neither right nor left. "Why don't you collect our payment for previous services?" she suggested to Galen. "I'll wait outside."

Anela beckoned him to follow her to her own desk, where she counted out coins from a lock-drawer. She held out the bag, and Galen took it.

"A moment." She opened a lower drawer with her wooden hand. "I asked Brother Lucaw to make a list before he left. He didn't have all the materials, but he wrote down what he could. Here's a copy." She twisted to retrieve something and then passed a sheet to Galen.

He glanced at the uncertain script. *Singer — red — perception, Painter — gold, Storyteller, Dancer, Player — violet, Poet, Sculptor — opalescent — strength.* "Uh, thanks."

She nodded. "Safe travels." Her eyes lingered on Galen for an instant, and she smiled, and then she looked to her work-filled desk, dismissing him.

Galen walked into the sunlight to rejoin Lisveth. "I feel as if something large just walked past me, and I missed it."

Lisveth nodded slowly. "I think we were just given a highly unofficial commission."

"We're supposed to protect the amulets?"

"In one way or another."

Galen turned up his palms. "But if a cohort of soldiers can't guard the temples, what are we supposed to do?"

"Prince Kayvin can't steal something that isn't there."

"So we steal it first. You're saying the general wants us to steal the amulets."

"Of course not." Lisveth took an indignant tone. "The general cannot tell us, a pair of raggedy bandit hunters, to steal cultural artifacts from the religious houses of our land. That would be ridiculous."

"Watch how you say raggedy," Galen warned, straightening his jacket.

"No, the general could never be caught saying such a thing," Lisveth continued. "Nor would the general gainsay the Octovirate's decision to focus their resources on guarding the remote roads from known bandits rather than on guarding city temples."

"I see."

"What the general might do, in good conscience, is reminisce about the verified artifact she saw once, and she might reflect that while it's not likely to be a useful weapon to anyone, it's still an heirloom, and one that may hold magic or recoverable magic, and something that should be preserved in Sayinia, rather than carried off to a foreign land."

Galen put a dramatically thoughtful finger to his chin. "Did she speak of preserving heirlooms?"

Lisveth elbowed him, but gently. "She meant it. Anyway, she knows we've already delivered one amulet to keep it safe, so we're at least a little bit trustworthy."

Galen thought of the dull red eye, unblinking and unremarkable. "What she said about the power of the amulets fading—what do you think about that? Clearly some are still working."

"But not all," Lisveth confessed. "I put the Singer's Eye on briefly. Nothing happened."

Galen was not surprised. He'd considered trying it, too. "Maybe you couldn't recognize the effect because it wasn't for you," he protested logically. "Like the Painter's Eye does not make you forget yourself, it blurs you for others' thoughts."

She nodded. "I thought of that. But the Singer's Eye is one we know, and it's said to enhance the wearer's perception. But I couldn't detect any enhancement, not in sight or hearing or smelling or, well, anything."

"Oh, right." He drew out the list. "That's what it says here: Singer, red, perception."

Lisveth took the list. "Hmm. Well, at least this is something."

"So you tested the Singer's Eye? With your own magic?"

She nodded. "Ran a little tingle of power through it. No blink, no flicker, nothing at all."

"So it was dead, or depleted, or something. Or it was never one of the real amulets to start."

"I guess either could be true." She returned the sheet and crossed her arms, tucking the little pouch of coins close to her torso. "Anyway, we have money to travel, and nothing to hold us here."

"And a dozen or more possible amulets, real or imagined." Galen turned his eyes out to the great beyond. "How could we hope to find any real ones to protect and steal, outside of the capital, when even the state mages think little of them?"

"If there's one thing I've learned, it's to give half a rotten fig for what a state mage thinks," Lisveth said with disgust. "And a pair of not-so-raggedy bandit hunters is less likely to be blinded by our own importance."

"You think they cannot imagine a true amulet that isn't preserved in the capital treasures?" Galen felt the weight of his own bumping gently against his chest as they walked.

"It wouldn't be the first time." Lisveth turned toward their room. "The *Fable May* was a merchant ship lost in the Bay of Blue Ice, about fifteen years ago. There was a terrible storm, and it never arrived. The guild said it was gone, the local authorities said it was gone, even the ship's owners gave up the search for it. Everyone ignored the local village who kept outfitting their homes and selling expensive new materials that weren't in their local markets, who whenever asked politely explained they were taking them from the grounded ship. It was three years before someone from the guild went out and found the wreckage of the *Fable May* sitting on a ledge, twenty leagues from her destination but providing nicely for a remote village too unimportant to be listened to."

"You don't have to convince me," Galen said. "I already know there was an amulet in the Heel."

"And that sounds unbelievable," Lisveth said frankly. "Even to my open mind. But another example: Way in the south, there's a series of rapids in the Tomold River that makes it unnavigable for a half-mile or so, that a local legend said was once a stone walkway over the river until struck down by an angry god. Of course, the learned men all knew the legend to be balderdash—divine miracles occur only when observed by priests—until some clever person found a cave of preserved manuscripts that not only mentioned this pathway, but illustrated it, a natural stone arch over the river."

"Now you're just showing off," Galen said. "Mocking the learned men."

She nodded in amiable agreement. "I'm willing to bet once the state mages couldn't resurrect the Sculptor's Eye in the capital, they gave less credence to the stories of amulets in lesser towns. Even if the amulets might be real, they were more or less worthless. The point is, the puppet show was true, in its way, and the provenance of your own amulet was true, and I think we'll do better than the state mages if we start by assuming the stories exist for a reason."

"And if the amulets have lost their power?"

She shrugged. "Then at the very least, we have a cultural heirloom to redeem to the Octovirate."

CHAPTER 77

THEY'D WALKED THROUGH A long stretch of forest, dense with old trees that creaked in the wind and whispered ancient secrets, and Galen was beginning to understand where frightening legends of spirits in the dark came from, when at last the trees began to thin and clear meadow showed ahead. As they stepped into the light, however, Lisveth swore and jerked back, and Galen found himself ducking and stumbling back with her without quite knowing why. "What was that?"

Lisveth put a hand over her eyes and blew out her breath in an irritated snort. "We just ran away from a dragon."

"A dragon?" Galen made a face. Even in the Heel, they knew dragons were either extinct or practically so, certainly no longer in Sayinia.

But when he followed Lisveth's gaze, he saw the dragon. It hung in the sky, wings spread to catch the wind, and its long tail swam snakelike, stabilizing it. It was mostly red, with a darker underbelly, and its head tipped down toward the earth as it hovered.

Dragons weren't supposed to hover.

Galen blinked, and the dragon resolved into a kite, all cloth and paper and cord. A cluster of people stood below, watching in awe.

"Idiot," Lisveth muttered, but he didn't think it was for the kite or the audience. He followed her out of the sheltering trees. He also felt foolish for ducking back—but it was astounding, really, how instinct had taken over, prompting him to hide before he'd even identified the ostensible danger.

The kite was enormous—probably not quite the size of an actual dragon, if legends were to be believed, but impressive. It was hard to guess, with the kite suspended midair, but Galen supposed three men could have lain head to toe across the wingspan.

A team of men and women were working the lines that bound the kite to earth. Their faces shone with pride and delight as Galen and Lisveth drew near enough to see them.

"You scared us half to death with that thing," Lisveth called by way of greeting, her tone making it a compliment.

"Apologies," called a young woman, and her tone made it a friendly joke. "She gets frisky at times."

"How'd you come by a dragon kite?" Galen asked.

"We're getting her ready for the festival," the woman answered. "What do you think, do we have a chance at the prize this year?"

Galen didn't know the festival she meant, but a nearby man provided, "Up in Taniman City."

Galen thought that was to the north—probably a lot of wind, good for a kite festival.

"She would take any prize I offered," Lisveth assured them. "Good luck with her."

"Thanks! We based her on an old bestiary illustration. It's nice to hear she looks the part."

Lisveth turned to another spectator. "If we wanted a town not plagued by dragons, where we could get a safe meal and a bed, is this the road to take?"

The man chuckled. "This one makes sure there are no other dragons around to make trouble. Territorial, you know. And I have a public room that's going to open as soon as we're done here. Would that be the kind of thing you're looking for?"

"If you'll have hot food, it's exactly the thing."

"We've got beds, too. I can make you a price for the both."

"We'll wait here and follow you back."

Two days on, Galen lay on his back, looking up at the night. It would be cool and damp before morning, but sometimes there were few alternatives to sleeping along the road.

They'd found a good location for tonight, at least. The meadow had thick grass to cushion them and shield them from any late or early passersby on the road a stone's throw behind them. A flock of sheep were gathered within earshot, murmuring to one another quietly, with the breeze in the right direction for the smell. And the sky was clear, promising beautiful stars to guard them.

Lisveth had rolled into her cloak and nestled into the meadow grasses, an arm's reach away. It wasn't cold enough for them to lie back to back, not tonight. The scent of the crushed grasses tickled Galen's nose.

"Aren't you asleep?" Lisveth asked without turning.

"No." Galen propped his head on an arm. "It's early yet."

"It is. Too early to sleep and too dark to do anything useful." She rolled to face him. "It's an annoying time, an in-between time."

"A time for remembering and reflecting," Galen suggested with a smile. "A time for recalling how far we've come, and where we are now. A time for thinking of how far we have yet to go."

She closed her eyes. "As I said, an annoying time."

Galen felt rebuffed. He'd been joking, but he hadn't been obnoxious. "I certainly never thought I'd be on an errand for a general, even unofficially."

She opened her eyes again and looked at him. "I suppose this is pretty far from what you expected, farm boy." The words could have been mocking, but her tone was almost gentle.

"I suppose it is." He shrugged. "You too, because when I met you, you were a notorious highwaywoman. Now you're taking legitimate payment from the army."

She made a sound like a disgruntled pig and rolled onto her back. "Don't make it sound so respectable. Besides, this is still under the table. We don't have a clear and legal commission."

"Whatever makes you able to sleep at night." But he pressed, "After all, you weren't a very good highwaywoman."

"I beg your pardon?" Lisveth fixed her gaze on him in mostly mock offense. "I did well enough."

"You did, and you had the infamous reputation to match. But you told me, when I came that first night, that you had to take precautions in towns, lest people suspect a single woman traveling alone as the Fire Brigand did."

"And that means I wasn't good at it?"

"You didn't need to be suspected; you could have looked like anything. And you didn't need to be a highwaywoman at all." Galen gave her a significant look. "If your illusions are so good—and they are," he added quickly, "and if no one even suspects they could be illusions, you could have walked into any shop in any town and picked up whatever you wanted. You could have made yourself look like someone else, or nothing at all. You could have been a thief who didn't even exist. You could have stolen anything from anyone, without the hazard of a reputation or of caravan guards fighting back. So why didn't you?"

"That's a good question, farm boy." Her voice was sober in the twilight. "You do use your brain sometimes."

But it wasn't praise for an idea that had never occurred to her; it was a reluctant acknowledgment that he'd thought of something logical.

"I wasn't here yet to try to talk you out of it," he pressed. "You were already a thief. Why take the more dangerous path?"

She gave a flat little laugh. "And who would speak ill of a thief who wasn't even known to exist?"

"What?"

But she was already rolling away from him, facing into the tall grass. "Good stargazing conditions, I think. Good night."

"Wait, were you—what did that mean?"

She didn't answer, and the silence felt heavy.

Galen looked at her back. What she'd said made no sense. Had she wanted the Octovirate to send soldiers after her? That was ridiculous.

Crickets sang from the grasses around them. Galen adjusted his shoulder to a more comfortable position and traced the path of the Ladle's Pour as the stars emerged from the darkening sky.

HOSTAGE

CHAPTER 78

KAYVIN'S PULSE WAS AN unwelcome percussion in his ears, and he caught himself shifting his weight and tapping his fidgeting fingers against one another as if fretting an instrument. He forced himself to be still—the Amethyst Prince, rather than a nervous child hoping for praise.

On either side, two steps behind, Yovela and Dielo stood at easy attention, their practiced poses of casual display making him almost envious. Their role in this audience was simple: bring attention and lend status to their master.

But he was the Amethyst Prince. He was the one with honor and status and prestige. He was the one bringing Pasiphae Jade what she needed, condescending to aid her, offering her what she lacked. He drew himself straight and waited for permission to enter.

She kept him waiting just long enough to emphasize that the Amethyst Prince still waited upon the Arch Potentate, and then he was admitted.

He chose to employ all his court manners, treating this audience in the grand way she might prefer. He swept into her apartment and sailed toward her dais, trailing Yovela and Dielo like bejeweled barques in his wake, and when he reached the appropriate distance he bowed low. On either side of him Dielo and Yovela knelt in liquid movement, heads low, gems flashing.

"My prince." Pasiphae Jade's voice was smooth and almost warm. "Welcome home. We are glad your journey has ended safely."

This audience was not private. Yovela and Dielo were there, of course, and several of Pasiphae Jade's own sera qadra, but there were also a handful of courtiers, lounging or standing about the room, anxious to observe and be observed near the seat of power.

Let them stare. Let them see that Kayvin could play the game as well, that he could know his own place even as he humored Pasiphae Jade's wishes. Today he would present what Pasiphae Jade so desperately wanted, and she would return his mother to him—and then he would be free to act.

He straightened. "I am happy I was able to come safely to you, to deliver what you requested."

Requested. It was a generous word to use when bartering with his mother's life, but he would play the game. And using that word stole a little power back for himself.

Yovela and Dielo rose in unison. Kayvin brought out the amulet, tied in richly dyed fabric, and held it out. One of Pasiphae Jade's beautiful servants hurried to collect it, bowing, and then delivered it safely into her mistress's hand, where she worked the knot until the cloth slid free. An unseeing violet eye stared toward the painted ceiling.

Pasiphae Jade looked down at the amulet on her palm, her expression shadowed. Kayvin pressed his lips together, controlling his smile.

At last she raised her head. "This?"

A stab of uncertainty pierced him. "That is one of the great amulets," he said. "I tested it."

"You tested it," Pasiphae Jade repeated, looking at it. "And then you brought it to me."

"Yes."

"It."

"Yes." He did not understand.

"You've brought me a single amulet."

He stared at her. "I brought you an artifact. I stole it from a temple. I did—do you know what I went through for that? Sleeping in inns, trying to pass as a human—doing a remarkable job of it for the most part, actually, and—"

"One amulet?" she interrupted, her voice rising. "What am I to do with a single amulet?"

He turned his hands up in savage ignorance. "I don't know what you intend to do with a dozen amulets. I don't know anything of your plans. You told me to bring an amulet to redeem my mother, and I've done it. And now you say it's not enough."

"It is not enough!" Her fingers clenched white on the jewelry, and the eye winked between her fingers. "One amulet will not save anyone. You have the temerity to stand there and claim you deserve consideration because you have stayed at inns, common inns, with common people, with no one to serve you but your *sera qadra woman!*" She flung a gesture at Yovela, who remained quiet and expressionless. "Well, look at what I have done, while you suffered in an ordinary inn with ordinary people. I have watched my body sold, I have hidden my mind and played a fool, I have murdered my lord, I have negotiated with nobles who disdain me and cooperate with me only for what power and favor I can provide, and I live every moment knowing I manage an ally who would kill me if he dared."

Kayvin's chest tightened. If one of the nobles would kill her—if he could make a friend of this unreliable ally...

She leaned forward, her eyes glittering. "But he won't dare, because while I've killed more than once to take and hold the only seat where I can do good, he has been struggling with the overwhelming challenge of lying to foolish humans."

Kayvin. She meant Kayvin. He had no hidden allies, no possible friends. There were only the nobles who despised him for his weakness, just as she did.

They were not wrong.

Too many feelings whirled inside him, fury at being denied success and the return of his mother, shock at being called her nearest ally, despair at realizing she was right to belittle him when he could never stop her. His tangled emotions blurred into a grey skein of noise, a cacophony without individual voices.

"Get out," she snapped, but her order was not for him. Her sera qadra drew themselves up from their various lounges and filed out of the room. The courtiers moved more slowly, lingering in the hope of drama, but they had to eventually reach the doors.

Yovela did not move. Dielo shifted his weight, slid one foot to the side, and then steadied. Kayvin wanted to embrace them and wanted to shout at them to go.

Pasiphae Jade ignored them, chaff in the gale of her anger. She rose and advanced upon Kayvin. "You useless heap. You absolute blob of sickly jelly. You are so like your father, except you can't even be bothered to stir yourself for lovemaking, or even the sanitized war of a royal court." She stabbed a finger at him. "You had one task, and you went how many times into Sayinia? How many times? And you bring one amulet. One! Just one. As if I am to save the kingdom with one amulet."

He shook his head in futile protest. "The amulets are scattered. No one knows where they all are." He was not speaking well in his agitation. "I was proud to have found that one, and to have stolen it safely."

"I don't care how you acquired it! I care only that you bring me sufficient tools to preserve us when the spawning comes."

"How many amulets do you need?" He was afraid of the question, more afraid of the answer, but his mother's life depended on knowing.

"As many as you can find!" she snapped. "Half a dozen. A dozen!" She returned to sink into her chair and put her face into her hand. "I have done everything to be in the right place, and to have the ability to do what must be done. I have sacrificed my lord and made myself a monster, all because I knew I would be justified in the end. And without the amulets, I will not be justified."

A fresh ember of anger stirred in the ash of Kayvin's dismay and horror. "Nothing can justify what you have done."

She raised her face. "You say that because you have never faced the spawning without hope. You have not read the accounts of those who were there, who survived. You would think differently if you were standing in your garden, facing death, watching those around you die, knowing this could have been stopped."

He did not understand, and he did not want to. Fire burned within him, shaking him, and he was afraid he would crack apart in the center of the room, breaking apart before her, helpless in his rage.

"Get me another amulet. Get me another amulet, or I will break pieces off of that ice, taking part of her with each shattered fragment. I don't care if the amulets are hidden or lost, I don't care if they are in palace or temple—get them for me." She drew an audible breath. "I believe I will need five even to attempt this, six to be sure, and all seven to do it with the least risk to myself. I do not care what it costs, whether money or jewels or an Amethyst Prince, only get me those amulets."

Energy ran through Kayvin, making him tremble, making him want to shout, making him want to strangle her, making him want to flee from her. His arms prickled with it, and his stomach twisted as if on a roasting spit.

"Get out," she ordered tersely, with a flick of her hand. "You fail me and you disgust me. Get out."

Kayvin wanted to speak, but the words were bound up in him, tangled in the rage that made him shiver and burn.

Yovela stepped close to him, her arm nearly brushing his, and she bowed. On his opposite side, Dielo moved forward, bending low in front of Kayvin, glittering with oil and tiny crushed precious stones. "Your Illustrious Excellency, my lady, an Arch Potentate must not be unfair. The prince has brought you an amulet with his best effort—"

"Get out!"

Kayvin was guided backward by Yovela's magnetic draw. He got out of the audience room without remembering exactly how. He stared at the closed doors, and his mouth burned with poison.

"Not here," Yovela murmured.

"My prince," Dielo said aloud, "let us return to your apartments. I shall play for you there."

Kayvin knew he was being herded, but he was too angry to speak. He wanted to argue, just to assert himself—but they were all too near Pasiphae Jade's door, and she would hear his redirected anger, and she would enjoy it.

CHAPTER 79

HE WAS A FOOL. He had been a fool. He had humiliated himself before all, dressing in his court garments and going to Pasiphae Jade like a toddler anxious to show off his childish drawing. He had failed—failed not just to bring enough amulets, but failed in believing he could please her, failed in presenting himself as a prince with dignity, failed to redeem his mother.

He had stood quietly for her mockery and had protested feebly under her rebuke, and he was not an Amethyst Prince, not a prince, not a son, not a man. He was a fool.

They reached his apartments and he plunged through the door into the shelter, his only reprieve from Pasiphae Jade's sphere. But that wasn't quite true; he was sure her influence reached through some of his servants.

And there was Dielo.

Kayvin advanced through his primary rooms to a balcony and glared at the plants below as if they were at fault.

"My lord," Dielo said quietly, from a little distance. "Let us soothe you."

"I don't want to be soothed!" Kayvin slammed his fist onto the balustrade. "I want to burn the palace down, with her in it." He sent a little blast of fire down into the ruined plantings, where it sizzled out.

Dielo's lips compressed, and he slid away. Kayvin watched as the virilo rushed ahead, sweeping pillows into a pile—Kayvin did not want pillows, he did not want to sit, he wanted to burn things—and scurried for refreshments, and the sight was so pathetic, Kayvin could not send him away. Drinks and snacks would not mitigate a single word Pasiphae Jade had said, but the virilo could do only as he'd been trained, and even in his fury Kayvin did not have the heart to mock him.

Yovela slid a hand around his wrist. "I'm sorry," she whispered, and it should have been as useless as Dielo's silly pillows, but it was not.

He dropped his head and closed his eyes. Part of his garden was visible from other palace corridors, and someone might have seen his tantrum. He was a fool.

Yovela lifted his wrist with a feather's weight of pressure. He went with her, noticing that his apartments were now deserted but for the three of them. He wondered briefly if that was due to his rage or to some signal from his minimal sera qadra.

She settled him on Dielo's ridiculous pillows and knelt beside him. Her expression was tight, and she said nothing. But what was there to say?

Dielo knelt in front of him, his posture more formal than Yovela's and his manner subdued. He kept his eyes low. "What would my lord prefer?"

Kayvin did not want to answer questions, and he especially did not want to answer silly questions from a pleasure slave trying to distract him, like offering sweets to a crying child. He flapped a hand to dismiss the query.

Dielo flinched and bowed lower. "I could bring oils and scents."

Kayvin's irritation grew, blending with his stoked anger. "What are you doing? I've said I don't—" He stopped, because Dielo had bobbed lower, tucking his head. "What is that?" he demanded. "It's not as if I'm going to strike you."

Dielo did not lift his head, only waited.

"What? What is it?"

Dielo bent his head and waited.

"When a man is angry," Yovela supplied tersely, "he may often dominate another, in conquest or in brutality, or in both."

Kayvin stared at her, momentarily stunned from his rage. "That's..."

"Very common, my lord. It's a chief purpose for those sold for men's entertainment."

Kayvin shook his head. "That's—unreasonable. Horrific."

Yovela blinked once, her face an unfeeling mask, and then her eyes flicked to Dielo. "And he is cowering because some, feeling themselves slighted, find solace in being feared. Your virilo has been trained to offer that."

"I... I wouldn't..."

Yovela glanced back at the balcony over the garden.

Kayvin felt ill. He turned away from them, wanting to vomit up what he had just heard, what he had been expected to do.

Dielo slid backward, retreating.

It was too much. Kayvin was powerless, he was assumed to be a monster, he was incapable of being the monster that respected courtiers were. He was nothing, he was an embarrassment, he was useless.

"I don't want to hurt anyone here. I just want—to destroy something." He felt childish even as he spoke.

Dielo went to the desk across the room, where he twisted a sheet of paper into a bent stick. He rolled another, and wrapped them together, and after a moment he held up a lopsided figure with head, arms, and uneven legs. "A target, my lord," he said. "Shall I put him in the garden for you?"

Kayvin stared at the little figure. "That's about the quality of the foe I should face," he said bitterly. "That's the strength of the enemy I might fight."

Dielo's expression faltered as he tried to work out whether Kayvin was chastising him. Kayvin sighed and sagged upon the silly pillows. "You were right, Yovela, when you argued I was naïve to believe her."

Yovela was merciful. "You thought you were bringing what she wanted."

Dielo came again and sat down at a distance, the poppet loose in his hand. He looked lost. "Would my lord care for music? I could play for you."

Kayvin suppressed the desire to snap at him. "Just—just let me be. You don't need to—you can't soothe this away. I have humiliated myself before the court, and my mother remains imprisoned in ice, and I don't want to pretend it hasn't happened."

Dielo looked down, chagrined. Kayvin almost regretted his words; he did only as he'd been told.

Kayvin reached for the twisted paper doll and held it in two hands. "I hate her," he said, trying to keep his voice steady. "I hate her so much. I would do anything—I would take any opportunity—but she has my mother." He drew a long breath and squeezed the doll. "And maybe I should accept that you're right, Yovela, and she will never return her. Maybe—maybe she isn't even still alive. Maybe that ice is a coffin, rather than a prison."

Yovela dropped her eyes. Dielo gazed at him with heartbreak in his face.

Kayvin let fire rise from his palms and lick up the body of the poppet. "But I can't. As long as there is a chance... I can't risk killing my mother, not even to avenge my father or take a throne." He squeezed the burning doll and admitted something shameful. "And I don't know that I want to take back the throne. She's right about me; I'm a weak blob of jelly who doesn't want to fight for it. I just don't want her to have won it."

"You're not weak," Yovela said, putting a hand atop his. "I have seen you outside the palace. You are your own man."

"You're not weak," Dielo offered quietly. "You don't need to prove yourself upon someone else."

"I am nothing but weak," Kayvin insisted softly.

"Then we will help you," Dielo said quickly. "I will study for you. Yovela will go with you. We will support you, and you will be strong."

"I won't be strong until I have a cadre of nobles supporting my claim," Kayvin said bitterly, "but at any rate, thank you."

CHAPTER 80

KAYVIN PRACTICED HIS MAGIC, throwing fire at the upright stones in his garden. He made a pitiful show of defiance, sending a note to Pasiphae Jade declaring he would remain in the palace until Lord Trerin's egg hatched in the next week so that he could make the appropriate visitation to an esteemed courtier. He did these small things, and he lay alone in his sleeping pit and wished they were more.

"My lord?"

At Dielo's voice, Kayvin dropped the magic from his hands and turned to the side of the garden. "Finished already?"

"I have read the next chapters as you asked, yes. But I wanted to—I found this in the book."

"What's that?"

Dielo came further into the garden and extended a folded letter. It was unopened, with the complicated cuts and folds that locked it still intact. "It was tucked into the pages. I first thought it was to mark a place, but then I saw it was unopened."

There was a bird inked on the outside of the letter. A kestrel. Facing left.

Kayvin snatched the letter. Had Lord Narrim's alliance survived him? Did Kayvin have allies he did not know?

But as he tore the letterlocking open, he saw the writing was in Lord Narrim's hand. This was an old note, then, delivered too carefully and so not found until now. It could offer no fresh hope.

Still, he flattened the letter on his thigh, smoothing it to read.

Lord Fretton has been bought for her service with the promise of marital alliance. Not to the usurper herself—she will not share a throne—but she has a daughter, and he has sold his allegiance to sire a new dynasty for his sons. This daughter would make a precious hostage for exchange. I believe the usurper would wish to keep her near enough for oversight, and so she is likely not too far from the palace. I will continue to search.

Kayvin crumpled the letter. If Lord Narrim had not found this mysterious daughter before his death, there was little Kayvin could do without spies or allies after it. "A daughter," he muttered. "Pasiphae Jade's own daughter. But no one could know where she is."

"Actually..." Dielo looked down at the creased paper, and his expression drew taut. "I might."

The three of them sat close, heads together, not daring to let a breath of sound escape. Around them the damaged garden waved gently in the breeze, and browned blooms fell in the cool sun.

"She never called her a daughter," Dielo said carefully. "But the care she took to keep her secret... If she indeed has a daughter, Lirin is my best guess."

"And this girl is a maid?"

Dielo nodded. "A maid, and there was some talk of protection. Lirin believes, like so many, that rising to mistress or courtesan is her best path to a better life. To that end, she is open to interest from the nobility—though it's not as if, as a maid, she could refuse for long. But she told me when someone began to browse around her, her aunt put a stop to it." He shrugged. "She might have been protecting the secret of her daughter, as much as protecting her daughter. But in either case, it is an unusual amount of discouragement away from a mere maid."

Kayvin nodded. "Without any other prospects, I agree she seems the most likely choice."

"What do you mean to do?" asked Yovela.

"Pasiphae Jade has a hostage to bind me," Kayvin said fiercely. "It's time I have one to even the scales."

Yovela said nothing, her hands stiff on the dead ground cover.

Kayvin looked at Dielo. "You know her already. Will you bring her?"

"Bring her?"

Kayvin nodded. "We must have her within my reach, or there is no threat to it. Will you bring her into my apartments? After all, you know how it is done."

Dielo blinked. "My lord?"

"You said she is interested in becoming a courtesan. You know how one can be talked into that life. Go and do the same."

Dielo looked at his lap and squeezed his hands together. "I—I will try, my lord."

"You'll have to do better than that. If she does not come directly with you, and if word gets back to Pasiphae Jade, then that same protection will descend. You'll have to bring her with your first invitation, or we'll have to bring her by force. We can't afford to let Pasiphae Jade know what we intend until we have her safely here."

Yovela twisted her fingers in the dead ground cover, making it crackle. "And what will you do with her once she is here?"

Kayvin shrugged. "That doesn't matter now. The important part is that we have a hostage of comparable value."

Dielo had never expected to think back on it.

He had been a child when his parents were approached. Their son was exceptional, they were told. He had striking good looks and a pleasant, even eager personality. He could rise; they could give him so much more than what awaited him in a swampy farming village.

He had not thought on it for years—what was the point of remembering? He knew he had been given a choice, and he knew he had chosen, and he knew he had been chosen to serve great men and to rise to great station.

But Prince Kayvin had so naturally assumed that Dielo had been persuaded, just as Yovela had accused his selection of being exploitive. Now he remembered, and he knew he remembered through a lens of years of training, and he almost recognized...

But it did no good to think on that now. There was no benefit to believing, or suspecting, or knowing, or whatever one might call it—there was no benefit to questioning how he had come here. There was no benefit to believing his parents had been influenced with profit or prestige. There was no benefit to believing he was anything but a valuable elite, trained to a position few others would gain.

Realization could not bring freedom, only fury without a safe target.

And no matter what he thought he might realize, if he did think back, today's concerns were more urgent. He needed Prince Kayvin to like him and to keep him close. He needed Prince Kayvin to see Dielo helping him against the grasping Arch Potentate Pasiphae Jade. He needed to bring Prince Kayvin the girl Lirin.

And he knew, from their time in the kitchen and at the servants' party, how to do it. It would be easy to dangle an offer of elevated status, of duties other than a maid's drudgery, of glamor and privilege and of being desired instead of ignored. It would be the work of a conversation.

She once had hoped to use him to climb to others' notice; he had only to concede to what she had already wanted. She would not wait to consider the ridiculous question of remaining a maid.

And so Dielo dressed himself in fine garments, the clothing of a rich man's favorite, and went out into the palace. He found Lirin in an ostensible coincidence and fell into easy conversation with her. He let slip that the prince was looking for additional servants, preferably beautiful young women. He let himself be talked into taking Lirin to interview with Arad, and he amiably advised her when she asked his opinion between two hairstyles to make a good impression.

And then she was settling her small box of belongings in the servant's quarters, and Dielo was sitting in his sleeping pit, staring numbly at the wall opposite.

He had done what his master had asked, and he had fulfilled Lirin's own dream. Both would be satisfied. Both would be grateful to Dielo. He had pleased everyone.

He did not know why he did not feel proud.

CHAPTER 81

KAYVIN WALKED INTO HIS study to find it in disarray. His books and scrolls for human culture were stacked upon his desk, but the texts from his tutelage were pulled down from their storage and piled irregularly upon the floor, where Yovela was putting them into two open chests.

"What is all this?"

She did not look up. "I'm tidying for you," she said. "You don't have a full staff of servants, and those you have won't know enough to sort these properly, as you're not in the habit of discussing your preferences and conclusions with them."

Still confused, he advanced into the midst of the fray. Philosophy texts, discussions of ethics, religious scriptures and commentaries, all were going into the chest without order.

"I don't understand," he protested.

She slammed a heavy book into a stack. "I'm packing away the moral high ground, since you have no use for it any longer and will undoubtedly resent being reminded of it."

Kayvin tensed. "What?"

"Oh, don't pretend you have no idea what I'm talking about!" Yovela burst. "You know there's a new girl in the servants' quarters. You know she came here dreaming of something else. You know—"

"And you know I haven't touched her," Kayvin interrupted. "You know she's here only as leverage—"

"Yes, exactly! She's a tool to you now and she'll be a tool all her life, and you just—you just—oh, I can't even say it, because I keep hoping against all reason that it can't be true. But here you are"—she made a savage gesture to encompass him, the apartment, the palace—"exactly where you belong, and I'm the fool if I deny what I see happening."

She was wrong to accuse him. He was doing only what he had to, the only option he had to fight the greater evil of Pasiphae Jade. "You're being ridiculous."

She scooped an armful of scrolls into the chest.

"Stop! You'll damage them."

"What do you care? They're only words. They don't mean anything."

"Stop making me out to be—I'm not! I'm only doing what I have to do—the only way I can do it. I need leverage, for my mother and for Nala and for all of you. I do it to protect others!"

"So do they," she snapped without looking at him.

"What?"

"I have heard Pasiphae Jade say the same to justify her actions. I don't see the difference."

He seized her arm and jerked her up from the floor. She flinched.

He froze. He was uncomfortably aware of his fingers bruising her, his other hand hanging like a raptor about to dive.

She glared up at him, daring him, eyes glittering with fury. "Go ahead. There's nothing to hold you back. This is who you are now."

He wanted to strike her, for those words as much as for her previous accusations. He wanted to silence her unreasonable insults. But in that heartbeat of self-awareness, he did not want to strike her.

It was not fury that made her eyes glitter, but tears. She was blinking back tears. The realization filled him with fresh rage, at her for her manipulation and at himself for having somehow brought her to this and at her for putting him in this situation.

She saw his anger, and she dropped her eyes. He released her abruptly, stepping back, and lowered his hands. He was in the right here. He had not hit her. He was in the right.

Yovela sank slowly to the floor, drawing her knees to her chest, folding her head over them. Her hair spilled out over her arms and shielded her face.

She had come into his study to make a scene and accuse him of being what he fought against. She had no right to cry, no right to make him feel...however he felt in this moment. This was her doing.

"You think I am doing this for the wrong reasons," he said, trying to keep his tone level. "But I am doing this to fight against something terrible."

She lifted her head, but she did not look at him. She stared across the room, her face blotchy and red, her hair disheveled. She was not crying, not quite, but tears gleamed in her eyes and her breathing was uneven. She shook her head.

Anger flared. "How dare you accuse me of being everything you hate? You see what I'm doing only through your own experience—not mine. You choose to think the worst of me and attack me for deeds I have not yet committed."

Her face crumpled, contorting into ugly tears. "Yes!" she sobbed, the word twisted too. She shifted forward, her hands on the floor, speaking fast in the direction of his desk. "Yes, exactly. I see with my experience. I hear what you say here just as I hear what she says, and I hear the echo. Empty void, that is why—oh, I'm crying, and I hate that, because you will think I am weak and you will disregard what I say."

"I disregard what you say because it is ridiculous and unfair."

"Is it?" she snapped, looking at him for the first time. "Am I crying because it is ridiculous?" She shook her head. "No one has ever respected the words of a woman in tears. But you would not hear me if I spoke in measured tones, either. You are gone, or disappearing."

Such drama, such hysteria. Kayvin understood for the first time the complaints he had heard from his father and from courtiers. He had been fortunate to have avoided such a display for so long. Dielo at least was too well-trained to have such a tantrum.

"It is Pasiphae Jade who wants me gone," he growled, going around to his chair. "And it seems you would have me give in."

"I never—absolutely not." She swallowed. "I'd have you fight her rather than become her."

"Again you accuse me—"

"Do you know what you are?" She looked directly at him, challenging, accusing. Before he could answer, she continued, "Do you know what the Amethyst Prince is?"

He knew his royal history better than she. "Of course."

"The amethyst is prized for its purity and its ability to resist intoxication. An amethyst is used to keep one's head despite extravagance." She folded her arms across herself. "I was so glad to have found an Amethyst Prince who remained pure in a whirlpool of poisons."

He had never guessed she might think of his namesake stone against the court's hedonism and Pasiphae Jade's machinations. He stared at her.

She shook her head. Her words were difficult to understand now. "But now you have the same taint. The Amethyst Prince is now just another of the same. That is why I cry."

He shoved himself out of the chair, "Shut up," he snarled. "Get these books and scrolls back on—no, I'll have Arad do it. I cannot trust you to do it safely. Get out."

But he left the room first, leaving her sobbing on the floor.

Dielo had heard. He had heard Yovela accuse Prince Kayvin—bold, dangerous, unwise—and heard her fail and sob. He stepped back into the corridor as the prince stalked out of the study. He was not hiding, not exactly, he only did not present himself while his master was in such a furious state and did not wish to be interrupted. A moment later, he heard the terse order to Arad to have the study reorganized.

Yovela needed another moment to gather herself, and then she emerged from the room, walking with her arms folded tightly and her head down and an expression that threatened to crush through any obstacle in her path. Dielo let her pass, unwilling to speak where the prince might hear. She would not go to the women's quarters, not now that Lirin might be near. Yovela would not risk being asked what troubled her by the very evidence of her troubles.

He would follow in a moment.

He found Yovela in the garden, nestled beside a trellis of faded vines. He circled so that she could see him approach, and he stopped a short distance away. "May I join you?"

She did not look up. "It doesn't matter."

It did matter. He sat with his shoulder toward her, leaving a little space. "You were right."

She lifted her head and rubbed her face. "Right about the prince?" She waved a hand toward the balcony and the apartment beyond. "I assume you heard some of that."

"Right about me," he said heavily. "When I invited Lirin here... I knew what I was doing. I knew what she wanted, and how to offer it without saying it too plainly. I knew how to entice her to agree to something she did not fully understand."

She sniffed and glared at the ground.

He picked a handful of dry grass, tearing it apart in his fingers. "You were right about me, as a child."

She nodded. "And then you went and did the same to another."

The words slid easily between his ribs. "I know," he whispered. He twisted the grass. "But I could not refuse him."

"You could," she replied shortly.

He did not argue. There was no point to it.

He did not know why he had told her. Perhaps it was easier to tell her than to tell himself. Perhaps she would shout at him and make him defensive, let him deny it all. Perhaps she would express the anger he still could not.

But she only sniffed again. "You..." She shook her head and wiped her face. "He was different," she said, and her tone was almost plaintive. "He was different. And now, he's someone else. Or maybe he never was what I thought. Maybe I haven't been betrayed; maybe I'm just stupid. I'm the fool, for ever having trusted."

"He was different," Dielo assured her. "But he is also desperate. And he will try anything, especially what he can see is working for them."

She let out a long sigh. "Then we've lost him. And you."

The words stabbed again. Yes, he was only a tool for his master. That did not absolve Dielo; that made them doubly guilty.

"I'm sorry," he said, and he did not know what specific thing he apologized for, but there was enough to apologize for.

For a long moment they sat, separated by two arms' lengths, heads bowed, not speaking.

Finally he stood. "I'll go back first." They should not be seen alone together, not again.

But he wished they could talk.

CHAPTER 82

LIRIN WAS PETITE, PRETTY, smiling, and everything a prince should want in a palace maid. She straightened and beamed at Kayvin, her arms full of scrolls, as he returned to the study. "My lord! I'm still on working on these, I'm sorry."

"It's fine." He went to his desk.

"I'm trying to guess how they were ordered," she continued. "By author, some of them, but it looks like others were maybe by topic or theme?"

Kayvin looked across the room. "That—the blue one—that's a treatise by Demfast. Music theory. It should be on the second shelf on the right."

"Oh, thank you!" She slid the book into place.

Kayvin turned his attention to the stack still on his desk. Yovela had not disturbed the materials for his studies. He selected a book of soft paper, bound with knotted silk thread, and opened it on the desktop.

"Ason writes about music also, is that right?"

He answered without looking up. "Yes, of course. Or, he did."

"I didn't know anyone could write so much about, you know, songs."

He lifted his head. "It's not just writing about the songs, it's writing about how to make songs, how songs affect us, the math of the best songs."

She was holding four books in her arms, trying to compare the title pages inside the covers without dropping them. "The math of songs?" She laughed, but in amused incredulity rather than mockery. "Isn't it just, you know, singing?"

She was not accusing or challenging. She had just been left uneducated in a kitchen. Kayvin put his hands on the desk. "One can just sing, yes, just as one can just throw a stone. But if one wants to make war, it's better to understand the physics of that stone and to develop a better weapon from it."

She shook her head and laughed again. "But singing isn't war." She set a book on a shelf, looked at another title page, and sighed. "My aunt always said I should read, but it's not as if I had time or books in the closets."

"Can you read?"

"Yes!" she said proudly. "Some. Enough."

"Can you read a book?"

She looked up suddenly from her armload, as if she had just realized something. Kayvin felt a faint prickle at the back of his neck. She put down the books and came around the desk, sliding close to him. "What are these books about?"

"Sayinia," he answered. "I'm continuing to study."

She gave a little gasp. "There are books about humans?"

Maybe she was only pretending to flatter and engage him, maybe she was really interested—but she was still speaking to him, and he did not care which. "Of course. How else could I study to find the amulets?"

"I don't know what these amulets are, anyway."

"We forged them long ago, during the age of skin and scales. They were meant to help fight against dragons. We shared them with our human allies, who then left us in our time of need and kept the amulets for themselves."

They had claimed ignorance of this history, but who could admit treachery while intending to negotiate?

She shook her head. "I don't know much about the old times. Are the books only about history, or do they tell more about the humans?"

He turned the book so she could better see it. "This chapter is about temple culture and its variants across the land."

"May I?" She knelt beside the desk, leaning over the pages. "So many..." She placed a finger to track the words as she haltingly began, "In remote places, edu—cation is often entirely the..."

"Purview," Kayvin supplied. "It means concern or influence. Education is supplied by the temples in some rural areas, instead of private academies or the state."

"The state? For study?"

"Yes, Sayinia has open schools." He looked at her. "Would you like to study?"

"Oh!" Her smile widened. "My aunt would be pleased."

Kayvin doubted that; Pasiphae Jade might or might not want Lirin educated, but she could not be glad of her tutor. "But would you be pleased?"

The smile deepened, and the eyes latched onto his. "You would teach me?"

He was disinterested, not ignorant. He knew what she tried, however clumsily. But he needed her close. "Move your things into the women's quarters. So you'll be close to the study."

A close sequence of expressions flashed through her eyes—excitement, fear, achievement—and she nodded. "Oh, thank you, Your Highness!" She beamed. "In the—in the sera qadra?"

"Mm, yes, I think so."

"Your Highness!"

He looked at the stack and drew out a thin volume. "You may start with this one."

She looked a little confused—perhaps she had not expected his teaching to start with a book—but he did not give her time to suggest other areas of practice. "Now I must read. You can take that with you, and finish the shelves later."

"I... Thank you, Your Highness." She retreated with the thin book.

Now he had her safely, entirely within his realm. Now she would appear in his retinue, and Pasiphae Jade could not protest without revealing her secret, and Kayvin had a hostage of his own.

For the first time, he looked forward to the next court function.

The opportunity came quickly. Lord Trerin's second wife's egg hatched, and there must be a social gathering to honor the occasion. It was not a court function, but it was a chance to parade his sera qadra and its newest member in public, and that was all Kayvin needed.

He brandished the invitation to Dielo and Yovela. "This is the moment. It must be carefully choreographed—we must be seen by all, but there must be no moment of inattention when Pasiphae Jade's agents can entice Lirin away from us."

"Her agents?" Dielo asked.

"The Arch Potentate herself cannot show particular interest without drawing attention and questions," Kayvin explained. "But she will see Lirin—it is my intention that she sees Lirin—and she will certainly send someone else to draw her away."

It was for Lirin's good as well as Kayvin's. If Pasiphae Jade stole her back, her disappearance from Kayvin's sera qadra would make court gossip and Lirin's identity might be exposed, making her a greater target for others who wanted to use her.

Yovela had the flat mask of an expression she usually wore these days. He wished she would be more reasonable. It benefited her, too, if Kayvin regained enough footing to protect his own household.

Yovela asked, her voice as level as her expression, "So we are all to visit the new child?"

"Yes, of course, that's what I've just said." Belatedly he recalled, and a sick guilt writhed in him. "That is...I would like to have you there. But..."

But Yovela had collapsed with a nervous hallucination when they had visited the laying-in for the egg.

Dielo looked anxiously from Yovela to Kayvin.

Kayvin rubbed his hand across his face. "I'll understand if you stay behind. I can take Dielo and Lirin. That will work just as well. Symmetrical."

"We could say you'd taken ill and did not want to risk carrying a cold to the new baby," Dielo offered. "Then there would be less loss of place when Lirin was there instead of you."

Poor Dielo still thought in terms of rank within the sera qadra. Kayvin preferred to think on more important things, such as regaining his standing against Pasiphae Jade.

Yovela nodded once.

Kayvin turned to Dielo. "It will be your responsibility then to see that Lirin is kept close."

"I think she'll be anxious to stay in formation," Dielo answered. "She's very excited by her new position."

"Then see that she's fitted out properly, and let's prepare for tomorrow."

Lirin would borrow from Yovela's wardrobe, as she didn't yet have her own collection. Yovela declined to be present at the selection, however.

Lirin seemed to take this as something to be expected. "After all, I am the new rival," she confided to Dielo, "and she was told to let me use her clothing. It must feel threatening."

"I do not think Yovela feels threatened," Dielo said mildly, browsing through a stack of folded pieces and considering colors.

"No? You don't think she'd view me as a younger rival?"

He had once thought Yovela jealous, too, and he had been mistaken. "Yovela knows our prince better than either of us."

"Oh? Then maybe I'll have to get his attention, so she notices me." Lirin giggled.

Dielo tugged a sage green gown from the bottom of the stack. "If you'll take my advice, Lirin, you'll quietly enjoy your new privileges without trying to make waves."

"But if I don't please the prince, how—"

"You'll best please His Highness by not creating strife in his court," Dielo said firmly. "What do you think of this color?"

"It's pretty. What does it do for my eyes?" She held it below her chin.

"I suggested it for your eyes," Dielo said practically. "Try it on. We'll have to tie it up or wrap it." Yovela was taller than Lirin.

"It's a little tight," Lirin reported from behind the dressing screen.

"Yovela is a dancer."

She came from behind the screen, frowning at the comparison, and smoothed the sage dress as she looked down at the excess fabric brushing her toes. "Well, she may be a dancer, but His Highness likes that I'm studying, He says I'm clever and could learn anything I set my mind to."

Dielo nodded, already weary of her enthusiastic competitions.

"And I've been reading the wildest things! This morning I had a paper on human physio...anatomy. I did not understand most of it, but there were parts—Dielo! Did you know that humans have more than one opening?"

He was choosing between three necklaces and not paying close attention. "What?"

"They have more than one opening. Down there. Separate for piss and crap! Can you imagine? What would that even feel like, trying to sort it out?"

Dielo's attention was finally torn from the jewelry. "What?" he repeated.

"And for lovemaking—there's another one! How do they know which to use? Wouldn't that be awkward, trying to aim properly?"

Dielo already regretted bringing Lirin as a willing hostage, and he was coming to regret bringing her for other reasons.

"I knew they have live births—and that must be so odd, can you imagine?—not even an egg but an actual baby, and oh, it just makes me shudder to even think about it."

"Then don't think about it," Prince Kayvin said flatly as he entered. "There's more to that report than the anatomy of human lovemaking. Did you try the coronet yet?"

The ceremonial headpieces of the sera qadra were glorious, and Lirin's face lit up at his suggestion. But Dielo looked at the prince. "My lord, it is not a court affair. The headpieces will not be expected."

"I want you to wear them," Kayvin said. "They will identify my sera qadra, and I want to make clear how it has grown."

Finery would make Lirin stand out. The courtiers and nobles would not know her, but that was an advantage. It meant Pasiphae Jade could hope to keep her secret if she conceded to Kayvin.

Dielo understood, but he tried again. "It will invite discussion."

"I want to wear it," Lirin said plaintively.

Dielo shook his head. "You will be considered grasping—my lord, I mean, but Lirin as well. It would be inappropriate for the occasion. You do not want to appear too eager."

Kayvin agreed with a small shrug. "But then put yourself and Lirin in similar attire, so that it's obvious you are both sera qadra. And play up your virilo look; I need all the status and all the implication."

Lirin grinned at the news of better clothes and matching a virilo. Dielo nodded. "I have an idea of what to do."

CHAPTER 83

THERE WERE MULTIPLE ROOMS in the prince's apartments, and the sera qadra was divided into separate men's and women's quarters. For all that, with Lirin's addition, there was little privacy. When Yovela could bear it no longer, she went out into the garden to cry.

She did not know what had finally brought her to tears. It might have been the sound of Kayvin's voice, speaking to Lirin in his study. It might have been a dark, shuttered look from Arad as he passed on his duties. She was not sure; she only knew that suddenly her throat squeezed tight and she knew she could not hold back the tears she had not felt a moment before. She drew a a scarf over her head, a frail concealment, and slipped out.

The garden was long and curved, and while part was visible from palace walkways, a segment was hidden. There was a bench made of curved wood, grown in precise curls, nestled beneath an arbor weighted with a flowering vine. It offered relative concealment, and she folded there as the anguish began to shudder loose, unable to stop the tears and the rising, choking sobs.

Empty void, it was too much.

She tried to muffle the sound, afraid someone would hear from the balconies. She did not want Kayvin to hear. She did not want him to ask. She did not want him to fail to ask.

There was a rustle behind her, and her chest convulsed painfully. But no, it would be Dielo. He was always careful to make a sound when he approached.

He knelt behind the bench, addressing her over the curled back. "Can I help?"

A wretched, sobbing laugh broke from her, shaking her and making her bray and choke. "No, you can't. Especially..."

He waited. He did not ask what troubled her; he already knew.

She sniffed. "We're going to die, you know."

He said nothing. She didn't turn toward him, but she could feel him watching.

"He's going to lose whatever this court game is, and she'll kill him like she killed the Arch Potentate. And his household will be killed with him, the sera qadra first." She rubbed the back of her hand against her streaming nose. "And I don't think I'd mind dying with him so much, if he were still himself. But..." She couldn't bring herself to say the final words.

There was a long pause. She had said something dangerous, something disloyal, but it could not be any more dangerous than their current position. But it might be too disloyal for the virilo to listen.

He extended an arm over the back of the bench, leaning against the wood. His hand waited, open.

There was no good way to take his hand, at this awkward angle, but the gesture softened her. She began to cry harder, and she bent her head to hide her shame. She reached across to take the hand, as if it could do anything. She was helpless, she was in danger, and her only friend in this place, her only friend in years, had become a stranger who preyed on others like she had been. She held the hand, and she wept.

As her fingers closed on his palm Dielo shifted, bringing his arm closer and slipping the other around her, bracing her against the bench's back. He kept his head low and slightly turned, somehow giving her space even as he held her. The contact undid her entirely, and the last dam shattered.

She cried uncontrollably, mourning the loss of Kayvin, the loss of Lirin's innocence, the loss of her own unborn child, the loss of her unconventional safety in the sera qadra. She did not cry prettily.

It did not last long. The flood exhausted itself, and the sobs slowed. Dielo's head was close behind her shoulder, and she imagined she could feel the warmth of his cheek.

When she had quieted for a moment, he made a small movement as if to withdraw. But she kept her light hold on his hand, and he stayed.

Her voice was too thick with crying to be understood at first, and she had to try again. "I'm sorry."

He shook his head, and now his breath did brush her shoulder. "They're only tears. There is nothing to apologize for." His voice was hoarse.

She let go, reluctantly, and his arms slipped away, cleanly and without pulling across her. She took a deep breath, unsure if it was in relief or in preparation for another strain.

"You miss him," Dielo said softly. "You miss the prince he was."

She nodded silently.

"Me, too. I didn't know him as well, but I can see the change." His voice was unsteady, too. He drew a breath.

"We—we won't get him back, will we." It was not a question. A question held hope.

Dielo was wise enough not to lie. He said nothing.

Lirin's laughter rang out above them, and they both jumped in place. Yovela did not know whether it was alarm at being caught crying or at being caught together. But Lirin couldn't see here; it was why Yovela had chosen this place.

"We'd best go back," she said, rubbing her face. "We can't both be missing." She stood and turned.

Dielo looked away. He started to speak and then stopped, and he nodded.

Yovela went first. She looked up at the balcony, seeing it empty. Lirin was further inside.

"You'll stay with him, though?" Dielo's voice was quiet under the sheltering vine, barely carrying to her.

She nodded without looking back. "Of course. Where else would I go?" She crossed her arms, pressing her fingers into her flesh. "And whatever else, he offered me shelter I did not expect, and I owe him some loyalty for that."

"Even if he becomes someone you loathe?"

She squeezed her eyes shut. "No. But then—then, I still have nowhere else to go."

She hurried forward before he could answer and tell her she was wrong. She did have somewhere else to go; if she fled now and threw herself into the arms of another courtier, she might bring enough prestige, a prize stolen from the Amethyst Prince's sera qadra, to be taken in. But she did not want to think about that.

She wanted to return well away from Dielo, rather than coming back together. But when she re-entered the apartment, Kayvin was adjusting Lirin's fingers on a lute, and he did not even glance toward Yovela. She pressed her lips together, telling herself she was glad and it was good he had not noticed her tears, and she went to the women's quarters.

CHAPTER 84

DIELO SAT IN THE dark, weighing the slight mass of his chit on his open palm.

He had not given it to Prince Kayvin, not yet. The stunning disappointment and humiliation at the prince's homecoming had not been the time, and then Kayvin had sent Dielo to bring Lirin, and that had felt... Dielo did not have the words, not yet, but he knew it was not the time to present his chit to his master. Not while the prince collected more for his sera qadra. Not while he brought a girl to use as a tool and a pawn.

There were no lights burning in the men's quarters, but the moon provided a scant gleam on the polished floor, pocked with empty sleeping pits. Dielo got his feet under him and rose to put the chit in his trunk of accessories and jewelry.

There was a scuff of feet in the corridor.

Dielo tightened his jaw and hurried out to intercept her. "Lirin."

She jumped, turning back to him. She was dressed in a gauzy robe, slipping from one shoulder, and little else. "Oh!"

He smothered a sigh. "Go back to bed, Lirin."

"I'm cold."

"You would be, in such an outfit. Go back to your furs and blankets."

She persisted. "The nights are cold. I'm cold, in my own little sleeping pit, so I'm sure he must be cold in that enormous one. I'm going to warm his furs."

"Lirin..."

"And then maybe he'll ask me to stay."

"Lirin," Dielo repeated, trying to gentle his irritated tone. "Don't get greedy."

"Greedy?" She raised her hands in self-evident indignation. "I have been here four days, and nothing. I am a member of the sera qadra. This is nothing like I thought it would be. Why am I here, if I am not—"

"Your purpose," snapped Dielo, "is to be a young woman, cleverer than she's been told but not as clever as she thinks herself. You've been offered books and study, you've been offered music, you could learn dancing or maths or medicine. Or you could take this luxury of time, now you're not scrubbing tiles or chopping fruits, to discover who you are when you have a few moments to yourself. You might find you wish you were someone else." He put his hands on Lirin's shoulders, cool to the touch. "You might do so much beyond warming a bed, if you take time to consider it."

She stared up at him, startled and a little in awe.

He squeezed her shoulders and released her. "I'm sorry. I only mean you shouldn't hang all your hopes on catching his heart. He's particular, and you...you have a whole life before you, and only so much of it can be in a sleeping pit."

Her lip jutted in suspicion.

He was uncomfortably aware of his bare chest and loosely wrapped trousers. It had been a long time since he'd felt self-conscious in that way. He pretended he did not notice her glances. "Go to bed, Lirin. If you'll hear nothing else, it's rude to wake him."

"Why are you up?" she challenged.

"I couldn't sleep. But you know I was in my quarters."

She did; she'd seen him come from the door. "Fine. But I'm not giving up."

He decided not to answer this, and he waited while she returned to the women's quarters. She glanced back once at the door, and then she disappeared.

Dielo exhaled, tired beyond his lack of sleep. Once, he would have worried about dark circles, a dull complexion, a slower wit. Now, blooming skin was the least of his insufficiencies.

Someone moved in the shadow beyond the women's door; Yovela must have slipped out of the women's quarters while they were talking. Dielo nodded to her, polite and exhausted.

She came closer, an arm's reach away. "I heard what you told her," she said softly, "I was surprised to hear it."

Shame burned up his neck. "I didn't mean to say anything more than what I told her," he said quickly. "His only intent for her is political. It would be better for everyone if she did not believe it to be more than it is."

"We don't want her thinking it is what it is, either," Yovela cautioned gently.

Dielo let out a long breath. "He likes her, you know. Not in that way—he does not want her as a courtesan. But I think he likes her more than he realizes, for herself."

"She's a child. And she can be an annoying one."

"We are all aware," Dielo agreed with unaccustomed frankness. "But he's never had a younger sibling, has he? Not near to him. The courtesans' children are all in a far wing. Our prince has never had someone to teach and encourage, or to comfort, or to watch over." He paused. "I think she's good for him, in a way. He's not brooding as badly."

"He's not brooding," she allowed. "But still, he keeps her here."

That was true, and he understood. He wished he had a better explanation than that Kayvin meant to use Lirin just as Pasiphae Jade had used his mother and Dielo and others. But Dielo had nothing to say.

Yovela was still looking at him. Again he felt an embarrassed awareness of his bare skin, unadorned and unprepared. Yovela did not assess him, though, not like others did.

"I'm glad you told her," Yovela said, her voice nearly too quiet to hear. "Even if she didn't listen, I'm glad you told her."

"He'll have to go again soon. He'll have to leave her."

None of them had a solution for holding Lirin, should she decide to leave once Kayvin left the palace again. Dielo thought the prestige of being in a sera qadra would be enough to keep her, even with her frustrations. But if not...

"Get some sleep," Yovela said softly.

Loneliness struck him like a wet towel at the thought of walking back into that empty room. But he nodded. "You, too."

CHAPTER 85

LORD TRERIN'S SECOND WIFE was seated with her new child, a son, on a dais at the far end of the room, where she and her accomplishment could be admired by the circulating guests. Lord Trerin, with his tight-faced first wife at his side—she had given only daughters so far—accepted congratulations and well wishes from all in turn, and members of his sera qadra drifted about the room with refreshments. A small band of musicians played near the door, but the sleeping infant did not note them or the noisy guests.

Kayvin would have to hope Dielo's rapid schooling had taken root despite Lirin's excitement at her first public appearance in the sera qadra. At least she was in enough awe of the virilo to respect his instruction; he would know how she could increase her own standing.

Dielo had done as he'd promised, and he looked splendid in bloused green trousers and an open vest, with armbands trailing matching ribbons and golden ear cuffs flashing from his dark hair.

Lirin was in a gown of nearly the same green, borrowed from Yovela, and she was weighted with more jewelry than was tasteful. Ground mica had been brushed around their eyes and over their cheekbones, making them gleam. Identical scarves completed the implicating imagery; Dielo and Lirin were a set, flanking Kayvin on his path through the guests. Pasiphae Jade could not fail to comprehend.

And now she was arriving, honoring the occasion with a visit from the Arch Potentate. She would surely present a gold coin to the baby, Kayvin had already heard it speculated; Lord Trerin was an ardent supporter of the new ruler and popular in the court. A silver coin was the traditional gift from a ruler to a courtier's new son, but there was room for gold if warranted.

Kayvin had a silver coin tucked within his sash. After Pasiphae Jade had seen his new sera qadra member and recognized his fortified position, he would present the coin to the child, a symbolic gesture to the watching court and a thumbing of his nose to the interloper.

Kayvin stood to the side, patiently waiting to be eclipsed by the Arch Potentate's arrival. That was fine; he could wait for Pasiphae Jade to target him for a cutting barb and then to abruptly pause, recognizing who followed him. He smiled to himself.

Lirin was trying to appear cool and haughty, but her eyes kept roving, greedy for the splendor of the nobility. She stayed close to Kayvin and Dielo, though, as instructed. She was anxious to hold formation and prove her suitability for the sera qadra. Her new life was too exalted and exciting to risk by wandering.

Now Pasiphae Jade was speaking to Lord Trerin and his first wife. The first wife was making a determined attempt to regain status as a hostess, and she escorted Pasiphae Jade to the second wife and the new child. A coin was granted—gold, as supposed—and there was general approbation around the room. Fresh drinks were brought out.

Pasiphae Jade, trailed by four glittering sera qadra members on each side, made a slow revolution of the room, accepting bows and greetings. Kayvin waited.

At last she approached his little group. It was a slight, coming late to him as if he were not a prince and fellow royalty, but for once he was glad. It would make the strike against her that much more satisfying.

"Ah, Prince Kayvin," she said, coming to stand before him. "I hope you have enjoyed Lord Tre—" She stopped.

Kayvin permitted himself a small smile. Subtlety was key here, and he had to show his pleasure at having turned the tables without giving away his secret to other courtiers. "Good afternoon. It was good of you to honor the child with a coin."

She did not reply to the rote phrases. Kayvin watched her face tighten, straining to conceal the rising storm within. He smiled—small, pleased, a smile borrowed from her own supply.

At last she spoke. "What have you done?" she demanded in a low, terse tone.

The words were not for Kayvin.

Kayvin did not look back at Lirin. He had imagined her reaction already—first pride at having achieved such an exalted position, and then alarm at her ostensible aunt's silent and inexplicable anger, and finally resentment at the unreasonable restriction and a renewed determination to stay with Kayvin.

But Pasiphae Jade could not converse long with Lirin or demand of Kayvin why she was there, not if she wished to avoid drawing attention to her. Instead she said, "I see you have taken a fresh interest in your serving men and women."

"I have," Kayvin answered levelly. "I am, after all, a prince. I should have priority over others, even those of high station."

Her pinched face went white with shock and fury. Now she knew that he knew how Lirin had been promised to Lord Fretton, payment for his support. That meant he knew Lirin's true identity. That meant he had a hostage of equal value to Raea, the Shining Gem.

For the first time in a long time, Kayvin felt powerful.

The beautiful people behind Pasiphae Jade had recognized their mistress was angry, but they could not place a cause. Around them, guests stared, aware that something dangerous writhed in the crackling glares between the Arch Potentate and Amethyst Prince, but they could hear nothing telling.

For a long moment they looked at one another, and at last Pasiphae Jade said, "I like the new girl. Perhaps you'll let her visit me sometime."

Lirin slid nearer to Dielo. Kayvin made himself smile, polite and toothy. "Oh, I couldn't give her up just yet, I'm afraid."

Pasiphae Jade's mouth curved on one side, though her eyes stayed cold. "Fortunately, I hold a chit, if I should find need of another companion."

Kayvin's savage glee faded. She still had claim on Dielo—she could recall him, or even send guards to seize him, without drawing attention to Lirin. Kayvin could keep some leverage, but he would sacrifice Dielo to hold this ground.

His sudden, chilling dismay must have shown, because she smiled again—more pleased, this time—and walked away, trailing her sera qadra.

Kayvin could feel Dielo's eyes. He did not turn to meet them. He would walk out as if he had gained his footing. He would find the next step, something to keep Lirin and Dielo and Yovela in his household.

Pasiphae Jade was on the other side of the room now. Kayvin started forward, trusting Dielo to follow and bring Lirin. He had stayed long enough; now they could go.

He kept his eyes forward, his chin raised, his jaw firm. His fingernails tore at his palms. She had almost countered him; he could not hold a hostage without losing one of his own. Now he had to decide how to proceed.

Dielo followed Prince Kayvin from the festivities, staying only a stride behind. Beside him Lirin nearly trotted, struggling to keep pace with the frustrated prince. Dielo glanced at her, but he did not slow. He, too, wanted to be well away.

But Prince Kayvin did not return to his own rooms. He turned aside in the corridor and paused in an open walkway, where fruit trees lined the shaded hall and where a little fountain burbled, muffling sounds around them—and their own conversation.

"I can't believe she—" Lirin stopped abruptly, glancing at Dielo to see if he'd heard. He pretended he had not. She should not reveal her relationship with the Arch Potentate to Prince Kayvin any more than Pasiphae Jade could to the court. Prince Kayvin could not reveal to her that he already knew—indeed, knew better than she did herself, Dielo suspected.

Lies. They all lived in lies, and secrets, and threats.

Kayvin had not heard her. He stared down at the fountain, clenching his jaw, flexing his fingers. "We shouldn't be seen to rush back," he said at last, his voice quiet beneath the splashing water. "I am not escaping. I am out enjoying the day with my sera qadra."

"Of course." Dielo nodded and looked at Lirin. "Should we gather some flowers for you? Attend you on a garden bench? Anyone in the passages above could look down and see you enjoying the day."

Kayvin blew out his breath. "I don't think I have the skill to look indolent and reposed on a bench while you bring me flowers and fruit. I want to..." He stopped, worked his jaw, glared at the fountain. Then he looked at Dielo. "You heard what she said?"

Fortunately, I hold a chit, if I should find need of another. Dielo could hardly have missed it. She had addressed Kayvin, but the words had burned into Dielo.

If she went to her cabinet for Dielo's chit, she would discover it missing. That would start questions to make trouble for Prince Kayvin and far more trouble for Dielo. He had hardly drawn a full breath since she'd spoken.

"I heard her, but I didn't understand," Lirin said.

Dielo, drawn tight with the unspoken threat, could not bear her ignorant questions.

"She has lots of virilos," Lirin continued. "Why mention having a chit?"

Kayvin, with more charity and patience left in him, answered briefly, "She holds Dielo's chit. He is lent to me, but he is hers. She was threatening to take him back."

"Oh!" The single syllable held surprise, confusion, and dismay. When she looked at Dielo, she had a small twist to her mouth, perhaps imagining him with her middle-aged aunt and recalling how she had leaned into him, asked him to plait her hair, silently suggested more.

Kayvin did not address this response, if he even perceived it. He crouched and extended a hand to toy with the burbling water, filling time. "I was so near..."

Dielo did not know exactly what the prince had been near. He thought, watching the prince's eyes shift, Kayvin might be weighing whether to give up Dielo to keep Lirin. Certainly that made sense; he would not give up his valuable hostage to keep a disused virilo.

Dielo stood silently, dizzy with the pounding of his pulse.

Lirin crouched across from Kayvin, putting her own hand into the water. "If you want to look unbothered, then there should be play." She turned her open palm and slapped water toward him.

Kayvin gasped with the shock of the cool water over his face and arm, and for a moment there was a suspended amazement at what she had done. But her suggestion had been wise, and Kayvin coughed out a laugh and slapped water back at her, making her squeal and duck.

Dielo stepped back as they traded splashes. The dress could be saved, and she had been clever. Kayvin's expression was loosening, and perhaps it was real relief rather than playacting for observers outside the little courtyard.

Yes, it would make sense to keep Lirin, both valuable and cheerful. Prince Kayvin would sacrifice Dielo to keep a better playing piece. Dielo felt ill.

At last Prince Kayvin straightened, brushing down his damp clothing. "All right, that's long enough. They know I didn't run home with my tail between my legs. Let's go."

Dielo stayed a stride behind the prince's shoulder, pacing Lirin, but Kayvin didn't look back. His jaw was set again—the water fight had not dispelled his worries—and he pressed down the corridors at a brisk pace. Dielo was not sure he would hear even if Dielo spoke to him.

They turned into a narrow passage, one where they were unlikely to meet others in palace traffic. Their palace slippers made little sound on the tiles. Dielo crushed the hem of his scarf in his hand, wishing he had something to barter. If only—

Something slid around his throat, a necklace drawn too brutally tight. He was pulled backward, stumbling, as he clawed desperately at the cord biting into his neck. He tried to call for help, but he could make no sound. He saw Kayvin continuing down the corridor, never pausing, never looking back, and then his vision blurred to darkness.

CHAPTER 86

YOVELA HEARD THE RATTLE of the door and the muted greeting of the doorman. Kayvin and the others had returned.

She did not want to go to them. She did not want to hear how Kayvin's plan had worked to hold off Pasiphae Jade. She did not want to hear how it had failed and Lirin had been taken back by her aunt or mother. She did not want to think about any of it.

But her feet carried her out of her wearied pacing and toward the primary rooms, and against her will she blurted, "Are you all right?"

"It's early to say," Kayvin growled, coming into the room. He shrugged out of a silk over-robe and tossed it toward a chair. "She indeed recognized—" He stopped, catching himself before admitting he knew the Arch Potentate could recognize an elevated maid. "The celebration was elaborate. The child was well-received."

Yovela goggled at his indifference. "But where is she? Did she take her? What about Dielo?"

"She said she had..." Kayvin stopped, a confused lock at his face, and turned back. Then he whirled back to Yovela. "Where?"

"Where are Dielo and Lirin?" she demanded, not understanding him.

"They were behind me," he answered, disbelieving. "They were walking behind me." He turned back. "Where are they?"

She gave him an incredulous stare and then bolted for the door. Stupid! How could he be so stupid?

"Let me go!" Lirin pulled back, but his grip was a vise, and she twisted and folded in pain.

The man dragging her down the corridor was dressed in courtier's robes, unlike the guards who had first seized her. She thought she recognized him, someone she'd seen at a distance, but she could not recall his name.

"She's kept you from me for too long," he snarled, "and for him? I won't stand for it." He chuckled. "And neither will you."

Lirin was crying now, with the pain of her wrist and with her terror. "Let me go!"

"Lirin!"

That was Yovela's voice! Lirin twisted to look. "Help me!"

Yovela's filmy skirt caught about her legs and flared as she ran. She slid, and she kicked off her slippers and came on at a full sprint. "Get away from her!"

The man jerked Lirin back, out of the way. As Yovela reached them, he slapped her with his free hand, snapping her head to the side with the force of his blow and her rush. She stumbled and fell against the far wall, her mouth open with shock and pain.

"I should take both of you," he growled. "That would show him. But I need only the little princess."

Yovela pushed away from the wall, swaying with shock but her eyes fixed on the court lord. "Kayvin," she breathed. "Kayvin!"

"Oh, shut up." He dragged Lirin forward again. She pried at his fingers, but it was useless. "Stop it! You only make it difficult for yourself. There's no reason for all this fuss! I promised to make you a wife."

Lirin couldn't fight him. She pulled back, but she could not fight him.

"Get away from her!" Kayvin snarled, seizing the man's upper arm.

Lirin's heart leapt. Prince Kayvin!

The courtier shoved him hard, an open hand to the chest. "Don't touch me."

Kayvin caught himself, straightened, tried again. "Leave her alone."

"Or what?" His lip curled. "Or what, Your Highness? You'll forbid me?" He snorted. "You're so ignorant, you haven't even realized what you are not. Go back and play your flute, Lilac Prince. Leave the men to their court business." He turned away from the prince, hauling Lirin gasping with him, and took her other wrist. "Now..."

A flaming hand reached over his shoulder and grasped his face, pulling him backward. He screamed and clawed at it, and Kayvin flung him to the floor and slammed another bolt of fire into him.

Yovela seized Lirin and drew her back, wrapping her in an embrace away from the man screaming on the floor.

Kayvin lifted his hand for a third fire strike, but the lord was huddled and wailing, writhing as he tried to touch his blistered face. Kayvin hesitated, and then he backed away. "Let's go."

Lirin clung to Yovela as they passed through the maze of the palace. Yovela tried to hush her—the guards were probably still in the corridors—but Lirin could not stop crying.

Once within the prince's apartments, they sank to the floor on silken cushions, leaning against one another. She should have felt relieved to be safe, but the sobs only came harder.

Yovela had her arms around Lirin, but she fixed her glare on Kayvin. "Are you pleased now?" she demanded in a low, fierce tone.

"He saved me," Lirin choked.

Kayvin looked away, and Yovela raised her voice. "Well? Are you satisfied?"

"I don't understand," Lirin wheezed. "Why are you angry with him? He saved me!"

"Shut—" Yovela bit off the reprimand and only squeezed Lirin more tightly. "You're right. You don't understand."

Kayvin sat on another cushion, one knee high, still avoiding Yovela's gaze. "He wanted to strike at me. He wanted to take something of mine, to make a stand in court, to show my weakness."

"Yes, you were the most wronged here." Yovela's voice was savage over Lirin's shoulder. She gave a little hiss of breath. "You were the one to make her a prize. Of course someone else would want to win it." Yovela was angry, frighteningly angry, and her mouth was bleeding, and Lirin was afraid of her too, even in her embrace. She didn't understand what Yovela was talking about. What had Lirin done?

Her throat hurt. Her wrist hurt. Her face hurt, where he had slapped her when she'd first tried to run. She was still crying.

Yovela was saying something, loud and urgent, directed now at Lirin and not Kayvin. Lirin squinted up at her.

"Lirin!" Yovela repeated. "Where is Dielo?"

Lirin looked from Yovela to Prince Kayvin, staring intently at her. How did they not know? "You said she wanted to take him back," she choked.

Yovela gaped at Kayvin. "You let her take him?"

"I don't know anything about it!" He turned on Lirin. "Did you see?"

She wailed. "When they grabbed us—I saw him on his knees, and then he slumped over. She wouldn't take him back like that, would she? Is he dead?"

Yovela turned, open-mouthed, to Kayvin, silently imploring him to do something. He stared at Lirin, horrified.

CHAPTER 87

KAYVIN COULD NOT BOTH stay and go. Yovela had tried to stand, ready to rush out of the apartments again, but Lirin had clutched her and sobbed. So Kayvin, pinned by Yovela's horrified, accusing stare and ill with his own sick realization and guilt, had gone by himself to look for his missing virilo.

He might have asked Arad or other servants to go with him, but he did not know if he trusted them, and he did not know if he might lose another servant to the corridors. He did not think they would take him. Not yet.

He was not worth taking.

Lord Fretton had spelled it out plainly. *You're so ignorant, you haven't even realized what you are not.* Kayvin was such a useless laughingstock, the courtiers did not fear even to steal his sera qadra woman from him.

Lilac Prince.

He retraced their path to the little courtyard, and there was no one. He did not want to return to the servants' wing where he had left Lord Fretton; someone would have found him by now. Kayvin had burned him badly... Kayvin felt sickened, and furious.

Lirin and Dielo had been seized at the same time, so Lord Fretton's men had taken both. Kayvin strained to think, wishing he were better at intrigue. They probably would not have taken Dielo to Pasiphae Jade; Fretton would not want to admit to raiding Kayvin's sera qadra and stealing Pasiphae Jade's daughter. Or would he, as a threat to the new Arch Potentate? Or had he kept Dielo for himself? Or had he killed him?

Kayvin could protect no one.

He had to find Dielo, who deserved better than this. He put a hand over his eyes, blocking out the sunlight and the memory of Yovela's glare. Yovela despised Dielo, and yet her expression when she realized Kayvin had not brought him... How had he missed the attack? Both of them, abducted while he had plowed ahead, caught up in his own thoughts...

He could not go back without Dielo. He could not face Yovela's accusing eyes if he walked in alone. He could not lose another person, not even the virilo pressed into his household to embarrass him and spy on him.

He stopped in an open passage, a bridge between wings, and looked down to the garden below. It was empty of people. It was more neatly maintained than his own garden, with no flower out of place and no sooty damage from fire practice.

He had burned Lord Fretton. He had assaulted one of the most powerful men in the nation, and he couldn't imagine what consequences lay ahead. His stomach churned.

Something lay near a dense hedge of greenery, a darker shadow beneath the shrubbery. Kayvin leaned over the parapet, as if he could see more clearly with a few more inches, and tried to discern the irregular shape.

Yes, it was a man.

He looked left and right, trying to determine the nearest route down. He found a stairway and descended, glancing around the empty yard as he entered. He did not want to be caught as Dielo had.

He did not want to confirm Dielo's corpse.

But Dielo struggled to rise as Kayvin approached, pulling himself upright. He was covered in scrapes and punctures, oozing blood from his face, arms, and bare chest. His green trousers were torn and he was missing a sandal. Kayvin dropped to one knee beside him. "What happened?"

Dielo tried to speak, but his voice only croaked. His arm gestured toward the hedge, crushed and broken, and the open passage above.

Had they thrown him over? "Can you walk? Let's go." Kayvin took Dielo's arm and pulled him upright. The virilo sucked in a breath but came up, and his legs stayed beneath him. Nothing broken, or nothing critical. Kayvin pulled him close, putting Dielo's arm over his shoulders and holding his waist for support. They should travel as quickly as possible.

"They took Lirin," Dielo whispered hoarsely.

"She's safe." Then Kayvin wondered if that was still true. If someone had gone to his apartments while he was here...

He couldn't afford to think that way, or he would lose his mind.

He couldn't afford not to think that way, or he would lose his friends.

He couldn't think, not now, so he half-dragged Dielo along the palace corridors. Once or twice servants came into the passages and immediately disappeared around distant corners before he could call them.

Even the maids had a better sense for palace intrigue than he did.

Dielo was walking better now, limping but mostly supporting himself. "Sorry," he offered, still hoarse.

"Hush. We'll talk later." Kayvin wanted only to reach the illusory safety of his own rooms.

And then they were there, and Kayvin pulled Dielo in and ordered the doorkeeper to set locks. Before they could get through the dog-legged entrance, Yovela was rushing around the corner, eyes wide.

Kayvin looked at her, and then at Dielo. Dielo's head hung low. Yovela rushed to gather his other arm and lead him inside.

Lirin, seated on a cushion and wrapped in a fur, wailed when she saw Dielo. They lowered him to the floor, and Kayvin ordered Arad to call a physician.

"And hot water and cloths and soap," Yovela added. "Hot tea. More blankets."

Lirin was crying. Kayvin tried not to be frustrated by this. "Dielo, what happened?"

"Threw me," he answered, his voice soft and rasping.

"Threw you? What?"

"He's been strangled," Yovela said curtly. She rose and walked to the pitcher on a nearby table, dipping a scarf into it. "We need cold compresses, quickly, before the swelling worsens."

Kayvin stared at her and then looked back at Dielo. There was a line wrapping his neck, the mark of a wire or cord.

Yovela knelt and pressed the wet scarf around his throat. "It can swell inside. It's dangerous."

"He—he fell." Kayvin thought back to the courtyard, now that they were safely inside. "I think he fell onto a hedge."

She bent to meet Dielo's eyes. "I'm going to tie this in place, but loosely. Say something if—if you want."

Dielo nodded once.

"Lirin, come here." Yovela glanced over her shoulder. "I need your help."

Lirin, still sniffing, let the fur fall and crawled nearer, her sage green gown slipping.

"These cuts need to be washed. Carefully—there are bits of bark and grit here, see? They need cleaning to heal."

Lirin nodded, sniffing, and took the cloths and hot water from the maid who brought them. "I can help."

Kayvin nodded to himself; Lirin was not as efficient as the maid or Yovela, but the task steadied her, and her crying was slowing.

There was a wet scarf on her neck as well. "Did they grab you by the throat?" he asked.

"I couldn't shout." Fear was in her voice. "Him, too—they had a cord for him. I didn't see—he went on his knees, and they took me away. I didn't..."

She might have thought him dead. She wouldn't have had much time to think on it before she was passed to Lord Fretton, waiting nearby. If he had not taken her through the roundabout side corridors instead of directly through the main passage...

"Threw me over," Dielo rasped.

The passage was only a short height above the courtyard, not even the height of two grown men. The fall had not been meant to kill him, only to get him out of the way. He wasn't worth a proper disposal.

Kayvin slid closer and braced Dielo's wavering torso. "Here, sit back. We have you."

Yovela and Lirin worked meticulously over the seeping wounds. When the physician arrived, he frowned. "Empty void, what happened here?"

"He fell into a bush," Kayvin said curtly.

"By his neck?" The physician twisted his mouth.

"I'm..." Dielo didn't complete the sentence.

"Show me your eyes." The physician stared into each of Dielo's eyes for a moment, and then he leaned to examine the bruising and cut on his neck. He pressed his lips together and turned back to his carry-box of supplies.

He did not ask how it had happened, Kayvin noted. A sera qadra was to be patched up when things went too far.

"Here's a salve for that cut. And this is a powder to add to some tea; you're going to have quite a headache for a while. You may not want to swallow much, but take small sips, and it will help. Now, let me see these."

There were a few painful moments when splinters had to be pulled, but the physician declared that Dielo had been fortunate and had not taken a stick directly to an organ or an eye. At last it was done, and bandaged Dielo sank against Kayvin's supporting shoulder with an exhausted sigh. Lirin, still sniffing, let the physician examine her and applaud the application of the cold compress. He gave her some powder as well. Then he gave a little vial of salve to Yovela for her bleeding mouth and told her to apply a cold compress to her face as well. He asked no questions.

When the physician had gone, the room was suddenly and keenly quiet, with only Dielo's breathing and Lirin's residual sniffing breaking the silence.

Yovela sat a little distance away and twisted the cleaning cloths into ropes, looking at nothing. Kayvin wished desperately for another task, something to blunt the terrible sharp questions that remained.

"Why?" Lirin blurted suddenly. "What happened? It was only a party!"

Kayvin's stomach churned. "What do we do with you now?"

"Why not give her a purse of coins?" Yovela's tone was acid as she fixed her eyes on Kayvin. "Give her some money, and a beautiful new outfit, and send her away. Isn't that the precedent?"

The words lanced him like ice.

Lirin, confused, looked at Yovela. "I don't want to go! I haven't done anything wrong, have I?"

Kayvin looked down, his eyes resting on Dielo's torn shoulder and half-removed vest. "You need some proper clothes," he said, grateful for the distraction. "You're shivering. Go and dress."

Dielo moved to obey without replying, shifting his weight. Yovela stood and extended a hand to help him up.

They had gone only a few steps when loud voices came from the entrance. Kayvin jerked around, and his doorman bolted into the room. "My lord," he began, and then a liveried guard pushed him aside.

Pasiphae Jade stalked in. Behind her stood four guards, armed within the Amethyst Prince's quarters.

CHAPTER 88

KAYVIN GOT TO HIS feet, facing her. Behind him, the others froze in place.

Pasiphae Jade looked over them all with a cool assessment, her eyes resting first on Dielo and his bandages and torn clothing, and then on Lirin. Her face darkened at the sight of Lirin's tears.

Kayvin's pulse was pounding, but he tried to keep his tone cool. "I did not expect the honor of the Arch Potentate in my own rooms."

"I can see you were unprepared to receive guests." Her voice was barely restrained, dripping with disdain and fury.

Neither Dielo nor Yovela moved forward to offer proper greetings or services. Kayvin did not look back at them. "Come into my study, and we can talk." He gave a pointed glance at the guards. "Unless you are not here to talk."

"Lord Fretton has been assaulted and burned," she said curtly. "I'm told he's badly injured."

"That's too bad," Kayvin answered flatly. "I wish him all the healing he deserves."

She pursed her lips, and for just a heartbeat he thought she was...amused, maybe? Perhaps she had thought him beaten beyond caustic remarks. But anger churned in him, and he was on the edge of saying unwise things.

She gestured at the guards behind her. "We'll go to your study to speak. They will see that no one disturbs us."

Kayvin led the way through the door, his back prickling behind his heart where she might slam an icicle.

She took his chair, turning it behind the desk stacked with books and notes. "You brought someone new into your sera qadra."

Kayvin set his jaw. "Are we going to pretend each of us is ignorant?"

Pasiphae Jade gave a single nod. "Then let's not be coy, and you can answer my questions directly. I went to great lengths to keep that secret. I have spent a great deal of money and effort to know whether Lord Fretton knew her identity, and I'd thought I'd been successful. How did you learn it?"

Kayvin attempted to counter. "She does not know, either. Not the whole truth."

Pasiphae Jade's face went still. It was a terrifying effect, a mask concealing both her rage and her furious calculations. At last she said, "When you brought her into your sera qadra, you identified her to Lord Fretton."

"I did not," Kayvin said quickly. "He would have taken little notice of a member of my household, even in my sera qadra. It was your own interest in her that gave her away."

"You could not expect me to remain unmoved when you bring my—her into a court event and display her as your own. You have endangered her."

"No more than she was—and she is in fact safer now." Kayvin spoke quickly, hoping he could think fast enough. "Lord Fretton cannot touch her while she is in my sera qadra."

Her mouth twisted. "I suppose his present injury is due to clumsily tripping into a midday candle?"

Kayvin did not answer.

She crossed her arms. "I went to him first, when I'd been informed of his condition. He did not seem pleased by my visit, but I suppose anyone in that sort of pain and distress might not appreciate even a royal visitor." She tipped her head. "When I asked how he had come to be injured, he insisted he had been assaulted from behind while alone, and he had no idea who his fire-wielding assailant could have been." She raised an eyebrow and waited.

Kayvin's mind spun. Why wouldn't Fretton have identified Kayvin? He had no reason to protect Kayvin and every justification to punish him. Even as a prince, Kayvin couldn't assault a high courtier, and Fretton was close to Pasiphae Jade, who should have welcomed an opportunity to censure the prince...

But Lord Fretton couldn't have told Pasiphae Jade he had tried to abduct her daughter. He could flout Kayvin's standing, but not hers.

Pasiphae Jade was still waiting. Kayvin shook his head. "It's upsetting, to hear of an attack so blatant, and within the palace. I hope he takes more caution in the future."

One corner of her mouth curled in reluctant appreciation of his circumspection. "I thought we were not being coy."

Kayvin tried to swallow, but his mouth was dry and his throat tight. "Then, if we are being very candid, I should point out that you cannot take Lirin from here without declaring to all the court she is more than a maid who has caught my eye. Lord Fretton was looking for a young woman you withheld from him; I doubt others have any particular interest in her yet. If Lord Fretton had, perhaps, attempted to steal one of my sera qadra and failed, he certainly would not share that story with others. But if you take her from here, you will make her even more of a target."

"And what do you intend to do with her?" Pasiphae Jade's voice was coldly crystalline and dangerous.

Kayvin took a breath. "You have someone dear to me and I have someone dear to you. We could each welcome back a family member. Give me my mother."

Pasiphae Jade's mouth curled into a tiny, dismissive smile "No."

Kayvin stared at her, disbelieving.

"You look surprised? Let us examine the offer you bring." She sat forward in the chair. "I have only one piece of leverage to keep the angry son of the former Arch Potentate focused on bringing the amulets I desperately need. I cannot afford to let you be distracted from this task, and so I cannot afford to release her. Meanwhile—" she turned up one palm—"you have ruined Lirin's value in my negotiations. You seem to know she was promised to a dedicated retainer, but now? What great lord would want to found a new dynasty with a woman possibly carrying the old regime's heir? Even if he waited until any coming eggs were laid in, he would still be taking a fallen prince's castoff. By bringing her into your sera qadra, you have ruined her hopes for a fine marriage."

Kayvin tried to follow her explanation, but he was too stunned by her refusal. All this—all this was to rescue his mother, and now... "You were going to give her to Lord Fretton."

"And what else should I have done with her?" Her anger flared. "I meant her to have a secure position, a wife instead of a courtesan. She might eventually lose a place to a younger wife, but she wouldn't be cast away to a cheaphouse, not if she bore royal heirs. I had planned the best possible future for her." She shook her head. "And now you have ruined that. I cannot trade your mother for a sera qadra girl."

He was losing control of this exchange. "Wait! I— Aren't you afraid for her?"

She tipped her head to regard him, almost curiously.

"Don't you fear for her safety?"

She blew out a little breath. Then she raised her voice. "Bring me the girl Lirin, from His Highness's sera qadra."

A moment later a guard escorted Lirin in. Pasiphae Jade waved him out, and Lirin stood beside the desk, looking anxiously between her seated mother and Kayvin standing.

"Lirin," Pasiphae Jade said, turning and extending her hands, "are you all right?" The façade was gone, and Kayvin thought he saw real concern.

Lirin seized her mother's hands and nodded, though her eyes began to tear again.

"Has he hurt you?"

"No!" Lirin burst anxiously. "No, it wasn't—it was Lord Fretton today. Prince Kayvin has been—it's fine, everything is fine. He's been very good, he's teaching me reading and music, and he—he hasn't hurt me, not in any way. I haven't done anything wrong! Don't make me go."

Kayvin's heart sank.

Pasiphae Jade kept her eyes on the girl. "Are you sure?"

Lirin nodded. "Please—I want to stay."

Pasiphae Jade smiled kindly. "All right, I'll think about it. Go on and let us finish here."

Lirin nodded and threw a quick, hopeful glance at Kayvin. Then she went out, leaving Pasiphae Jade turning smugly back to face him.

"You were disturbed when I had a servant slapped, and you brought my virilo into your household rather than even hear his punishment. You are not the kind to hurt Lirin, not even to reach me."

Kayvin had no footing and no words. "But..."

"And I still hold Dielo, who I think has become a companion of sorts to you. If you did not want him beaten even before you knew him, you would be more careful of him now."

"But..."

She shook her head. "Even if someday you do take her fully into your sera qadra, she will not suffer, not more than as a maid. I had intended her for a man who would value her for the sons she will bear; you will not do worse."

"I..."

Her eyes hardened. "And if you do, then I will kill your mother before your eyes, and then I will kill you, and I will scatter both of you over the hills without burial."

Kayvin's chest clenched and his stomach churned, but he made himself return a glare of his own. "Do not threaten me."

She gave that infuriating little smile. "I'm sorry. I know I don't have to."

Kayvin stared, speechless.

"Lirin wishes to stay with you, for now. But you will not be here. When you return to Sayinia to search for the amulets, I will require an extra hold on your loyalty, and I will therefore keep your remaining sera qadra in my own household as surety until your return."

Holding Dielo to be ransomed with another amulet, and keeping Lirin secure from Lord Fretton without admitting their relationship. He was begrudgingly impressed by her quick rationalization.

She stood. "And now, I will take my leave. It's a pity about Lord Fretton's injury, but I suppose these things can happen. No doubt some intrigue or squabble among the nobles, but perhaps we'll never know."

She went out into the main room, where Lirin, Dielo, and Yovela waited on the cushions, not looking at the armed guards. Lirin half-stood. "Can I...?"

"You may stay," Pasiphae Jade said graciously, "at least until he departs again for Sayinia. I'll see you tomorrow." She gave Lirin a kiss on the cheek, and then she swept out, drawing her guards with her.

CHAPTER 89

FOR A MOMENT, EVERYONE was still, afraid to break whatever spell protected them. Then Lirin's face crumpled. "I'm sorry," she began, her voice breaking. "I'm sorry. I should have—I couldn't tell you. But I got you into trouble."

Kayvin turned to her, his heart sinking and stomach churning. "You did not get me into trouble."

"I did! I couldn't tell you, but you didn't know." She choked. "I'm... I am..."

Kayvin went to stand before her. "Your aunt is Pasiphae Jade," he said quietly.

She nodded. "I'm sorry."

"I knew. This wasn't your fault."

She stared at him. "You knew?"

"I knew you were told to keep it secret. You were right not to tell." Kayvin couldn't think clearly, but she probably deserved the truth. He knelt to face her. "But Pasiphae Jade is not your aunt," he said as gently as he could. "She is your mother."

Lirin blinked at him. "My..." She gulped. "I..."

Yovela and Dielo were staring, but Kayvin did not look at them. There was no reason to lie to Lirin, not now.

Lirin's bruised throat worked. "I...I didn't... But it—it makes sense, doesn't it?"

Yovela leaned forward. "Lirin..."

But Lirin nodded. "She—she was only trying to protect me. She was always trying to protect me." She began to cry again.

Kayvin leaned forward and embraced her. Lirin was right; Pasiphae Jade had protected her daughter, in the only way she knew. And he had first put her in an illusion of danger, and then in actual danger.

"Your Highness." Yovela's voice was curt. "Dielo is still in his court clothes. I'll take him for something warmer."

He nodded over Lirin's shoulder.

"I'm taking him to his own quarters."

He nodded again. Lirin turned her head and squeezed his arms, sobbing and coughing, and he closed his eyes, wishing he could take back everything.

Dielo was towed by his wrist away from Prince Kayvin and Lirin, down the short corridor to the sera qadra's quarters. Yovela led him into the men's room and kept going. "Which is yours?"

He drew back against her fingers, his stomach churning. "I..."

She looked back at him. "Oh, stop it. You heard me tell Kayvin where we were going. You saw how little he noted it." She looked ahead and identified the chest against the wall, distinct in the sparse furniture. "That's it." She went to it. "You need something warm to wear. You've been shivering, and I know it wasn't from cold, but you shouldn't be cold, either."

She wasn't supposed to be here. This was the men's quarters; the sera qadra was not to mingle, not alone.

"Come on. It's fine." She looked away. "Besides, you came to the women's quarters once."

He had, when he had heard her in distress. She was right, and Kayvin had not seemed to mind, not in the way that others would. He had worried for Yovela, but without jealousy.

Dielo tried to crouch beside the chest, but he slid onto the floor. His head ached, as predicted. He drew out a tunic and leggings.

"Go ahead," Yovela said, flipping a hand at him. "You haven't got anything I haven't seen more than enough of." But she turned her back. "The laces might be difficult."

They were. It was easy enough to slide out of his loose vest and ruined trousers, but his curiously numbed fingers struggled to pick at the laces. "I..."

She glanced over her shoulder, and then she sighed and came to him. "Let me do it."

He stood still, like a chastened child, and tried to look away. Her dark hair brushed his chin as she closed the tunic roughly, and he fought the urge to pull back. Her fingers never touched his skin.

Then she stepped away. "Sit down," she ordered, "and I'll make tea for your powder."

He sat against the wall, well away from the sleeping pit and an arm's reach from his open trunk. His discarded clothing lay in front of it, puddled on the floor. He wondered where his other sandal had been lost.

Yovela was restarting the banked small-hearth in the corner, angrily pumping the miniature bellows to bring the embers into a glow. It should have been a servant's task, but Kayvin's household was short on servants. Dielo was glad of that just now; he did not want anyone else to watch him humiliated and reproached.

She set a kettle atop the small-hearth and then fetched two cups from the wall shelf. Dielo winced as she slapped them down on the edge of the small-hearth to warm. Somehow neither broke.

She was going to shout at him, and he could only wait for it, and he couldn't even shout in return, even if he'd had the strength or the will.

She left the water to boil and came back to him, dropping into a squat to peer at his neck. "How's the compress?" Her voice was terse as she touched it. "Could be colder, it's warming now. Pressure?"

He couldn't bear it any longer—not today. He looked at his hands and whispered, "I'm sorry."

Her hand stilled on the cloth. "Sorry?"

"I'm—sorry." *Please don't revile or scorn me. Not today. Not now.*

She drew back her hand and shifted to look at his face. "What are you sorry for?" she demanded.

She wanted him to list his offenses, to apologize properly, and he couldn't. He closed his eyes. "For all of it. For whatever has angered you. Just...please..."

There was a moment of silence, and then she burst, "You? Do you think I'm angry at *you?*"

He opened his eyes, looking down, almost holding his breath.

"Empty void, I'm not angry with you." She stood, stalked to a small table, snatched a pitcher. "I'm furious. But not with you." She returned, sat beside him, reached for his neck. He flinched.

She stopped and blew out a breath. "I'm sorry. Let me wet it again."

"I can." He unwound the compress from his neck, and the air brushed his damp skin.

She sighed again, longer. "I'm sorry. I'm not angry at you, not for this. This is all his doing."

Dielo kept his eyes on the cloth in his hands. "If not for this," he rasped, "then for what?"

She stiffened. At last she said, "For accepting it. For wanting what they told you to want and giving up anything else. For believing what they told you." Her hands balled into fists. "But you were a child, and you were taught that is all you were meant for. I understand that. But still, I wish you hadn't accepted, or wanted, or believed."

She took the cloth from his hands, again without brushing his skin, and dunked it into the pitcher. Then she wrung it out and lifted it. "May I?"

He could have wrapped it himself, even with his unreliable fingers, but he nodded.

She leaned close and deftly wound the cloth, spreading cool damp over his bruised throat. He made himself breathe. Then she was done, pulling away. Her hands rested on her legs.

He looked at his hands. "What would you have me do instead?"

"What?"

"Instead of believing and wanting—what should I have done?" It was partly a challenge to her derision, and partly a desperate question.

"I don't know." The words were curt, but it wasn't quite a snap. He thought her voice might be shaking beneath her irritation. "I don't know. You were a child—but you aren't now. You could—at least be angry. Be resentful. Know what you've lost."

His heart sank. "So I could mourn every day?"

She slumped beside him, one hand on the floor, her hair hanging. "No. Maybe. I don't know."

His heart pounded as if he were dancing or running. His throat was tight even inside the bruising and cool compress. He laced his fingers together and squeezed them pale. "Go look in the little drawer."

"What?"

"The little drawer in the top of the chest." He couldn't release his fingers to point. "Look there."

After a few heartbeats of hesitation, she stood and went around him to the open chest. The drawer was easy to find. "The jewelry? What am I to see in—oh!"

He squeezed his hands. He could not feel his fingers.

She rushed back to kneel beside him, and her voice dropped to a whisper. "Is this your chit?"

She was holding it gingerly, a little dusky gold kilted figure with black hair. He jerked his head in a nod.

"Oh, Dielo," she breathed.

It was not anger. It was—it was a little afraid, but it was not fear. He bit the inside of his lip.

"Dielo..."

He raised his head to venture a glance at her. She was staring at him.

He had never drunk such a heady wine as the shine in her eyes. She regarded him not with appreciation of his physique, not admiration, not envy, but an awe of who he was and what he had done. He would walk on live coals if he could ever get that look again.

She cradled the little figure as if it were alive, a tiny fragile bird. "When?"

"When you and Prince Kayvin were away. I visited Her Illustrious Excellency, because there was no one here, and..." He tried to smile, but his cheeks were stiff. "I took it."

"That was bold."

He huffed a small, embarrassed chuckle. "I did not feel bold. Well, maybe a little reckless. But I was too afraid to be bold.'

"Then maybe you were bolder than you thought." She let the figurine lie in the palm of her hand, and she extended a finger to press it. "What will—"

He reached to cover the chit. "Don't—there's magic in it."

She glanced at him. "What magic?"

He shook his head. "I know only some of it."

The kettle whistled, and Yovela jumped in place. She gave him an embarrassed smile and then tipped the chit into his hand. "You hold this, then."

She got up and went to the small-hearth, beginning the mundane routine of tea. She added the physician's powder to one cup, mixing it with the brewing leaves, and came back to sit beside Dielo. "Here."

His head pounded with the beat of his heart, and he was not sure how much was from the strangulation and how much from the terror of showing her his stolen chit. He took the tea—too hot, too bitter with medicine—and sucked it down, scorching his tongue. She sat beside him, leaning against the wall, and wrapped her fingers around her cup.

"You can't keep it," she said suddenly.

His chest tightened.

"In the drawer of your own chest? It will be found immediately. It has to be hidden." She looked at him. "Will the magic draw her? If she looks for it?"

"I don't know."

"You don't know?"

"We weren't taught much about the chits' workings—only that they were symbols." Almost sacred symbols, inviolate in their symbolism. He was a thief, having stolen himself.

She shook her head. "Regardless, you can't keep it here."

"I—I thought of giving it to Prince Kayvin." He felt almost ashamed as he said the words, knowing she would disapprove. But then, at least he would belong to the prince, a proper member of his household. It was better than being lent and discarded.

But she did not scold him. Instead she waited a moment, looking into her tea, and then she asked, "Is that what you want?"

What he wanted, he realized, was for someone to look at him like that again—to look at him, at who he was and what he had done, as if he were someone brave who had accomplished something impressive, as if they respected him. But Prince Kayvin would never need to look at him that way.

He wished he had more tea, to drink and delay answering. But now she was watching him expectantly.

"I want someone to want me," he blurted, too anxious to say something to cover the truthful silence, and immediately he cringed. "I mean, if someone wants to hold my chit—if they want a..."

It was too late. The words could not be called back.

But Yovela did not curl her lip. She looked back at her tea. "I used to dream of someone like that. I imagined he would come to one of our shows—I was a dancer in a troop, before..." She waved a hand to encompass the palace and more. "He would come to one of our shows, and he would stay after, and he would say such nice things, and he would take me away to someplace wonderful." She smiled ruefully. "I was a foolish girl, with foolish dreams."

When he looked at her, her eyes were too bright, brimming with unshed tears. When she saw him looking, she quickly turned her head. "It's all right to laugh at me. I didn't know any better then."

"I don't think it was so foolish," he said. "I don't know about—but you wanted something better, didn't you?"

She sniffed. "I suppose this is it, though. I have a life of luxury, with a master who does not use me poorly, and I can be quite comfortable until Pasiphae Jade has us killed." She gave a coughing little chuckle.

It was too near a possibility, even without considering the penalty for a virilo who stole his chit and violated his purpose. Quickly he asked, "What do you want now? When you dream?"

"Oh, I haven't dreamed in a long time. Not like that." She took a drink.

He stared down into his cup. His head still hurt, but distantly. He thought his cup looked farther away than it felt. He wondered what the headache powder was.

Yovela glanced toward him. "Your tea's empty. Let me refill it." She took the cup, again without brushing his fingers.

His fingers were no longer numb and stiff. He flexed them, watching them work as if the mechanism were unfamiliar.

Yovela gave him another cup of tea and settled against the wall again. She took a drink. "What about you? What do you really want?"

She was giving him another chance, to cover his embarrassing answer. He should say something important, something impressive, something powerful. He should... He looked into his cup, watching the broken tea leaves swirl.

"I want someone to run their fingers through my hair," he said aloud to the tea leaves.

Yovela blinked at him. "What?"

"If he has a great chair, in court or at a banquet or what have you, and the favorite sits at the front... That was my dream, to be the favorite, to be shown off because he was proud of me." He smiled, wistful. He was saying too much, but the tea leaves were swirling and his head was pounding, too far away, and the words kept coming. "And I imagined he would drop his hand from the armrest to touch my head, and he would run his fingers through my hair, just a small touch while we sat in court, and I would know he was proud of me."

Yovela was staring at him, and he had the sense he had said something wrong. Or, not wrong, but not right. He tried to shrug his stiffening shoulders.

"His hand?" she repeated, leaning a little on the first word.

He understood the question, and he crooked his mouth in a self-mocking grin. "Well, it would have been a man, obviously. I only ever thought of serving great men. No one had heard of a woman with a virilo, much less as Arch Potentate."

"But now, we have."

He licked his lips. "I don't think I want to be her favorite," he admitted in a treasonous whisper.

His cup was wavering. Yovela frowned. "Let me have that." When she reached for it, his unsteady hand bumped hers. "Empty void! You're too cold. Get into your pit."

The sleeping pit yawned in the floor in front of him, only a body length away but dauntingly far. She took his hand and tugged him toward it, and he undulated across the floor and slid over the edge. Yovela descended after him and pushed pillows together. "Sleep with your head raised, just in case. Here, like this. Put your arm in so I can cover it." She put blankets over him, frowning. "That medicine should have come with a warning."

Dielo thought there were too many things that needed warnings, but the blankets were comfortably heavy. He took her hand as she pulled a blanket into place. The warmth of her fingers felt good—a sweet warmth, a cocooning grasp. It had been a long time since he'd shared companionable touch.

She drew her hand away, leaving his fingers lonely and aching. "You need rest, and I can't stay here."

The words were sad, somehow. But he was tired. He closed his eyes without protest—always be agreeable—and sank into the slope of pillows.

CHAPTER 90

FOR A MOMENT, BENEATH the warm blankets, Dielo imagined a choking darkness, and then he came fully awake.

His mind was clear, he was in a sleeping pit, and he was holding someone's hand.

He looked up, following the arm which dangled into his sleeping pit, to Yovela. She lay on the floor, one borrowed pillow beneath her cheek. With a little start of horror, he released her and drew his cold hand beneath his blankets.

His heart was already racing. Yovela had stayed in the men's quarters all night—even if she had not been in his sleeping pit, they had invited punishment. And he had held her hand, and yet he could remember her pulling her hand away, and he could not—he could not imagine Yovela offering him her hand. Not even the strangely tolerant Yovela of last night, brewing him tea that had made him say things, oh empty void, had he really said such things? To her, to confident, forthright Yovela, who despised him? Maybe the tea had made him imagine rather than speak...

He slid down against the pillows and wriggled away from her, catching his breath as he moved. Everything had stiffened as he slept, and the bruising had deepened. He swallowed tentatively—it hurt, but it was manageable and he could breathe well—and turned back.

She lay asleep, undisturbed by his movement. Her cheek was deeply colored with the mark of a hand. Her legs were drawn up and her other arm was tucked to her chest; guiltily he realized she was cold. He climbed stiffly out of the sleeping pit, bringing a blanket with him, and he spread it over her, sucking his breath a little as he stooped and his muscles pulled.

He should have woken her, should have urged her back to the women's quarters before they were caught. But if he woke her, he would see in her face what she remembered and what he had said aloud the night before, and so instead he fled the room, putting distance between them.

He went out into the primary rooms, remembering belatedly that he had not combed his hair or checked his clothing or considered kohl for his eyes. No, he must still have kohl and mica from the day before, now hopelessly smeared. Quickly he smoothed his tunic and pushed his hands back through his hair. He should wash before the prince saw him.

Lirin was sitting on the balcony floor, looking out through the balusters. She must have heard him, for she turned her head and then, seeing who it was, gave him a weak, weary smile.

Dielo could wash later. He went to sit beside her, an arm's length between them. "Good morning."

"Good morning, I suppose. You look terrible." She looked out again, not really seeing the garden.

He wondered whether she meant the smeared kohl or his scraped face. He searched for a suitable expression of concern that was not too probing a question. "How do you feel?"

"Stupid." She shrugged. "I should have known, I guess. About my mother. Because once you say it, it just makes sense. If she lied to others about us not being related at all, then why not a lesser lie to me about being a niece instead of a daughter?" She huffed a dismissive sigh. "I don't remember my mother, and that's probably because I didn't have another mother."

"I'm sorry you learned this way." It was all Dielo could think to say.

"And I should have guessed he didn't want me for me," she continued in the same dull tone. "That also just makes sense—why would a prince want a maid? I should have realized he needed me for a plot."

Dielo's stomach sank.

"And you, too." She looked at him. "You'd already turned me down, and it was too good to be true when you came and invited me here. I thought—but I was stupid."

He felt ill. "I..."

"All that scolding about the servants' affair, and then you invited me for your own purpose as well. I should have guessed, only I was too flattered. You're more used to flattery, I suppose."

"Lirin, I'm sorry."

"It's—"

"No! I am sorry, and I have to say it. I—I thought it would be all right. I thought it was different. And it was different, but it wasn't different enough. I'm sorry."

She shrugged and gave him a sad smile. "He told me he ordered you to do it, said it was his fault, not yours. I told him—well, he told me Lord Fretton is the one I was promised to, the one he sort of stole me from by bringing me here. And... Well, if things had to be wrong, I suppose I'd rather they be wrong this way and not that way. Do you see what I mean?"

He did, but that did not excuse what they had done. Things had nearly gone very wrong in another way.

She looked at him a moment, and then she sighed. "Look, I know you think I'm young and foolish—and I am, both of those things."

"It wasn't your fault you were misled—"

"Just let me say this." She took a breath. "She'd protected me so far, but I was a drudge maid. I wasn't ignorant. We all knew we could expect to be pushed against a wall every so often and then go back to our scrubbing. At least in a sera qadra we could have some luxuries for the same work. Of course we dream of catching a virilo's eye and being invited into a prince's household." She stopped, looking as if she meant to go on but was not sure how to say more.

"I'm sorry," Dielo said. He understood. He'd dreamed, too, of a touch on his hair.

Lirin chewed her lip, and then she gave a little shake of her head and started anew. "He said you and I will stay with—her when he goes away again."

Dielo's stomach twisted further. He did not want to be left alone again—but he did not want to go to Pasiphae Jade...

His chit! Where was it now? Yovela had given it to him, and then he had taken the tea. But then the medicine had started to take effect, and he could not remember if he had set it down, or where. He had to find it, so he could hide it. Yovela was right; keeping it among his own things was too obvious.

But if Pasiphae Jade noticed it was missing, what hiding place could save him?

Lirin read his worry as for another cause. "It's all right. I won't tell her about the servants' affair or about you bringing me here. His Highness says she has your chit anyway, so it should be the same as before for you."

It would not be the same as before. It would never the same as before; now Dielo knew too much, had seen too much, had drunk the tea and said too much.

Lirin sighed. "I want breakfast."

Yovela woke beneath a blanket; Dielo must have already awakened. Her cheek was swollen and aching, and the cut in her mouth was tender.

She rose, passed down the corridor, and turned in at the prince's sleeping room.

His pit was long and deep, and she went down carefully. He was awake, but lying still on his left side, his eyes flicking to her and then back to an unfocused stare toward the wall.

She took a seat near his feet. "Do you see it now?"

"No one likes a gloater," he said hoarsely. "Saying 'I told you so' is rarely attractive."

"Fortunately, I don't care," Yovela retorted. "A retainer owes honesty before flattery and affinity."

"Retainer." He tried to smile, but his lips didn't quite make the curve. "I hardly can claim a retainer."

"Quit feeling sorry for yourself."

"I am feeling sorry," he said, "but not for myself." He sighed, long and heavy. "I know why you were angry. I thought I was doing something different, but I was playing to their rules, and I know why it angered you. And you weren't wrong."

"I wasn't wrong? Is that all you have to say?" Anger rose again in her, like an overfilling well, and hot rage bubbled up and spilled out through fresh tears. "I trusted you. Do you understand that? After everything—after everything, you were someone else, someone safe, and I trusted you! And then—and then you lied to bring her here, you used her, and your entire plan hinged on threat, and—" And she couldn't say any more, because the hot rage caught in her throat and she was dangerously close to sobbing.

Kayvin looked at her, and then he jerked upright. He reached for her, but she slapped his hand aside. She shoved away tears, hating that in fear and fury she cried, wishing she could be upset in a way that could be respected instead of pitied or disdained.

Kayvin pulled his hand back, and he shifted onto his knees. "Yovela. I'm sorry. I was wrong, for most of the reasons you've said. But I wouldn't have hurt her."

"No, you would have let her believe it was something more than a political calculation, you would have flattered and enticed her, you would have lured her to—"

"No!"

"You're not incapable, and to pin Pasiphae Jade you would use her daughter like—"

"No!" This time he reached out and caught her wrist, but the touch was light. He shook his head. "Yovela, among all other reasons, she is most likely my sister."

"Do you think that has stopped other men?" she snarled.

"It would stop me! And also—"

She quieted, staring at him, waiting.

"And aside from that..." He paused, bent his head, took a breath. He turned his palm up, letting her wrist lie loosely across it. "I've seen things now I couldn't see before, for standing too near to them. I've heard you, even when you didn't use words. Before, when I felt the weight of their derision on me—but now... I know better now. Or I'm learning."

She swallowed hard. He did not meet her eyes. "I'm sorry," she whispered as she wiped away more tears.

"No. No, you trusted me, and I...I made you afraid."

He had. That was why she had been angry. She had trusted him, and then he had done untrustworthy things.

She firmed her mouth. "You need to apologize."

"I've said I am sorry. I still am."

"Not just to me."

He nodded once. "Right."

"To both of them."

He nodded again. After a moment he continued, "I keep thinking I—but then I don't know how to be different. But it has to change. I have to change. I cannot be what this place makes us."

She looked at him and waited.

He balled his fists on his thighs. "I loathe what we are doing. I loathe this place, and how it forces us into such things." His mouth twisted about the words. "I tried to play their games as they did, and look at what it did to the only people who—it should have been me." He looked ill, as if he had taken a bite of rotten meat. "I hate the ostentation of it, the pretense of it, the obligation of it. Flaunt a greater disregard for others to show your own power, as if it costs more to gain than to give."

She nodded, having no words.

"And yet they prevail. Every one of those fine lords at her banquet, each one of them who boasts and promises, all of them who compliment one another on their honor—of all of those clever men, not one of them would hold a conviction instead of a coattail. They know how the game is played. They know words mean one thing for their subjects and another for themselves. They are cunning and clever, and not one would stand for a conviction."

Her voice cracked when she spoke. "You're standing for a conviction now."

He tried to smile and nearly succeeded. "I am not clever."

"Kayvin..."

"I have lost my only leverage, and my mother is as far from ransom as ever while I have made many new enemies. Lord Fretton and the other courtiers have thought me useless and ignorant and harmless, but now I've opened battle with them and set the stakes at a mortal level. And I still have no more amulets, or much idea where to find them."

She reached for his hands, wrapping them in her own. She could not offer more comfort.

"We need to go." His throat worked, and he took a breath. "I said I would stay until the hatching, and that's done. I said I would give up the throne and only try to get my mother freed, and my plan failed. I am thoroughly done with trying to reason as they do, in intrigue or otherwise. Now I have only the amulets for bargaining. We have to find them."

She nodded, though she had neither hope nor expectations.

CHAPTER 91

A MOVEMENT SHADOWED HIS desk, and Kayvin glanced up from his book. Yovela leaned against the study door's frame, eying him. "Come, Amethyst Prince, I hear you play a little. Give us some music, so I can dance."

Kayvin gave her a weary glance. "I haven't the spirit for dance music."

"Then play something maudlin. But play." She took a gittern from a shelf and pushed it into his hands.

He was exhausted with frustration and despair. Tomorrow he would leave his palace and go again into a hostile nation to search for lost artifacts, equipped only with memories of his failures, and she stood before him with a bruised and swollen face suffered at the failure of his plan, and he could not even recall a melody in this moment.

But Yovela had taken a position a few paces in front of him. "Please." Her teasing tone of a moment before was now strained. "I want—I need to dance."

He was so tired, and he did not want to play, but he owed her something after the debacle of bringing Lirin here. He set his fingers to the strings and played a melancholy arpeggio. Yovela inclined her head expectantly. He repeated the arpeggio, still unable to recall a melody, and she began to move. Her head drooped, her arms swung low, she swayed like a willow tree in drought.

Kayvin repeated the notes, slowly, and she twisted in place, bending deeply backward, showing him a distorted frown and eyes rolling to search the ceiling in hyperbolic despair.

Kayvin snorted.

She paused, flicked her gaze to him, waited.

He played a chord, slowly progressed to another, fingered a resolution. She moved at the cautious pace of his fingers, straightening and raising her arms and eyes.

She was an excellent dancer, even with the poor accompaniment he was providing. He shifted keys and watched her spin and step into the new tones, one arm passing over her head as if peeling back a shell.

More movement—he glanced to the doorway, where Lirin was watching with rapt fascination. He jerked his head to beckon her in, and she beamed, a child permitted to join an adults' feast.

It was no feast; Yovela was making the best of his meager music, but they could do better. She dropped low, turned, looked at him with a challenge. Almost without thinking he slapped the face of the gittern and strummed more fiercely, and she clapped her hands overhead and wheeled, her long tunic flaring over her trousers.

Lirin came to stand beside him, her hands clasped as she watched Yovela. He noted how her eyes followed the dancer and her own weight shifted as Yovela moved. But Lirin stayed in place. She did not know how to dance, not like Yovela's art.

Then a flash of orange silk came in, and Dielo stepped alongside Yovela while picking out a simple syncopation on the hand drum he cradled. His movement was stiff, and a little hesitant, and scabbed scrapes were visible across his face and where the silk fluttered, but he was smiling. Yovela grinned and twisted, inviting him to follow, and Kayvin plucked a run of quick liquid notes from the strings. They were in a major key now, a key for high arms and bright eyes.

Lirin was clapping now, swaying with Dielo's percussion, and with a toss of her hair Yovela suddenly reached and caught Lirin's wrist, pulling her into the dance. Lirin ducked her face, embarrassed, but quickly tried to follow. She did not dance as Yovela did, her movement neither a story nor an emotion, and Kayvin guessed she was trying to entice. She knew only one purpose for dance. He looked away.

Dielo stopped drumming and took Lirin's hands, and he began to spin the two of them in place. She laughed, and clutched his hands, and only wheeled with the music Kayvin played and the beat of Yovela's quick feet. Her face showed joy.

And then Yovela leapt forward and tugged Kayvin's arm, and after a brief moment of resistance he let himself be drawn into their gyre. He strummed and trailed awkwardly after them—he was a musician, not a dancer—and grinned with them.

For a moment, they were happy.

Kayvin quickened the strumming, and they all faced him and clapped, faster and faster, until they reached a crescendo of clapping and laughing, and he slapped a final chord from the strings as they cheered. They dropped their arms and smiled around at one another, winded and relieved.

Kayvin lowered the gittern and nodded to Yovela. "It had been too long since you danced for me."

"It has been too long since I danced for me. I needed that, too."

Dielo unslung the drum from his shoulder and set it on the book-stacked desk. His face, though bruised and scabbed, looked more relaxed and open than Kayvin could recall in recent days. Beside him, Lirin was smiling for the first time since they had gone to Lord Trerin's reception.

Kayvin returned to his chair. "Maybe we could work on a song next. We could have food brought and eat as we hum and write the score." He should be preparing to go—he would leave in the morning—but joy was precious, and music was freeing.

"I wish you didn't have to go," Lirin said abruptly, and the mood cooled.

Kayvin took a breath. "She wants the amulets for the spawning. I've brought her one, but she says that is not enough."

He wondered suddenly if Lirin had inherited her mother's skill with ice magic. Could she unwork the spell holding his mother in the frozen fountain?

But a maid didn't have the time or education to practice magic, and Pasiphae Jade wouldn't have risked Lirin betraying herself with such pursuits. Any skill she had was insufficient to risk Raea's life.

"I wish I could stay here while you're gone," Lirin went on, looking about the study. "I could keep reading. My au—my mother would like that, wouldn't she?"

"She would rather have you under her protection," Kayvin answered tiredly, "where Lord Fretton daren't try anything again."

Lirin nodded soberly. "But at least Dielo will be with me there."

Dielo's face tightened. Kayvin understood; he would be a hostage, and with someone who had already proved ready to harm him as she felt necessary.

The joy was rapidly slipping away. Kayvin sighed. "Dielo, go and tell Arad I'll need the travel money, please. I haven't seen it yet, and I'll want to leave early."

"I'm coming with you," Yovela said. "You need someone, and no one has a right to keep me here."

He did not like to think on how much he did not want to leave her behind. "Yes, of course."

Dielo left the study in search of Arad. Lirin pulled a chair toward the desk.

Dielo chewed his lip as he passed through the prince's apartments. Where was his chit? He had looked through his chest, and around the men's room where they had been sitting, and it wasn't there. Had Yovela taken it?

Arad nodded when Dielo relayed the prince's request. "I have the money. I'll bring it to the study."

"I can take it," Dielo said helpfully.

Arad fit a key into a lockbox and retrieved the leather purse of coins. "The Arch Potentate sends these, sourced from the traders down on the south border," he explained. "Sayinia takes these coins as their own."

Dielo nodded in due appreciation of their rarity.

Arad handed over the purse. "You'll stay here again, I suppose?" He did not sound welcoming.

Dielo shook his head. "The Arch Potentate has invited Lirin and me to stay with her."

Arad gave Dielo an appraising glance. "If she wants."

Dielo pushed aside the humiliation. "Thank you for the coins. I'll take them directly."

And he did, going straight toward the study. Along the way, he drew out a handful and slipped them, clinking quietly, into a small vase behind stacked musical notations. Then he went into the study and set the purse on Kayvin's desk.

Kayvin was sharing a scroll with Lirin. He glanced up and nodded thanks to Dielo. Dielo went out again in search of Yovela.

He found her on a balcony, looking over the garden. He leaned on the balustrade. "Thank you for the dance."

"I needed to dance. I thought he must, too." She sighed. "It helps, sometimes."

"It did."

"But then it ended." She shook her head. "I'm sorry I... I'm glad Lirin is going back to her mother. I think she'll be safer there than hiding as a maid, now that Lord Fretton's tried and failed."

Dielo's throat tightened, and he resisted the urge to touch the bruising.

"I wish you didn't have to go with her."

"I...I could come with you."

"To Sayinia?"

She sounded so surprised that Dielo was ashamed to continue. He asked instead, "Have you seen my..." He glanced around, but there was no one else to hear. "My chit?"

She gave him a worried glance. "Pasiphae Jade will be looking for it, won't she?"

He did not need to answer that. They both knew Pasiphae Jade needed to remind Kayvin of the hold she had over the people around him.

"If I give it back to you," Yovela said slowly, "will you give it back to her?"

Dielo felt ill. He did not want to. He had felt something new and thrilling when he had taken it from the cabinet, and he treasured the brief look Yovela had given him when he'd shown her what he had done. But if the Arch Potentate found the chit was missing, she would need to make an example, both for all virilos and to Prince Kayvin.

He gave a small, tight nod.

Yovela exhaled, and though it was not a sigh of disappointment, Dielo's heart sank.

She wore a long, flowing blue tunic over bloused grey trousers, and she hitched up the fabric until the tunic rose above her waist. A narrow thong was tied there, and tucked into a loop of thong was his chit.

She undid the knot and held it out.

He took it, every movement heavy. To fill the silence, he began to pick out the simple half hitch that held the chit.

"I wanted to keep it hidden," she said at last. "I was going to take it out of the palace. I don't know what the magic does, but I thought it could be carried away."

"At least you didn't tie it about the neck," Dielo observed.

She burst out a choked sob of laughter and covered her mouth. "I'm—I'm sorry. That wasn't—I'm so sorry."

He smiled. "It's all right. I wouldn't want to *waste* your effort."

She tipped her head and furrowed her brows. "Was that—was that a pun?"

"If you have to ask, it wasn't a very good one."

"It really wasn't," she said, but her voice was light.

"I haven't had much practice." Wordplay wasn't what virilos were wanted for.

She sobered. "When you said at least it wasn't tied about the neck—that isn't what the magic does, is it? I mean, it wouldn't throttle you, would it? You didn't feel it about your waist, either?"

He shook his head. "Not at all. I don't think carrying it would do anything." He handed her back the empty thong. "Thank you for trying to help," he said softly, his voice almost a whisper.

"I'm sorry I can't do more." Her voice was thick.

"So am I." Dielo looked out into the garden, wishing it was dark, wishing he had the tea to ease his bruises and make speaking hard things simpler. Shame weighted him like a heavy rug.

"Does it hurt?"

Her question confused him at first; he hadn't realized he was touching his neck. "A bit."

"Do you need something?"

A protector. Escape. A hug. "I'll be fine."

She did not look convinced. "Do you want me to find more of that medicine?"

"Empty void, no." He tried to cover his vehemence with a belated grin.

She smiled, and it cut him, for it meant she remembered what he had said.

"I should go and, er, put things together for moving to the Arch Potentate's rooms," he said awkwardly. "And I'm sure you have packing as well." He stepped back.

But she didn't move. "Be careful," she said softly. "And I know that's an unfair thing to say, because it's not your fault if—but be careful."

He understood, and he nodded.

Then he went out into the main room, and, after glancing around to be sure he was alone, he retrieved the coins from the vase. Then he went to the lonely men's quarters, and he tucked the chit into a small drawer with some jewelry.

ON HIS OWN

CHAPTER 92

THE GUARDS CAME FOR Dielo and Lirin before Kayvin left.

Dielo had known they would; Pasiphae Jade would want the Amethyst Prince's last sight to be his household in her power. He and Lirin bade safe travels to the prince, departing again across the mountains to the human country, and then followed the guards to the Arch Potentate's royal apartments.

Lirin had few belongings, and Dielo had split the load with her, bearing two baskets. The escort guards had not thought to ask whether there was more, so when two hours later Dielo asked if he could go and fetch his own belongings, the chief servant scolded him and then sent him to bring his things. This time he traveled without guards, as Kayvin was not there to see the demonstration of power and a virilo would return promptly.

Dielo knelt beside his chest and took out the little satchel he'd hidden at the bottom. A smaller bag held some of his less ostentatious jewelry and the little figurine of himself. He set his least favorite ear cuff into place. He added a cape to the satchel—made more for drama than warmth, but it was what he had—and his plainest trousers. Then he put on a linen shirt meant for seductive layering and slipped the satchel's strap over his head.

His heart was pounding. His fingers fumbled on the buckle closure.

On his way through the prince's apartments, he passed a shelf with a table game, left arranged mid-game though he had never seen the prince play. The figurines on the inlaid board were cut of semi-precious stones in varying colors, and after a moment's hesitation he swept them into his bag.

He went down to the palace exit he had used when buying for Nala. "I'm off to the market again," he said in a neutral, cheerful voice.

"I'll need—my, you look a mess." The guard's forehead crinkled in faint disgust or concern. "What happened to you?"

"I lost a fight with a hedge," Dielo said as casually as he could. "Do you need to see my authorization?"

"Yes," the guard said, but his heart wasn't in it. "Hedge got you by the neck, I see. Shopping again?"

Dielo held up the palace pass he'd taken from Kayvin's desk. "One has to maintain novelty, after all."

The guard didn't want to be bothered with a virilo's efforts. "Go on."

Dielo put the pass in his bag and, with his heart pulsing in his throat, went out the gate.

His first task was to sell the ear cuff. This wasn't unusual; it was common knowledge that gifts of jewelry were gifts of cash. He went next to the cobbler, for shoes sturdy enough for roads. He sold his palace slippers for a few additional coins.

He had lost two or three hours by now. He would have to hurry.

Dielo did not overtake Kayvin and Yovela on the road. Once he saw them, distantly ahead, as he crested a steep slope. He shouted, but they did not turn, and a moment later they were out of sight beyond a rolling hill.

But he was mostly confident of his directions, and he knew he would close on them eventually. When he came to the passage entrance, he found the way just as the instructions on Kayvin's desk had said. He was still too far behind to sight them, but there was nowhere for them to turn off; they and he, could only continue on to Sayinia.

It was a long and daunting journey. At last he emerged in what must be Sayinia. Human ground. He looked around, but there was nothing in the remote mountain foothills to suggest a different race or society. Looking down the rocky slope, he saw two figures descending toward the distant road. He shouted, and they lifted their heads. Kayvin turned, as if scanning the horizon. Dielo called again. But his voice was lost in the distance or the wind, and they started forward once more.

But he was close. He would have them in another hour or two.

When at last he came to the road, however, he paused with dismay. It ran north and south, roughly paralleling the Sung Mountains range. When he looked in both directions, squinting against the eastern light, he saw no one.

Which way had they gone?

Surely he was not so far behind. He only had to guess which direction they had taken, and he would overtake them tonight. His stomach was growling, and his feet were aching, and he was thirsty, as his water had given out. But he was so close, and he only had to guess correctly.

At last he turned north, and he set off at the fastest pace he could manage.

CHAPTER 93

"Empty void, it's cold." Yovela squeezed her arms more tightly across her chest, but it did not help. "And it gets colder still in winter? How do people live here?"

"They were born here," Kayvin answered flatly. "They did not know they had better options."

She huffed a chuckle and clenched her fingers into fists.

"I thought there would be a town," he said apologetically. "There should have been one by now. Maybe we didn't make the distance we thought."

Yovela was weary enough to have walked to two towns, but that was partly the cold. She did not like the advancing season here across the mountains. Her ear tips were numb and her fingers icy against her arms.

"There!" Kayvin nodded ahead, his own arms huddled inside his cloak. "Lights."

The lamps gleamed in the evening light, drawing her eye to the darker shape of buildings against the rolling landscape. She let out a grateful groan. "I hope they have hot soup."

Half an hour later, though, the town did not look promising. It was small, more a village than a town, and the few signs hanging over the doors were faded, suggesting these businesses served familiar locals more than travelers who needed to identify the shops.

They selected the public room and went in. "Hello!" Kayvin began. "Is there a place to buy a bed in this town?"

The customers paused their conversations to ogle the strangers, and one at last volunteered, "No inn, if that's what you mean, but you can ask Martin if he's got room out back."

"Thank you," Kayvin said, but Yovela did not like the sound of the answer.

"Martin's over there." He pointed to a corner where a man was refilling drinks.

At a table, another man grinned over his tankard, and Yovela's gut tightened. She reached to Kayvin's arm. "Let's go," she whispered.

"I'll go speak to Martin."

"No, let's go." She kept her voice soft, barely enough for him to hear.

He gave her a confused and irritated look. "I thought you wanted out of the cold."

She could not explain exactly what it was, but she knew... It was something in their eyes. Not all towns had liked traveling troupes. This wasn't exactly the same, but it was something near enough.

But Kayvin was already crossing the room to speak to Martin, and Yovela suddenly felt very alone. She turned, so she wouldn't see their eyes on her, and estimated the steps back to the door.

Kayvin's hood was still up, and she couldn't see his face. But the exchange went as one might expect, and a moment later Martin and Kayvin returned together. "He has a place for us," Kayvin said. "Let's drink something, and then he'll take us back."

He was already taking a seat at a roomy table before Yovela could protest, and she followed him reluctantly. She took a small lamp from a table as she passed and sat facing him. "We should go."

"Where? There's nowhere else."

"Anywhere. Away from here." She set the lamp at the table's edge, where it did not cast glare into her view of him.

"What's wrong?"

It was hard to explain. "We're not welcome here."

"But they'll take our coin well enough." Kayvin scowled faintly. "He said it's two taler for the night, which seems high, especially for a mattress that looks my own age. But he said the next town is Briarbend ten miles on."

Yovela shook her head. "He's lying about the distance."

"You don't know this area."

"No, but I know we shouldn't stay here."

"Why not?"

But she couldn't list the warning signs, she could only say she had known there was danger. It frustrated her, not least because he didn't believe her and she couldn't properly explain why he should.

"Ales for you," Martin the landlord said. "I'll be back in a minute for supper."

When he was gone, Kayvin nodded in the landlord's direction. "What's wrong with that?"

"Kayvin."

"What did you see?" he pressed. "Was it something they said?"

"It's not so specific!" she snapped. "It's—look, you are a man, and you are a prince. You have never had to think on these things."

He was quiet a moment. At last he said, "I am a prince, and I have seen how I can assume a regard that isn't there. But I saw a robbery once before at an inn, and they targeted a man, a musician, and—"

She reached across the table and put a hand over his mouth.

After a moment of surprise, he nodded, and she took away her hand. Kayvin nodded again, his gaze flicking between her and the tabletop. "All right. I'll go and pay for the ales."

"We can just leave them—"

But he was already walking away, tugging his hood closer.

The men moved quickly, sliding onto the benches about her table. There were four of them. Not everyone in the public room, but enough. Yovela's chest tightened.

"Strangers can make trouble in towns," a man with a faded blue cloth about his neck said. "It'd be nice of you to make a show of goodwill."

"I'm not carrying the coin." This was partly true.

She expected the next line. "There's more than one kind of goodwill." The man grinned.

"He keeps that hood tight. Don't suppose that's red hair?" Another man squinted after Kayvin. "Well, that settles it. We're not letting any red stay here without some sort of premium for good behavior. And with a woman, even. Got to be careful." He looked at Yovela. "Wouldn't you like a taste of something better than what that maple-headed steer can offer?"

Yovela's heart was racing, but she kept her expression firm. "He's paying for the drinks, and then we're leaving."

"Leaving? This late in the day?"

Despite herself, Yovela glanced back at Kayvin, arriving again at the table with a wary look. "I see we've made acquaintances."

"Lady says you're thinking of leaving."

"We just stopped for some drinks."

"And you've not even touched them." The man rubbed a finger across the rim of the nearest cup. "So you wouldn't mind making a little contribution to our drinking funds, just to show you're friendly?"

"We don't mean any harm," Kayvin said instead.

The third man nodded toward the moneybag still in his hand. "That would do for a start."

Kayvin shook his head. "I don't want trouble."

"Then you should agree, real friendly." The first man reached forward for the bag.

Yovela slapped the lamp so that it spun across the table, making him leap back. It struck him in the chest and fell, spilling oil and then crashing onto the floor. Flame leaped across the trail of oil and licked up his leg.

Shouts went up all around as Kayvin gestured, and fire sprang from the man's leg to the next man, blossoming into hungry flames. Heat rushed over Yovela's face. Men shouted and staggered backward, slapping tentatively at the fire with their unprotected hands.

Kayvin threw two more quick bursts and then rushed forward, with Yovela close behind. They pushed through the distracted men and out the door. Yovela caught a glimpse through the window—Martin had a pitcher in his hand and was bellowing something into the room—and then they ran along the buildings toward the edge of the village.

Yovela thought they would be chased, but there was no pursuit. The men had not expected that kind of resistance, and they were undoubtedly putting out the fire and arguing with Martin over the damage.

Kayvin and Yovela ran a short distance, finally slowing on the far side of a hill where they could no longer see the town. They panted for a moment, and at last Kayvin commented, "Empty void." He paused, his hands on his knees. "How did you know?"

She shook her head. "I'd seen it before. With the troupe."

"I hope their town burns." He straightened. "There's a building over there. No lights. Shall we look?"

She had missed it in the deepening twilight, but he was right. It was an outbuilding of some sort, small and standing alone, maybe a quarter mile away. Still, she hesitated.

"We don't have anything else to try," Kayvin said. "Ten miles to Briarbend, he said."

"Innkeepers will lie to get a night's fee." They didn't know, though. "We could sleep in a field," Yovela said desperately, but she didn't mean it. Even after the panicked run, she couldn't feel her ears or fingers.

It was a shed full of threshings, cheap winter fodder for goats or cattle. The door was loose, barely enough to bar the animals from the feed, but there was enough straw and chaff to make a nest. A metal bucket full of dirty rainwater stood outside the door. It would have to do.

Yovela was seized with urgency, now that the immediate danger had ended. "I'm going to relieve myself," she said, heading beyond the shed.

She took longer than necessary, hugging herself and trying to slow her breathing. She had been afraid, and Kayvin hadn't known enough to be afraid with her. It could have gone differently...

She went back to the shed. Inside, it was nearly too dark to see, but she could just make out Kayvin crouched beside the bucket, his hands flat against the sides. "Here," he called as she entered.

She picked her way toward him, careful of the uneven dirt floor. He reached for her hand and guided it down, drawing it into the water.

It was warm. Blissfully warm. Painfully warm.

She flinched as her hand began to sting, but she knelt and slid her other hand into the water alongside it. She couldn't feel steam on her face; it wasn't dangerously hot. She shivered incongruously and flexed her cold fingers.

Kayvin scooped warm water to her ears, wetting them and covering them with his warm hands. She shivered. He dunked his hands again and put them to her cheeks, her neck, her ears again. She closed her eyes and savored the heat.

The burning in her hands faded, and now she could feel his fingers against her ears. She opened her eyes. "Thank you."

Kayvin buffed her face dry with the edge of her cloak. "Come on. We'll pull the straw over us. It will be almost like a sleeping pit."

It was not like a sleeping pit, but it was better than a field, and she was exhausted with the cold and her fear. She held his shoulder close, craving his warmth.

"How did you know?" he asked after a moment. "It wasn't so different from when we've asked for rooms before. Was it the size of the village?"

"No. A—feeling. You wouldn't have had reason to develop it."

"I'm sorry I needed convincing." He turned his head toward her. "You did well with the lamp."

"I thought that would give them explanation for the fire, if it came to that. Better than them forming a party to come after us."

"It was clever." Kayvin shifted, pulling some straw higher around them. "Are you comfortable?"

"Not at all." She chuckled grimly. "But I'm warmer, thank you."

"I wonder what Dielo is doing," he said. "He must be idling to boredom, waiting for us. Perhaps he's grown out a beard. A big one, down to his collarbones."

Yovela snorted. She couldn't imagine the trim, glossy-skinned virilo with an enormous beard. "He probably oils it daily and rubs mica into it to sparkle."

Kayvin laughed, but it was not cruel. Yovela liked that. In truth, Dielo was in Pasiphae Jade's oversight, possibly still hiding his stolen chit. Yovela hoped he was comfortable enough to be bored.

She leaned into Kayvin's warm shoulder, and she slept.

CHAPTER 94

DIELO TOOK A BREATH and pushed himself into the public room.

All around farmers, tanners, cobblers, apothecaries, and more humans were clustering into noisy groups, exchanging stories and calling to one another and sharing drinks. Though the village populace was broken into a dozen fragments, they seemed impenetrable.

But they were sharing stories and drinks and laughter, the same as anyone might, and they no doubt had the same emotions and desires as those he'd left in his homeland. He could approach them in the same way. He had only to stop thinking of them as humans and start thinking of them as people.

"Hello, friend!" A man in a dusty vest put a hand on his shoulder, surprising Dielo. "Yours isn't a face I know. Just passing through, or come to stay?"

Dielo pushed a smile onto his face, letting his training lead him. *Ease and flattery.* "Just passing through, I'm afraid, though this looks like a place to make one wish he were staying."

"Fairly spoken, that is! Come here, and let's get you a drink, and you can tell us whatever news you carry."

Dielo went with him, mind racing. He had no news, and he didn't know this land well enough to invent something convincing. Nor did he want to face questions about where he'd come from.

"What's your name?" asked the man in the vest, taking an ale from a crowded table and handing it to him. The others at the table looked up expectantly, with friendly, curious expressions.

"Dielo."

"What kind of name is that?"

Not one to blend with the local human culture, apparently. "My parents were a bit eccentric. My mother named me for my great-grandfather."

One of the men at the table nodded. "From the northwest, your people are?"

Near the mountains, but not near where he'd crossed. "Pretty far north, right."

The man nodded again at this confirmation. "You've got the vowels of the mountain folk, I think. And they've kept some older names up there. What brings you down here?"

Foolish Dielo, not to have prepared a story in advance. He should have known better. There would be questions, at least nominal interest, and in a small, rural village, the interest would be more than nominal.

Fortunately Dielo knew that while people loved to hear interesting news, they loved even more to talk about themselves and their own news.

He slid onto only the end of a bench. "I was on a little farm in the middle of a mountain's backside, just me and my parents and my little brother and sister, and twice a year we'd see the tinker come through. And I got tired of waiting six months to see a different face, and so I came out here. I'm hoping to walk around and see some of the world, and find some people who will be patient with my ignorance."

The men around the table laughed. "Well, son, you keep talking like that, and you'll find someone to fleece you, anyway," one advised. "Which way are you going?"

He had no idea, now that he had lost Prince Kayvin and Yovela. "Westward," he said, "and I'm not particular."

"I've got a mule train going out in the morning. A farm boy should have some useful skills, I think. Care to come with me? I can promise you a fair wage for a few days, at least."

He had none of the farm skills that would be expected, but he could pretend for a day and then leave the train, he thought. And he'd be traveling, at least, getting nearer to Prince Kayvin or nearer to an amulet, or at least not staying still and useless. "Yes, thank you."

Dielo sat on a bench with his head back against the wall and his eyes mostly closed, and he listened to the conversations around him. He heard the name Kels used first for a tall man with dark hair and then again for a short man; so names could be reused here. That was good. He could select one that would invite fewer questions than his own.

He caught Kels for a third man, and then Tor used twice, and Frank several times. But another name he counted a full seven times as the travelers bustled through the crossroads, proving it sufficiently common and unremarkable. He rose, adjusted his hood to conceal his ears—more out of worry than overt reason, as no one had commented on them so far—and started walking to the next village.

Dielo was good at talking stories out of people. His training had been perfectly suited for this, in fact, all flattery and interest and encouraging others to feel at ease. Conversation, storytelling, and music had been as important as more erotic skills. This new task was much the same as the ordinary entertainment duties.

And it was good for them as much as for Dielo, he decided. What was the harm in flattery? If a merchant believed he told a good story about a broken wheel, what did it hurt? If he thought Dielo truly fascinated by his visits to the distant coast, who suffered? And if he then also told a story of a collector who had purchased an amulet eye, what trouble was that?

"Good evening, good evening!" The merchant in question beamed around at the others as they formed a loose circle in the early evening chill. "Good to meet you all! I am Rodd, as you mostly know, and it'll be my oxen drawing the wagons." He gestured to Dielo. "And this is Henry, traveling with us for a bit."

The others made their own introductions, and Dielo nodded to them each in turn.

"I've got you figured out," said a young woman with chestnut hair and deep brown eyes, once conversation had begun to flow. "I've been watching you all day. I know who you really are."

Dielo's heart went still, but he only smiled at her. "Is that so?"

"You're no farmer. You're just drifting along, getting drinks and stories out of people." She grinned. "You're a rich runaway, off to see the world when your father said you shouldn't."

Dielo started breathing again. He grinned. "You know if that were true, I wouldn't admit to it."

"But you haven't denied it, at least." She pushed her hair over one shoulder.

"Enough of that," Rodd said in a good-natured grumble. "Flirt on the road, where there's time to kill. For now, let's order supper and settle our business."

They left together the next morning. It was a pleasant walk, north and west, with Dielo moving from group to group, listening and nodding. Traveling this way was useful to observe human manners, to see when others laughed genuinely or out of social obligation, or how offers of assistance could be made sincerely or in hopes of being turned down, or how idioms could obscure or clarify conversation. The study came naturally to him—observing and following a conversation had been important teaching—and strangely, he soon felt at least as comfortable walking along this human road as he had in the Mandoral palace, waiting for Prince Kayvin's return. In both places he tried hard to make others comfortable and become what they wanted, but somehow it felt more genuine here as he tried to match another culture.

He was learning other skills, too. He'd never handled cattle before, and his initial wary awe at the big creatures was maturing to fondness as he helped to feed and care for them. The oxen that drew the wagons were steers from a sturdy breed prized for milking in the rocky Tendertooth Hills. They were primarily black-coated, though a half-dozen had a diluted blue color. Rodd admitted some of the larger western breeds might have been a better choice for draft animals, but he confessed an affection for the breed of his homeland. "They bred the reds out, you know," he explained to Dielo. "The Ruby Devons were the foundation stock, but no one in the Tendertooth will keep a red if they can help it. Too much of the Selk in the hills' past. So they breed mostly black and blue now, just a few reds now and again."

Dielo had heard aspersions on red before, but it had been so generally understood, he'd known asking about it would betray him as an outsider. This was the first hint of the prejudice's origin, and it had something to do with the Rideis. He nodded and tucked the tidbit away for later use, when he might hear another piece to fit with it. Small clues of the Rideis would eventually lead him to the amulets' hiding places.

"I'm starting to think, Henry, that girl might be right," Rodd said one evening as they brushed down the oxen and measured out their feed.

"What's that?" Dielo asked.

"Vanessa. The one that says you're a nobleman's son out to see the world." Rodd ran a finger through the grain, frowning as he tested for damp, and then set the bucket down for Fawn, a friendly steer. "You know precious little about oxen or wagons, or roads, or anything, and you're about as ignorant as anyone I've ever seen."

Dielo looked down, stomach clenching. "I..."

"But then you can't be a nobleman's son, either, because you're a good worker, with a mind set to learn new tasks faster than any spoiled boy ever has, and you're friendly and interested without a speck of the wrong kind of pride in you." Rodd grinned.

Dielo released a nervous chuckle, still looking away. "I'm sorry—that is, I'm trying to learn. I hope I'm doing all right." He put a hand on the ox's shoulder. "I wouldn't want Fawn to be disappointed in me."

"He'll think you're all right." Rodd nodded. "I don't much care, as long as Fawn has a good opinion."

"I'll make sure to slip him an extra measure of feed tonight, then." Dielo ventured a grin.

"Go ahead, bribe the stock. But it won't hurt either if you sing us a song tonight after dinner. Something else like the last one. I didn't think I liked melancholy songs of unspent love, but I suppose they don't have to be just for the girls, do they?"

It had taken Dielo a whole week's worth of courage to sing the night before, but his story of unrequited longing and distant hope had been well received. He thought that, as his traveling companions had never heard Rideis songs before, his renditions could only be the best version they'd heard. "I think I have another," he said, feeling pleased. "If you want."

CHAPTER 95

DIELO HAD ONLY A single blanket to wrap around himself, which seemed unfair on the colder plains of Sayinia when he would have had both blankets and furs to burrow into in his sleeping pit at home. But if he pulled it tight, covering his head and exhaling into the space at his chest, he could sleep without shivering.

Some of the travelers slept close to share warmth. Some slept close for other reasons, too, and he was not sure how to approach for the first without appearing to invite the other. He was not sure enough of his understanding of human customs to risk that.

This hesitancy was a curious thing to note in himself. It wasn't that he felt too much loyalty to his chit and his master; he'd stolen the chit, and Prince Kayvin clearly didn't care for Dielo in the way he'd been taught to expect. Kayvin would never know if Dielo frivolled with humans here, and Dielo could probably pass without detection as a Rideis more easily than Yovela or another Rideis woman. And, if he was honest, a night of lovemaking might be a welcome comfort, if temporary.

But he did not approach anyone. Yovela's words, from that awful night with the tea and the raw humiliating honesty, still wandered in his mind.

From childhood, from the beginning, he'd been told his greatest aspiration was to be the favored companion of a powerful man. He'd never questioned that. Then he had gone to the palace and nothing had been as he'd expected.

Ah! Clarity came in hindsight. Riolo had been unkind because Dielo had gone to a prince and Riolo to a woman, even a woman on the throne, and Dielo had not realized the jealousy. But Dielo had been jealous, too, of Riolo sitting beside a banquet chair and posing in proud display, a valued figurine in the court's social games while Dielo could not win even a touch from his disinterested prince.

But now... As a child, undergoing his selection, he had called both the men and the women beautiful pictured in their court clothing. But he had been a child, not understanding the question, and perhaps Yovela had been right to say the well-paid selectors might have had their own motives in interpreting his answers.

Now, Rodd and the others spoke to him as an equal, and while Dielo had always known his position was an elite one, it had held him apart from others. Now he had whole conversations about meals or harnesses or grain markets without ever feeling the other was guessing at his particular skills or imagining him in their own sleeping pit—not that there were any pits here, of course, but the concept remained.

And Dielo thought he liked it.

He was not an equal, of course. He was ignorant of so many practical things, and even more so in this strange country, and he owed much to the travelers around him. He knew it was Rodd's kindness that kept him fed rather than any competence of his own. He could be an elite again any time he chose by crossing the mountains and returning to the palace, and he would return, eventually—but for now, he was someone else, someone new, someone at whom Yovela might gaze with those shining, awed eyes as he showed his stolen chit.

So he had approached no one, and each night he wrapped his blanket tightly about his head and body and lay alone at the end of the line of wagons, and so he was taken entirely by surprise when he heard himself being discussed around a watchfire.

"The pretty one, the skinny pretty one," a man said gruffly. "What's his name."

"Henry, you mean?"

"Yeah, Henry. He's one. I can smell them a mile away, and he's definitely one."

"I think you're right."

"Wouldn't surprise me if he made a hobby of it, or a business."

"I think you're right."

There were three of them, sitting close around a tiny fire. It was late, and Dielo should have been asleep, but he'd ventured in the cold air for an extra trip to the dug privy. He hadn't intentionally passed near enough to the fire to listen, and now the words alarmed him.

"We could go and get him. I'll bet he'll wake up quick enough. His purse is thin, and he'll be reasonable."

Dielo's chest squeezed tight, and for a moment he couldn't breathe. And that was foolish—he was lonely, and he knew how to serve, he knew how to accommodate...and he wanted none of it.

He could work out his reluctance later. Now, as the shapes rose around the fire, he ran.

The half-moon provided enough light for his path, but it also betrayed him to the others once they were away from the little fire. Someone called out, and he ignored them, rushing to the safety of the wagons.

But there was no safety here. He usually slept under a wagon bed at the end of the line, and that could not shield him. He rushed to the other side, out of their immediate sight, but that would not shield him for long, either.

"Here!"

The harsh whisper came just before a tug on his shoulder, and Dielo turned in startled hope. Then he climbed into the wagon bed, obeying the pull on his shirt. "Get down," Vanessa warned, and she drew a tarp over him.

Dielo curled small beside bushels of vegetables, trying to muffle his breath. Vanessa lay down again, her blanket over her, and feigned sleep. For long moments they were still, as Dielo strained to listen for the men outside the wagon. He heard muted voices, and then nothing.

At last Vanessa rolled onto her side and tugged back part of the tarp. "Well, that was an adventure."

Dielo's heart still pounded in his ears, and he was giddy with his escape. He had been trained his entire life to acquiesce, and he had defied it. "I'm sorry—they wanted..."

"I can guess. There aren't too many reasons to follow someone at this time of night."

He laughed, high and frantic.

"It's all right," Vanessa said, tugging him close and embracing him. "How awful! But it's all right now."

Dielo let her hold him close, and the comforting pressure of her arms quelled his racing pulse. The men were gone, they were alone, the wagon bed offered a simple shelter, and her embrace in his loneliness was like a steaming bath after hours in the cold.

"I'm sorry," he said, though he wasn't sure what he was apologizing for.

"I'm glad I was here," she said warmly, and she laughed.

Dielo didn't see the humor, but he nodded agreeably. "Thank you. Now I'll go—"

"Not yet," she said teasingly, pulling herself closer. "Now we can enjoy ourselves."

Suddenly her hands felt different, though little had changed. He stiffened.

"Oh, come on," she said, partly teasing and partly chiding. "I saved you from them. This is the least you can do, and surely I'm a better prospect?" She moved into him, and his skin fired obediently at her touch.

She hadn't saved him. She had only taken him for the same purpose.

What did the flattery hurt, he had wondered. Nothing and no one. And this... This hurt no one, too. Vanessa came to him of her own will.

But she had come to Henry, not to Dielo. She had come to an itinerant noble son of Sayinia, perhaps going home again to a rich inheritance, not to a Rideis virilo. This...this was perhaps where he crossed the line from flattery to thievery.

And this could be where he crossed the line from fine tool to free person, declining what he was expected to give.

"Vanessa," he said, unsure and stalling.

She giggled and tried to hide her nervousness with bold words. "What's the matter, Henry? I think part of you has already agreed."

He flinched as she brushed him, and his first thought was that he should not have, that it would offend her. A heartbeat later, he recalled he was not a virilo to her, she did not hold his chit, and he did not have to lie with her if he did not want to.

He caught her hand and held it, trading one physical contact for another he might direct. He had no practice in denying, and there were no well-rehearsed words to follow. "Vanessa," he said, and all his easy speech was gone. "I'm so honored—but I cannot."

"I think you can," she answered with a teasing smile. She wriggled against him. "If you put your mind to it."

"I can't," he repeated. "I... There's someone else."

"No one here," she countered. "How would she know? I won't tell if you won't."

How difficult it was to simply speak a refusal, when he had always been schooled to be careful of disappointing. "I don't... I can't. Please. I'm sorry."

Her anger flashed. "What's the matter? Are you too fine and proud for a village girl?" She rocked back, propped on her elbow, glaring in the thin moonlight. "Or are you some sort of judgmental prig?"

"It's none of that. You're a wonderful girl, and I'm glad to have met you. I've enjoyed traveling and talking with you."

She considered this, and then she shifted again toward him. "Then what is it? Don't you even care about me?"

Dielo had been conditioned for years to know the right answer—of course he cared, he would do anything to please her, it had been a misunderstanding but he was sorry, and he could never deny her what she wanted. The words sprang to his lips, automatic and soothing. His blood rushed through his ears and toward his tightening trousers.

Yet a small part of his mind, gleeful and reckless in his newfound freedom, pointed out how she betrayed her own lack of caring by her very insistence, putting her own desire over his hesitation.

He marveled at how quickly his guilt had obediently risen at her accusation, pressing him to assent lest he embarrass her.

He could not think such unfamiliar thoughts quickly enough while she waited, staring. "I'm sorry," he said hoarsely. "I need a moment, please."

"I'll not sit here while you try to decide if you care for me." Her voice was terse. "Make up your mind."

She knew, or she suspected, that he could not think while she pressed. He would collapse beneath her expectation and will. If he hesitated now, he would obey.

For the first time since he could remember, he spoke refusal. "I'm sorry. No."

It was a mild denial, but it piqued her anger. "You misleading slag," she snapped. "Making all those eyes and jokes and meaning none of it, just to bait and tease."

He shook his head. "I never meant to bait or tease, I only—"

"It doesn't matter now, does it? You've embarrassed me, whether you meant it or not."

"I'm sorry," he tried, but she spat an expletive at him and shoved him away.

He scrambled out of the wagon, burning beneath her words, and walked down the line. He did not go to his usual place, in case the watchers were still looking for him, but stopped at a cart and sat on the tail. His well-trained body had answered her call, at least, and he needed time to reflect and to calm himself.

Part of him worried that he had hurt her, that she would be upset with him in the morning, that he had lost her friendship and possibly the hospitality of the group. Another part scolded him for his conditioned thoughts and reminded him that even a virilo owed no pleasure to those he was not bound to, and here he could choose his own actions and mates. That part of him, smaller and weaker but rooting in its new soil, resented how quickly she had blamed and resented him for his reluctance.

Just as he had done to his master.

Chill raced through him, cooling the last of his physical response. His task, his single duty that all others supported, was to support the prince, and he instead had resented him, criticizing a grieving son struggling to keep his place in the court for not catering to Dielo's own feelings of worth. Prince Kayvin had not been interested, and instead of respecting his wish, Dielo had tried to persuade him otherwise. He had, in the name of devotion, done the opposite of devotion.

The sera qadra exists to support our master, and not just by pleasure.

Curse Yovela and her accusing truth. Respite and pleasure were valuable gifts, but the training that taught they were his only tools, that a lord would find his other support in his noble peers, had been a lie. Dielo could do more. *Was* doing more, even now, as he sought the amulet.

He slid under the cart and wriggled into a less-uncomfortable position on the uneven ground. He was close, surely. He would find it soon.

Dielo did not wait for morning. He slept only fitfully, and then he rose while it was still dark, with only a pale edge to the eastern sky to suggest dawn was coming. He had to go now, before he could face Vanessa in the morning. She would be embarrassed, and perhaps therefore cruel, and he did not want to argue with her or involve others in her embarrassment.

Besides, he had traveled in this direction long enough, and this group had not brought him any nearer to major temples or treasure houses. He should take another path.

He set off down the road. He could move faster than the group, especially given the time needed to break camp. He could take another route at the next crossroads. If he met someone else on the road, he could ask directions to a city—he was growing confident enough to enter one—with a temple. Prince Kayvin and Yovela had found an amulet in a temple; another would be the best place to look.

CHAPTER 96

THE ROAD WAS WIDE and empty, with fields of a green-gold shrub stretching on either side between hamlets and households. Dielo didn't know the crop. He didn't know many things, it seemed.

Dielo was on his own again, but he could find others and listen to their stories, clap to their songs, walk to their destinations. He was good at listening, and the stakes here were only an amulet to save the lives of thousands, and not his soul.

He passed a large stone building, alone on the road, fenced but with an open gate. A statue of a man, extending one hand and holding a stringed instrument in the other, stood just past the gate as if to welcome visitors.

Dielo thought of Prince Kayvin, playing his horned lyre, and wondered if they would someday gather with Yovela again to make music.

He walked another quarter mile, listening to birdsong and the breeze, and wondering when the next town would appear and whether he would find welcome.

A different sound caught his ear, and Dielo paused. Was that a sob? He turned on the road, seeing no one behind him, and then looked down the slope of the elevated road into the irrigation ditch alongside. A young woman curled on the grassy slope, half hidden by the growth, clutching her torso and weeping.

Dielo slipped down the short slope. "What's wrong? Can I help?" Her abdomen was unnaturally swollen; she must be in dire pain.

She turned wild eyes on him. "The baby—I have to reach the Hallowed Patrick."

Dielo saw a wet stain low on her tunic. "Is the baby at the hollow? Where is the baby?"

"Help me," she said with difficulty. "I need the Hallowed Patrick hospital."

This at least he understood. "Which way?"

Her head rolled back the way he'd come. He remembered the stone building with the open gate. "I've seen it, I think. Let's go." He gathered her into his arms with some difficulty and started up the road.

She gripped her abdomen as if wanting to hold it closer, and with a start he remembered that humans bore their offspring differently. She was giving live birth. His stomach churned.

She was young by human standards, he thought, and young to become a mother. Was she a new bride? An abandoned plaything? She should not have been left alone.

He was a Rideis of only average size, but he kept himself fit, and she was petite and the situation urgent. His arms burned as he carried her into the open gate. "Help! Is someone there? Hello?"

A woman came to the door and, sighting them, called back into the building for assistance. Then she waved to Dielo. "This way!"

He followed the woman out of the bright sunlight into the dark entry, and for a moment he was blinded. He hesitated, afraid to trip and drop the young mother in his arms.

"This way!"

A hand on his upper arm guided him. He saw an open bed before him, and he laid the crying girl upon it.

An older woman appeared and drew up the girl's skirt. "I'm Tilly, and I'm here to help you. Hold on, my dear, let's see what you have here. Ah, no time to lose, my dear."

The girl clung to Dielo's hand as he watched the medicals work. She lifted her head to try to look. "Is the baby all right?"

"Your baby's in a hurry," Tilly said with a smile. "But it looks like you and she haven't been working together. Let's get you up and squatting, that will help you."

"I tried," the girl said.

"You did nothing wrong. Sometimes it's just hard to get things started. Up now."

Dielo helped the girl up, wincing with her. He glanced at the doctor, suspicious of her easy tone; even a first egg-laying was not this difficult. The woman's worried expression as she gave quiet, terse instructions to another confirmed his guess.

She saw him watching and gave him a fierce glare. "Why did you wait so long?" she demanded.

Dielo needed a moment to realize she thought him the mate of this young woman. He shook his head. "I found her on the road," he tried, but his voice was quiet in his confusion, and Tilly was already working again on her struggling patient.

The girl squatted as instructed, holding the footboard for balance as he knelt beside her. She grimaced at him. "Thank you for your help," she whispered.

Pain creased her face. She needed conversation and distraction. He nodded. "I'm glad I happened upon you."

"Could I hold your hand?"

He offered it, steadying her.

"What's your name?"

"I'm Dielo," he answered without thinking. "What are you called?"

"Bekah." She sucked a ragged breath. "Things felt wrong. I didn't know what it should be like, but it felt wrong. I wanted to come here for the memento."

Dielo didn't understand. "What memento?"

Behind Bekah, the younger doctor rolled her eyes. Bekah squeezed Dielo's hands and leaned into him.

"I see your baby," announced the older doctor with pleasure. "You're almost there."

Bekah gave a little gasping laugh. Dielo stared back at the doctors in a kind of disbelief. They could see the child?

But Bekah was trembling on her legs. She'd been weak even before she had begun to squat. "I can't," she panted.

Another helper brought a pillow. "Lean against the bed here," she said. "You'll be up again in a bit, but it's all right to rest."

The doctor arranged Bekah's limbs, coaxing and coaching, and she curled over her legs with her knees and elbows out, one hand gripping Dielo's like a drowning man clutching a rope. He glanced down and saw the top of a tiny red face emerge from her, squished and slimy and squinting. His stomach roiled and he swayed, bracing his free hand on the floor.

"Steady," chuckled Tilly. "We can't take time to pick you up. You should have thought of this before you went in."

"I didn't," Dielo tried to say, the words thick in his mouth.

The doctor pulled at Bekah's forearms. "Up, now. You're almost there."

But the baby did not come further as she squatted and pushed and squeezed tears from her eyes. "I need the memento," Bekah panted.

"Oh, child," said Tilly with a sad smile. "That light went out long ago."

Bekah's confused expression vanished as another contraction struck her. Her face screwed with effort, but nothing happened.

"Shoulder's caught," observed the doctor. She leaned forward and guided Bekah's knees toward her shoulders. "I'm going to try to nudge the baby down."

Before he could stop himself, Dielo looked down at the child's red head, and his stomach heaved. He squeezed Bekah's fingers as hard as she held his.

Tilly balled her fist and pressed down into the flesh just above Bekah's groin. Bekah groaned.

"It's not working," observed a second doctor.

Tilly scowled to indicate that she could see that herself, but her next words were for Bekah and Dielo. "Now we have to act promptly. Roll over, girl. Hands and knees. You help her.'

Dielo supported Bekah as her arms shook. She grunted with the effort of another contraction. Dielo gritted his teeth against his revulsion and horror. "Hold on," he said. "They'll make it right." He had no idea if this could be true, but Bekah needed hopeful words.

Tilly consulted with the second doctor in quiet, rapid tones. Bekah leaned more heavily into Dielo's grip, her breath fast and ragged. "Where is the memento? What are you saying about my baby?"

"I'm going to reach inside and reposition the baby," Tilly said. "Turn back to face me, and lean against your young man there. We're going to get you on the bed so I can reach. You, you're going to have to hold her. She's tired, and this won't be easy."

Dielo helped lift Bekah, trembling with exhaustion, onto the bed, and then he slipped behind her and she fell against him. He wrapped his arms about her, letting her hold his forearms and brace against him. Tilly crouched low and slipped her hands inside Bekah along the puff-faced infant.

Bekah jerked back against Dielo and wailed. She braced hard, digging her fingers into his arms, and Dielo watched in fascinated horror as Tilly twisted the baby. A moment later, Bekah sobbed and pushed again, and the bloody, stringy body slid into Tilly's hands.

Bekah shuddered and sighed. "You have a boy," Tilly declared. "And he's going to be just fine. We were quick enough."

Bekah wept and dropped her head against Dielo's shoulder. The doctors fussed over the infant for a moment and then set him, wet and bloody, on her chest. She smiled tiredly and cupped one arm about him, her head still against Dielo.

Tilly looked down at Bekah and swore quietly.

Bekah's head grew heavier against Dielo. "Beautiful..."

Tilly snapped an order and began pressing a towel hard against Bekah, and it reddened immediately. The other doctor rushed to an herbal cabinet across the room.

Bekah was exhausted, but not ignorant. "What's wrong? My baby?"

"Your baby is fine," Tilly said, shifting the towel. "You're bleeding."

Bekah licked her lips. "The memento," she whispered.

"We need to get something into you to slow the bleeding. We're mixing you a dose now."

The second doctor came to the bed and poured a small cup into Bekah's mouth, and she swallowed with only a little dribbling, screwing her face against the taste. "Am I going to die?"

"We just need to stop this bleeding," Tilly said evenly. "And that will be easier if you lie still and let the medicine work. The more you fret, the faster your heart will beat, and we need you to be calm."

"The memento," breathed Bekah.

Tilly turned a frustrated glare on the second doctor. "Give her the thing, just to quiet her," she muttered. "We have to get her heart to slow."

Bekah's head lolled, and Dielo looked from her to the bloody towel and back. "Hold on, Bekah," he whispered, more helpless than ever.

The assistant returned and pressed an object into Bekah's free hand. "Here. Here's the memento. Now you can rest."

Bekah didn't answer. Dielo bent over her, his chest spasming in helpless fear. "I—I think she's in trouble."

Tilly didn't look up. "I know."

Dielo took Bekah's other hand. She held a bronze metallic object with a splash of orange—

An amulet. She held one of the amulets.

This amulet was weathered, the details of the wires worn down with frequent touching, rubbing, the oils and acids of skin. This amulet had been held and squeezed over a long time. And it was drained, Dielo could see, dead and dull in Bekah's hand.

The assistant moved around Tilly and began to press and rub into Bekah's lower torso below a small circular scar. She looked up at Dielo's confusion and misunderstood it. "Once, the memento helped those who came here. The Hallowed Patrick was known for it. But it has been dead for decades now." She shook her head, still rubbing. "But stories persist, and so people like her try to come here even when they should not."

Long ago, the amulet had been a powerful artifact. Now Dielo had found exactly what he'd come for, and it was useless, drained and broken, and this strange woman was dying in his arms.

He closed his hand about hers, squeezing the amulet between them. Shock raced up his arm and he jerked. Bekah did not respond.

He closed his eyes and let the amulet warm between their palms, listening to the urgent murmuring between the doctors. He sagged against the bed, aching from carrying and holding the exhausted Bekah. There were bloody gouges in his arm where she had gripped him.

"Young man?"

He was tired beyond reason, tired from carrying Bekah to the hospital, tired from holding her, tired from the horror of an infant pushing its way not through a shell but through a living body.

"It's slowing."

He should move, should ask Tilly about Bekah and the child, but he slept as Bekah lay still against him.

CHAPTER 97

DIELO WOKE TO GOLDEN light spilling over him, the wall, the thin mat he lay on. He sat up, wincing against the headache that began pounding in his temples.

Someone was moving nearby. He looked through a doorway and saw Tilly working at a table, deftly sorting herbs. He pushed himself to his feet, lost his balance, and sat down heavily.

"Oh, wait a moment!" Tilly left her work and came to him. "Are you all right?"

He kept a hand to his head, but it didn't help. "How is she?"

"Bekah? She and the baby are well. We were able to stop the bleeding." Tilly looked at him. "You fell asleep with her. You must have carried her quite a way, to drop off at such a key moment." There was only the faintest of accusations in her tone, mixed with concern. She tipped her head to regard him. "How are you?"

"Headache," he said, ashamed. Bekah had been bleeding to death, and he had slept and complained of headache.

"At first we thought it was the blood—many do slip away for a moment if they see that, you know—but then that's usually only for a moment." Tilly gave him a concerned look. "Are you all right? Was it only the carrying?"

He nodded and regretted it.

"I'll make a tincture for your head."

"Thank you." He closed his eyes and listened to her pick through bottles and splash water. "May I see her?"

"Of course." Tilly brought him a glass. "Here, this should help. How do you know her?"

"I found her on the road. She'd fallen, trying to reach this place." He drank. The medicine had a faintly sweet taste.

"You did a good thing. She would not have been able to deliver that baby on her own, not with the shoulder caught. You saved her life getting her here. The child's, too."

Dielo smiled through the throbbing pain.

"She's in the next room, not far."

Bekah was lying in bed, cradling her infant. The child was clean now, and sleeping against his mother's chest. Dielo thought Bekah asleep as well, but she turned her head as he approached. "Hello."

"Hello." He wasn't sure what to say.

She turned so that her nose touched her sleeping child. "This is Dielo."

He bent to look at the infant. It looked less terrifying now, wrinkled and squinched like a normal hatchling. "It's nice to meet you, little one."

She smiled tiredly. "No, he is Dielo. Like you. I've named him for you."

A rush of hot emotion ran through him, from his stomach to his heart. "No—you can't, I'm just—you don't even know me."

"I know you helped us. That's enough."

He sat on the edge of the bed and pushed her damp hair back from her face. "I am so glad I could."

"I needed to reach the memento," she said. "I knew I had to birth here."

He looked at the blanket where she had left the amulet, lying on her abdomen. The orange eye seemed a little brighter than he remembered, though that might have been the effect of the headache and contrast with the terror of the birth.

"It was left long ago for the needy here." She closed her eyes. "I knew I would need it."

"You found the best place for your child."

"For Dielo."

He smiled, warmed somewhere deep within. Then he teased a sticking tendril away from her eye, since her arms were occupied with the baby.

"Thanks." She gave him an embarrassed smile. "They cleaned me up after the birth, but my hair is sticky with sweat and road grime. I must look a mess."

"Would you like me to comb it?" Dielo offered without thinking.

She looked startled. "I..."

"I wouldn't mind," he said quickly, "but only if you wouldn't mind, either."

"That might be nice," she agreed.

He didn't know where to find a comb, but he had plenty of time, and so he drew a chair close behind the bed and began to draw her hair back. "I'd wash it, but I'm not sure there's room here without soaking the pillows." He picked out the tangles, working out the dirty knots. Washing would be best, but it could wait. Live birthing had looked like such an ordeal, and she should rest.

Bekah relaxed beneath his rhythmic work, stirring only when the baby made a sound in his sleep. Dielo glanced up once to see

Tilly watching from the doorway, and when their eyes met, she nodded and went on her way.

"Thanks," Bekah breathed. "I need to say it before I fall asleep."

"Go ahead and sleep," he replied softly. He gathered her hair and coiled it on the pillow.

Another assistant entered and with a smile quietly gathered the baby, tucking him into a basket alongside the bed. Dielo looked in at the sleeping child and then bade Bekah sweet dreams. The assistant nodded at Dielo and left. He stepped back from the bed, marveling in Bekah's contented expression.

The amulet on the blanket lay still and empty. Curious, he reached out to pick it up, and it stung him, as when sparks leapt from metal to skin in the winter. Energy tingled through him, burning in his forearm and hand. Immediately the throb in his head worsened, and he wanted nothing more than to lie down beside Bekah and sleep.

The amulet wanted power. It wanted to restore its exhausted vacuum, and Dielo was Rideis as it was. It was drawing energy from him.

He released the amulet and shook himself. If that were so, then perhaps the amulet could be restored—but not here, not by the humans in this hospital.

Dielo drew his sleeve down over his hand and collected the amulet once more. With a guilty glance around him, he tucked it into his hand and folded it into hiding.

It was left for the needy.

He had come prepared to steal the amulet from a hoarding warlord. This was a hospital.

He left Bekah's room and went into one of the large wards, where rows of beds held patients of all ages and ailments. Nearest to the door was an older human woman, propped on a tall mound of pillows and blankets. Her breath rattled in her chest, like popping cartilage, and when she coughed it was a thick, brutal sound that seemed to be more effort than she could sustain. She was pale, her skin nearly translucent, and Dielo's heart shivered when he saw her.

She regarded him with watery, unfocused eyes. "I'm not ready yet, Arthur," she whispered. "I need to watch the children."

Dielo reached out his hand to cover hers, and her fingers barely flexed in return. "Good mother," he said softly. Then he fingered back the protective sleeve and pressed the amulet into his flesh.

Invisible fingers wrapped about his head and pressed into his temples, and his eyelids sagged. He concentrated on the sting against his hand to fight the pressure and exhaustion.

On the bed, the old woman's lungs crackled, and she coughed with more strength than before. Her face flushed, and her fingers tightened on Dielo's. Then she coughed again, hacking up spittle and phlegm, and when she wiped her mouth her lips held more color. The crack and rattle of her breath slowed.

He did not know how much time passed. At last Dielo swayed, and he forced the amulet away from his skin. He was kneeling beside the bed, leaning upon it. Before him, the woman blinked at him, a faint frown on her face. "You don't look well, son," she observed.

He shook his head. "I'm sorry. How are you? Are you feeling better?"

It was an unnecessary question. She had been half-hallucinating when he'd found her barely breathing. Now she knew him for a stranger.

"I've been napping, and it's done me a world of good. You should try the same."

He nodded wearily. "I will, good mother, I promise."

But he was too tired to stand, and he waited there, trying to keep his eyes open. After a moment, she placed a dry hand on his arm, and he felt himself drawn to it like a plant to sunlight. Now he could not pull away from the friendly touch.

"Sleep here, if you want," she said. "I wouldn't mind. It's been a long while since I had someone to watch over."

He smiled. "I don't know how much watching I need."

"Psh. Everyone needs watching, at least once in a while. Go to sleep."

He didn't mean to put his head down, but her hand was warm and the blanket was soothing and he was so very tired... His thoughts whirled, uncontrolled in his exhaustion.

It worked. The amulet worked, just as Bekah had believed. But, just as Tilly had said, it could no longer work on its own. It needed a Rideis to restore its depleted magic, and he could not sufficiently fuel it. Already he was unsteady with its effect.

But no human could restore it, either. As powerful as it was, it was useless here.

He had come to steal the amulet, but not to steal it from a house of healing. But was it wrong to steal it from a place where it could be of no use, and take it to a place where it could be restored?

"Why, Almar, you look brighter this afternoon!"

Dielo blinked awake and tightened his fingers about the amulet. It was securely in his palm, barricaded with his pulled sleeve. His other hand lay over the woman's on his arm. He sat gently upright, without pulling away.

"It's him, I think," Almar answered, and Dielo's heart began to pound. Did they know about the amulet? Did they know a Rideis could partly restore it?

But she continued, "It's been too long since I had a visitor, or someone to coddle. I needed some coddling, I think. And look at him, sleeping by my hospital bed as if I was someone special." She chuckled, her voice cracking.

"You are someone special," Dielo told her, giving her a warm smile. "It's only a pity there isn't anyone to regularly remind you."

"Now, that's the sweetest thing to say." This was the woman who had assisted Tilly. Dielo shifted backward to make room for her to set down her tray. A mug of broth steamed on it as she put a hand on Almar's forehead.

It had been a lucky guess. Almar had mentioned children, and someone called Arthur, but she had probably outlived at least some. She was in hospice here and not with family, as surely was more natural even in human society. Dielo was glad to have been here for her, even briefly.

The physician looked satisfied with her assessment of Almar, and she passed her the broth. "Take your time with that; it's fresh and hot. I think I can safely leave you to hold it, yes? And I may borrow your young man, if you don't mind."

"I knew he was too good to last," Almar said with a chuckle, her hands on the soup.

Dielo got up and followed the physician out. Once they were in the corridor, she turned to him. "I should scold you for wandering about the wards, but I haven't seen Almar that comfortable in a month. If all she needed was someone to fuss over... But you look like a forgotten porridge. You need to lie down, and I'll find someone to take a look over you."

Dielo shook his head, though it felt heavy when he did. "I'm only tired. I just need to sleep."

"Don't argue with someone who treats the ill every day. You need more than a nap."

Maybe he did; he didn't know how the amulet wanted to restore itself. But he knew he couldn't explain that he was exhausted from feeding an amulet everyone had thought dead for years because he was a demon from over the mountains. He nodded and went acquiescently back to his mat. It felt good to lie down, even exposed on the wide floor.

A thrill of rare joy still tingled through him. He had helped the old woman Almar. She could breathe freely now because of his action. Bekah was alive because of his action. He had helped them, in a way he had never helped anyone before.

He had been taught that providing a respite from a difficult day was helping. And it was, he was sure. But the sensation of seeing a suffering woman draw an easier breath, or of watching Bekah cuddle her tiny red infant, was entirely different than watching a lord relax contentedly upon a mound of pillows as Dielo rubbed his feet. There were different ways of serving, of course, but he had never known that he might offer more.

But he could not think clearly on these treacherous ideas with the amulet's burden thumping in his head. He rolled himself into the thin blanket, the amulet tucked safely beneath his pillow.

He did not wake until late in the evening, when twilight showed in the window. There was a cooled cup of soup beside his mat, and he drank it and lay down again to return to sleep.

He woke late, when the hospital was silent and only one lamp burned, far down the corridor. In the night, he came to a decision.

Dielo could lend enough of his Rideis essence to save one woman, but he could not give enough to restore the amulet for the centuries of healing aid it had offered.

He had come to Sayinia to steal an amulet. Thinking of Bekah, remembering the tiny baby curling fingers in her hair, it was more difficult to take it. Yet leaving it was no gift, if only Rideis magic could restore it. His master needed an amulet more than the humans needed an expired trinket.

In the grey before dawn, he rose and went to where Bekah and her infant slept. He bent and gave her a chaste kiss on the forehead. "Be well, with your child." She smiled without opening her eyes.

He secured the amulet into the small pouch at his belt. His heart burned with delighted anticipation. Prince Kayvin would return home, and Dielo would be waiting there with an amulet to present.

CHAPTER 98

LIRIN CREPT THROUGH THE rooms to her mother's study, placing her bare feet carefully on the tile floor so as not to make a sound. It was still new and somewhat awkward to think of Pasiphae Jade as her mother. After a lifetime of thinking of her as an aunt, and hardly ever addressing her even as that, there was a hollow feeling to the word *mother*.

She understood. Especially after Lord Fretton's threatened assault, she knew why Pasiphae Jade had kept the truth of their relationship a secret. But there was still a wrench in knowing her mother had not been lost, as she had long believed, but had been denied.

Pasiphae Jade still had not told her the truth. Lirin did not know if she knew that Lirin knew. But Prince Kayvin did not benefit from lying about it, and Lord Fretton had hinted she was a prize, and...it felt true.

It was late. She did not know the time, but the moon had been up for two or three hours, and all the rest of the royal apartments lay silent. Lirin had looked first into the royal sleeping pit, large enough to hold a small crowd and therefore somehow no longer luxurious or comfortable, before she began her explorations. She had learned that sleeping the night through was granted to hardworking servants; the rich and powerful rose during the night to pick out soft melodies on muted instruments or to wander the shadows like a ghost, or to read in their studies full of books and knowledge.

Lirin leaned into the study doorway silently. A single lamp sat on the desk, guttering with ill maintenance. Pasiphae Jade leaned heavily on one hand, with the other brushing her eyes. Lirin thought uncharitably that if she read during the day as ordinary people did, her eyes would not be strained. Or now she could add more oil to the lamp; she could certainly afford it in her newly exalted position.

Lirin did not know why she'd come tonight. She had nothing to ask; she already had the answers, and asking again would not bring different or better answers. She thought she wanted to see if the woman who was both her mother and the Arch Potentate would have a different face in the night, just as the prince who played soft notes in the night wore a different face than the one who played by day. As she waited in the dark, hardly daring to breathe, she knew she was not meant to see this face. This was something meant to be private, secret and the fragile ties of their relationship could not stand the strain of this insight.

A pen and a jar of ink lay beside the open scroll, half-filled with uncertain notations. Ink dripped from the nib and dried there, clogging the pen. In the trembling dim light it was difficult to be sure, but Lirin thought there were dark smudges on Pasiphae Jade's face that were more than the lack of sleep. She held her breath and watched as Pasiphae Jade lowered her face into both her hands, heedless of ink or decorum.

Lirin did not know how to retreat. She dared not stay and see this; she could not retreat. The Arch Potentate was a force of nature, an incarnation of the powerful Bull Throne, the strength to defend the nation and the people. Maybe this weakness of tears was why women were not meant to hold such positions.

She did not know what sound it was—her bare foot against a tile, or the catch of breath in her throat—but Pasiphae Jade lifted her face and looked into the dark doorway. Lirin stared at her, mouth agape, heart pounding. "I'm sorry," she breathed, hardly making a sound. "I only..."

Pasiphae Jade stared at her for a long moment, and then she put her hands on the desk. "Come in."

Lirin stepped inside, somehow feeling chastened.

"Is it only you?"

She nodded. "I couldn't sleep, and I thought..." She trailed off, lacking a suitable explanation. *I wanted to see who you were at night* sounded ridiculous.

Pasiphae Jade wiped tears from her face, leaving faint streaks. "I'm sorry you found me like this."

Lirin's throat closed, and she wanted to ask if she was a daughter. She wanted to hear it said aloud. But the question was too large to fit through her tight throat, and so she said instead, "What's wrong?"

A simple question, a childish question. A cowardly question.

Pasiphae Jade looked at the scroll. "I'm working out the calculations, again. I'll have one chance, and it will be difficult and rushed. I have to get it right."

"For what?"

Pasiphae Jade brought up one corner of her mouth in an exhausted half-smile. "Don't you know why I'm the Arch Potentate? I'm here to save us all. I'm going to save the world, or at least our nation. All Mandoral is in danger, and I'm the only one who can help."

Lirin stared down at the obscure notations.

"I killed Gromgest in his sleeping pit. I took the Bull Throne by force and secret alliances, narrowly bought with promises of power and prestige. I took a royal wife hostage and made her a prisoner of ice, and I suppressed all resistance, both in intrigue and in open revolt. I've spun so many plates atop so many sticks, and I have not yet dropped one."

Lirin nodded mutely. No matter what else, she had done the impossible and more.

"And then..." Pasiphae Jade rubbed her face. "If I do not work this magic, if I do not bring one more miracle that no one has ever done, it will all be for nothing. Worse than nothing, for I will be the greatest villain of legend, a murderous courtesan who craved power instead of a heroine who foresaw and forestalled disaster."

"But can't you do it?" Lirin asked bluntly. "Didn't you take the throne to do it?"

"I took the throne to try." Pasiphae Jade blew out her breath. "I need the amulets, or as many as I can get. Even then it will be difficult. I won't have a chance to practice, and I won't have time to adjust my calculations if they're not quite correct. And if they're not, I will be one of the most hated people of all history."

Lirin slid onto another chair. "But you will have done more than anyone else to stop the spawning."

"Oh, child." She gave a sad little huff of bitter laughter. "The only thing people mock more than someone who made no effort at all is someone who made a real effort and failed. It reminds them that they did not try at all, and they resent that."

"But if you try to save their lives..."

"Hundreds of lives. Thousands." Pasiphae Jade nodded. "Those who die in the spawning itself, and those who die after when the farms are untended or the booths and workshops are abandoned as people flee. And the survivors will be furious, and they will need someone to blame, and it will be the whore who killed their Arch Potentate and then failed to save them."

Lirin pressed her fists into her legs. "But you're trying. And Prince Kayvin is trying to help you."

She scowled, despair momentarily relieved by disgust. "He is a weak little man, not even a man."

"He's—" Lirin stopped. Kayvin was kind, and thoughtful, and dedicated to rescuing his mother. He was indeed unlike the courtiers Lirin had seen, but she thought she liked the difference. But she could not explain any of this, and not aloud to the mother she hadn't known or the Arch Potentate who despised her displaced rival. Finally she said instead, "I like him better than Lord Fretton."

Pasiphae Jade's expression tightened. "I don't believe you'll have to worry about Lord Fretton again. He tried to take you from me, and I cannot let that stand."

Lirin noted the affront was to Pasiphae Jade's authority, not to Lirin's safety. She also recalled it was Prince Kayvin who had come for her. Yes, they said Lord Fretton would not have known her if she had not been with the prince—but Kayvin had come for her, not Pasiphae Jade.

Still, Pasiphae Jade was the only family she had, and she was broken with worry, and Lirin had few options in the palace. She slid off the chair and went to embrace her. "I'm sorry for all that's gone wrong. I hope you work out the magic you need."

Pasiphae Jade put her arms around Lirin, tightly, and for a moment there was no confusion or deception between them. "I will. I will save you and everyone in this city and beyond. I will, because I have to."

CHAPTER 99

GALEN WAS COUNTING ON his fingers. "The Sculptor's Eye is in the capital with the state jewels. The Player's Eye was in Barkerton, but Kayvin has it now. The Painter's Eye was in the pawnshop. The Singer's Eye was in the Pradford temple. That leaves the Poet's Eye, the Storyteller's Eye, and the Dancer's Eye." He tipped his amulet up to study it. "Which do you think this is?"

"Well, it can't be the Storyteller's Eye, that's certain." Lisveth stretched her arms overhead.

"How do you know?"

"Because you won't tell me a story."

Galen gave a little huff of indignant chuckle. "That was unfair."

"You could prove me wrong at any time." She shrugged.

The road stretched before them like an unspooled ribbon, pale and dusty in the dry autumn. Galen was ready for a break, but he didn't want to be the first to mention it. "I should never have confessed to making up stories. I should have known you would be irresponsible with any secret knowledge."

"I haven't sold it to the Rideis," Lisveth protested mildly. "I only keep it for my own purposes." She glanced at him. "Why won't you?"

"What?"

"Why won't you tell me a story?"

Galen frowned and looked across the field. "It's stupid."

"The reason?"

"No, the..." He struggled for words. "You were right, of course, when you said they called it foolish. But they were right, too. Stories aren't real."

"Neither are my illusions, but you seem to like them at times."

"That's different." Galen looked ahead and then back at the field, anywhere but her. "If I tell you a silly little story, something rote and safe, it won't matter if you laugh at it. And even if you somehow like it, that won't mean anything, because it was a silly little story, rote and safe. No one deserves praise for dropping an apple into a bushel basket."

Lisveth mercifully remained quiet, letting him finish.

"And if I tell a grander story, something I put my heart into... Then it's my heart you'll laugh at." He said it quietly, perhaps too quietly, and facing the field, but she seemed to understand him anyway.

"Why do you think I'd laugh?"

"So many reasons... Because they're foolish stories that don't change anything. If I told the best story in the world about two friends who found themselves at a feast of roast beef and buttered potatoes, if I made you weep with sentiment and drool with poetic description, we'd still be on this road with a handful of dry jerky, only sadder now for the contrast. How is that not foolish?"

She didn't answer, and he couldn't read her silence. They walked on, and he wondered what he should have said differently. He hadn't tried to explain it before.

Perhaps twenty minutes had passed when Lisveth turned her head to him. "You're hoping I'll suggest a rest, aren't you?"

"What makes you say that?"

"I've walked a thousand leagues with you, farm boy. I know when you're tired. And I'm tired, too. It's too bad they built this road over so many hills."

The rush came over the crest of the hill, three men charging, and Galen barely had time to reach for a weapon.

"Eyes!" Lisveth snapped, and Galen tucked his face hard into his elbow. There was a muffled sound, and three men cried in startled pain. Galen uncovered his eyes and rushed into their confused disarray, striking quickly as they reeled and blinked, trying to clear their vision.

Lisveth knifed one from behind, and Galen finished the others quickly. He looked around—no one else was coming—and then braced for the sick disorientation he knew would come. It was never easy, even when it was self-defense.

Lisveth crouched over the dead. "These are Rideis, I think. More bandits."

"Only three together?"

"This isn't exactly a high road, and we were only two together. They would have had little trouble with anyone who didn't put a fireball in their path."

Galen sat down so his legs wouldn't shake. "What do we do with them?"

She shook her head. "Leave them. Not on the road, that won't be pleasant for anyone coming along—but there's not much else we can reasonably do."

"Feels wrong."

"It does. But that doesn't mean there's a better solution. This ground is dry and hard and we don't have tools, even if we wanted to dig a three-man grave, and we can't carry three bodies to the next town, which undoubtedly doesn't want them either."

The conversation wasn't settling Galen's stomach, but he had no counter-argument. "We'll at least tell someone in the next town."

"Obviously." She came over to him and held out a hand. "Let's take that rest a little further on, if you don't mind."

He agreed. She helped him up, and they moved the bodies off the road, and they walked on.

Two hills over, by unspoken agreement, they paused and sat in a patch of thick grass that hadn't gone too prickly yet. Galen felt exhausted, drained from the walk and the fight and the futile killing. He propped an elbow on his bent knee and leaned his head on his arm.

After a moment, Lisveth's hand rested on his back. "Have some water."

He hadn't realized he was thirsty, but she was right. He gulped greedily from the water bag, and a little life came back into him.

Lisveth stayed where she was, her hand on his shoulders, her face slightly behind him. He was glad of the touch. "Thanks for the fireball. That was quick."

"So was your duck."

They worked well together. He turned his head. "Are you all right?"

"I'm fine." But she shifted close, her side to his.

He slid an arm around her. "Are you all right?" he asked again, more softly. "It was sudden, and...it was three dead."

"They came for us. There wasn't much option but to do what we did." She blew out a breath. "It's just..."

"Is it something other than the fight?" Galen felt his way carefully through the words. "I thought—I wondered if you were, maybe, a little off..." It had been a vague feeling, for the last few days, but nothing he could identify or even ask about.

"No, it's fine, I'm fine."

Galen grasped for something else to say. "I've never been to Atalasu City. I hope the general's coin buys us some nice accommodations."

Lisveth tightened her arms against her body. "I suppose."

It wasn't the answer he expected, but she'd already said repeatedly she was fine. He didn't know what else to ask.

"That was the last of the water, so we should start walking again," she said abruptly. "We can't be that far out, not this late in the day. Let's go."

They came upon the next town after another hour or so, a surprisingly accommodating hub for merchant trains and farm markets. Galen was grateful; such a town would have plenty of rooms and food. And he was developing a blister on his left foot.

From the looks of things, at least two, maybe more merchant trains were in town for the night. Accommodations might be scarce, and they'd likely have to share tables, but it was still a welcome break.

But the first place they stopped, a serving man waved them to a small table against the wall. "Just cleared," he said. "Take a seat and I'll be right over."

Galen stretched his aching legs under the table, feeling the pull in his hamstrings. Lisveth left room for his ankles. "I hope he's got something warm in the kitchen."

The kitchen offered only lamb stew, but that was welcome. As the serving man set down their bowls, Lisveth asked, "Where would we find a sheriff? A town this size should have one, or someone else we can talk to."

"Certainly. I hope you didn't have too much trouble?" He waited anxiously.

"Bandits on the road. We came out all right, but the sheriff should know."

"Oh, of course. I'm..." His eyes fell on Galen's hair. "We don't want any trouble here."

Heat scorched through Galen's neck. "I didn't bring any trouble."

"We want to report the bandits," Lisveth said firmly. "The Selk bandits, the ones we fought. Not us."

The man had the conscience to look ashamed. "I'm glad you made it safely. You'll want Sheriff Cordon, and he's probably three doors up, either in the Mickle Pickle or in his office beside it. Short man, shoulders nearly as wide as his height, dark blond beard down to his heart. You can't mistake him."

"Thanks," Galen said.

"I'll go," Lisveth told him. "You're limping."

"I think I'd make it three doors, but thank you."

"You arrange for some beds, then. I'll find you when I'm back."

They both brightened with supper in them, and after Lisveth scraped her bowl clean, she left to find Sheriff Cordon. Galen adjusted his seat, stretching his legs again.

"Did she get away?"

He glanced toward the next table, filled with caravan folk. "What's that?"

A man gestured about the table with a foamy mug. "We're over here trading stories of the ones who got away, and then suddenly you're alone. Do we need to buy you a drink in sympathy?"

Galen grinned. "We're working partners, nothing else, and she's coming back, but I'll take a drink with you in good company."

"Come on over, then." The man slapped an empty stool at the table.

It had been a long time since Galen had sat with caravan guards, and he'd never completed a full route as a guard, but still it felt nice to be included. They introduced themselves, a loose fellowship from three caravans pausing in town. Regulars on this key route often met up when their itineraries overlapped, they explained.

"I'm not a guard," Galen answered when they asked. "I was, once, but that was years ago, and brief. Now I do odd jobs for hire."

"With that partner of yours?"

"That's right."

"That makes a sort of sense. Was she a guard before, too?"

Galen grinned. "No."

Another man leaned forward. "And you're sure she's not—that is, she didn't get away, right? Because you aren't, you know, with her?"

Galen gave him a suspicious look. "We're not together, no." But he said it more slowly than warranted.

"Maybe you'd like to be, though?" One guffawed.

Another elbowed the mocker. "He's just looking out for his partner, once he saw the likes of you in the building."

"Leave him alone," ordered the man who'd first invited Galen, "or you'll run him off two minutes after he sits down. Now, I believe it was Lewis's turn, wasn't it?"

All eyes turned to Lewis, whose hands were braced on a half-full tankard. He grinned nervously. "Aw, c'mon, fellows. I don't have..."

"Set up, Lewis. Even the new guy, what's his name, even Gralen can see you're pining."

Galen couldn't, but Lewis looked to be in only mild distress, so he merely grinned. He remembered both male and female guards when he'd joined up in Abbay, so long ago, but if there were any female guards here, they'd abandoned this table. Perhaps that was what had inspired the conversation.

Lewis looked down into his tankard. "Aw, you'll laugh."

"Of course. That's the whole point of this. Set up anyway."

"She's got freckles."

"Good start, not enough."

"She's got a fine job, and she's too good at it to need me." He grinned hollowly.

"Good moping, Lewis, but you're not getting out that easy. The rule is to describe her so we can drink to her with a proper picture in mind. After that you can bemoan how she got away."

Lewis conceded. "Chestnut hair, a bit wispy. Too fine to stay fixed in place, which is a bit of a problem in the military."

"Oh, a soldier girl!" Several chuckled. "Keep going. She's too good at soldiering to take up with you?"

"She's aide to a general."

With that distinguishing detail, Galen could suddenly recognize the chestnut hair and freckles. "Lost a hand?"

Lewis looked at him sharply. "That's right."

"That's Anela, isn't it?"

Lewis flushed. "Well, isn't that my luck, that someone would know her."

Galen was thinking back. If Anela, looking for love had turned Lewis down, she must have been disinterested for a reason. But aloud he said, "Yes, I know her. And I'll certainly drink to her, if that's the next step."

"It is indeed," said someone else. "To Anela!"

They drank, and then Galen looked back at Lewis. "So she got away?"

"Oh, she was nice enough about it," he said hurriedly. "She let me down real easy: I asked if she wanted to step out with me, and she said they had a meeting with a march lord. I can't compete with that." He laughed nervously.

Something shifted in the back of Galen's memory. "Was this the night before your caravan rolled out?"

"Of course. I wasn't going to ask her until I had another job ready; what if she'd turned me down, and then I had to awkwardly see her every day for another week or so? I'm not a complete fool. I waited until I had an escape if it went poorly."

Galen shook his head. "You're more of a fool than you feared."

Lewis stared at him, tankard half-raised, eyes simultaneously suspicious and guardedly curious.

"She thinks you saw her hand and left."

Lewis's jaw dropped. "What? No!" He shook his head. "I'd known of course—but she always kept it back, so I thought she didn't want to—no!"

This response pleased Galen. "She's in Lord Bryuki's house now, with the general, or was not that long ago." He took a drink.

"Fair night." Lewis put his tankard down without drinking. "Where's that?"

One of the other men laughed. "Need to make another contract when this one's done, Lewis?"

"She thinks I left because of that? How heartless she must have thought me. Must think me. Where's that Lord Bru... What's his name?"

A few minutes later, Lewis was on his way to buy out his contract with his current caravan and try to beg a place on another heading in the right direction, and his friends, after affectionately mocking him during his departure, were drinking to his new endeavor. Galen was roundly praised for his deep knowledge of generals' aides, and two more rounds of drinks were purchased.

Galen realized, partway through the second, Lisveth should have had plenty of time to report to the sheriff. "Maybe I should go to check on my friend. She's been away for a while."

"What? No, she's back. Been there for a bit, now." The first guard nodded toward Galen's previous table. Galen twisted and saw Lisveth sitting crossways in the chair, leaning against the wall with her arm draped over the chair's back. She nodded and smiled as they looked at her.

"And you just let me sit here?" Galen protested.

"She shook her head when I started to say something. Seemed like she was happy to wait. Doesn't look mad now, either."

She didn't, but Galen felt bad for carrying on without her. "I'll go anyway. Thanks for asking me to join you."

When he reached Lisveth, she shook her head. "You don't have to come away if you don't want."

"I had no idea you were back. Why didn't you join us?"

"Do you think I'd want to sit at a table full of caravan guards?"

He chuckled. "All right, fair enough. But you could have come to get me."

"You looked like you were having a good time." She said it lightly, but the words felt like a mask, disguising something else.

Again, he had the impression that something was wrong, and yet there was nothing to identify.

"I was. I think I just played matchmaker."

She laughed. "You?"

"For Anela. She told me once about a man who'd left her, and then he was here tonight, thinking she'd turned him down."

"And you got that sorted? Well done." She smiled, but it was a fragile smile. "Are you sure you don't want to go back to the guards?"

"No, they're going to finish up soon enough. Most of them are leaving in the morning, so it won't be a late night for them."

There was a slight pause. "All right."

Again, there was something... But then Galen remembered. "Oh! I forgot to ask about beds."

"Too good a time with your friends," Lisveth said without rebuke. "Let's do it now."

CHAPTER 100

LISVETH CURSED FREELY AS a wagon rolled by too close in the street.

"Careful," Galen said. "Busy place, Atalasu City."

"This is a midden of a place." She tugged at her hood, up despite the warmth of the sun.

Atalasu City was indeed busy, and growing. They passed through an area of buildings that were all plainly newer than other parts of the city, though they were too far within the gates to be new settlement. The mystery was solved when Galen noticed old soot on some walls; this was reconstruction after a fire, possibly the one of Anela's accident. Rural life was dangerous, but cities had their own risks.

The Vernal House temple lay near the city center, and they found it without difficulty. Galen started for the gate.

"Hold on," said Lisveth. "I'm hungry."

"We can eat after we check the treasury," Galen said. "We're already right here."

"And it's not going anywhere," she answered irritably. "I'll be back in a minute. Here, hold this."

She put the Painter's Eye into his hand. Galen frowned. "Why are—"

"Just hold onto it, okay? For today. I'll be right back."

She disappeared into the market spreading out from the temple gate. Galen stared after her, and then he sighed and squatted against the wall to wait, dropping the amulet into his belt pouch.

If the temple indeed held one of the other amulets, they would have to keep it safe from Kayvin and Yovela. That meant staying out of ready sight, lest they alert the Rideis that an amulet was nearby. Perhaps Lisveth had been right to cover her head. He pulled his hood up as well, snagging it on his distinctive hair.

He watched the faithful enter the temple, noting that many rubbed the portal post as they entered. Some kissed their palms and then pressed them to the wood, passing on the kiss. It was a curious custom he had not seen in the Heel, though the obeisance was easy enough to recognize.

Lisveth emerged from the crowd, her mouth set in a hard line. "All right, let's go."

She did not offer him a hand up as usual, and Galen got to his feet. He inhaled as he stood and hesitated. "Were you—drinking?"

"Free ale with the vegetable pie."

"That's not ale."

"Are we going to argue over my lunch or retrieve the amulet? Let's go." She set off into the temple gate, shoulders hunched.

Galen blinked after her. Definitely an off day. Perhaps she had a headache or upset belly, or maybe it was her time of the month and she was experiencing more pain than usual. He followed, catching up easily.

Near the gate, Lisveth put her hand to her mouth, as if warding off a cough or sneeze. She passed close by the portal post and brushed it with her fingers. Galen noted the gesture; why had Lisveth seemed to subtly kiss the gate, as the more dedicated adherents did, when he'd never known her to visit temples? But today clearly was not the day to ask.

Lisveth folded her arms and barreled through the courtyard, crossing the circles of Love, Joy, and Peace as if there were a prize for finishing first. Galen trailed her, understanding she did not want company. Halfway through Patience she nearly plowed through a robed junior priest, who recoiled at their collision and began an apology. "I'm sorry, I—wait!" He leaned forward. "Are—Luana? Where have you—"

Lisveth punched the junior priest in the nose.

Galen gaped for a second and then leaped forward to steady the junior priest. "Fair night! Are you all right? Here, pinch that, right here." He looked around to see Lisveth sprinting toward the gate. "I'm so sorry."

"Whad I say?" The junior priest was bewildered and pained. "Why'd she hid me?"

"I can't say," Galen answered apologetically. "Do you know her?"

He shook his head, still holding his bloodied nose. "Apparently nod."

"You thought she was someone—Luana?"

"Luana would neber punch me. 'Scuse me, I'll go inside."

Galen let the junior priest retreat toward the nearest building, and he turned to retrace his steps across the virtue circles to the temple gate.

It took him a few minutes to find Lisveth, pressed between two market stalls. She was hugging herself, her hood pulled low, and she rubbed at her face as she spotted him. "I'm sorry," she said, her voice low and rough. "I shouldn't have hit him."

"Probably not," Galen agreed mildly. He slipped an arm about her. "Come on."

She offered only token resistance and then followed him down the street, keeping her face down. Galen led her to a tavern front and pressed her gently onto a bench against the wall. "Stay here until I get back?"

She nodded, eyes on the street.

He went inside and bought two tankards of ale, which he carried out and handed to Lisveth. Then he dragged the bench to the side alley of the building, somewhat less visible to the passersby.

Lisveth sank onto the bench and pushed one tankard back at him. She stared into the other.

Galen sat down beside her, extended his legs, and stared at nothing across the way. "That was a bit unfair."

She sniffed and nodded. "I'm sorry I hit him."

"Why did you do it?"

Lisveth stared into the dark ale, her hood shielding her face.

Galen blew out his breath and drew his feet back. "I suppose I could go ask him," he said lightly.

Lisveth's hand shot out and clamped onto his forearm, pinching hard. He flinched. A few rapid heartbeats later, she drew her hand back. "I'm sorry."

"It was a joke."

"I—I know."

But she hadn't known, not for a moment. Galen waited a moment before asking the question. "What he called you—is Luana your real name?"

She shook her head. "No. I'm Lisveth, I really am." She rubbed at ale spilled on her thigh. "I didn't lie to you."

And she wouldn't now, if he did not press for explanations.

Galen took a drink—the ale wasn't very good—and tried to think on how to proceed.

Her fingers were pale on the tankard, and tiny ripples in the ale's surface marked her tense grip. She did not look up.

Galen chewed his lip. "I'm not going to ask you."

The ale settled in her hand, but she did not move.

A hundred possibilities spun through his head. Someone might have—hurt her. She might have stolen from this temple long ago, and maybe something had gone wrong in the theft, as with his father and uncles. That might explain why she refused to steal from one again. The junior priest had not seemed alarmed to see her, but he'd also thought she was someone else.

Assuming she was not lying about her name.

He waited, having promised not to ask, to see if she would offer unasked.

Lisveth sat for a long moment. At last she lifted the ale and took a drink. "This is pretty terrible," she said.

"It is," Galen agreed.

Lisveth drank it anyway. When she finished, she set down the empty one without speaking and took Galen's, and she drank it as well.

Galen waited. This was her fourth drink, if she'd really had a free ale as well as her other earlier drink. He tried to remember if he'd seen her drink so much before. He could recall only twice, both on chilly spring nights, when she had drunk more heavily, but they had been safely lodged in taverns where she could go immediately to bed. Not before she would go to navigate a strange city and negotiate for a priceless artifact to save their world.

Lisveth set down the second tankard. She put her hand to her mouth, and he wondered if she meant to say something. Then she belched.

He wanted to stand and walk away. She was being ridiculous and secretive and somehow he felt she was blaming him, as irrational as that sounded, and somehow, just as irrationally, he was angry at her for whatever had happened here that made her so oblique to him now. If she would tell him what the junior priest had done, he would know how to respond, know whether to hit the man again instead of apologizing and pinching his nose.

But it wasn't the junior priest's fault. Without knowing anything else, Galen knew that.

She pushed her palms down her thighs. "I suppose we should go back for the amulet."

That was it, then. She wasn't going to talk about it. Galen took a breath. "I suppose we should."

He returned the tankards, pocketed his coin, and came back to the bench. Lisveth was standing, one foot propped on the seat, rubbing her fist against her nose. She nodded once at him. "Ready?"

He nodded back.

They walked side by side toward the temple, and Galen wondered if her pace was quicker than usual so that she would not appear to be hesitating. His longer legs easily matched her strides, but he slowed to watch as she passed through the gate. Yes, her hand went to her face and then to the post.

She tugged at her hood, and this time she went up the side of the virtue circles, avoiding the few adherents making their way along the labyrinthine paths. She crossed her arms and kept her head low.

Galen stepped close beside her. "Why not use a different face?"

"What?"

"You clearly don't want to be recognized. Use an illusion."

She shook her head, almost unseen within her hood. "Can't."

Of course she could. "I know you can use magic in a temple. You made an amulet appear to be a chicken bone; altering your face can't be more magic than that. Or—we have the Painter's Eye." His hand went to his pouch. "Why don't you—"

"No!" She shoved his hand down, pinning it against his belt so that he could not draw out the amulet. "I gave that to you so—so I wouldn't use it. I can't use it. Not here."

He stared at her. "Not here?"

She withdrew her hand and looked down. "We bring our true selves into the Vernal House. No lies, no illusions."

"You made the amulet look like a chicken bone," Galen said flatly. "In a temple."

"No illusions," she repeated, her voice stretched like fraying fabric. "Not in the Vernal House." She turned and walked on, her head bowed so that her hood hung over her cheeks.

Galen gave an exasperated sigh and followed.

CHAPTER 101

IN PRADFORD, THEY HAD needed the letters of authorization from General Artextra and Lord Bryuki to persuade the temple authorities. Their warnings of a coming theft, with the credentials to prove they weren't the thieves themselves, had eventually won the priests' assistance, so that they agreed to lead the described visitors to the treasure room and the trap Lisveth and Galen had laid. They had been even less inclined to allow them to carry away the amulet, but they had done it, assured that it was necessary for the protection of Sayinia and that the Octovirate would reward their help.

Here in Atalasu City, at the Vernal House, Lisveth did not hesitate. She did not look left or right, just paced quickly through the corridors and halls, keeping near the walls, winding through the temple passages as if she knew them well. Obviously, she did.

Galen shook his head and tried not to wonder.

They came to a long, rearward corridor, blocked by a gate of wrought iron. Lisveth leaned close and whispered to it, and the gate swung open. Galen gaped. Lisveth gave no explanation as she walked on. She drew a candle from her bag and handed it to him, sparking a tiny flame as he took it. He shielded the flame as they walked along the passage, away from the light.

The corridor ran unlit to another set of gates, heavier and enameled with fanciful beasts and vining flowers. There was no latch Galen could see; it seemed fused from hinge to hinge, clearly divisible by its mirrored pattern but without so much as a keyhole.

Lisveth put a hand on the gate, palm resting on a gryphon's wing. She hesitated a moment, and then again she leaned close and whispered. A seam opened vertically in the iron, working around the animals and plants where they crossed the center line, and the gate swung smoothly inward.

"Lisveth..." Galen breathed.

She shook her head sharply and walked on.

They were in the treasury now. As in the other temples, there were many fine items, but more than Galen had imagined or could identify. Some were rich in materials, golden coffers and jeweled lamp stands, but he guessed most had a greater significance that the rich materials had been meant to honor.

Lisveth turned in place, for the first time unsure of her direction. At last she seemed to settle on a cabinet, and she approached it and, very gently, eased a silver-gilded door open.

Inside sat a book with a cover of set gems, a reliquary containing a piece of carved ivory, and an amulet resting on a coiled chain.

Lisveth lifted the amulet—the eye was forest green, the color of summer fields and sunny meadows—and stared at it. Her hood had slipped, and Galen thought he saw the candlelight glisten in a streak on her cheek.

She took a paper from her bag, rolled and tied with an expensive indigo ribbon. She placed it into the cabinet where the amulet had been, and she closed the silver door.

Then she put the amulet into her bag and turned away. "Let's go."

They had not spoken to the priests. They had not shown their letters and explained their need. They had stolen from a temple.

Galen thought about the rolled note in the ribbon as they passed out of the treasury, out of the seamless gates, out of the iron gate. He trailed Lisveth's unhesitating path through the deep temple and into the courtyard, along the circles' edges, to the main gate and into the street.

Lisveth stopped, took a breath, and started walking again. Galen fell into step beside her. "Do you want to talk about it?"

"No."

"Do you want a drink?"

"...Yes." She pointed. "There's a disreputable tavern three streets that way. It'll do."

The Sweet Jester's signboard was chipped and half moldy, which Galen took as a kindness given what he could make out of the design, but it was crowded with locals, which spoke well for the food and drink. Galen pointed to a small empty table for Lisveth and then went to the bar to order. He opted for wine—it had been a rough day, whatever the cause, and she likely needed something stronger than ale—and asked for beef sandwiches to follow. A splurge, for their success.

When he reached the table, Lisveth was sitting still, her hands folded tightly on the scarred wood, her hood still shielding her eyes. He slid the wine across to her and waited.

After a moment, her hands unlocked and she took the drink. He waited until she'd put half down and replaced the cup before he finally spoke. "Air feels a bit damp. Might rain tonight."

Her concealing hood gave a deprecatory sniff.

"Be good if it did. Been a bit dry lately. I don't know if you paid attention to the fields on the way here, but they were drooping. Not too badly; they'll perk up with one good drenching. Just have to hope that tonight's the night." He rotated his cup in his hand. "I don't know that you would have noticed, not having the expertise of a field-raised eye. You'll just have to trust me on that. But you can."

She lifted her head, and her mouth twisted into a sad smile. "Thanks, farm boy."

He took a drink of wine and thought he might be hungry enough for a sandwich after all.

"What's this?" a voice boomed over Galen's shoulder.

Lisveth was swearing before she even looked up. She flung her wine cup, making Galen instinctively flinch as it sprayed over him and the man behind him. Galen saw her face change to a stranger's, and then she flung the table to the side and dove at him.

Galen stumbled backward, trying to catch her in his arms, and he stepped into the robed man. The man gave him a quick, dismissive glance and then turned back to the rocking table. "Luana!" he snapped. "I've found you!"

Galen shoved him. The robed man staggered and then raised his hand, and light crackled around Galen in a way that he did not understand but recognized. Years of practice of moving through illusory magic let him step into position without recoiling.

The man did not expect Galen to come through the magical assault, and he did not expect the punch. Galen's fist put him on the floor, and Galen did not wait to see how quickly he stood. Lisveth was already gone, and so he ran for the door.

She was not in the street, or at least no one he recognized was in the street. He jogged away from the tavern—no one was following him, which was good—and scanned the people on either side for her familiar walk. After a moment he stopped; she might be waiting to catch up with him, as he would be easier to find.

He leaned against a wall and waited. Minutes passed. No one glanced at him, no one spoke his name, no one tugged his sleeve.

He put his hand into his waist pouch to find something to fiddle with, to make his waiting more plausible to anyone looking. The absence struck him immediately.

The amulet was gone. Not the one they had just taken from the Vernal House; Lisveth had carried that. The Painter's Eye was missing.

So that was why she had crashed into him after tipping the table. She had the Golden Eye, and he would never find her if she did not want to be found.

He would not meet her in the city, of that he was certain. He hoped she would be waiting outside the city gates. He began walking.

CHAPTER 102

GALEN WALKED A QUARTER mile from the city walls, near enough to be visible and far enough to be unrecognizable by anyone standing in the gate. He thought Lisveth would not show herself, altered appearance or not, while within easy eye-shot. Maybe the road, lined with shops and stalls outside the city walls, was still too near, but he could not leave it behind entirely. He sat by the road and idly watched the passing traffic.

The man in the tavern had worn robes, a uniform of some sort. Galen hadn't had time to observe them, but he might have been a state mage. He had certainly used magic on Galen. Galen couldn't identify much magic, but he had a sense of when something was more or less powerful, and that had been meant to put him on the ground, at least. Yes, Galen had shoved him first, but that wouldn't have done lasting harm. That spell... It might have.

Lisveth had mentioned state mages. Only a dislike, no details.

He waited in the cool autumn air, weaving drifted leaves into a disheveled chain. The sky began to darken, and the stream of traffic became a trickle. He put the leaves aside. With the Painter's Eye in Lisveth's possession, he would never find her until she wanted to be found.

He would wait another hour, and then he would seek a place to shelter for the night.

The state mage had called her Luana. The junior priest had called her the same name. Lisveth had said it was not her name, but both men had used it.

Galen began to shred the chain of leaves, dropping cracked pieces across the ground. His arm twinged, and he rolled up his sleeve to find a bruise, in long narrow streaks. It was the shape of Lisveth's fingers, where she had stopped him from going to ask the junior priest why she'd hit him.

The two men had said the strange name differently. The junior priest had been hopeful when he recognized her, while the state mage had used a tone of anger or disgust, or both. Galen thought that was why he had shoved him.

He ran out of leaves and sighed. The logical choice was to take lodging in one of the rooms just inside the city gate, where he could have supper and a warm bed and be well away from anyone who might have been near the Vernal House. But even so far from the temple, Lisveth wouldn't come back to the city.

He blew out his breath and got to his feet.

Something tugged at his sleeve. "Hey."

He half-turned and tried to focus his eyes. But it was a trick of the wind; he should go and find a room for the night—

"Hey." Lisveth took the amulet from her neck and puddled the chain in her hand. She did not look at him.

For a second he stared at her, shaking off the effect of the Eye. Then he embraced her, hard and fast. He pulled her head beneath his chin and enveloped her as if he could hide her himself

She sank into him, and she began to cry. Then she swore.

He did not release her. "I thought you might have gone. Really gone. Without me." It was easier to admit, now that it wasn't true. His throat was tight.

"Fair night," she choked. "I thought I was done with this." She drew back and rubbed her face. "I should be dried up by now. Like your stupid fields." She jerked her head to indicate up the road. "There's a place in the village with a couple of rooms for those who miss the gates closing. We can stop there."

Galen put his arm around her shoulders and walked with her. He left her in the twilight while he asked for a room, and the landlord gave him the last remaining. He stepped outside for Lisveth and then led her around the back to the rear door.

"Beside the privy," she said in a hoarse voice. "How convenient."

"And hardly any smell," he replied, wrinkling his nose.

He dropped his pack on the dusty floor. There was one bed against the wall, just wide enough to share.

Lisveth sank onto the bed and leaned against the wall. "I was so stupid. I never should have gone, no matter what we thought. I was stupid, and then I was so...distracted that I forgot to mask up when we left the temple, and no one can be that stupid but obviously I am." She sniffed. "And I can't stop crying, and it's not doing any good, and I shouldn't have come..."

Galen arranged their bags beside the door, and then he rearranged them.

She rubbed her face again. "Go ahead."

"Are you sure?"

She nodded tightly.

Galen sat down beside her and stared at the opposite wall. "I think you've been to Atalasu City before."

She laughed, a choked, pained sound. "Very clever."

"I think you understand why Kayvin killed the Rideis bandit."

She didn't answer.

Galen waited a moment before asking the question. "Is Luana your real name?"

She shook her head. "I told you it isn't. I really am Lisveth. I kept that." She took a shaky breath. "Luana's my sister." Her throat worked. "Was my sister."

Galen's stomach lurched, but he waited.

"We were three years apart, but we could be confused. That wasn't hard, when everyone knew her better." Lisveth leaned her head against the wall. "Luana was an acolyte at the Vernal House. I was too, but... Everyone adored her. She was studying to be a temple mage. Do you have those, out in the Heel?"

Galen shook his head.

"Our parents were very proud of her. They were proud of me too, I suppose, but it was easy to be proud of Luana."

Galen nodded.

"She was selected as the Cerule Herald for the spring bells ceremony. That's the ritual that welcomes the peregrine gods back to the temple and renews the magic in the virtue circles. The Cerule Herald is... It's a role, chosen each year, it's...it doesn't matter right now. It was a great honor, and she trained for weeks. It's an important ritual, and it requires power and precision. And faith."

She seemed to have exhausted her words for the moment, and so Galen offered, "That's the ritual with the bells people wear. They'll ring, even while you're standing completely still, when the magic is renewed."

She nodded. "It's incredible. The bells sewn on everyone's clothing chime all day as they walk around, during the festival, and then everyone goes still just before... There's a branch, cut from the sacred tree, and it blossoms when the Herald presents it. Then the bells ring on their own. It's incredible."

Galen nodded and waited.

Lisveth licked her lips. "On the day of the ceremony, I went to the temple tower to wish her well." She nodded jerkily in the direction of the city. "I found her at the top, sitting on the floor, frozen up with fear."

"She was nervous about the ceremony?"

"There were two state mages, she said. They'd approached her—they said—fair night, I'm not going to..." She sucked a breath. Galen put an arm around her, and she did not pull away. "They said if the sacred branch failed to bloom when she lifted it on the tower, it would affect everyone who had come to watch. If she'd made an error, or if she wasn't worthy, if she didn't please the gods, it wouldn't bloom, and she couldn't let them down or betray their faith. The mages had a hothouse branch she could lift instead, to ensure all the faithful saw the annual miracle as intended."

Galen's jaw clenched, but he waited.

"She did not want to betray the ritual and use the false branch. But what if—it wasn't that she did not believe the gods had returned, but what if she was unworthy? What if she shouldn't have been chosen, if she wasn't the true Cerule Herald, and the buds didn't open? What if someone's faith was damaged, because of her?" Lisveth sniffed and she shook her head. "She had more failings than anyone knew, she said, she wasn't ready to be the Cerule Herald, and if she failed in this enormous and visible task, she would be responsible for people losing faith."

"That can't be true," Galen said without reason, feeling a stab of empathetic pain years late for a girl he had never known.

"I don't think so, either. But Luana... I never knew until then how she felt she was made of her achievements. And telling her someone else would falter because of her—that was cruel and calculating, and exactly what she would most fear."

Galen nodded, not quite understanding but accepting.

"And..." The word clotted in her throat, refusing to be spoken. "And someone let them in. The state mages—someone brought them to the temple tower for that." She was rigid beneath his arm. "I thought—maybe this wasn't the first time state mages had come to the Cerule Herald. Maybe the previous ceremonies and miracles hadn't been real, either—maybe none of it... Maybe everyone knew it was just a game we played together, except us." Lisveth shook her head sharply. "You have to understand how terrified she was. Not like we're talking quite reasonably here now." She sniffed in bitter irony. "She was paralyzed, she was ready to give it all up."

"And you encouraged her?"

"I tried." Lisveth's face crumpled, but she squeezed her eyes shut and kept going. "And then the two mages came, and they started in on her again. They were—it was awful. They said they would work an illusion for the first sound of the bells, and then the rest would be carried out by people moving in unconscious response to those, and all would be well. And—that was anathema too. There are no lies and no illusions in the Vernal House; you bring your true self to the gods, no pretenses. To work a false miracle with forbidden magic... It was unthinkable, in so many ways."

Unthinkable enough that years later, Lisveth had risked discovery rather than conceal herself. She had given him the amulet to carry so that she could not be tempted into hiding herself. Galen bowed his head over hers.

"So there she was, hugging her knees on the floor, crying that what if it had always been an illusion? What if the branch had never bloomed at all, and we'd always seen a false miracle? But that couldn't be true, this was a test to prove her worth, to see whether she would choose faith or whether she possessed a false pride in taking a role she did not deserve, and what if she failed... I was so furious at the blasphemous mages, and she was panic-stricken, just frozen in place. And the entire city was waiting below, and it was past time and I could see people getting restless in the courtyards, and if someone came because of the delay and found her like this, that would ruin her in all the ways she was afraid of, and...and I decided to do it myself, to stop the mages and to cover for her."

Lisveth put her hand over her mouth, as if she could stop the story and so stop the history.

Galen tightened his arm, and this time she drew away. She shook her head. "I did it. I wasn't the Cerule Herald, but I knew the necessary magic. I made the invocation." She squeezed her hands in her lap. "I did it because I had to help her. And I was so angry at the mages, wanting her to betray her faith like they did. But also...what if I did it because I could and she couldn't? What if I wanted to finally outshine her? What if...what if I wanted to hurt her?" She choked. "I—I don't know. I didn't take time to think; the ritual was late and the mages were shouting and... I did it. I invoked the magic, though I wasn't the Cerule Herald. And it all went wrong."

She stopped. After a moment Galen, caught despite himself, prompted, "How wrong?"

Lisveth closed her eyes. Her voice came out hoarse. "The magic turned back. The tower exploded. Luana probably died within the first few seconds." She flipped her hand in the direction they'd come. "I set fire to the city, a swath from the temple through the northwest. Everything was burning. People were fleeing, trampling each other, tearing down shops and booths and houses to try to make a firebreak. It was horrific."

Galen stared down at her, caught between empathy and horror.

"The state mages, too. I worked the spell, so I had outflowing magic between me and the backlash. I survived. It wasn't fair. But I was—Luana was dead, and I'd set fire to Atalast City, and... I just ran."

Galen nodded and wished for words that might somehow help. Of course there were none.

"I couldn't—I killed her. I killed people in the city, worshipers watching the ritual or people in the districts that burned. I was the only one alive in what was left of the tower. How could I say I had done it for such a foolish reason as to save my sister's face by working her holy magic?"

"And so—"

She nodded once. "I ran. No one stopped me; there was the fire."

Galen said nothing.

"It wasn't until days later that I heard the stories carried out of the city. They thought Luana had lost control of the magic. They thought it was my burned body they found, thought *me* dead in *her* blast. It was Luana who went missing." She shook her head. "There were stories and speculation, rumors that she had been attacked during the ritual or that the relics had been sabotaged so the ceremony would go wrong. Everyone was looking for the missing Cerule Herald."

He still did not know how to answer. What could be said?

"At least no one thought she had done something wrong. They still believed she was exceptional. I killed her, but I saved her good name." Lisveth's shoulders moved in a jerky shrug.

Galen hugged her close. After a moment he tried, "And so you became the Fire Brigand."

"Eventually. What's a little theft, once you've burned a city? And after that..." She shook her head and forced the next words. "You understand a little bit that my illusions are better than average, but... It was never to my advantage to school you on exactly how much better they are. Most illusions are like a puppet show, something people choose to go along with for temporary entertainment. No one, *no one*, does illusions like mine, convincing people against the reality they know. I don't know how, but—I was immersed in divine magic. I think that's it. Divine magic for my lie of being the chosen and hubris to act in her place." She shook her head. "Now I have unnaturally good illusions, and the rest of my magic is still only average. I guess it just burned away all the dross to show my true nature. A charlatan and a thief."

"No," Galen said without hesitation.

She was still speaking, gaining speed as if it were a race to get the words out. "And now you know, finally, and I understand, you can take the whole purse with you, you deserve it, and—"

Galen's gut twisted. He blinked back blurring tears and embraced her. "Oh, Lisveth. I am so sorry."

She sniffed and pulled back weakly. "For what? You did nothing. You were busy chasing pigs or something."

He did not let her go. "For everything. For your sister dying, and for not knowing, and for bringing you back here, and for not understanding." For her belief for years, and now, that he would leave her if he knew.

She stopped resisting. She took a tremulous breath, her back moving against him.

For a long moment, they did not speak. Her hair snagged on Galen's unshaven cheek, but he did not brush it away. The candle flickered and steadied.

"I have a question," Galen ventured quietly.

She tensed against him, but she gave a quick jerk of a nod.

"How did an acolyte know the magic to pass through to the temple treasury?"

Lisveth pulled back and stared at him. "*That's* your question?"

"What?" He made the question defensive. "I want to know."

"Fair night." She stared across the room.

Galen understood. She'd lived in terror of this conversation, and she'd struck first the priest and then the mage to prevent it. She'd finally confessed she'd killed her sister and hundreds of others, and she believed Galen would be horrified.

He *was* horrified. He would need time to think on this, to understand how it had happened and what it had made her. He was horrified. But even if she had acted in jealousy, as she feared, surely she had never meant to burn a city. He knew her as a thief and a brigand, but one who had robbed with illusions instead of real harm.

"That is my question," he answered quietly. "Maybe not my only one, but it's my first. A mere acolyte shouldn't know the inner magic to reach the treasures."

She sniffed and curled one corner of her mouth. "There are supposed to be collections of phrases to guard the passage. But the grand priest was getting older, and he kept forgetting the complex spell-words, and he didn't like to admit his memory was going. They had to reset all the gates twice when he forgot, and he was humiliated. So he made his own as well, easier to remember."

"And you were prowling and spying through the temple even then?"

"I wasn't hard to overlook, and I was curious. He had a favorite kitten. The cat's long grown by now, but his name still works."

"...The great Vernal House's treasure store is protected by the name of a pet kitten?" Galen adjusted his back against the wall as he laughed. "I don't know what to say to that."

"Not much to say," she agreed.

He waited a moment. "I have another question."

She braced.

"Two men saw you today. What will you do about that?"

She blew out her breath, and the moment of reprieve faded. "If it hadn't been two of them, I'd be fine. Others have falsely claimed to have seen Luana before now."

"Why?"

"You aren't the only one with a bounty," she said bitterly. "My father calls it a reward, but it's the same thing. Especially if they knew I was the one who lived."

"Your father—don't your parents know you're alive?"

"Everyone thinks Lisveth died in the tower," she repeated, her voice nearly rasping. "They think Luana fled after her ritual was sabotaged. She fled from the person who attacked her and ruined the magic, or she pursued those who sabotaged it, or any number of other stories. She's a heroine, or maybe a martyr. I can't disillusion them just to tell them I killed her." She choked. "What would that help?"

He stared at her. "They would have a daughter."

"They would have a daughter who had killed their other daughter. They would have a daughter who had burned a swath of city, in place of an honored missing temple herald still lauded and mourned. I can't do that, to any of us."

"They—"

"No. That's it. We're not talking about it again." Her words had an unfamiliar, icy core that surprised Galen into silence.

The candlewick popped.

A moment later Lisveth continued, "Two reports together will sound more plausible and more than just a grab for the reward, but they'll still have nothing but their claims. Neither can prove anything. Either they'll be ignored, lacking evidence, or rumor will invent some reason for Luana to have returned and struck a state mage. That story will be at least as good as anything I could come up with; people are good at inventing tales to support what they want to believe. Anyway, there won't be another sighting."

Galen nodded.

The forest green amulet was the only thing that could have coaxed Lisveth back. With it safely in their possession, they would not return to Atalasu City.

They sat a long while, as the room cooled in the deepening dark and the candle smoldered and failed.

CHAPTER 103

THE ROAD STRETCHED LONG and flat. Lisveth did not fill the morning with anxious chatter to cover the revelations of the night before. Galen was grateful.

She was clever enough to know he needed to think, now that the initial shock was done. Possibly she meant to give him a chance to reconsider taking their purse and going his own way. Possibly she did not yet trust that he was unshaken.

He *was* shaken. How could he not be? Only distance and isolation had kept him ignorant of the shattering disaster, which must have been a subject of rumor and speculation for months. To learn that such a thing had not been an unfortunate happenstance but had been caused by deliberate action...

But not deliberate murder. Lisveth might have been jealous of her sister, might have wanted to show her up, might even have wanted to humiliate and surpass her—but he could not imagine Lisveth at her worst wanting to murder anyone, much less burn a city to do so. But what Lisveth might recall, or imagine she recalled in the horror of surviving...

Galen had sometimes wondered, in the silence of the long nights, what might have transpired at the farmhouse after he'd gone. He'd hoped Idorn and Parn had focused their shared rage on an absent nephew, ending their feud in a common cause. Or, they might have turned on his mother as a more accessible target. He had never let himself think on it for long.

What if he knew the answer, and it was the worst possible outcome?

Love could not tolerate harm to the beloved. The mind might bend to relieve that pain.

Galen had also acted rashly to save his family. Still...Galen had given up everything to protect his family, a knowing sacrifice to save even the uncles who had killed his father. Lisveth had acted on impulse, possibly in jealousy, and had sacrificed her sister and countless others. It was not an easy difference to reconcile.

Around midday, Lisveth slid her pack around and rummaged in it. "I bought some apples," she said, her first words for hours. "Want one?"

"Thanks." Galen took it. The moment felt somehow solemn.

It was too early in the season for apples; it was a little hard and not yet sweet. Galen ate it to the seeds.

Lisveth made a face at her apple, but she finished it, too. They had plenty of coin now, but old habits died hard.

She had not always been poor, though. She had not said as much directly, but temple acolytes came more often from noble families than from the streets, and her father's offered reward was enough to have invited many false claims.

Some things made sense now, in hindsight. Galen wasn't sure he liked recognizing that. He wondered if he would guess at second meanings regularly now. He disliked how now, after years of comfortable apathy, he found himself analyzing her past and guessing at her previous position.

He wished he could think of anything else.

"It was a great show of faith from the general," he said at last, desperate to drown out his own thoughts. "Sending us so far to bring back an amulet. She might never have heard from us again."

Lisveth shrugged. "She didn't know we've already taken one. And we gave her the Singer's Eye. She doesn't know she can't trust us."

The words felt more loaded, now, and Galen hated it. "We told her where the Player's Eye was, before it was taken. We probably seemed like a good bet."

"Well, let's not tell her about yours."

"But we're giving her the new one, from the Vernal House."

"The Dancer's Eye." Lisveth nodded. "When this is all over, it can go back to the temple."

"Just one left," he mused. "Even if Kayvin found it, would it be enough to do what they need?"

"That's not the point," Lisveth reminded him. "The problem is not whether he can use them, but whether the Rideis will wreak havoc and raid to get them."

Galen shook his head. "That's so, but... General Artextra has to be intending something more than just hoping we're quick enough to find the amulets before the Rideis do. She expects us to bring them back to her. They aren't...weapons to her, are they?"

Lisveth did not deny it as quickly as he would have liked. After a long moment she said, "Pasiphae Jade wants them to save the Rideis, or that's what I took from our conversation. Even in all Kayvin's frothing about her, he's always said she wants to save the people. And one does not save a nation by protecting one person at a time from magical attack."

"So they also do something else."

"Or they can do something else together, at least." She blew out her breath. "That's a little worrying."

It was. But now Galen was no longer thinking about her calling down magic that killed her sister, so it was a bit of an improvement.

The afternoon passed a little more easily, despite ominous suppositions about the amulets' capability. But as the western sky darkened, Lisveth began to look doubtful. "I don't like that weather," she said at last. "It's going to be nasty tonight."

Galen agreed. "Should we turn off early?"

"There's a town north of here, if you remember. A little out of our way, but worth the detour if the storm delivers what that sky is promising."

As if to underscore her words, lightning flickered in the clouds, too distant still for thunder but a clear warning.

"We won't lose much time," Galen said. "It's not as if the general expects us on a particular day."

She nodded, and they took the next crossroad.

They were half a mile out of town when they caught up with a traveling group. The first to greet them was a family, moving to join relatives on a distant farm, whose four children ran in noisy circles around their slower-moving wagon. The oxen did not so much as flick an ear as the children passed; they had long grown accustomed to the play. There was also a vegetable peddler, taking his donkey cart of leftovers to another village market, and a man in scholar's robes and a backpack of books, whom they seemed to have caught mid-lecture.

"As I was saying," he continued once the polite greetings were done, in a tone that suggested interruption for such frivolity was an affront, "there should be laws against it. They shouldn't be allowed so freely everywhere, and certainly not in schools or temples. It's all right if they're in the service of the government, in some cases, but there's no reason the ordinary people should be using magic without some sort of control."

Galen gave him a sidelong glance. "Sorcerers and mages? Who would control them?"

"That is the point, exactly! They are difficult to control, and so they must be controlled, or there will be no controlling them when they need to be controlled."

"Do they all need to be controlled?" Galen immediately regretted his question; he had only encouraged the man. But he didn't like what was being said beside Lisveth, already fragile.

Indeed, the lecturer was already nodding vigorously. "Yes, of course. Anyone with an unfair advantage should be reined in."

Galen nodded toward the laughing children ahead of them. "You and I are bigger and stronger than they are. What should be done about our unfair advantage?"

The man harrumphed. "Obviously I am not a danger to them. I'm a ordinary man, without any advantages. And I'm a father with a son at home, so one can see I'd be trustworthy."

"I see," Galen replied, letting his tone suggest he observed more than the stated point.

"But sorcerers are suspicious. They make the laws of nature lie."

"It's not a lie if it works," Galen said in what he thought was a practical tone.

"Magic violates nature and the right order of things."

"You cannot fly above the ground," Lisveth said at last. "Your feet stay firmly on the road. But if you jump, you can leave the ground, even fairly high with enough effort. You'll come back down; the effect is not permanent. But for a brief moment, you violated the laws of nature."

"That's different," he said stiffly.

"How is it different?"

"Jumping is a natural thing."

"For those who can jump, yes. Magic is a natural thing, for those who can work magic."

"But magic is learned."

"You've got a son?" Lisveth gave him a sidelong glance. "Did he start jumping as soon as he hit the floor, still damp from birth? Or did he need a year or two of rolling and crawling and walking and then, with a few falls, some tentative first jumps?"

The man scowled. "It's no secret a babe must learn to crawl and walk. But magic is learned later."

"Like abstract reasoning," Lisveth commented blandly. "I suppose both abstract reasoning and jumping must be harder than crawling."

Galen smiled to himself. Then the man called Lisveth a word Galen hadn't heard in years, even in the dingiest of public rooms.

Lisveth's head snapped toward him, her eyes narrowed. Galen took two quick steps to put himself between them, and he gave the stranger a disapproving look. "That's unkind and unnecessary."

"I don't—"

A hole opened in the road beneath the man's next step, and he yelped and wheeled his arms as he stumbled to the side, trying to catch himself. His foot hit the edge, just saving him, and he took a few quick steps to regain his balance. "What was that?" he demanded, amazed and breathless.

"You should have jumped," Lisveth said flatly.

He looked back. Galen glanced back, too, and saw a shallow rut, much smaller than it had appeared a moment before. The other man made a confused sound. "I thought..."

He thought he'd seen a greater danger, though his foot had remained safely on the road. Galen did not bother to summon much sympathy for the man who, now somewhat embarrassed, fell silent. No one asked him to resume.

The town turned out to be larger than Galen had expected, with a small partial wall of its own and a respectable staging ground for merchant caravans. The family turned aside before the gate, as they planned to stay with their wagon. The sullen scholar bade terse farewells to the group and went his own way. The peddler advised Galen and Lisveth on the most likely street for lodging and then turned toward a friend's home.

The streets were busy—they were not the only ones seeking early shelter—and Galen hoped they would find a decent room still available.

Lisveth caught his arm and jerked him backward. "Watch out!"

"What?" He let her drag him to the nearest corner.

"Kayvin and Yovela." She peered around the wall. "I think I saw them."

Galen looked through the traffic. "Are you sure?"

"Not really. But enough to be careful."

Galen leaned with her. "Why would they be here?"

"I don't know. Get back!"

"You're looking."

"You're easier to pick out in a crowd."

He scowled at her. "Rude, but not inaccurate. Let's just find someplace to sleep before all the rooms are spoken for."

"Wait—is that...? I think she was looking back at us."

Galen peered out again, feeling foolish. "If they're here. then they're looking for shelter, too, and we're going to be angry if they take the last room."

Lisveth elbowed him, but gently, and she pulled back from the crowded street. "All right, then. See if they kill us in our sleep. It'd serve you right."

Galen laughed, just happy that she was elbowing him and joking again.

The first three inquiries they made were rejected, all rooms being rented for the night. But the fourth house had one room left, which Galen took without question. Then they sat down to supper.

Outside, the wind picked up, blowing trash in the street and crowding the public room with more people. Lisveth rested her chin in her hand, watching the door. "If Kayvin walks into this house," she said through a mouthful of cooked greens, "you take the Painter's Eye—that's the golden one—and disappear. I can hide myself."

"Are we sure someone can wear two amulets at a time?"

"Oh." Lisveth frowned. "Hm. I wonder if they might interact in some way. Probably not an experiment for a crowded public room."

But only traders and craftsmen came in from the weather as the windows darkened.

"You were a little troublesome tonight," Galen said after a moment, giving her a crooked grin. "Not that he—that purported scholar—didn't have it coming."

"What else could one expect from a degenerate sorceress?"

"He shouldn't have said that about your magic."

"That isn't why I did it," Lisveth said flatly. "It was for the much shorter name he called me."

"Fair," Galen conceded. "But he was still wrong to criticize you for using magic."

"He was wrong about the reason," she agreed.

Galen glanced at her. "And for saying you were suspicious and a liar."

Lisveth didn't answer.

Galen, suddenly worried, reached out to tap her forearm. "Hey. He was wrong to say you were suspicious and a liar."

"I did lie."

"You didn't."

"I didn't tell the truth."

Galen could argue, but it would do little good. "You're not suspicious."

"I am the most suspicious," she countered sharply. "I had a bandit name of my own, you may recall. I was a plague and a warning." She looked straight ahead. "He's wrong about the magic, but he's not wrong about me."

Galen leaned on his elbows. "Have you thought all this time that—that you were..." He couldn't figure out how to say it without sounding both ridiculous and heartless.

She did not look at him. "Someone who shouldn't be welcome in a temple?"

"You're not. I mean, you're not someone who shouldn't be. You know what I mean—you should be."

"I'm about the worst person you could welcome in a temple. I've burned one and I've robbed two."

"You..." Galen strained for something to say. "Look, you could have used an illusion any time you bought a pie or a purse, to make the shopkeeper think you were giving them the right number of coins. Have you done that?"

"I've thought of it, yes."

"But have you done it?"

"No."

"See? Then you're not as bad as you think."

Lisveth pushed herself back from the table and cocked her head to squint at him. "Is that what they taught you at your temple lessons, farm boy?"

"No."

"Good. Because that's the stupidest thing I've ever heard said aloud."

Galen was stunned. "What? No, it's..."

"If a man stole a chicken but did not steal a wheelbarrow, wouldn't you still call him a thief? Or if a man forced three women but did not force a child, would you say he wasn't so bad, really? Or what about a man who had forced just one woman? Would you think ill of him only until you met the man who had forced three?"

Galen shook his head, his footing lost. "That's not what I meant."

"That's exactly what you meant, only you hadn't thought it through to that point yet. There will always be someone whose crime is just a little worse, a little more horrific, and it's absurd to argue the possibility of a worse crime absolves an ordinary one. A sliding morality is no morality at all. Fair night, you'd have us all kicking puppies because at least we weren't skinning kittens."

Galen pressed his lips together. "I only thought..."

"I know what you thought," she said more gently. "But you won't make me feel better by speaking to me as if I'm stupid."

"I never meant you were stupid."

"Then let's not pretend we're anything but what we are." She lifted her mug to signal for a refill. "Thirsty, and maudlin, and ready for a change in subject."

Galen put down his half-finished drink. "I'm going to the privy. You'll...be here when I get back?"

Lisveth shrugged. "Where would I go?"

He didn't know. That wasn't exactly the question he wanted to ask, but he didn't know how to ask another one. "I'll be back shortly."

CHAPTER 104

GALEN HAD TO STAND in line, and when at last it was his turn, the privy stank. He hurried as best he could, and then he made his way back into the public room. The timbre of the room was mostly the same; nothing had happened while he was outside.

He didn't know what he was afraid of, exactly. He did not expect Lisveth to start a brawl, or for her to be recognized in this place, or anything else he could name. He only felt unsettled, and he did not know how to rectify it.

Lisveth was leaning against the wall, standing behind the bench. She didn't see him, approaching from the side, as she stared into the tawny liquid of her mug. He stopped a few paces away, observing her, wondering what he could say to her.

"Hey."

Lisveth glanced up from her drink and set her eyes on the young man approaching across the narrow table. She blinked twice, as if to fix him in focus. Galen watched him, ready to step in if...but Lisveth could always handle herself.

"Hey," the young man repeated. "My friend over there says you're mercenaries for hire. I want you to beat up someone for me."

Lisveth's face and voice remained flat. "What?"

It wasn't a *what?* of interested inquiry, more a *what?* of polite disbelief and a chance to retract or refine his words, but he did not pick up the difference. "I was supposed to get a position at the carpenter's shop, where I've been apprenticing. I've been expecting it for a while now. But this other one, he's getting the position, and I've got to stay on as apprentice."

To judge by her eyes, the story could not have interested Lisveth less.

"Not only that, but then he's gone around town and told everyone, proud of himself. And sure, it would have been common knowledge in the end, but he didn't have to make out that he was grand by telling everyone I'd have to work under him. And now he's in here—that's him, in the corner, in the green jacket, you see?—he's in here talking about his great future and the plans he has to add another workshop and hire more workers, as if it's his shop, and he knows this is where I drink. He's come just to make trouble, and I want to hire you to give it to him." He dumped a handful of coins onto the table. "I've got money. I have two taler here, and if he can't use a hand or arm for a while, I can double that."

Lisveth sighed as if she'd decided against her better judgment to make the effort to correct him and already regretted it. "There are something like a half dozen things wrong with what you've just said, and I won't bother with most of them. But several of them work out to nearly the same thing, which is that nothing has been injured except your pride."

"My pride?" he burst. "What about him bragging about taking my place, rubbing my nose in it?"

"What about it? Sure, it's a poor look for him too, if he's bragging and not just sharing news, and now you're both wallowing in the mud. But what does that change? It's still just your pride. Do you think it's an actual trespass that he's more skilled than you?" She pointed a finger from her mug. "I doubt you expect life to be so fair when the odds are in your favor. Well, nor do I; I certainly don't feel like gifting you any of my own sense to make up for your lack. No, you're just stung that you were shown up, and that's the whole of your complaint."

"A man's got to have pride," he retorted.

"He does," Lisveth agreed easily with a lift of her mug. 'But a man's pride isn't such a blushing baby's bottom pale, shrinking from every little brush and showing every minor mark."

He swelled in anger. "You can't—"

"And see, thanks for proving my point. Look at you, ready to throw knuckles because I said you were too easily provoked."

He bit off his words, clenching his jaw. Galen suppressed a smile.

Lisveth propped one foot on the bench and leaned forward, her drink hand resting across her knee. "Go back and get over it."

He scowled. "Now who's proud? Don't pretend you're so high and holy! Don't tell me you've never wanted revenge for something."

Lisveth's expression went still and cool. "Oh, I've wanted revenge. I've poured my soul into dreams of revenge, and for something much greater than stung pride."

"See?" But his voice was weaker before the dark of her expression.

"But then I stopped thinking like an un-napped child, and I considered it more clearly. What did I want revenge for? For someone being more gifted than me? For someone offering temptation? For the outcome of my own actions?"

His tone was skeptical. "You're trying to tell me revenge won't change anything."

"People who say revenge won't change anything are short-sighted. Revenge wouldn't bring back the dead, that's true. But it would change many things." She paused for a drink. "If I took a life for a life, the pinnacle of vengeance, it wouldn't make the world as if those I hated had never existed. They would be killed, and others would feel that. And then one of them would seek revenge, and a new ripple would start, and on it would continue, forever." She looked at him. "Or did you think the world would stop on the day you won your petty battle?"

"I wouldn't..."

"You want me to maybe maim someone in your village, and you think nothing else would happen? You think no one would strike back, at me or at you or at your little brother they mistook for you in the dark?"

"I..."

Lisveth shook her head. "Revenge would only continue the disaster they started, and I refused to do their work for them. Instead, to balance the disaster, I wanted to do something great and heroic. I dreamed I'd save a town from a landslide just before it was buried, or fight away one last dragon from a guildhall, or something like that." She shook her head. "But I don't have that kind of magic. All I'm really good at is lies. And lies are never going to save the world."

Confused, he frowned. "I don't care—"

"Shut up. My wish to do something heroic, to save a thousand lives—that was just another kind of revenge. And it wasn't any more possible than the first kind, and it still wouldn't change what had already happened. Saving a thousand lives won't undo a thousand deaths, and breaking another man's arm won't make you any better at turning a lathe. You need to learn that early."

"You're not so much older than me."

"I am; I'm just prettier. As I was saying, I was lucky enough to meet someone who could talk me into something else. I realized I can't be a great hero or do anything to change what's already been done."

He started to stand from the bench. "I don't see how any of this matters to my—"

"Sit down!" she snapped. "I'm not saying this for your benefit. I need to say it, and I'm saying it to you because I can't tell anyone whose opinion I care about."

He blinked as he worked through this.

Lisveth continued speaking over his confusion. "I'll never make a great difference. But I can make a small difference, again and again, and that's worth more than a silly dream of stopping a landslide. That will do more to correct the broken world than my best revenge." She waved her hand in a lazily derisive gesture. "I know you don't understand. Pray you're fortunate enough to never understand."

He screwed up his face and delivered his best dismissal. "So you think you're a tiny hero, now? A savior of small things?"

Lisveth leaned over the table. "Even on my tiniest day, I am still not the hero of taking up a shopboy's petty fight in a village pub for scraped together change. If you can't be enough of a man to admit someone else's skill, then at least be a big enough boy to have your own tantrums." She gestured with her drink, sloshing. "Go."

He scowled, but he had no comeback, and he pushed away from the table and retreated across the room.

Galen held his breath, not daring to move. Lisveth remained bent over the table, her head lowered. After a moment she asked, "Did you hear all that?"

Galen hadn't realized she knew he was there. "...Yes."

She nodded once, a jerky, curt movement. "Good." She straightened and drained her drink.

Galen wanted to tell her he was glad he'd heard, he was glad to hear she had found some solace in their tiny heroics. But she had said she could not talk with him, and he would not cross that. Not yet.

He sat down and reached for his half-empty drink. Lisveth did not look at him. He kept his own eyes on his hands, wrapped around the cup.

She had thought he would leave. She had been afraid, for years, that he would go if he learned who she was.

She thought her true self had been a secret from him.

She looked into her empty cup. "I need another drink."

Galen raised his hand, and a serving woman across the room nodded and turned for a pitcher. He had maybe half a minute.

He leaned closer to Lisveth's shoulder and put his mouth close to her ear, so that he could speak softly in the lively room. "You don't need to say anything. Just hear me out."

She started to turn. "What—"

He moved closer, dodging her eyes, and spoke over her. "I have lived with you for three years, and you are my closest friend. I have gone to sleep beside you and shared meals with you, and I have fought beside you and with you at my back, and I have covered my eyes in the face of attack when you asked me to trust you. It doesn't matter what name you were called by, or what you wore, or what great men your father sat beside. I know who you really are, who you are today. I know why I am grateful to you and why I admire you."

She sat absolutely still, rigid and silent. He drew back and smiled at the approaching serving woman as she reached for Lisveth's cup. Lisveth moved as if cracking a rime of ice from her skin and smiled stiffly at the woman as Galen extended his cup for his own refill.

He drank, keeping his eyes forward but keenly aware of the warmth of her shoulder beside his. Lisveth did not drink, not right away, but at last she lifted the cup and sipped. When he glanced toward her, her cheeks were streaked with damp, but she clutched her cup and looked ahead.

Around them, patrons called to one another and laughed at shared stories. A few minutes later, two plates of vegetable stew were brought to them. Galen began eating, and after a moment, Lisveth did, too.

She relaxed as she ate, surreptitiously wiping her face dry and scraping her plate with a hunk of bread. Galen found himself breathing more easily, too. At last they finished their meal and went upstairs to their tiny room.

"Cramped, isn't it," Lisveth observed flatly.

"Choice is for those who stop earlier in the day."

"At least the bed looks free of bugs."

The room was warm with the heat rising from the rest of the house. They lay back to back, not quite touching, and listened in the dark to the rain falling overhead.

CHAPTER 105

GALEN WAS AWAKENED BY a persistent low knock at the door. It continued, not a pounding of urgent emergency but a continuous quiet annoyance, irritating and unrelenting in the quiet after the rain. At last he rolled out of bed, coiling his blanket to hold its warmth, and made his bleary way to the door.

Lisveth propped her head upon her arm. "If they want payment for the room, they can have it in the morning, minus eight percent for every minute it takes me to fall asleep again."

"And another eight percent for me." Galen pushed a hand across his eyes and opened the door.

Yovela waited outside, a canvas satchel in her hands, her eyes flicking from Galen to the empty corridor and back. "I'm sorry to wake you, but I could not miss this chance. I did not know when we might cross paths again. May I come in?"

Galen glanced at Lisveth and stepped back, making room for the Rideis to enter.

Lisveth rolled upright in the bed, hugging her blanket around her. "Good morning, or whatever unpleasant time it is." She yawned. "I suppose this is important? And secretive?"

Yovela was appraising them in evident surprise. Lisveth was in her daily clothes, as they usually slept, but without her jacket and cloak, as the room was warm. Galen was mostly dressed as well. He hadn't thought of the picture they might present—or might not present—until Yovela's open observation.

"Are you not lovers?" she asked bluntly.

Lisveth blinked. "Fair night, I did not wake for this. I'm going back to sleep." She slumped back into the bed.

An awkward feeling stabbed through Galen's stomach as Yovela looked at him. "I—we're—"

"Why would you assume we were?" Lisveth asked from the pillow. "It's not obligatory between any given pair."

Yovela held up a placating hand. "I'm sorry, I did not mean to be rude. Please, let us talk."

"I suppose you might not realize the question is rude," Lisveth said through a yawn, pushing upright again and crossing her legs, "since your prince declared your own position clearly enough."

Position. Galen snorted. Lisveth threw him an irritated glance.

"I am in his sera qadra," Yovela said evenly, "but I am not his lover."

"Hold on." Galen went to the fire and crouched to stir it into life. "What is this sera qadra? I don't think we have such a term."

She frowned. "It is an elite group of pleasure servants within the household."

Lisveth made a gagging noise.

Yovela magnificently ignored her. "It is for pleasures of all sorts, body and mind. Prince Kayvin chose his sera qadra primarily for their voices, to best serve his music."

"I guess everyone has a type," Lisveth said dryly. "So how many people might a sera qadra contain?"

"The last Arch Potentate, Gromgest, had a sera qadra of forty."

"Sounds expensive."

"A sera qadra illustrates its master's prestige, and a royal sera qadra in particular. Most courtiers would not have nearly so many."

"And your prince?" asked Galen.

"He had twelve, before he sent them away."

Lisveth raised an eyebrow. "Sent them away?"

Yovela nodded. "Pasiphae Jade was a royal concubine. The day she killed the Arch Potentate and took the Shining Gem, Prince Kayvin dismissed his own sera qadra. He sent all of them away but for me."

"Just couldn't do without you," drawled Lisveth.

Yovela's expression remained flat. "I stayed because he could trust me even in a palace of enemies."

"How sweet. Just the two of you. And Dielo, I think."

"And Dielo, placed into the prince's sera qadra by Pasiphae Jade."

"A possible traitor?" Galen recalled.

"Possible," she agreed. "First to the prince, but now to the usurper."

"That sounds promising," Lisveth said, straightening and tugging at the blanket. "What has brought him to your side?"

Yovela opened her mouth, looked down, and said nothing.

"Ah," Lisveth observed wryly.

"It's not like that," Yovela said quickly. "He is a virilo bound to the prince. But he is becoming something more."

"And you like that."

"I respect that." Yovela's expression hardened. "I did not come here to speak of the sera qadra, but of the usurper. It is my duty to my prince to stop her."

"Indeed? And will you be your prince's assassin against his father's murderer?"

Yovela shook her head. "He would never permit it while she holds his mother hostage." She looked from Galen to Lisveth, holding their eyes. "That is why I have come to you."

"We've never taken an assassination." Lisveth gestured to the single chair. "But please, have a seat, and tell us what you have in mind."

Yovela seated herself where she could look at both Galen, squatting beside the revived fire, and Lisveth on the bed. She folded her arms on the satchel in her lap. "You are mercenaries, as I understand it. You will take any job for hire."

"Not quite, but you have the general idea," Galen said. "We have some guidelines."

Yovela waved a hand in dismissal. "You have fought bandits, and I have seen you challenge my prince. You are not afraid of combat. And you are a sorceress," she said to Lisveth. "You have magic."

"Enough," agreed Lisveth non-specifically.

"Then I wish to retain your services. I want you to go to Saragu, the capital of the Rideis kingdom, and free my prince to take his stand against Pasiphae Jade."

"Wait." Galen was briefly stunned. "You want us to go into the Rideis land? Across the mountains?"

She nodded. "Prince Kayvin is stronger than he appears, but he cannot openly counter her as long as she holds his mother captive." Yovela's mouth thinned. "Pasiphae Jade has imprisoned Shining Gem Raea within a block of ice in a fountain, held right within the throne room for all to observe."

"That's confidence," Lisveth observed in quiet horror. "And the court accepted this?"

"There was a faction devoted to restoring the Amethyst Prince, but the leader was executed. Whatever remained has disappeared, while Pasiphae Jade rules and Prince Kayvin is limited. But if he were to challenge her himself, the nobility might stand with him. She is generous and clever, but a woman has never before been Arch Potentate, and she is not loved."

"Then why doesn't he just rise against her?" Galen asked.

"She has already frozen and melted one of his servants, disfiguring her to demonstrate the threat. She could do worse to his mother."

"Frozen and melted..." Galen needed a moment to process the words, and his stomach heaved.

"This is the reason I come privately to you. He dares not oppose her directly."

"If he kills Pasiphae Jade, will that release his mother?"

Yovela shook her head. "If Pasiphae Jade dies, the Shining Gem dies within the spell."

Galen looked at Lisveth. "That's possible?"

Lisveth was pursing her lips and looking toward the ceiling, as if a spell reference were written there. "I can't say it's something I've come across before, but it might be possible. I mean, it seems it *is* possible, just not a branch of magic I've studied."

"But you can undo it," Yovela said urgently. "If you rescue the Shining Gem, then Prince Kayvin can oppose Pasiphae Jade without hesitation."

Galen was not quite sure how to frame this idea in his mind. "But if we cross the mountains, isn't that—wouldn't we be opening a war? Sayinia against the Rideis ruler?"

"The Rideis interloper," Yovela corrected. "Who has already sent bandits into your land, and who will send an invading army if she does not get what she wants."

"What does she want?"

Yovela's mouth turned down. "I would have thought she might have been satisfied with ruling as Arch Potentate. But she wants Prince Kayvin bent to her will, and she sends him on these impossible errands. How can he be expected to find artifacts lost for so long? She put a ring through his nose with her talk of saving the people from the spawning, but I am not convinced the danger is real. No one else has predicted a coming spawning, and we have only stories from the past. It might even be legend."

"What is a spawning?" Galen asked practically.

"Monsters hatch, all at once, and surface to feed."

"Like cicadas?"

"Yes—cicadas that eat you. It's said they feed on Rideis and on livestock." She shook her head. "But again, we have only stories. Even cicadas do not lie so long in wait, but appear again and again within a normal lifetime. She speaks of monsters that might appear every two hundred years." Her lips thinned. "It is an unsound claim with which to taunt and threaten a prince."

"You do not think these brooding monsters are real?"

"I do not know. But our histories say we once fought dragons; I cannot believe we should give up our Amethyst Prince for something less."

Galen looked at Lisveth. "It's not our prince."

Yovela turned to him. "Again, she has already sent bandits, and she will send warriors. You would be protecting your own people. And you would have the gratitude of the Rideis throne once the thing was done."

"Gratitude is a wonderful thing," Lisveth interjected, "but it buys precious little at the market. We are mercenaries for hire, as you said, and we would require hire."

Yovela nodded. "I thought that would be the case." She unfastened the satchel in her lap and withdrew a leather case dyed in deep purple, round and flat, a bit over a handspan wide with roughly a finger's depth. Galen had never seen anything like it before. Yovela unclasped the case to reveal a coronet.

Lisveth leaned forward. "Fair night."

The coronet was worked of gold, with curls and twists all along the band as if it were a wave just breaking upon the shore in little bursts of artistry. Within each twist was set a cut gem the size of Lisveth's smallest fingernail, a rainbow of faceted firelight.

It was enough to buy them a cottage, a bit of farm, starter livestock, and perhaps a small castle with an accompanying title in case they wanted to join the local nobility.

"This is a court headdress for the royal sera qadra," Yovela explained. "I brought it in case I needed money to help my lord. Now I offer it to you as payment for this task."

Galen was dazzled, and a little afraid of what the glittering coronet represented. He struggled for an excuse. "But won't it be missed? Won't you get into trouble if you've stolen it?"

Yovela's mouth quirked into a grim smile. "If Pasiphae Jade falls, my lord will forgive me for buying him an ally. If Pasiphae Jade remains on the throne, I am a dead woman anyway, once she no longer needs the prince, and a misplaced headpiece will be the least of my worries."

Lisveth's eyes were locked on the coronet. Galen, watching, knew the power of its draw for her. "I don't know if we can accept this charge," he began. "We don't know the magic involved, and—"

"We will do it." Lisveth looked at Galen. "The magic will be my worry, and I'll take responsibility for that." Her eyes drifted back to the coronet. "And if General Artextra has finished with us here, there's no reason we can't cross the mountains on our own volition, no longer contracted to the state army."

"Wait," Galen said. "I think I should have some say in this, too."

Lisveth looked back to him. "Does your say have enough gold and gems to buy us a few years where we could each have our own mattress, every single night?"

"It might have something about living to enjoy those mattresses."

"Does it have anything about surviving in a land overrun by Rideis soldiers ransacking for food and taking human prisoners?" Lisveth frowned and looked at Yovela. "We would not be prisoners, yes? We would be safe in—what was the city?"

"Saragu," Yovela answered, "and while I believe Prince Kayvin would grant you safety once you'd rendered him such a favor, of course Pasiphae Jade would not forgive you if you are captured. But you would have the advantage of entering her palace unknown, and with a guide to the palace. It's probably less risky than some of your other hired work."

Lisveth turned back to Galen. "See? Less risky, pays well, saves their land and ours. Now, what's your say?"

Galen sighed. "So, to be clear, you are asking us only to unwork the magic spell that holds the queen? Not to fight Pasiphae Jade ourselves, or her guards, or the Rideis army?"

Yovela shook her head. "You can go in by night—the fountain is not guarded, she is confident in her spellworking—and do what you must, and in the morning, with his mother released, the prince will be free to exert himself against Pasiphae Jade like a Rideis warrior."

"So we just go into the palace with you, break the queen out of her magical ice, and we're free to go with the payment? Even before the general uprising?"

Yovela nodded. "Exactly."

Galen exhaled. "Then I suppose we're in."

Lisveth grinned. Yovela nodded again, pleased. "Thank you. Now, we're returning to Mandoral in the morning. Follow us when we depart today, but at a distance."

"Giving up on finding any more amulets?" Lisveth gave her a cheeky grin.

"Delivering the amulet we have acquired." Yovela smiled at Lisveth's dismay. "We have the red eye you left with the general."

"How?" Lisveth demanded.

"We took it from the aide. Don't wo—"

"Anela?" Galen leaned forward. "Did you harm her?"

"Don't worry, I said. She is well, only a little frightened and probably roundly scolded for answering the door. But His Highness wouldn't return without one, and now we have one. Please do not try to take it from us; I've worked very hard to convince him we can return with just this one. That is your chance to follow."

Galen sat back, suspicious but placated for the moment.

"He will not want you to know the way, so stay behind, but you will need to watch carefully. Stop outside Saragu, in the trees, and I will come back along the road for you by night. I'll pay you once the spell is broken."

Galen nodded. "We'll find a secluded place and wait for you."

Yovela buckled the satchel and stood. "And now I must return to my lord, before he wakes and misses me."

Lisveth raised an eyebrow. "I thought you were not lovers?"

"People may stay together even if they are not lovers," Yovela said, lifting her chin slightly. "They do it for practicality, for warmth, for companionship. Or did you think the state of lovers obligatory between any given pair?"

She went to the door and out into the dark corridor, leaving Lisveth gaping angrily behind her.

CHAPTER 106

GALEN CLOSED THE DOOR and stared at the wooden planks for a moment, his shadow wavering in the firelight.

"She did see us in the street," Lisveth muttered behind him. "Followed us here. Asked the landlord what room we were in. Waited to come in the night." She huffed and jerked at the blanket. "I think I'll take that eight percent for his giving up our room so easily."

Galen returned to the bed, where he sat on the edge.

Lisveth looked at him, and her expression faltered from irritation to worry. "You all right?"

Galen didn't know how to answer. "I hope Anela's all right."

She nodded. A moment later she said, "I should have let you argue more about the job. But...fair night, Galen, that's a rich prize."

"I know." Galen turned to her and tipped his head. "We could have just taken it from her. She's not a sorceress or a fighter."

Lisveth snorted. "We wouldn't just steal it—" She stopped.

He raised an eyebrow. "We aren't thieves?"

Lisveth didn't smile. She fixed her eyes on the woven blanket. "You were thinking, we aren't killers. But you're also thinking, that's not true, is it."

Galen's stomach wrenched. "That's not what I meant."

"But you have to think of it now. And now you're sitting on the far edge of the bed, remembering you thought you could make me something better than a thief, and thinking how little you knew then."

He shook his head. How quickly she'd forgotten when he'd tried to say... But how could a few words overwrite years?

"And I—I can do this thing she asks. I can help. Kayvin said he's trying to save his people. Yovela says it will save ours. Think of what it..." Her voice faded. She looked down, ashamed, and dug her fingers into the blanket. Her next words were small and quiet. "This is the landslide. The dragon. This is my chance."

Galen's stomach twisted, and he shifted fully onto the bed, leaving a small space between them. "Think of Andrea, going safely home instead of being lost in a bandit gang. Think of, what was his name, Rolf and his stolen land, returned to him. Remember when we—"

"I know what you're trying to do," Lisveth cut him off.

"Didn't you mean what you told that apprentice tonight?"

"That was when there was no dragon!" She caught herself. "I know what you mean. But you know, even as you say those things, you're wondering how many people died in that fire in Atalasu City."

Galen didn't answer. He had wondered.

"No matter what you say, no matter what I do, that fire will still be on my hands. And you're always going to remember that."

He could not tell her she was wrong, and that cut him. He wanted to tell her she was wrong. But she would hear the doubt in his voice.

He looked down at his knees, avoiding her eyes.

"It's all right," Lisveth said quietly. "I knew this might happen someday. That you would find out. I might have wanted it, in some way."

Galen looked at her, but her eyes were on the blanket. He supposed aloud, "Because you didn't lie to me."

She didn't answer.

"You told me your real name, when you could have been anyone. You didn't tell me a false history, when I'd have had no reason to doubt it. You gave me an incriminating explanation after the temple, when I would have believed any tale you spun about assault or theft or treachery." He jerked his head to the side. "At any moment, you could make me believe I was walking a country road and walk me off a cliff to protect your secret. And you haven't."

Her lips twitched, but she did not answer.

"You did not lie to me, because you are a more honest thief than you pretend even to yourself. And you might have wanted it, in some way, to know if you could trust me—"

"That's—"

"—the way I trust you."

She went still. He had stunned her.

For a long moment, she did not move. He hardly breathed. Finally she asked, in a voice smaller than he'd ever heard from her, "Still?"

"More than ever." The words scraped his soul raw, bared him. He was supposed to be reassuring her, but it felt as if he was the one balancing on needles.

She twisted her fingers into the blanket. A long moment passed, and he wasn't sure either of them was breathing. The flames sank into the embers, leaving a glow.

"Tell me a secret," she whispered. "The deepest, darkest secret you have. Something that needs me to trust you."

Without thinking, he leaned forward and kissed her.

It was quick, and light, and unpracticed. He drew back, shocked and ashamed, but the warmth of her stayed on his lips.

He looked down, certain he had trespassed. This secret, buried and hidden even from himself, was too much, even for her whispered demand. "I'm sorry," he tried, his voice unsteady. "I shouldn't have done that."

She still hadn't moved. Finally she said, "I asked for your secret that required the most trust."

"I didn't..." But he could not explain what he had done. Not to himself, not to her.

Lisveth stared at the blanket bunched in her hands.

Galen swallowed and reached for his pillow. "I'll sleep on the floor."

"No." She reached for his arm, but without the force of the day before. "Don't go."

For one irrational instant, his chest tightened with surprised hope—but she was not confessing a similar secret. He looked down, heat burning his face and ears as he flushed in the way he hated. "I don't want to make it awkward."

"Then don't make it awkward." Her throat worked. "Fair night, I only just told you I killed my sister and ruined a city. I need a moment to think through anything more." Her voice dropped. "But I can't—that's too much like leaving, and I...I can't. Not just now."

He turned his arm and slid her hand into his. "I'm not leaving."

Her sigh was soft, almost imperceptible, but it felt like a weight slipping away. She squeezed his hand, and then she gently pulled away, somehow again the self-possessed Lisveth he'd always known. "There's no one I'd rather have at my back than you, farm boy. But keep your back close, so you don't hoard the blanket. We have an early start if we want to watch for the Rideis leaving town." She turned and settled into the mattress, pulling the blanket to her shoulder.

Galen nodded. He lay down, his back just touching hers, and tugged the blanket into place.

He watched the embers flicker and fade, brief warmth melting back into the darkness. He thought about how he would not be able to face her in the morning light. He thought about how ironic it was that her doubt of him had underscored his trust of her. He thought about atonement, and whether it was possible in a lifetime.

He lay on his pillow and watched the embers darken and cool.

CHAPTER 107

GALEN PULLED THE LIGHT chain over his head and looked at the amulet in his hand. "I feel a little odd, parting with it."

"You don't have to leave it." Lisveth's arms were crossed over her chest.

He shook his head. "I'm not carrying an amulet to them. This whole premise could be a trap to get these."

"I already told you, Yovela and Kayvin can't know we have more than one. They weren't at the pawnshop or at the Vernal House. And if they're after yours, I can think of a dozen traps less outlandish than hiring us to invade the Mandoral palace."

"Still. I don't want to worry about it." He handed the amulet to Lisveth, who dropped it into a bag with the others. Then she set the bag into a shallow hole nestled between two young elms, and she began to scrape the dirt back over it.

"Do you see them yet?" she asked.

Galen looked back toward the road. "No one, not yet. It's pretty early still."

They waited in a patch of trees outside the town until they saw Kayvin and Yovela, carrying light packs and shading their eyes from the rising sun as they headed east. "I suppose we follow them," Galen said, watching them walk toward the mountains. "But not too closely."

"Nor so far behind that we lose them," Lisveth said, shouldering her pack.

They did not. The first day they walked due east, staying mostly to one of the king's roads and finally keeping east when the road did not. Galen and Lisveth hung back a little more than half a mile, easily able to sight the Rideis among the other light traffic on the ground rising toward the mountains.

They camped at a distance, keeping their fire small and shaded, and the next morning they followed east again.

When they came to the foothills, they saw Kayvin and Yovela turn south from the road for several miles, until they came to a river that cut its way from the higher ground. "They must follow a river pass," Lisverth observed, as they prepared to spend a second night on the track. "That would be the obvious choice."

But the next morning the Rideis passed over the river and climbed a little way, finally entering a dry rocky ravine that led east again. Galen and Lisveth had to follow more closely in order not to lose them in the steep ground. Galen was the first to see their confusing destination, coming over a ridge and walking into a small box canyon. "Um, it might be I'm not the most perceptive, but do you see anyone here?"

Lisveth swiveled to examine the rocks. "Steep walls, no Rideis. They vanished."

"Is that a magical thing?"

"No. And if it were, she wouldn't have expected us to follow them."

"You have an amulet that lets you disappear," Galen pointed out.

"Right, but even if they'd stolen it, they couldn't have both used it."

Galen nodded. "Good point." He started walking, examining the ground and walls. "But Yovela wanted us to follow, and she must have known this would be difficult, so did she leave us a clue?"

"Or another sign." Lisveth closed her eyes and took a long, slow breath, and Galen stopped walking.

Lisveth exhaled, just as slowly, and turned quietly in a sunwise circle, facing outward to all the points of the compass. She completed five full rotations, her face upturned as she spiraled her magic outward and waited for its reverberations. Then she turned anti-sunwise once. She raised her hand and pointed. "There."

Galen followed her gesture. "Are you sure?"

"I'm sure." She opened her eyes. "Oh."

She was pointing at the end of the box canyon, directly into the wall.

Galen followed the line of her finger, picking his way until he reached the rough rocky jumble. "I don't want to belittle your magic, but I don't think this is our best—wait, what's this?"

A glove lay on the ground, crumpled as if it had fallen, with a single finger extended toward the rock wall.

Lisveth came to stand beside him, looking at the sign. "If the Rideis magic can walk them straight into a mountain, then I'm afraid I'm outclassed."

Galen frowned. "We're on the right track. We have to be close." He crouched to frown at the glove. "Surely she wouldn't—ch!"

Crouching brought his sight line below the largest of the rocky tumble, and he could see a dark gap behind the fallen boulders.

Lisveth squatted beside him. "Well, I suppose we're walking straight into a mountain."

"This was not what I imagined," Galen said. "Fair night. I don't want to crawl through the dark."

"Maybe it's not dark all the way through," Lisveth said cheerily. "Let's see where it goes."

She went first, and Galen crawled after.

It remained dark. Galen felt for each new measure of ground, unreasonably afraid the low path would open abruptly into a subterranean pit even though he knew Lisveth would encounter any such sudden abyss first. They crawled for long minutes, so that he imagined they must have crawled for half a mile, though he told himself he overestimated the distance. His eyes began to play with the unrelenting dark, reporting indistinct colors and shapes that were certainly not there,

"Fair night," grumbled Lisveth, winded with the unusual effort, "are we going to crawl through this entire mountain range?"

Galen did not trust his voice to answer.

And then the sounds of Lisveth's progress stopped, and Galen's heart twisted with irrational fear. But when she spoke, her voice held no fear. "Fair night," she breathed again, this time in awe. "Wow."

"What is it?" Galen asked, wondering if he should reach forward to feel for her trailing boot. "What happened?"

She moved again, and he heard the scuff of her crawling change. When she spoke, she whispered. "I'm standing up. Come on out."

Come out? Into what? But as she moved aside, Galen could perceive rather than see a widening in the tunnel, and then he saw the lights.

The tunnel left off being a narrow tube just large enough for crawling and opened into a larger corridor, twice as tall as a tall man and perfectly round in shape, as if an enormous earthworm had burrowed it into the mountain's base. The walls and ceiling, one smooth surface, bore a hundred million blue-green pricks of faint light, marking a long tube in either direction. To the right, the lights wrapped all of the tunnel, but to the left, there was a narrow strip of darkness along the floor.

Lisveth set her hand on the wall and stifled a giggle. 'They squirm! Oh, they're tiny animals, I suppose." She withdrew her hand, and a dark spot marked her touch. "And they don't like being disturbed."

"No question which way they went, then," Galen said, turning toward the footpath. "I wonder how long the lights stay out?"

Lisveth leaned toward her mark on the wall, faintly silhouetted by the points of eerie light. "There are a few faint dots still here."

Insight came to Galen. "That's a solid track, not individual footprints," he pointed out. "That's not the steps of two people. It's a trail left by many people. The lights don't recover, not quickly if at all."

Lisveth straightened beside him. "Good observation. That means we don't have to follow too closely behind—which is good, since this tunnel will funnel our sounds clearly."

"So move quietly," Galen said, adjusting his pack. "Let's go."

CHAPTER 108

THEY WALKED FOUR DAYS in the dark.

Occasionally they heard laughter ringing down the tunnel toward them. They did not smell any fire—which made sense, given the limited atmosphere—and did not make a fire themselves. Several times they saw black pools of darkness where the pinpricks of blue-green light had been extinguished and smelled the urine or dung of previous travelers. Lisveth, crouching and wrinkling her nose, thought there might have been even tinier spots of light forming in the older piles, perhaps recovering or even feeding upon the waste. Galen did not care enough to investigate.

They stayed as quiet as possible, picking their way along the nearly perfectly smooth trail and communicating when they needed mostly in gestures. Galen began to feel panicky for the light and occasionally he gasped for air, though there was no lack. His eyes had adjusted remarkably well, distinguishing the millions of blue-green pricks of light on the enveloping walls that defined all of their world. He knew Lisveth by her silhouette; even after days in the dark, it was not enough light to make out her face.

They counted the days by when they slept, which they did when they heard the voices ahead of them stop in one place. Often there was singing at these times, faint and indistinct, but Galen thought he liked it.

There was another music in the tunnel, which did not come down from Kayvin and Yovela but somehow through the walls. Galen sensed it more than heard it, and for a long time he thought he only imagined the song as he had imagined colors and shapes to fill the dark. At last he whispered to Lisveth, "Do you hear that?"

"I thought it was my imagination," she answered with a sense of relief. "What is it?"

Galen stopped walking and dropped his mouth open to listen better. He thought the soles of his feet rumbled slightly with the sound. "It's like the rock is singing."

"It's a mountain," Lisveth said practically. "Mountains don't sing."

Now that he knew it was real, he could track it better, a rise and fall of profoundly deep tones. It seemed the melody hung in the dark just out of his grasp, as if he could almost touch it but could not quite hear it, as if it were not for his ears.

It stopped after a few hours, and resumed hours later. Was it constant, and the tunnel took them near its source only occasionally? Or was someone else traveling in the tunnel and singing?

But that night, Galen was awakened by the sense of overpowering song, though he could hardly hear it. He sat up on one elbow, as if he could peer into the dark.

Beside him Lisveth rolled to face him, and she whispered, 'I feel it, too."

He could feel it—that was the better word. The song rumbled in his chest and tickled his ears, as if a hair had lodged within. He had the most peculiar sensation that something was about to happen, something that would leave him awestruck. He looked up the tunnel.

The blue-green specks of light went out.

The tiny stars around Lisveth and Galen still glowed their faint light, but the end of the tunnel had gone entirely dark. Galen's stomach caught, and he blinked hard despite the futility.

The lights rippled. What could put out the tiny lights? So far only contact or damage had darkened them, and Galen couldn't imagine anything affecting the entire circumference at once. This looked more as if—as if something had blocked out the entire tunnel.

Lisveth's hand fell on the back of his wrist and held tightly, as if in warning. But Galen could not have made a sound.

The enormous shape glided across the far end of the tunnel, blotting out the light and the air, and the rock rumbled with the sound that was almost music, and Galen did not breathe.

And then the pinpricks of light reappeared, rippling into view, and the creature—or whatever it had been—was gone.

After a long moment, Lisveth spoke in a soft, shaken voice. "What do you think that was?"

Galen shook his head, though she couldn't see, and answered with another question. "What do you suppose made these tunnels?"

"Fair night. I would have preferred to wonder about that from outside the mountain."

They lay awake a long time, but the song of the mountain remained quiet, and they did not see another enormous shape blot out the lights.

On the fourth day, Galen and Lisveth followed the trail to another branch tunnel that led off at crawling height. The dark foot trail ended at its mouth.

"I never thought I'd be glad to crawl through a rocky gullet," Galen said, pushing his pack back so he could fit more comfortably. "I even feel I'll be grateful to enter the Rideis kingdom. At least they'll have sunshine and breezes."

They crawled a long way, until at last light began streaming down the sides of the tunnel around Lisveth's body. Galen squinted against it, his eyes aching with the adjustment, and then realized it was cold and silver instead of warm and golden. They had come out in the dark.

"That's good," Lisveth observed. "Gives our eyes a night to recover before the sun."

The moonlight was brilliant enough, Galen decided. When they finally emerged, he cupped his hands about his eyes to shade them as if it were noon.

"Where to?" Lisveth wondered aloud. "I almost miss that dark little trail. At least it was easy to follow."

They picked their way down the slope from which they had emerged, and the answer became obvious. Far beyond them, silver and white in the light of the half moon, rose a city of colonnaded buildings and vaulted roofs.

"Saragu," Galen supposed. "It is beautiful, I guess. That tall overwrought bit might be the royal palace."

"So I guess we go close enough that Yovela can find us and bring us inside," Lisveth said. "At least we're in the open. If you see a slow-moving rabbit, hit it with a rock. I'd sell a shoe for some hot food."

They'd gone about a mile when Galen did manage to catch a rabbit, and they settled down to butcher and cook it. Though they had no herbs or seasonings, Galen could not remember the last time anything had tasted so good.

The road after a few hours led into a wide gate, and outside it seemed the best place to wait for Yovela. They settled well off the road and behind deep brush—better to work harder to spot Yovela's approach than to risk being spotted by anyone else—and made themselves as comfortable as possible, which despite the cold seemed easier to Galen than it had inside the eternal tunnel.

Yovela did not come.

They waited a day, and then another, and at last they had to admit she was not coming to escort them inside. Perhaps she did not know where to find them, or perhaps the situation within the palace was not as she had left it and she had changed her mind.

"Even if that were the case," Lisveth mused, "you would think she would come to tell us. Even just to say we weren't needed and we should go home before someone finds us, lest we betray that we learned of the secret mountain tunnel by her."

"Then maybe she's not worried about someone finding us," Galen said. "I hope that doesn't mean she's sent someone to look for us."

Lisveth shook his head. "Not nearly enough guard traffic on the road for that, and I hope that doesn't mean she's not able to come for us. Maybe we weren't as quiet as we thought."

Now it was Galen's turn to disagree. "I don't think Kayvin would harm her even if he learned what she'd done. He may argue with her, but he's pretty fond of her."

Lisveth heaved a sigh and flopped onto the ground. "Then I guess we keep waiting."

HOMECOMING

CHAPTER 109

KAYVIN ENTERED THE PALACE with a curt nod to the guards—Pasiphae Jade's guards, and he would have to grow used to that somehow—and turned toward his quarters. Yovela walked a half-step behind, at his shoulder, her gaze roving over the guards and passages as if she had not seen them before. Well, it had been weeks, after all, and now that he thought of it, the breezy corridor did feel almost constricting after the open roads of Sayinia. That was due less to the painted ceilings, though, and more to the inescapable presence of the Arch Potentate.

The guards' messenger must have reached Pasiphae Jade's residence quickly. for Dielo was running up the hallway from the opposite direction as they neared Kayvin's own door. "My lord! You've come home." He looked as if he wanted to embrace the prince, but he did not.

"Obviously," Kayvin said, with a grin to blunt the jest. He shed his cloak and let the virilo take it. "I hope you've been well?'

"Well enough, thank you," answered Dielo.

But his expression countered the words, and a chill ran through Kayvin. Pasiphae Jade had held the virilo as another hostage, but there should have been no point to harming him if Kayvin were too far to know of it. Surely—and yet... He looked at the virilo appraisingly, and Dielo dropped his eyes. That was curious. "And Lirin? Is she well?"

"She is. She's at her lesson right now—her music lesson," Dielo added with a smile, raising his head. "She'll learn of your arrival when it's finished. I thought you might want time to rest before she demands to hear everything you saw over the mountains."

Kayvin gave a tired chuckle. "I can imagine her asking, yes. Music lessons, eh? Good for her."

"I will draw your bath, my lord," Dielo offered. "It's chilly today, and you have a long road to wash away."

"It's warmer than in Sayinia," Yovela said firmly. "But a hot bath sounds more than lovely. I'll take my own, I think."

Kayvin sent a servant to inform Pasiphae Jade he would come to her soon. Then he sat in his study, looking over his empty desk and wishing he could feel as if he'd come safely home from the human lands. But he felt no safety or relief here.

Yovela stood beside his chair like a bodyguard. "Promise her nothing. Give her the amulet, but promise her nothing. Swear her no allegiance."

"If she thought she had my allegiance, she would not need my mother. Or Dielo."

Yovela drew a quick, frustrated breath. "My lord, I will repeat yet again, her promise of your mother is—"

"It's not that." Kayvin took his time readying his next sentence, hating the words he had to tear from his chest. "It's not only that. But she says she can save the people."

She did not answer.

"It's not that I am happy to give up my birthright. It's not that I think she's a better ruler. Empty void, the woman is a murderer and more, and it pains me in every way to see her where she is." He shook his head. "But she understands the spawning, and if she can stop it—she can save people. My people. And as they are my people, then I must do everything possible to save them, even give up my throne to her."

Yovela's mouth made a firm, hard line. "If you cared for your people, you would not place a murderer over them."

"And was my father a more attentive Arch Potentate? She says she asked him to intervene, before she killed him to take his place. Who else remains, then? Lord Fretton? Or another courtier skilled in wringing power and wealth, without real concern for all those who died on that roadside beneath another man's banner?" Kayvin shook his head, weary beyond physical exhaustion. "And so she, as much as I hate her, may have the throne."

"For the time, perhaps. Until the spawning is done, and the people are saved, and you can take your place."

Kayvin forced a weak smile. "It almost sounds as if you wouldn't let me do anything else."

Yovela snorted. "I don't intend to live under her rule, my lord."

Kayvin's smile gained a little vitality. "Thank you, Yovela. I mean it."

Dielo appeared at the study door. "Your bath is ready."

At the bathing pool, Kayvin slid his legs into the water and waited as the prickle ran up them to make him shiver. "You were right; a bath will feel very good now that I'm home."

Another servant carried in a stack of towels. Dielo ran a scoop through the water to pour over his shoulders. "Weren't there baths in Sayinia?"

"Not quite like ours."

Dielo winced as he adjusted his position, and Kayvin again found himself suspicious. "Are you well?"

Dielo smiled an impeccably professional smile. "Of course, my lord. I am only glad to have you home."

Kayvin got fully into the bath and lay back, letting Dielo wash his hair. Soft steps marked the steady travel of servants between garden and bathing courtyard and apartment rooms, and he was vaguely irritated but too weary to order the untrained servants away. Dielo was undoubtedly giving them warning glances.

When at last Kayvin emerged from the water, shivering in the autumn air even in his protected courtyard garden, a warmed sheet was waiting for him. A maidservant extended a tray with scented oils, which he waved away.

Yovela did not answer his call as he walked back inside. She was probably lingering in her own bath, enjoying the warmth and privacy. That was just as well, as he wasn't sure he wanted her to accompany him to his report.

Kayvin hardly waited to be announced at the throne room entrance—of course she would receive him here, a merciless reminder—but strode directly in, holding Pasiphae Jade's eyes as he crossed the tile floor, now strewn with carpets for the cooler season. Once he reached the correct distance, he made a perfunctory bow, just enough to appease her without showing too much obeisance. Yovela would have liked that, at least.

"You're late," Pasiphae Jade said without preamble or welcome.

"It was time well spent."

"Are you certain you were not exploring the delights of the human lands with your sera qadra?"

"Yovela came to assist me. I cannot fault her for that."

"Yovela?" Pasiphae Jade stood, rolling her shoulders, and scowled as if he had lied. "I thought perhaps you had stopped to compose music, or whatever it is you do."

"What I do with my leisure time is my concern, not yours."

"It can become my concern," she warned. "When the prince I order to Sayinia spends his time playing at songs and ignoring the task at hand, then I must do something about it. You are wasting my time and yours." She came forward, disgusted. "You say you are both a poet and a warrior, but I see laziness, softness, decay. I see the reason you are a servant instead of a ruler. Poetry is not power."

Kayvin seized her arm, squeezing until he felt bone. "Roses are red, violets are blue. Bring harm to my mother, and I'll destroy you."

Pasiphae Jade's muscles ground under his thumb, and her eyes widened. That startled him. For the first time he thought of her as—as an opponent, someone he could physically resist, instead of a political and magical force. Did she in this moment fear him? For the first time, he felt a thin gold thread of hope as he faced her.

Pasiphae Jade pulled free of him with a little shake and turned her back on him. "Spend your breath on rhymes, then," she said coolly. "I think you should have more important tasks, but please yourself. Since you won't have your sera qadra woman to do it."

Kayvin needed a moment to follow her sentence. "What? What do you mean?"

Pasiphae Jade reached the other fountain at the front of the throne room, and Kayvin realized it was not running as usual. No water played over the top, and an inch of ice rose visibly above the basin's edge.

Kayvin's heart clenched in his chest. "What have you done?" he breathed.

Pasiphae Jade flicked a hand toward the fountain as she passed.

Kayvin did not want to approach the fountain, did not want to look, but his feet obeyed the murderess without his consent, and his eyes tracked down the fountain to the block of ice.

Yovela stared sightlessly up at him, her mouth open to scream or shout or call for help, one hand up to protect her eyes and the other extended as if reaching for her opponent.

Not her opponent, Kayvin thought. She had never been able to fight Pasiphae Jade.

His throat closed, and he could not breathe.

"I heard she had no intention to live beneath my rule," Pasiphae Jade said pointedly. "She may not have to."

He stared at the ice. Who had carried Yovela's words to her?

"Unfortunately, it takes such a great deal of effort to perform that spell," Pasiphae Jade said, crossing the floor to the first fountain. "I'm afraid my intense efforts there distracted me from maintaining the first one."

Kayvin spun, ice in his heart, and saw the first fountain's basin was still frozen. He went to it. The ice's surface dipped along one side, and there was a little pool of meltwater remaining on the top. Within that pool were the toes and arch of his mother's left foot, partially thawed and distorted with blobby, misshapen flesh.

"Thawing must be done so carefully if the integrity is to be maintained," Pasiphae Jade said. "But then, you already know that, as you've seen this before."

Nala's disfigured face.

Kayvin clenched his fists uselessly. "Why?" he managed, fighting down the taste of vomit. "Why did you do this? You had no right—you had no reason..."

"I have every reason," she snapped. "I have hundreds of reasons in this palace. I have thousands of reasons in this city. This is not only about me and about you, as you seem to pretend—it is about every person in this kingdom. And you are playing with your pleasure servants, just like your father, instead of bringing me what I need to save our people."

Kayvin tried to make his hand move, to touch his mother's foot, but he was terrified of what he might feel. He reached instead for the surface of the water and found it slushy and thick, refreezing.

"The rest of her is unharmed," Pasiphae Jade said, as if that should reassure him. "It's only a little damage. More can be prevented."

"I've brought you an amulet!"

He wanted to kill her. He wanted to seize her throat, call up his fire, burn her into ash on the throne room floor, and bury her soot deep in her own ice.

But that sagging, misshapen foot held him frozen in place, as helpless against Pasiphae Jade as his mother and Yovela.

"Did you? Good. Let's have it." The Arch Potentate turned toward the throne with measured strides, honed for long years to catch a man's eye. "And perhaps now you will give up trying to outmaneuver me as if we are playing with game pieces and perhaps now you will be able to focus entirely upon your task," Pasiphae Jade said archly. She looked over her shoulder at him. "Unless you think your virilo might be too distracting as well?"

Kayvin wheeled. "Leave him alone."

"Because if you think he might keep you from completing the tasks I have set you, I can remove that distraction as well."

"Leave him alone." His voice was tight, strained. "Don't touch Dielo, nor any other member of my household." Which was distressingly small now, he realized, and clearly full of her own agents.

She smiled. "I suppose you know best. And if it should turn out otherwise, I can always do what is necessary at that time." She seated herself on the throne and spread her gown like a spill of frost. "Now, the amulet?"

Kayvin swallowed hard against the stone in his throat, clenching his fists as he sucked air and tried to steady his voice. "The red eye." He brought out the wrapped amulet he'd taken from the general's aide's desk.

"Just one? Again?"

"They are more difficult to find than you thought." Kayvin shivered with the force of his despairing anger. Yovela's voice came again to him, the only part of her that could: *She will kill you both.* But it hadn't been Raea and Kayvin, not yet. It was Raea and Yovela.

He abruptly turned on Pasiphae Jade with murder in his heart. He dropped the amulet and seized her, his nails digging into her arms, heat pouring from him as if the fire wanted to burst from him. "You control me only as long as you threaten them. You cannot release them, lest you lose your hold over me. But as we both know that, you have denied me hope and thus have no control."

Pasiphae Jade smiled as if amused by a child's tantrum and threats. "My dear prince, son of my lover, heir to my throne. Let go of me."

"I should kill you."

"You cannot—and for the reason you already know, or else you would have already struck me down."

Kayvin shook her. "You cannot keep promising me you will release them. Either you hold their lives hostage, or you do not. I will not work toward a reward you cannot possibly give."

"You are remarkably bad at counting, my prince. Isn't that supposed to be important in music and poetry?" She nodded toward each of the fountains in turn. "I have two hostages."

He looked toward the fountains despite himself.

"I can give you one when you complete your task, and hold the other to ensure your good behavior toward your Arch Potentate."

Kayvin went still as he realized what she meant. Cold began to spread from his torso, cooling the fiery power in his limbs.

"Think on it, my loyal prince. I have promised to release one when you've done what I've told you. My promise is still good, my word uncompromised. I called you my heir, and that can be true: You can blend your father's rule and mine by keeping Lirin at your side, as Fretton wanted to do." She shook herself loose and stepped away, brushing her hair back into place. "And in the meantime, you can decide which of these you want to free."

Kill her. He would kill her. He would burn her—but he could not, not now, not now that he'd seen what would happen if she suspended her magic and let the frozen women blacken with frostbite, sloughing their melted flesh.

Kayvin ground his teeth and bowed, not in respect but so he could avoid her eyes and hide his own disgust. "Take the amulet I have brought. I will go and try again."

CHAPTER 110

KAYVIN STUMBLED INTO HIS quarters like a boat drifting into a mooring, aimless and unmanned. Dielo got up from the floor where he'd been sitting, his expression concerned. "My lord!"

The sight of him—returned safely from Pasiphae Jade's keeping—prompted Kayvin to think about when Pasiphae Jade had taken Yovela. She must have done it while he had been in the bath.

Had the virilo been part of it? Was he an agent of Pasiphae Jade, as Yovela had insisted? He had been near to hear where Yovela had said she did not mean to live beneath Pasiphae Jade's rule. It would have been easy for him to mislead Yovela out of her quarters to waiting guards. He could have done it while Kayvin was soaking or dressing.

But Pasiphae Jade would not have needed his assistance to take Yovela, and Kayvin could not live with more suspicion. He should send Dielo away now, he knew, but he was caught with the realization that the most likely traitor in his household was also his one remaining friend.

He needed a friend.

He walked past the watching virilo and sat down beside his lyre, pulling it into his lap and letting his fingers pass unthinking over the strings.

"Lirin sends her greetings. She would like to see you when you can."

Kayvin nodded. He would like to see her, too, but she could not offer the kind of steady friendship he needed now.

Galen and Lisveth, he thought, had been two people he might have called friends, in other circumstances. He had liked them when he first met them, all free travelers along the road exchanging stories on a friendly spring evening, and he thought they had liked him as well. That was, he suspected, why they had been upset to learn he was Rideis, and why he had wanted to keep it from them. Of course there would be distrust for their races' tumultuous history, but more, they had each felt betrayed by a friend, and he had wanted to prevent that.

Some feeling or respect had persisted, however. They had asked to talk at the temple treasury instead of seizing him, as they might have done.

But none of this mattered; Galen and Lisveth were leagues away on the other side of the mountains. He was here, alone with Dielo and a few servants, any or all of whom might have Pasiphae Jade's order to report on him or to kill him in his sleep.

He sighed and began to pick out one of his simpler melodies, a soothing roundelay he could reproduce without thought.

Dielo glanced out the door and then nodded toward the study. "Would you like to review your recent harmony notations?" he asked, in a manner nearly as awkward as the question. "Shall I bring you some refreshment while you work?"

Kayvin paused his playing and eyed the virilo. Was this some sort of trap? No, the study had a single door, but it was hardly necessary to trap Kayvin in it, not when he'd only just come from Pasiphae Jade. If she'd wanted him taken, it could have been done easily while he stood stunned over Yovela's icy prison. "Yes, I suppose so," he said slowly.

Dielo fairly danced his way to a table with, Kayvin saw now, a plate of sweets and fruit, and he paraded them into the study as if he served at one of the court banquets. Kayvin took his desk chair, sitting back to make room for his lyre, and watched the virilo put the plate on the far side of his desk. "Go ahead and play, my lord, please," he said quietly. Then he went to the tall shelves across the room, the ones Yovela had once emptied in fury.

Kayvin strummed absently, absorbed in watching Dielo. The virilo selected a scroll and partially unrolled it, tipping it upright, until a metallic object slid into his waiting palm. He replaced the scroll without rerolling it and turned excitedly to Kayvin. "My lord."

It was an amulet. Kayvin stared at it, leaving an unresolved chord hanging in the air. It was an orange-eyed amulet. "Where did you get this?"

"I tried to follow you," Dielo said, his tone a blend of apology and pride. "I lost you on the far side of the mountains, where the road split. I must have chosen the wrong direction, and I never caught up with you. But I was able to search where you did not, and I found an amulet, and I've brought it back."

Kayvin reached out to take it.

"It's exhausted, drained of magic, but I believe it can be revived. It seems to regain energy at least temporarily when it's been held," Dielo explained, like a small child with a favorite toy.

"And you brought this to me?" Kayvin shook his head. "But you clearly returned before me. How did you get permission to go in the first place?"

Again, that blend of apology and pride. "I did not ask. She was so certain in her authority, she bound me with words instead of cords, and I simply left after you did."

Kayvin stared at him. "You left! Empty void, I did not think…"

Dielo looked down. "I did not think I could, either. But I am glad I did."

"And when you came back?"

"She was displeased," Dielo admitted. "But you were not here to see if she punished me, and she is not one to waste her time or anger."

"That's a small relief, I suppose." Kayvin examined the amulet. It stung his fingers faintly, leaving a tingle through his hands and forearms. It was hungry.

"I kept it for you," Dielo said anxiously. He wanted to be acknowledged. "I didn't tell her about it, not even when she was angry. I kept it for you."

Kayvin nodded. "Thank you. I'll take this to her. Even exhausted, it's an amulet, and she can restore it as she wishes."

Dielo's hand hovered near the sash at his waist, fingers closed, but he said nothing. A moment later, he dropped his hand and stepped back from the desk. "I'll go and tell Yovela, if I may, that you have another amulet to offer."

Kayvin looked at him sharply. "Yovela?"

"Won't she be glad to hear another amulet has been found?"

Kayvin clenched his jaw. "Yovela was taken."

Dielo stared. "But—she came back with you, she was just here..."

"While I was in my bath, she was taken." Kayvin could hardly speak the words. "She's in the throne room fountain. In ice."

Dielo's dismay appeared genuine. He stared, jaw hanging, and then drew back. "No. No, we have to—we have to... She was only just here."

But there was nothing they could do. Kayvin would take the second amulet to Pasiphae Jade and hope it was enough, and even if it was, he would face an impossible choice.

But he had another amulet. It was a chance, and he had few of those.

Not today, though. He had to think of a plausible reason he had presented only one at first, without returning within an hour to give up another. He had to think on how he would demand a release. He had to think on which woman to ask for.

Across the room, Dielo had folded his hands to his torso and was staring down into a corner, frozen with the shock of Yovela's predicament. Kayvin wondered, almost against his will, whether the shock was feigned. The story Dielo had told was that he had left the palace on his own, had found an amulet, had returned without consequences and kept his prize from the Arch Potentate...

"I want to see Lirin," Kayvin said. "I hope she's well? I'd like to see her."

Lirin might dissemble for her mother's or Dielo's sake, but he thought she was not yet so skilled a liar as the others. He'd have the truth.

CHAPTER 111

LIRIN SHOWED LESS RESTRAINT than Dielo had, and she immediately flung her arms about Kayvin. "I'm so glad you're safely home! I worried about you every day."

Kayvin didn't mind the breach in protocol—she was either a member of his sera qadra or a princess, or both, and so a little forwardness could be overlooked—and hugged her in return. It felt good to embrace someone genuinely pleased to have him. "It's good to see you, too."

Lirin settled onto a cushion. "I asked for a map of Sayinia, to try to follow your path, but of course there was no way to know which roads you'd taken. But I wanted to look at all the cities and imagine where you were." She leaned forward. "Will you tell me everything? I want to know what they look like, what they talk like, what they do. Tell me about their buildings."

"Their buildings?" Kayvin suppressed a smile. "I'll tell you some, at least. But first, will you tell me what's happened here? I'm told you're taking music lessons."

"Oh!" She made a face. "He wasn't supposed to tell you. I wanted that to be a surprise."

"Well, I promise to be surprised when you play."

"Where's Yovela? Does she also know?"

Kayvin's stomach churned. "She's...not here."

Lirin went still, eyes wide. "Did something happen to her? Was it the humans?"

Kayvin made himself answer. "No, it was today. Pasiphae Jade took her."

Lirin did not move.

"She is in the courtyard with the Shining Gem."

At last Lirin looked down. "I'm sorry. I'm so sorry."

She sat rigidly in place, until her shoulders gave a little heave. Kayvin opened his arms, his throat too tight to speak, and she folded into him, beginning to cry. "I'm so sorry!"

He wished he had words to comfort her, but he had nothing to comfort himself.

"I'm so sorry," she sobbed after a moment. "For Yovela. I'm sorry." She drew back slightly. "And I'm sorry I'm crying, when I'm supposed to be welcoming you home, and the last you saw of me, I was crying then too." She rubbed her hand against her face. "I'm not much good for a sera qadra, am I?"

He looked at her, surprised. "Is that still what you want? Wouldn't you rather be a princess?"

"It's the same thing in the end, isn't it?" She sat back and sniffed. "I'm sorry. This was supposed to be a happy meeting."

Kayvin set his elbows on his knees and lowered his voice. "Can you tell me something?"

She leaned forward and nodded. "What?"

"Dielo said he left after I did, to go to Sayinia." If he made it sound as if he was unsure, she would speak more freely.

Lirin nodded again. "Oh, yes. He left the same day. Her Illustrious Excellency was furious, because she thought you'd arranged it. It wasn't until he came back alone that she considered maybe it wasn't your plan all along."

"And because it turned out not to be my plan against her, she forgave him?"

Lirin barked a dry little laugh and looked away.

"He said she was displeased, but she didn't punish him."

Lirin's mouth tightened, as if she were trying not to cry or to vomit. "She—she had his ankles tied behind a column, and his hands tied in front of him. And then his feet were flogged, and he—and we all had to watch."

Kayvin listened in sick horror. Flogging the soles of the feet was a brutal punishment, reserved for brutal crimes—or, he supposed, for virilos who embarrassed those they were meant to adorn.

"He said he'd gone to find you, but he gave up and came back to Saragu. She was so angry, because he'd gone of course and also because his chit was gone. She accused him of stealing it, but—I think he didn't, because he would have given it up, wouldn't he? Under that? I would have." She shook her head, eyes wide. "I would give it up right away."

"But he didn't have it?"

"He didn't have it. Eventually they stopped, and I suppose they think it was lost somehow or one of the other virilos hid it to make trouble, or something."

Where had the chit gone? Kayvin closed his eyes. *Dielo, why didn't you give up the amulet to save yourself?*

"After that, she took him to the throne room, and I don't know what happened. But he didn't scream." Her voice was small, and she had curled into herself on the cushion. "He was in bad shape when they carried him in. They put him in a pit in the men's quarters and left him for two days. I thought...I was scared for him. I didn't think foot flogging would do that. But then he came out, and he was all right, I suppose. He stayed quiet and out of the way. Until you came home." She brightened slightly.

Kayvin rested his face in his hands and tried to swallow his distress. Everyone around him, all suffered.

Lirin scooted closer to him. "I'm sorry. I thought you were asking what had happened to him."

"I was. I didn't know enough to ask specifically. Thank you for telling me." He looked at her. "Did he ask you not to tell me?"

She shook her head. "We never talked about it."

"Regardless, I'm glad you told me." Empty void, why hadn't Dielo said anything? But he wouldn't, and certainly not in front of the other servants, and...

Lirin was watching, unblinking, waiting for him to solve things. He could not, but he could talk of something else. He sighed and sat up. "Now, tell me about your music."

She gave him a sad, embarrassed smile. "It feels so silly, after Dielo and Yovela..."

"We have to acknowledge the good things, too. And I want to hear what you're doing."

"I asked to learn to play," she said shyly. "I thought it would be useful if I came back to your sera qadra."

He took a little breath. "Lirin—you know you'll never really be part of my sera qadra. You know—"

"I know you won't ever take me to your sleeping pit," she said bluntly. "And that's all right. Because you're the only man to treat me as a sister, and anyway I'd have to be some sort of fool to be a maid instead, wouldn't I?" She gave him a tentative smile.

Kayvin did not have the words to answer her. "You know, I might not have a sera qadra."

"What?"

"I might not be a prince." That was as much as he could say aloud, as yet. Whether he left the palace, if permitted, or whether Yovela was right and he would not survive his limited utility...

He smiled over Lirin's confusion. "What do you play?"

She was visibly relieved at his change of subject. "The psaltery! There was one I could use, and I thought I could also sing, if I'm ever good enough to do both at once."

Kayvin nodded toward his shelves. "Want to show me?"

"Oh, I'm not nearly good enough yet." But she got up and took down the instrument.

"I met a man who played the psaltery, the first time I went across the mountains," Kayvin mused. "He went from town to town, playing music and carrying news. Show me if you're ready to play from one garden to the next."

She laughed, and she began a very simple piece. Her rhythm hesitated beneath her nervousness, but the tune was recognizable, and Kayvin nodded along, adjusting when the beat faltered and smiling encouragement.

They had grown tired of waiting for Yovela. "We should go inside," Lisveth declared.

Galen boggled at her. "Are you crazy? Go into the Rideis palace? When we're practically at war, and when our only ally hasn't shown up as promised?"

"Exactly," Lisveth said. "We might have suspected she wasn't reliable. And really, the rest of it is to our advantage. Who will expect two humans to break into the Rideis palace?"

"I am not even going to bother to try answering that," Galen said. "Look, we said we would try. We've tried. Now we should go, while we still have a way home."

"We haven't tried. Not really. We haven't even attempted to get into the palace, much less to chip the queen out of her ice."

"And just how do you think we're going to get into the palace?"

Lisveth flopped onto the ground, extending her legs. "We don't look so very different. I can easily make our clothing match the guards' uniforms or something. And we have a little bauble that will help us to go unnoticed." She flipped back the soft flap of her bag and fished out the golden-eyed amulet.

Galen's chest tightened. "How—why do you have it? Where are the others?"

"They're all here." She drew them out almost apologetically.

"Lisveth! We left those in Sayinia! We weren't delivering them to Prince Kayvin!"

"And we won't. I think it's clear he didn't plan this; if we were going to be led into a trap, it would have happened already. If I'd planned such a trap, I would have grabbed us as we crawled blindly into the light. But we've been left here, free to wander or return home, so this wasn't just a ruse to draw us over."

"But now—"

"Now we can use them to complete the task we were hired for."

"You lied," Galen said flatly.

Lisveth's face went flat. After a moment she said quietly, "Yes, I suppose I did. Faced with bringing you into the home range of the most terrifying sorcerers of recorded history, without your protection against harmful magic—yes, I lied." She picked up his amulet and stared down at the deep blue eye. "And I would again."

Galen did not know how to answer.

Lisveth blew out her breath. "And as long as I was armoring you, it made sense to bring the others along, too. So here we have our small arms chest."

"All right." Galen gestured to the two remaining Eyes. "But if we lose these here, we are going to be in such trouble."

"Only if they discover the amulets are missing, and only if they know we were the ones to take them, and only if we don't return as heroes for preventing a destructive war. And if this goes poorly, we won't return at all. Overall, I feel our odds of escaping punishment are pretty good."

She dropped the golden Painter's Eye over her neck, and Galen's eyes slid off her as if she were oiled water. He blinked and concentrated to bring her back into view. "And what about me?"

"I'll be right beside you with an illusion, not to worry."

"And once we walk through the front gate without so much as a mild interrogation, where will we go?"

"We'll find a place to hide, a storage room or maybe one of the brothel quarters they seem to favor here, and look for Yovela. If we don't see her, we go ahead and find the frozen queen, as we agreed, and then we demand our reasonable payment."

CHAPTER 112

EVEN BY NIGHT, THE throne room was not hard to find. A strip of moonlight from the outer yard entered by the arcaded walkway and the massive doors, falling across the tiled floor. High above, skylights showed a splash of stars across the night sky, but they did little to light the way.

With the large doors safely closed behind them, Lisveth made a small torch of fire in her upturned palm, showing the dark reach of the hall. On either side of the door two fountains played, their bright splashing incongruous with the creeping shadows and Lisveth's and Galen's fear of discovery. At least the sound would help to cover their footsteps and whispers.

At the end of the long hall was a dais with a single throne, mounted with a bull's head that seemed to stare down at them in judgment. Lisveth made a rude gesture at it. "That's for centuries of invasion," she whispered. "Now we'll help your prince. You're welcome."

There were two more fountains on either side of the dais, but these were still. This was where they would find the queen, then. Galen chose the one on the left.

The wide basin that formed the base of the fountain was full of water, frozen so that it pushed above the lip of the fountain itself. As Lisveth came beside him, her light illuminated a dark shape trapped within the ice, a feminine form with upflung arms shielding her face. "Is that the queen?" she asked.

Galen had to try twice to answer. "No."

Lisveth pushed the fire further forward. "Fair night. That's Yovela."

For a long moment they stared at the woman they had known. She had plainly tried to escape the spell, tried to fight it, to no avail.

"Well, we know now why she did not come," Lisveth said heavily.

"Do they know she hired us?"

Lisveth took a slow breath. "I doubt it. No one was searching outside, and there aren't enough patrols inside. If they thought mercenaries had been hired, they would be looking for us. But we walked right in here, unhampered."

"So it's a trap," Galen suggested pragmatically.

"Would you lay a trap by letting a sorceress approach your magically sealed linchpins of leverage? I don't think so." Lisveth indicted Yovela. "I think she's here for other reasons."

"Well, then, sorceress, why don't you see what you can do about these magically sealed linchpins."

"I want to see the queen first."

They went to the other fountain and discovered an older woman, handsome and afraid, with part of one foot blackened and disfigured in shallower ice. Galen reached for it but didn't quite touch it. "Was that an accident?"

Lisveth, holding her hands just above the foot, shook her head. She closed her eyes to deepen her concentration. "I don't think so. This magic is newer—only just here. This tiny bit of spell was undone and remade."

"You mean—you mean she was thawed and refrozen? Just her foot?"

Lisveth opened her eyes. "I can't be certain. But I think we know why Prince Kayvin is so anxious to please this woman he hates so fiercely."

"Fair night." Galen couldn't think of many words beyond those. What monsters did they face here?

But Lisveth seemed to understand. "All right. Keep an eye on the door for me." She passed the fire from her palm to a thick candle she drew from her pack. "I'm going to go down pretty far into the spell, so I might not hear anything, even something you think should be terribly obvious. Wake me if something happens. I want to see this magic and work out how to undo it."

She knelt and braced herself against the edge of the fountain basin and placed her hands just over the surface of the ice, flinching a little with the unnatural cold. She closed her eyes and went still.

Galen watched her for a time, but it was deeply unnerving to see her and the queen frozen equally motionless on opposite sides of the ice. Eventually he stood, trying to remain quiet, but Lisveth did not seem to notice. He picked up the candle, irrelevant to Lisveth's closed eyes, and walked back to the first basin to look down at Yovela.

She was clearly the same woman who had hired them, but she looked different, supine and afraid in the ice. He did not like to see her either, he decided. He replaced the light near Lisveth and walked to the end of the throne room, where he peered between the closed doors for lights of passing guards. He saw nothing.

He made the long walk back to the head of the room, and he went to the throne.

It felt daring and disrespectful to mount the dais and approach a king's throne—or a queen's, he supposed—but there was no king or queen present. He circled the throne, examining the foreign carvings, and then stopped in front of it.

Dare he?

He turned to face the door, gazing over the empty hall. Three women remained utterly still before him, unseeing, unaware of his temptation. He took a step backward so that the seat brushed the back of his knees.

Lisveth's head jerked and she caught her breath, and Galen jumped. He left the dais and hurried toward her. "What did you find?"

Lisveth pulled her hands from the ice and folded them to her chest, suddenly shivering with unexpected violence. "Oh night. So cold. So cold."

Galen pulled a cloak free and threw it around her, and then he grasped her hands within his own. They were brutally cold. "You kept them on the ice too long."

She shook her head, hunching her shoulders. Her face was white and red even in the candlelight. "More than that. Fair night. So cold."

She sank from her knees to the ground, and Galen pulled her close, cradling her to share his heat. He reached for the little candle, brought it close, and held their folded hands over it.

Lisveth drew a shuddering breath. "I've never seen anything like this."

"I supposed as much," Galen answered. "I've never heard of anyone trapped in ice before."

She shook her head, her teeth chattering. "That's not what I mean. I've never seen anything on this level of skill. No mage, no sorcerer, no one I've ever known or studied under or studied as an example in history. This is a completely different scale of magic." She shook her head again, shivering against him. "No way can I work with this."

"What?" Galen looked down at her. "Can't you undo it? You're a sorceress."

She gave a little laugh. "Oh, Galen. Sorcerers are scary business, but we're still just people. Our skills may be freakish things like making fire out of what seems to be nothing, but we're just people with learned skills. And you know I'm good at only one thing.

"But even if I were skilled at all of it, even if I were among the best—this would still be beyond me." She jerked her head toward the woman in the fountain behind them. "This is powerful magic, Galen. I was only looking at it—not handling it, not trying to undo it—and I can't stop shaking. I think my hands are frostbitten."

Galen nodded. "It's obvious what the spell does. You're going to feel cold."

"Stop pretending to understand things you don't understand, farm boy." She took a breath. "You know how a good song or poem can make you feel something? Like, you can listen to a ballad of a storm at sea, and the rhythm of the words makes you feel the movement of the ship, and maybe you get a few goosebumps with a good line about the lightning?"

He nodded. "Of course."

"This is like listening to a song about a storm and ending up actually soaked to the skin, with your hair all frizzled with the lightning's passing." She shivered against him. "It's beyond me."

He tried to find words to counter and encourage her. "But you can learn it, if you take the time, right? The woman who did this, she's like any other sorcerer. They're just people with learned skills."

She blew out a little huff of laughter. "The Rideis may be people, Galen, but they're not human. This isn't human magic." She shook her head. "This is impossible."

Galen had no answer, so he opened his hands to examine her fingers. He thought she might be right about the frostbite. He closed his hands about hers again.

Her shivering was slowing. "Thanks. I think I'm warming now."

He released her, but she did not move away. "So what are we going to do?" he asked. "Yovela hired us to free the queen, and it doesn't seem we can do that, and Yovela isn't available to pay us now."

Lisveth finally shifted and leaned back against the fountain. "It's different now." Her voice was flat, hard.

"What do you mean?"

Lisveth gestured to encompass the fountains, the throne, the Rideis kingdom. "If this Pasiphae Jade, if she crosses into our human land—we can't stop her. If she can do this, and if she has more sorcerers, then not the state mages, not the army, nothing." She swallowed. "We have to stop her, and we can't stop her."

"Prince Kayvin said he did not want to invade us."

"It's a fair bet he didn't want Yovela in the ice, either, and we see how that ended." Lisveth chewed her lip. "Didn't she send the bandits, too, which he opposed?"

Galen conceded the point. "Then how do we stop her? If we can't fight her, and no one can?"

Lisveth pointed at the opposite fountain. "We can't fight her—but Yovela said Prince Kayvin can."

"But he won't, not unless we release his mother, and you just said you can't do that."

"I can't free her." Lisveth looked at Galen, and her face was grim. "But there's more than just the promise of getting his mother back alive. There's also the threat of killing her." She pointed at the damaged foot. "And it seems there's already been a demonstration of how the quasi-protection of stasis can be withdrawn if Pasiphae Jade is displeased."

Galen saw where she was going. "It's not just releasing her that would free him to act. He would also be free of the threat to her if..."

Lisveth nodded, her eyes dark. "If his mother and Yovela are dead, if the worst that can happen has already been done, then he has no reason to hold back."

"That's..." Galen struggled to find the words. "That's hideous. It's cruel."

"Imprisoning them in ice is cruel," Lisveth snapped. "Tormenting him with threats is cruel. Keeping him a puppet for their lives through months, years, maybe decades, is cruel. Freeing all of them at once?" She blew out her breath. "Yovela said if Pasiphae Jade lived, she would be dead anyway. I think she would approve this plan. She might have even thought of it already, but she asked first for release."

"And what about the queen? We don't even know her name. Do we know that she would want this?"

"Of course not! How could she? None of us want this!" Lisveth shook her head, looked around the dark room, bit her lip. "But would she, whoever she is, whatever kind of empress or mother she was, want her country stolen and her son tormented on her behalf?"

"And Kayvin? How do you think he is going to react if he finds you killed his mother and concubine, just to motivate him to fight?"

"We make certain he does not know it was us." Her voice was grim. "We make it Pasiphae Jade's work. Let him assume that she killed them, and let him take his revenge for father, mother, lover, and country all at once."

"And that will stop her coming across the mountains?"

"It might. And we would save all those people who have never heard of us and those who hate us." She elbowed Galen. "How would you like to save the lives of your uncles and cousins and the rest of your mule-bred family?"

For a moment he stared at her, and then he realized: This was a choice. She knew they would never be thanked for this, she knew it was dangerous, and she was offering him the worst of the bargain to refuse in case he did not want it.

To save his family? The men and women who killed each other, who beat him, who would have fled this palace with what they could steal on their way to the door?

And there was San, in his first job as caravan guard hireling, whom Galen had liked, and San had believed the worst of him and turned on him, leaving Galen to flee to Lisveth for his life. And there were all the hundreds of folk who pushed past him as he made his way through the street.

There were tens of thousands in any given city, good and cruel. None would ever know if Lisveth and Galen died to prevent an invasion that, when it did not manifest, would be dismissed as only rumor, if it was mentioned at all. Even those who remembered their names, like Anela, would never know why they had vanished with a bag of money and never returned with the stolen amulets.

"I'm going to do this," Lisveth whispered.

He guessed she had dropped to a whisper to hide the quiver in her voice. It only half worked. "You don't have to."

"I do." Her throat worked. "I already bear the stain. This time, I can save people instead of getting them killed. This is my dragon, my landslide. My chance."

She was frightening him. "Lisveth, you don't have to do this. You don't—my family is in the Heel, hundreds of leagues from any invasion. And they will never thank you for this, and you owe them nothing."

"Saving only people who deserve saving is not heroism."

Galen's pulse was pounding hard enough that he could feel it in his fingers. "Fair night. We're going to die."

"Maybe," Lisveth admitted. "Probably. Getting out of here after murdering a queen will certainly be harder than sneaking in at the tail end of a patrol line, and that's not counting whatever effects breaking the spell may have." She looked at him. "Aren't you glad I brought your amulet, now? You may make it out."

He shook his head. "Those guards carried swords and spears and bows, all of which would slide right through my amulet's protection. My only hope is to taunt them into using a fireball instead."

They shared a tiny chuckle at the unfunny joke, leaning together against the fountain's basin. Then they fell quiet.

After a moment, Lisveth sucked a long breath in. "Fair night. I can't do this."

"You..." Galen was unsure whether he wanted to encourage her in her magic or argue for her to give up the dangerous assassination.

"I mean, I can. One doesn't have to be very skilled to kill someone literally frozen in place. It will be the easiest assassination in history." She chewed her lip. "But I don't want to kill someone frozen in their sleep. Even on my worst days, even on my worst day, I didn't want that."

"We could fight Pasiphae Jade instead." Galen swallowed through his tight throat. "If we have to kill someone, let's make it the person who killed the king and put the queen and Ycvela into ice."

Lisveth shook her head. "If Pasiphae Jade can work this spell...I can't fight her. It wouldn't be a fight, it would be a mouse against a cartwheel. The only way the mouse will survive is by running away."

"And you want to run away?"

"No." Her voice shook. "I want to do something. I don't want to watch a war start and I don't want to see people die, and I don't want to know I knew it was coming and did nothing. I want to do something with every cord of my heart. But I also know there is nothing I can do except throw myself at this spell in a dramatic, symbolic gesture and die for it. That magic is too great, too...big. I can't hold a spell that large."

"Could you use another conduit?" Galen spoke slowly, not trusting his idea. If it could work, Lisveth should already have thought of it. "Could you put the magic into something other than yourself?"

"Possibly, I suppose. Like using tongs to handle heated iron. But it would have to be something incomprehensibly powerful."

"I don't know anything about what I'm saying, but... What about an incomprehensible artifact meant to hold powerful spells for a century or two at a time?"

Lisveth tipped her head toward him, her eyes slightly unfocused as she thought over his suggestion. "You're...a bit clever, farm boy."

"If Pasiphae Jade wanted them to work some great magic, then they must have a use beyond their individual spells. Maybe they could be reservoirs, or depositories, or storehouses."

"Not bad, farm boy." She sat forward, her elbows on her knees. "Let me think."

CHAPTER 113

GALEN SAT WHERE HE could see both Lisveth and the tall doors. It felt wrong to have the throne at his back, but that seemed the direction least likely to bring guards, and he needed to have an eye on Lisveth as she explored the spell.

He wished he could help. They had always been a team, with her handling the magic and him providing the muscle. But this job was entirely magic, and he could only watch uselessly as she slid deeper into the dangerous spell.

He thought very briefly of building a small fire to warm her when she came back from wherever she had gone, wholly immersed in the ice magic, but even a small fire would draw servants' attention, and they couldn't risk that. Nor did it seem wise to have a fire near the frozen fountains, though they did not seem susceptible to the room's temperature.

He wasn't sure how much time had passed. He wished he had an hourglass, or a candle clock, or anything more trustworthy than his nerves. How long had Lisveth been silent in the magic now?

At last she stirred, and he hurried to her and threw the cloak he'd been warming against his chest around her, blanketing her as he drew her back from the fountain. He folded her against him, pressing her frigid hands against his torso. "How are you?" he asked as she sucked a breath and began to shiver.

But she was grinning as her teeth chattered. "It's the f-fountain."

"What?"

"The spell's rooted in the fountain. Not the ice. She's using the fountain to maintain it." She gave a hard shake and burrowed in closer. "I'm not too cold? Is this all right?"

He thought he was losing a kidney where her cold hand slipped around him, but he shook his head. "It's fine. What about the fountain?"

"The fountain is a reservoir." Excitement bled through her muffled voice. "I don't know what it was first meant to do, because I can't imagine they thought to put four ice prisons in their throne room, but it's made to hold a deep spell for a long time. Exactly like the amulets, only much larger. And she's using that to hold the ice magic, rather than maintaining the spell all this time herself—which would have been terrifying power." She shivered. "Not that this isn't also terrifying. That spell isn't beginner work. But at least we know she isn't doing this in the back of her mind while also walking about and running a kingdom."

Galen nodded, as if it meant as much to him.

Lisveth slid her hands to the amulet on his chest. "Let me borrow this, please."

He unwrapped his arms and cloak from her long enough to slide the chain over his head, tugging it free of his lengthening hair.

She was trying to find the others in her bag, but her numb fingers weren't efficient. "These fountain reservoirs, whatever they are, they hold power to be drained slowly by the spell. But your amulet, it draws power, when magic is used against you."

"Yes?" Galen took the bag from her and felt for the pieces

"And if you think about it, the other Eyes do both. The one that enhances magic, that stores and expends magical energy. The one that protects from physical attack, that absorbs kinetic energy." She opened her hands, held together, and Galen placed the amulets into them.

"So you think another fountain should work to expend energy?" he asked.

She shook her head, rotating the Eyes so that they all lay in the same orientation. "I think the amulets must be able to work together in some way. If she only needed powerful sources of energy, well, she has them right here. There has to be some way to link them, pass energy between them, do something else with them."

"Maybe it's to carry magic from one place to another," Galen suggested. "The fountains are not very portable."

She nodded. "Yes, maybe something like that." She laid the amulets out on the tile, spaced equally apart, and sat cross-legged with one hand on the fountain basin and the other on the floor near the Eyes. "All right, give me some time with these."

"It will be dawn soon."

"I've got a couple of hours."

Galen withdrew to resume his watch.

Lisveth did not drop trancelike into the spell again but frowned at the amulets, rotating them, trading them in position, pressing them against the fountain, lying flat on the floor and pushing one toward the deep root of the fountain. She never looked up. Occasionally she wiped sweat from her forehead, so at least she was not feeling the unnatural cold of the spell.

Galen was frowning through the great door's hinge gap, wondering if that was a lightening in the sky, when she gave a little squeal. He whirled, ready for trouble, but she was focused on the two Eyes cradled in her hands. He relaxed and went toward her.

She glanced up at his approach, her eyes too wide as she grinned. "I have something."

"I hope it's a plan."

"Well, the plan is yours, to be honest."

"I don't remember having a plan." Galen crouched across from her.

She reached to put his amulet chain over his head. "You said earlier you would have to somehow taunt the guards into using a fireball instead of weapons. Only it's going to be Kayvin instead of the guards."

"Kayvin?"

"He'll be surprised to see you here. Use that against him. Get him mad, whatever it takes, and get him to throw magic at you."

"Couldn't we just...ask him to help?"

Lisveth shook her head. "Yovela said she came to us in the middle of the night because he wouldn't risk disrupting the spell that holds his mother. He'll be doubly cautious now; if this was going to tip him into rebellion, it would have already happened. He certainly won't help if he knows what we intend." She patted the amulet against his chest. "Make it a strong one. We know it can protect you from a killing bolt."

"Do we know it's still working? How would we know if it ran out, like the amulet in the capital?"

Lisveth gave the eye a little flick, and it blinked and seemed to swivel, as if looking up. Galen flinched away, a useless reaction while it hung from his neck.

"Still good," Lisveth pronounced with brave cheer. "Draw his fire. The biggest fireball you can provoke."

"And that's going to do it?"

Lisveth's smile tightened uncomfortably. "It's going to have to."

CHAPTER 114

LISVETH DID THE RECONNAISSANCE, going out with the Golden Eye and passing up and down long corridors, following servants in their early morning bustle. Galen sat in a corner of the throne room, hoping furiously that Lisveth was correct in her supposition that no one would have reason to enter it in the dawn.

At last Lisveth returned. "Down to the right is almost certainly the ruler's wing, given the kind of traffic going in and out. There are two other residence wings, and one of them is receiving a dozen trays of chopped fruit and porridge and small cups of milk, so I don't think that's the prince unless he's still living in the nursery. So I think the wing opposite the royal rooms is probably the one we want."

"You think? If I turn up in the wrong room..."

"I couldn't see inside, but I'm willing to gamble on it. Those are the only three places with breakfast delivered, and the one with the most traffic is also the one nearest this throne room, probably set close behind if we knew the right ways. I'll bet our sad prince is the one furthest from that."

Galen nodded. "And how do I get in?"

"There's a garden. Start there, and see what you can find. Remember, it's all right to make a little ruckus, as long as you draw Kayvin and not some guards."

"Right. Thanks." Galen blew out his breath. "Can I have the Golden Eye?"

Lisveth shook her head. "Sorry, I need it."

"Yeah, I figured as much. All right, I'm going. Out, to the right, and first left?"

She nodded. Then she moved forward to hug him. "Be careful."

"I wouldn't do anything else." He held her for a moment, wondering if she could feel his heart pounding. He didn't think he was taking full breaths. "Okay, let me go before I lose my nerve."

"Or before the corridors are too busy." She drew back and nodded. "Good luck." Then, as he stepped away, she caught his wrist. "Wait."

He watched as she closed her eyes, drew a circle upon her chest, and then looked up and pressed two fingers to his forehead. He did not recognize the ritual, but he stayed still beneath it.

"A blessing," she whispered. "Now go."

Galen found the prince's garden as described and climbed over the balustrade to jump into a young conifer, which swayed and bent until he finally dropped to the ground. He was scratched and scraped, but that would only add to his story.

He wandered through the garden, majestic with late-season blooms of chrysanthemums and aster but pockmarked with dark bare patches, and searched for an entry from the palace.

He would need to anger the prince into attacking him—but what could provoke a man who had already lost his mother and trusted companion? He would have to think Galen a threat—but why would he believe that when they had negotiated at last meeting? He would need a compelling tale.

There! He started toward the gate standing open to curving stone steps. That should lead inside to the prince's room, if Lisveth was correct.

But Kayvin was descending those steps.

Galen hesitated, drew back, and then he flung himself upon a nearby bench, as if he'd been waiting in the garden all this time. He crossed his arms with an impatient glower.

Kayvin stepped through the gate, both hands raised to his bent head to adjust his hair stick, his eyes low.

"So there you are." Galen made his voice a growl.

Kayvin jumped and looked forward, hardly settling when he recognized Galen. "You—what are you doing here? And, *here?* How did you get into the garden?"

"That's the least of your concerns." Galen stood and uncrossed his arms. "You told us a sad tale of a fallen prince, and yet you seem to be living well enough." He gestured about him.

Kayvin's expression tightened. "A garden does not make me a prince. But I did not think my position here was your concern."

"It wasn't." Galen couldn't bring Yovela into this; he needed to fight Kayvin, not entice questions. "But that was when you weren't a threat."

"A threat?" Kayvin looked legitimately confused. "To you?"

"To Sayinia."

The prince shook his head. "You know I want to stop—"

"I don't know anything but what you've told me, and I remember you started by telling me another story entirely." Galen took a step forward. "So I'm here to stop what you won't."

Kayvin hadn't called for help; he wasn't threatened, not yet. He stared, as if trying to find the right response.

Galen shook out his hands and rolled a shoulder. "You were there when the bandits came. You were stealing from our temples. You talked about a renegade queen, but I've never seen evidence of her meddling against our people. It's always been you." He faced Kayvin, arms slightly spread, ready to move. "There's only one way to settle this."

Kayvin stared at him. "You must have lost your mind."

"I have not."

"You know I will kill you."

"Then kill me." Galen gulped for air. Speaking bravado was one thing; feeling it was another. "Kill me. I have no reason to want otherwise."

Kayvin made an exasperated sound. "If this is a jest, it's not funny. My mother is dying a slow death in a prison of ice—perhaps tortured by the cold, I don't know, but I have nightmares about it. My—Yovela too is now a prisoner of ice. The woman who killed my father has ordered me to search your country for magical baubles, and I don't know if they can even help in the crisis she believes is coming. And you? You have skills to sell, people to buy them, a friend to travel with you. What have you suffered that is so grave?"

Galen grasped for the worst thing imaginable. "Lisveth is dead."

Kayvin flinched. "I am sorry to hear that. How?"

He needed a reason to fight Kayvin. "A Rideis bandit. Killed her as she slept—she never had a chance."

"I am very sorry." Kayvin pressed his lips together, looked away, swallowed. "I could tell you that was none of my doing, but you know—you know I never wanted that. For her or for anyone else."

"And yet, here we are."

"Here we are." Kayvin sighed. "Galen, let's not do this. Let me give you a place to stay, a meal to eat, time to think. We can talk. I can send you home with—I don't know, but let me try to help."

"I don't have a home." Galen pushed the words out, too fast to consider. "I left my home years ago, and I didn't know it was a nightmare until I could get away and wake up. I found a home that never stayed in place with Lisveth. She was the one who offered me a hand and company, negotiated our jobs, worked all the angles. She was a clever thing, and not always straightforward, but always reliable. If you could get her to give her word, she was a rock. And now she is dead."

The words were starting to take their own effect in Galen, even though he knew they were a lie. Well, a few of them were a lie.

Kayvin nodded solemnly. "You loved her."

Fair night. Galen had not expected the conversation to go this way. He should have attacked directly, forced Kayvin to strike him in self-defense. But now, now he had to answer, and in a way to make Kayvin believe in the fight.

"Yes. And now I must fight you for her sake."

"No, we don't need to do this."

Galen let his voice rasp. "I'm telling you in advance only as a courtesy."

Kayvin sighed. "I am sorry, Galen. This is not how I would have chosen it."

That was as close to an agreement as he was likely to get. Galen drew his sword and lunged at Kayvin.

Kayvin used magic and so relied upon range. He should not have allowed Galen to come so close in the first place. He threw up a shield that blocked Galen's rush—no! He needed magical energy to fuel the amulet! Galen stumbled back and charged again, more headstrong than calculating. Kayvin finally raised his other hand to attack.

Fire leaped from his palm and streamed over Galen. Heat flooded Galen, and his sword burned in his grip. He flinched against the heat, closed his eyes to protect them, and it felt as if his eyelashes were singeing off—but he did not burn.

On his chest, the amulet flared to life, and a feather-touch brushed his shirt as it blinked.

Kayvin stared at Galen, standing intact and unscorched before him. "Yes, you have one!" he gasped. He held out his hand. "Please. Give it to me. Let's end this nonsense and work together. If I can placate her with an amulet—please, we can help each other."

"You can't help anyone any longer," Galen snarled, hating the words and feeling like a traitor. A Heel, indeed. Kayvin was doing nothing wrong, and Galen had to abuse him, had to fight him, so they could break his heart.

With all the loathing he felt for his part in this, he attacked.

Kayvin reacted first with fire, his natural response. The amulet sucked at it like a hungry calf, pulling the danger into itself and leaving only a residual wash of heat for Galen. Galen did not hesitate. If Kayvin had time to think, he would use another defense, and they needed his fire. Galen pressed the attack and drove the prince backward, and Kayvin blocked Galen's blows with repeated bursts.

The amulet burned against Galen's chest, hot with the energy it drank, and Galen began to wonder if they would overwhelm it.

Did it have a limit to its protection? Could Galen taunt Kayvin to a point where the prince would push past the amulet and actually kill him?

His skin began to burn beneath the amulet, a hotter pain than the blunted arcane fire. The amulet had to be nearing its limit—or he would near his own.

He turned suddenly and ran from the prince. Galen scrabbled up a boulder, a tree, to the garden wall, and turned back to face the surprised prince. He leaned forward to look down, letting the amulet swing away from his chest within his blousing tunic.

Kayvin paused beneath him, wary of attack from above. "Why do you run, Galen? I thought you wanted to fight me."

"I am about to kill you," Galen said, making his voice pitiless. "But I will do it with my words."

Kayvin shook his head. "I don't understand what you mean."

"You don't think I came first to your garden, do you? Why should that be the first place I found when I entered your palace?"

Kayvin's face stiffened. "Where did you go?"

"I went to the throne room this morning. I wanted to see the queen you spoke of." Galen laced his voice with hatred, making himself gleeful to deliver the news. "I saw no evil queen, but I saw the others. They are both there, Kayvin. You lost Yovela, too. And she has already killed them."

Kayvin went rigid. "What?"

"Your Pasiphae Jade has already killed your mother and Yovela. I saw it done. There is nothing you can do to save them. They're not frozen, they're dead."

Kayvin roared incoherently and blasted Galen with a stream of fire like dragon's breath. Galen braced himself against the burn of the amulet as heat raced up the chain and bit into his neck.

At last the prince dropped his fire and turned to run into the palace. Galen gasped with relief and glanced down at his chest. A blackened oval showed where the amulet hung against his shirt.

He plucked the amulet outside of his shirt, grateful for the thin protection against the residual warmth, and climbed down from the wall. He had to find Lisveth and learn if their gamble had worked.

CHAPTER 115

KAYVIN RAN, FURIOUSLY DENYING Galen's words with each stride. His mother was alive, Yovela was alive, Pasiphae Jade could not afford to harm them further—

As he had thought before she had disfigured his mother's foot.

But surely she would not dare to kill them. Not both of them. Surely she would not—

The tall doors were open, and morning light streamed over the tiles, illuminating the two splashing fountains beside the entrance and stretching toward the two silent ones by the dais. But today no ice rose over the lips of the fountains, and he stopped in the middle of the tiled design, wanting to disbelieve what he saw.

A bare arm lay over the basin rim, dangling toward the wet floor.

His heart twisted despite all his fierce attempts to guard himself, and he broke into a run. "Mother!"

The wet floor about the fountain basin was slick, and he slipped as he approached. She lay across the basin under a handsbreadth of still water—but it was not his mother, not as he'd known her.

The body was misshapen and blackened with severe frostbite and melted flesh. Her clothing clung wetly to her body, but the cloth rose and fell in the wrong places. Her eyes stared blankly and hideously upward, as if she should see him and know him, but they were reddened with broken blood vessels, sightless.

Kayvin pushed himself away and vomited into the wide puddle on the floor, choking and spitting as he dropped to his knees.

Dead. *Dead*. And not only dead, but in such horrific fashion, such horror—he gasped and wheezed and choked. *Mother*.

Everything he had done, all his efforts, all his travels, all his humiliations before Pasiphae Jade, had come to nothing. She was lost forever.

On his hands and knees in the puddle of melt-water, he lifted his head and saw the second fountain opposite him. He pushed himself to his feet and staggered toward Yovela's ice prison.

She was dead, too. She lay on her back at the bottom of the pool, her mouth open and full of unmoving water, her eyes staring toward the surface she would never break. Half of her face had sloughed to one side, fallen under its own weight.

Kayvin howled with fury and anguish.

He blended tears and melt-water as he tore at his face and hair. He squeezed his eyes closed to block the sight of the distorted, hideous corpse and screamed his grief, his frustration, his fury, his hate.

But he could do nothing here. He pushed himself up and staggered on numb feet.

"My lord?" The tentative voice behind him belonged to a servant, clutching a bucket of cleaning supplies and another of water, staring wide-eyed.

"Pasiphae Jade," Kayvin growled.

"My lord?" The servant looked past him to the wet floor, the dangling arm, and she gasped.

There was a passage from the rear of the throne's dais to the Arch Potentate's rooms, but it would be locked, and he would not waste time beating on the door or demanding entry. He left by the side door, leaving the servant gaping in the entrance, and stalked through the corridors to the royal apartments.

The guard at the door put out a desultory arm in the usual fashion. "The Arch Potentate is not—"

"I will see her now." Kayvin kept walking.

"My lord, you must wait."

He struck the man in the chest and continued walking.

The guard fell against the wall and then leaped up, shouting. "Intruder! Stop!"

Kayvin did not stop. He passed through the dog-legged entrance and pushed through the door. He reached the central sitting room before the guards closed on him.

The first seized his arm and tried to wrench him to the ground, but Kayvin raised little tongues of flame in his hands and the man recoiled as the fire leaped upward. "I am the Amethyst Prince!" Kayvin snarled. "Stand out of my way."

Across the room, Pasiphae Jade looked up in first surprise and then suspicion. She rose from her seat, but she did not run. Instead she held up a calming hand. "His Highness clearly has something he desires to say." She managed to sound dismissive and curious at once.

"You did it," he snarled at her, his voice a feral thing that hardly owned him as master. "You really killed them."

Pasiphae Jade raised an eyebrow, as if mildly impressed with his newfound ferocity, and then regarded him in cold disdain. "What are you talking about?"

"You killed them. I did everything you asked of me, and still you killed them."

The guards stood close, hands shifting. Pasiphae Jade's order stayed them, but only for the moment. He could not bring himself to worry over that.

Pasiphae Jade took a step toward Kayvin, and her disdain faded to skepticism. "What are you talking about?"

"You've killed them!" Kayvin flung out an arm toward the door. "Look at what you have done!"

She held up a finger, perhaps asking for silence or asking him to wait a moment. She frowned in brief concentration, her eyes shifting to some upward part of the room, and then she looked again at him. "They are untouched."

"Liar! You've killed them both."

She scowled. "Then let us go and look at them, and we shall see who is lying."

He whirled in place, and the nearest guard shifted back. Kayvin did not wait for Pasiphae Jade to catch up. Let her follow him, for once. And if she chose to stab him in the back, well, that might be all right, too.

They went to the throne room, followed distantly by guards and servants. Kayvin's stomach clenched and rose as they neared the fountains, but he sucked a long, trembling breath and let his anger steady him.

Pasiphae Jade stopped, looking from fountain to fountain, mouth agape.

Kayvin threw a hand at his mother's body, fingers outstretched as if he could snatch a better world from the air. "There is no point to lying. You have killed her."

Pasiphae Jade shook her head in slow protest. "No. The magic is intact." She rushed to the fountain and ran a finger gingerly over the pool, rippling the surface. "I can't... This can't be."

"She is dead!" Kayvin swept his hand across the puddle, splashing it toward her. "What is the purpose of lying about it, even as we are looking at her body?"

She blinked as a few drops of water reached her, but she did not wipe it away. "Prince Kayvin—"

"Shut up!" There was no reason now to hold back. All that had kept his parents' murderer alive was now dead. Fire leaped from his hands, crawled up his arms, hissed in his ears. He wanted to strike her, but even now he hesitated. Worthless prince, unable even to avenge his dead. He clenched his fists and forced himself toward her.

"Think of Lirin." She spoke levelly, without hesitation, and the look she gave him was nearly expressionless. "You do not want to explain to Lirin that you have killed me."

That was true, and it galled him. "She would understand."

"She would understand, in part. Even if she did, she would never again look at you in the same way."

Kayvin clenched his fists until his nails threatened to draw blood from his palms. "Coward! Why do you always hide behind someone else?"

"Because no one ever stepped in front of me!"

For a moment they were each silent, each surprised by the words. Then Pasiphae Jade added darkly, "I learned to do whatever had to be done. And I will."

He hated her. He hated her so much, with every thought and breath and heartbeat, and he hated that he did not simply kill her.

She looked back toward the fountains, and her expression grew calculating. "But I am not alone in that, I see."

"I don't know what you mean."

"You did it, didn't you." It was not a question, and she regarded him with a horrified awe.

Kayvin scowled. "What?"

"My spell is intact, and yet they are melted and killed. That must have been your fire. You tried to burn them out, and that killed them, and now you blame me to justify your coup." She shook her head in disgusted wonder. "I confess, I would not have guessed you had it in you."

"How can you say such a thing? While they lie in your stolen fountains, destroyed with your magic?"

"Don't bother lying to me! My magic has held them safe all this while. Your impatience killed them, and now you mean to blame me for that as excuse for your revolt. But it will not work; no one will believe you at last rallied to avenge two dead women, one a servant, when you did not fight even for your royal father."

Kayvin ground his teeth, hating her and hating himself. 'I will not obey your orders again," he snarled in quiet warning. "I will not do your bidding. I will resist you with every waking thought, and in my dreams I will loathe you."

For just an instant, there was fear in her eyes. For the first time, she saw him as a threat.

And then the fear turned to something almost like regret, and her face went cold. "Then I am a little sorry, but I also will do what must be done. I didn't want to harm another royal. but I cannot have you undermining my work or trying to unseat me now. Lirin will never fully understand me, either. But she will be safe." She raised her voice. "Take the Amethyst Prince into custody."

"Stay back!" Kayvin's chest spasmed with the stunning realization that they were past all speech or retreat. This was real, as real as the loss beside him and the burial of his father and the futility of all his long searching.

The puddle in which he stood began to steam with the heat of his wrath and indecision. The guards approached. They spread on either side of him, and they reached for his arms.

He jerked away and ran, their fingers clawing down his arms as he twisted toward Pasiphae Jade. She struck aside his first fire with a spray of frost, surprised but quick. He pressed his attack with a flame at her unprotected side as the guards scattered. But a shield of ice rose to block his hand and shove him backward, and he slipped on the spilled water, now slushy with her magic. His flailing hand struck the basin and skidded down to his mother's leg, burning the sodden flesh with a sudden stench of seared meat.

He shrieked and burst upward, stumbling to one side. Instinctively he drew his arms in, expecting a blow to the torso he'd left unprotected. Pasiphae Jade threw a blast of ice crystals at him, but he ducked and they only pelted his shoulders and arms, stinging but not throwing him down.

She should be icing his footing, making him slip again. She should be striking him with ice honed to the piercing point that had killed his father. But of course—she had never been trained to fight, not with magic or with more common weapons. Kayvin was an incompletely trained and spoiled prince, but he'd at least had lessons and sparring, while she had none. She was a frightened courtesan with pretty ice magic, able to sneak upon a sleeping ruler or bespell a woman caught unaware, but she had never been permitted to resist, and she was not prepared to fight for her life.

Part of him was grieved by that. Part of him was joyous at his advantage.

"Guards!" she shrieked.

He threw a spray of flame across the room, pushing back the reluctant guards. He whirled toward her with both hands extended and a sheet of fire leaped toward her face. Pasiphae Jade brought a bar of ice down to split his fire and target his head, her movement quick but frantic. Kayvin wheeled his forearm to deflect the ice and melt it.

"Why?" she demanded, backing for space. "Why this, why now?"

"Why did you kill them?" he demanded, though her reason could make no difference anymore.

"I didn't!"

He roared fury at her lies, all her lies, so many lies and promises and manipulations, and he flung fire at her, alternating each hand, keeping a steady series of flaming projectiles flying toward her.

She struck aside each with icy shields, and her reactions were growing more controlled. "Fool, it's my own magic!"

"They are *dead*!" He shoved his two hands forward, pressing together at the heels, and spat liquid flame at her. He was using too much, he would drain himself, and he did not care.

She flung her arms upward and his fire crashed against a wall of ice that melted before it, but she was already safely away. She stepped aside and shot a staccato burst of icicle darts at him, and one pierced his upper arm. He howled with the unnatural pain of ice against his fire.

"Then shut up and die," she snarled, and she swept an arm around as if gathering snow, her fingers curling over empty air. His tears froze, pricking his face, and something moved inside Kayvin. His blood chilled and thickened, and for a moment his body bent toward her summoning arm, stiffening with cold.

And then his fire rose against the ice in his veins, and he roared fury. He rushed her, and an icicle tip sliced along his forearm. He overran her, seized her throat. She threw her arms between his wrists and flung herself backward, breaking his hold. He lunged again and caught her once more. She drove the icicle at him, tearing across his ribs. Her pale, ice-cold skin bit at his hot fingers, and he gasped with the shock of touching her, but he did not let go. She shrieked as her skin began to steam beneath his fingers, and she clawed at his face with icy daggers that cut him and boiled in his gashes.

He squeezed his hands together around her and called the greatest fire he knew to burn up from them. She screamed, shedding ice and water.

"No!" Someone struck Kayvin from the side, knocking him loose from Pasiphae Jade. He twisted, barely saving himself from falling, and struck out at his attacker. The blow landed without resistance, but Lirin only ducked her head and drove harder into him, squeezing her arms about his waist as if she could push him back with her useless weight. "No! Kayvin, don't!"

Pasiphae Jade was on her knees, one hand on the floor and the other to her throat, gasping. Steam wreathed her. Kayvin drew back his arm to throw fire.

"Kayvin!" Lirin caught at his arm.

He looked down at her, furious. "Get away! She's killed my mother!"

"And you're killing mine!"

Kayvin hesitated. Lirin sobbed against him, clutching him tightly. It wasn't fair. It wasn't at all fair. Kayvin only acted in answer to what Pasiphae Jade had already done.

"Don't," Lirin choked into his chest. "Please don't."

Kayvin stared over her at Pasiphade Jade, coughing into the puddle beneath her. She sat up unsteadily and fixed her eyes on him, raising a hand. But Lirin was between them, holding tightly to Kayvin.

The moment had passed, and Kayvin could not kill her, not over Lirin's pleading form. Pasiphae Jade hesitated, too, unwilling to blast murdering magic through her daughter's embrace.

To the side, the cowardly guards waited to see who would earn the right to command them.

Kayvin drew a breath. "Lord Fretton is incapacitated," he pronounced loudly. "You will answer to me now. Bind the usurper."

Lirin gave a wail of relief and squeezed Kayvin in wordless gratitude. He put his hands on her arms and began to peel her away. "Take her to a holding cell," he ordered, "and see her hands are bound behind her, to minimize her magic."

That wasn't a good solution. But he didn't have a good solution.

He extracted himself from Lirin's grip and pushed her away, too angry and too despairing to speak to her. Lirin stood a moment, one hand still awkwardly grasping toward him, and then she turned and ran to where the guards were taking hold of Pasiphae Jade. Little sprays of frost fell from the former courtesan's palms as they were forced behind her, but she was exhausted of magic. There was a series of cracks, and Pasiphae Jade gave a choking cry. Then they started out and Lirin followed, sobbing but not pressing too close.

Kayvin turned on the remaining guards, his fire still churning within him. "What are you waiting to see?" he demanded. "Go and be useful, help to transport the prisoner. Get out!"

They left.

Kayvin stood in place, panting. Then he turned, alone in the throne room with only the ruined bodies of his mother and friend.

He collapsed to the floor and screamed, furious that there was no one to fight, furious that he had been too weak to kill her, furious that he had been somehow glad of Lirin's interference, furious that now he could not kill his murdering tormentor except in impossible cold blood, furious that the two women he loved were half-melted behind him and he was still helpless to save them.

He fell forward, sobbing, and the exhausted fire in him at last burned low.

THE FALL

CHAPTER 116

KAYVIN WAS SLUMPED TO the floor amidst melting ice and broken tiles when Dielo came. He moved slowly, tentatively, looking from one fountain to the other and picking his way through the debris of power.

He came and knelt beside Kayvin, placing one hand ever so gently on his quivering shoulders. Kayvin wept and did not look up, until Dielo began to sing.

He sang the song Kayvin had written for his mother's birthday, wordless with a sweeping rising melody. Kayvin swallowed his sobs, coughed on them, and tried to join in. His voice cracked and broke, and then it found its footing, and the two voices rose in the vaulted hall, reverberating through the empty room and hanging over the two dead women.

Kayvin pushed himself upright to sit on his heels, and he sang the melody as if it held all the love and grief he could not sob out. Dielo shifted smoothly to harmony, supporting Kayvin's song, and together they sang through the complete composition, sharing the choral sections and blending where it was only melody.

At last they came to the end, and while their voices quavered in the final notes, they came to rest together, and Kayvin drew a full breath at the end of it. He reached a hand to Dielo, catching his forearm, and he squeezed it, hoping the gesture could convey what he could not yet trust his voice to say.

A slow, solitary clapping came from the far end of the courtyard, where the doors hung open. A heartbeat later a second pair of hands joined in. Kayvin's heart twisted—who dared to mock his pain so?—and pushed himself from the floor, fresh fire already sputtering in him.

His mother stood just within the tall doors, watching him and applauding.

Kayvin could not move, his muscles locked with disbelief and savage pain. He had not seen her—not seen her alive—in so long, and now that he knew she was dead, he was furious his mind should finally allow him to imagine what he had wished for so hard all those nights he had wanted to visit her.

Beside her stood Yovela, also clapping for his song, and she was smiling in a way he had never seen her smile, warm and beaming, so he knew she was dead.

The fire sank down in him, and he wanted to cry afresh.

And then his mother took a step forward, and she stumbled and fell. Yovela caught her, and from behind her Galen appeared to take her arm and help her upright again.

Kayvin knew his mind was under strain, but he could not imagine why it was choosing to include the red-haired human in his grief-fueled hallucinations.

Supported on two sides, his mother straightened and held her hand out to him. "Kayvin, come to me. It is hard for me to come to you."

His throat closed. Was she calling him to death, to join her and Yovela? Did she want him to die now, so soon upon Pasiphae Jade's defeat? Was Galen dead, too?

Dielo's fingers closed on Kayvin's upper arm. "My lord. How?"

This surprised Kayvin. "Can you see them, too?"

Dielo tore his eyes from the dead women and turned to Kayvin. "See them? They are here! They are alive!"

Kayvin blinked, and he saw the fountains before the dais were half-empty, only pools of still water. There were no bodies in the basins or on the floor.

He looked back at his mother, smiling with empathy and just beginning to cry as she realized he had not believed her to be real, and he bolted across the yard.

He enveloped them both in the largest hug he could encompass, unashamed of the fresh tears streaming down his face and the irrational laughter bubbling out of him. A moment later Dielo followed, and Kayvin pulled him into the group. His mother laughed and kissed them all, though she had never before seen Dielo.

As they rotated in their joyful embrace, Kayvin rocked near to where Galen was watching them, grinning with shared happiness. Kayvin broke away to face him. "What are you doing here?"

"We came to help," Galen said obliquely.

"By fighting me? Lying to me? You—you said *we*. Is Lisveth here?"

"Not that anyone would know it," came a weak voice to one side.

Kayvin turned toward the voice, and he saw Lisveth slumped on the floor, lying in the puddle between the fountains. When had she come? She looked pale and exhausted, and she made no move to rise from her place. Her face was turned to the side, barely out of the water, and her wet hair was frozen in several small chunks of ice. Each of Lisveth's outstretched hands held an amulet, each pressed toward a fountain that had once held a frozen woman.

"Lisveth!" Galen dashed forward and dropped into the puddle, splashing her.

"Careful, farm boy," she breathed as he lifted her. She let the amulets tumble from her stiff fingers.

Yovela clapped her hands. "You did it!"

Lisveth moved her head to nod weakly toward Kayvin. "You'd better say something before he thinks long enough to decide to kill us."

Kayvin took his mother's arm and followed, looking between Yovela and his mother. "What do you mean? What are you talking about?" He looked suspiciously from Lisveth to the empty fountains. "Did you—did you make me think they were dead?"

It wasn't possible; illusions were a false magic, barely useful. Even if Lisveth's temple guards had been convincing, that had been nothing like this fight, with dead bodies and burned flesh. No one had that kind of illusion skill.

"Yovela hired us to help you." Lisveth looked toward Galen. "We did. But I am absolutely bushed."

"How did you do it?" Yovela asked in wonder, grasping Lisveth's hand. "I don't remember anything but waking and hearing the fighting."

"It wasn't her magic, not entirely." Lisveth shook her head. "Could I explain later? I'm freezing. I'd love something warm to drink, and then a nap for maybe four or five days."

"Of course," Yovela said. "You can stay in the sera qadra's quarters with me. There's plenty of room for Galen, too; we have a men's and women's quarters."

"Wait a moment!" Kayvin demanded. "What's going on? How are either of you alive? Is that what you asked Lisveth to do?" He didn't think human magic was up to the match of countering Pasiphae Jade's spells. If Lisveth could unwork them, he would have to reevaluate his view of the human craft.

But Galen lifted Lisveth in his arms. "Later," he said firmly. "She's done a lot of magic, and she needs rest."

Lisveth dropped her head against his shoulder, eyelids drooping as if she might fall asleep before reaching the sera qadra's rooms. "I've never worked so hard in my life," she sighed. "Get the amulets."

"They're in my pocket."

Galen looked natural holding her. They had lied to Kayvin together—she had somehow worked the magic to make him see his mother and Yovela dead, and Galen had taunted him into coming here. They could not fight Pasiphae Jade directly, and so they had set him against her in vengeance.

It was a dangerous game, and brutally hard on all its players, but it had ended the terrible stalemate. There would be time later to wonder whether it had been right.

"Find servants," he said to Dielo, "and order hot food, hot drinks, a hot bath—"

"I'll drown," mumbled Lisveth.

"Hot stones and blankets for a sleeping pit," he amended. "And healers for my mother and Yovela."

Dielo nodded. He looked to Yovela, half-raising one hand, and he seemed about to speak. But she was following Galen and

Lisveth, her hand on Lisveth's arm, and he only nodded and went to carry Kayvin's orders.

Kayvin put one arm beneath his mother's, to support her, and wrapped the other to pull her close. "I'm afraid your rooms have been somewhat neglected," he said apologetically, "but let's get you back where you belong."

CHAPTER 117

THERE WAS TOO MUCH to be done, and too many decisions, and too much to be careful of.

The guards had obeyed Kayvin in the moment of his victory, as his flames leaped high, but even his dull court instincts knew his new position was far from secure. Lord Fretton was not an immediate threat, but that only meant a rip in the net of power. Another courtier might try to rise into the gap, either in the name of serving Kayvin or by making his own bid for the Bull Throne.

Kayvin was too exhausted to calculate the wisest next move. He had spent too much in the fight, and his grief and fury had sapped him beyond what even his following wild joy could support. He lasted long enough to commit his mother, now reclining on stacked pillows, to a physician, and to hear that Yovela and Lisveth had gone to his own rooms, and then he retreated to his mother's reading room, where he dropped onto a silk velvet couch.

"My lord, can I bring you anything?" This was Dielo, looking concerned.

Kayvin shook his head, and the room swam with the motion. "I need to rest. But they're going to come. I need to announce I'm now the Arch Potentate, but I can't do that while I'm collapsing." His eyes had closed while he was speaking, he realized. "Just...keep me safe. Guard the door."

"My lord." Dielo's voice was worried. "I am not a guard. I'm not enough. I cannot..."

Kayvin slid down on the couch, missing the pillow and not bothering to adjust his head. Whom else could they trust? "Then find Galen."

"The human? How do I ask him?"

But Kayvin wasn't awake to answer.

When Kayvin woke, he saw Galen on a stool, his back against one side of the door's frame and his scuffed boot braced on the other. He turned his head to look at Kayvin. "Are you awake?"

"I regret it, but yes." Kayvin sat up stiffly. His body ached, but that was the aftereffect of burning so much magic. He was thirsty.

"The other one, Dielo, he went to get some things."

"How long have I been asleep?"

"A couple of hours."

It should have been longer, after that expenditure of magic, but he was glad he'd woken early. "How's my mother? Yovela?"

"Your mother is fine; I can see the physician from here. I haven't heard anything from Yovela or Lisveth, but I hope they're sleeping, too."

"Is he awake?" Dielo stepped over Galen's leg without waiting for him to move. "My lord! How are you? I've brought you some appropriate clothes." He set down a basket filled with colorful garments.

"Appropriate?"

"For receiving. You have nobles waiting to see you."

Kayvin's stomach turned over, but he clenched his jaw and nodded. "Of course."

He thought furiously while Dielo dressed him. Where should he hear them? The throne room seemed too grand for a first conversation, though it might help to establish his authority. But it was spacious, providing ample room for attack if one of the courtiers chose to try a coup of his own.

The rooms of the Amethyst Prince would not speak to his new position. Likewise, receiving in the rooms of the Shining Gem would undermine his new rank. The Arch Potentate's receiving room would be both a firm message and a more secure setting, if he could trust the guards in it.

Kayvin gave Galen a sideways look. "Should I have a human as my honor guard, as I receive my first subjects? Or did General Artextra send you to take advantage of our unstable throne?"

"I'll answer in two parts." Galen held up a finger. "First, General Artextra thinks we're in Sayinia, collecting amulets before you can find them. She doesn't know we're here, and I'm certain she'd have someone much better for the task you mention." He tipped his head. "And second, with respect, you don't seem to have many other options, and I think you have far greater concerns than my uncertain loyalty."

"You did try to taunt me into killing you. If you are an agent of the general, your methods are unorthodox."

"And I sat in your doorway for two hours without taking advantage of the obvious assassination opportunity."

"You didn't have your partner with you for a hasty escape," Kayvin countered, but he didn't mean it. Galen and Lisveth had done things he would never have condoned, but they could have done more real harm and had not. He took a breath. "Please, will you stand near me, so that I appear properly equipped?"

"Lisveth will have my skin if I don't inform you we normally work for hire, but yes."

"I'll pay you from Pasiphae Jade's jewels."

"Which will you receive first?" Dielo asked, adjusting a sash.

"Who is waiting?"

Dielo began to list names, and Kayvin's heart sank. He needed someone to placate the courtiers as they waited and soothe those who saw someone go first. He needed someone who knew which Kayvin should see first. He needed someone who knew what Kayvin should say when he saw them.

Dielo was here, and anxious to be useful, but he wasn't trained in politics.

"What is it?"

Kayvin jumped a little in place and looked at Galen. "What?"

"What is it? You look like you've just remembered you owe money you don't have."

Kayvin tried to huff out a chuckle, but it failed. "I'm only remembering I lost this throne because the court was more willing to follow a murdering courtesan and an openly treacherous lord than an unimpressive and weak prince. Now she's gone, but I'm still just a weak prince."

"Weak? After that fire?"

Kayvin shook his head. "I've no head for court politics. I don't enjoy the competition of status and display, and I'd rather muddle through tax reports than try to guess which courtier actually supports a policy and which is merely pretending until he can switch his allegiance for another favor." He sighed. "I grew up here, and still I don't speak the language."

Galen gave a thoughtful half-frown and nodded. "You need Lisveth."

"What?"

"Or someone like her, but raised here. Lisveth is a sorceress with words, too. She could probably talk any courtier into whatever you wanted, but she doesn't know what you need them talked into. But there must be someone who knows what they really want."

"I don't know anyone like that." He hesitated. "At least, not that I can trust."

"Not even your mother?"

"What? No, she's the Shining Gem. She's..." Kayvin stopped, realizing why he'd impulsively refused. But Pasiphae Jade had studied the court well enough to negotiate secret alliances, and to check those who disapproved of her, and to form her own administration—which seemed to have run well enough, as there were few disasters in the countryside Kayvin passed through and no riots in the marketplaces or petitions for relief. Kayvin's father had refused advice from a knowledgeable woman; Kayvin would be a fool to repeat that mistake.

He turned to Dielo. "Go and see if the Shining Gem is awake. If she is, ask if she is well enough to advise me."

CHAPTER 118

KAYVIN HATED THE CHAIR. It was Pasiphae Jade's seat, the one
from which she had mocked him, the one she'd sprawled
comfortably in while he stood dripping and half-dressed to try
to warn her against harming his servants, the one from which
she'd ordered Dielo's flogging to force Kayvin's acceptance. It
sat in front of the display cabinet of virilo figurines—yes, there
was a gap in the row—and above the low table for light meals
with guests.

But there was no better seat to indicate he had taken
Pasiphae Jade's place.

No—to indicate he had taken his place, the one briefly
usurped by Pasiphae Jade.

Kayvin settled himself in the chair, surprisingly comfortable
despite its grandeur and history. Dielo conscripted Galen to help
move away the lower seats, leaving the table as a low bulwark
between Kayvin and his new subjects. Dielo then indicated where
Galen should stand, an arm's length from the display cabinet

behind Kayvin. Dielo then seated himself on the dais, just to the side of Kayvin's chair.

Kayvin hated this, too. Virilos had sat at the feet of his father and of Pasiphae Jade, and he wanted to be neither of them. Yet both of them had more firmly held the throne his fingers barely grasped, so he conceded to tradition for now.

His mother sat in the study, still stacked with Pasiphae Jade's books and papers. Kayvin had suggested she sit with him, to one side and lower as befit a retired royal wife, but she had protested vehemently. The nobles needed to see him, alone and proud and without womanly association. He'd tried to point out a woman had received them only yesterday, but the Shining Gem had been imprisoned through Pasiphae Jade's reign and kept insisting the court couldn't imagine an Arch Potentate influenced by a woman. Kayvin did not have the spirit or spite to argue with her, and he took his seat alone, with a virilo on display.

Arad—brought from Kayvin's rooms, though Kayvin was still faintly unsure of his loyalty—admitted the first noble visitor to congratulate Kayvin on his ascension, pledge his newly undying fealty that surely had never truly been meant for Pasiphae Jade, and hope for Kayvin's favor in the future.

But when Lord Scallong entered, he did not look like a supplicant or a sycophant. He approached directly, his eyes fixed on Kayvin, and gave only the slightest bow on the far side of the table. Kayvin stiffened, somehow even more unsettled than a moment before.

But he had the presence of mind to hold his tongue. He did not have to be the one to speak nervously to fill the gap; he could wait.

Lord Scallong, after a moment, inclined his head. "Your Illustrious Excellency."

This was a good start; he didn't dispute Kayvin's new title. It was a small victory, and perhaps temporary, but it was a good start.

"Lord Scallong. Thank you for coming."

Lord Scallong crossed his arms. "I have to admit, you have surprised me."

Kayvin tried to control his expression. "Oh?" he prompted.

"After Lord Narrim was killed at the banquet, I thought you were finished."

Kayvin kept his voice neutral. "You knew, then, why he was arrested and killed."

Lord Scallong chuckled. "Knew? I was supporting him."

Kayvin's heart leaped. Had he had a loyal backer all along?

"He was desperate, and that made him trusting, and that made him susceptible." Lord Scallong gave a little disapproving shake of his head.

Kayvin's heart settled a little lower than it had started. "You betrayed him?"

"I did not. That would have been at counter-purposes to supporting him, in the unlikely case that he succeeded. I will admit to you now I also backed Lord Fretton, because I am not a fool and a canny gambler may bet on two players. And I thought myself wise, after Narrim died. But today, you have surprised me."

Kayvin clenched his fist beside his leg, where he hoped it would not show. "Why would you be so frank with me about your support of my enemies?"

"Lord Fretton was not your enemy at the time, Your Illustrious Excellency, only an opportunist. Your attack on him came later."

"He supported Pasiphae Jade in exchange for the promise of her daughter and the establishment of his own sons on the Bull Throne. That makes him a usurper as well."

"Is that so?" Lord Scallong raised his eyebrows. "I thought him motivated by baser desires, led by a devious and compelling woman. I'm glad to hear he had some goal in mind, even if—"

"He tried to take the daughter from my sera qadra," Kayvin interrupted firmly. "That was the subject of our dispute."

He had impressed Scallong once more. "You killed him for a girl? I'd thought you disinterested."

Kayvin did not take the bait. "Lord Fretton is not dead."

"He is now."

Kayvin kept himself from asking and thought furiously. Had Fretton died while Kayvin was in Sayinia? Pasiphae Jade had not mentioned his passing, nor had the news come to the prince's quarters...

"Word will not have gone out yet beyond his court residence," Scallong explained with a generous nod. "You will be informed soon, I'm sure. I took the opportunity, before coming here, to settle my account in an investment that did not return well, and at the same time to invest in what I hope will be a more rewarding relationship with the new Arch Potentate."

Kayvin felt as if he were suspended in an oily pool, without ground to stand on and with reality strangely muffled. Had this man just...committed murder to bind them in political agreement?

He had to say something. Scallong was waiting, and Dielo was rigid beside his leg, and the chance to react was slipping away. "Keep talking," he managed.

"I have done you our first political favor, if we disregard my early encouragement of Narrim. It will be reported that Fretton succumbed to his injuries. Burns are nasty things, and since his disfigurement he was first bedridden and then has hardly left his rooms. No one will question that his condition at last proved fatal. It can be known that you struck him down to defend what belonged to you, both your sera qadra and your throne." He nodded once. "It will lend you credibility in your early days, when you otherwise have little."

"You..." Kayvin strained to speak through shock and outrage. "I do not want your political favors. I do not need your killing to take my place. I do not wish to win respect by squabbling over a sera qadra like dogs snarling over a bone. I will not begin my reign beholden to you for aid I never requested."

For a moment they looked at one another. Dielo drew a knee upward and rested his elbow upon it, tipping his head to coolly regard Scallong, playing his role.

Scallong raised a finger to scratch desultorily at his narrow beard. "I know your education has been lacking, and Narrim had confided to me how you struggled to follow political implications. So I will make myself clear." He fixed his gaze on Kayvin. "Why would I admit all this to you unless I required you to understand our positions? Know this, young prince: You will sit on your father's throne only because I permit it. I chose to watch two bears tear at one another in a pit, when I could have speared either at a time of my choosing. You are still in the pit, young prince. I watch because I am interested. But if you do not amuse me, or if you try to climb out of the pit, then I will do what is best for the nation and for myself."

Kayvin could not breathe. He could not think. This was everything he'd feared, everything he'd known to be secretly true, everything he knew others knew. Even as a new Arch Potentate, he was a laughingstock prince.

Beside Kayvin's leg, Dielo was fiercely rigid, nearly trembling. His fingers dug into the fur lying across the step.

Kayvin needed to say something. He needed to act. Scallong was waiting, the faintest of sneers on his lip. His mother was in the study, listening. Dielo was watching.

A foot scuffed the floor to Kayvin's left, and Galen moved just into the edge of his peripheral vision, adjusting his hand on his sword. "I can put anyone you like into a pit, Your Excellency."

Scallong snorted discreetly, and then he glanced again at Galen. "What's that?"

"A human," Kayvin answered evenly. "I found lots of them over the mountains."

"And you brought one back with you?"

"I find some of them are more trustworthy than even the noblest of the Mandoral court."

Scallong sighed. "It's a shame when a prince cannot trust his own people."

"My lord prince was not only speaking of moral character," Galen rumbled. "He meant effectiveness."

Scallong scowled. "I don't think—"

Galen moved in a sudden blur, landing one step down and reaching over the low table. His sword swept across Scallong's chest, tugging at the woven tunic and catching on a golden brooch. Scallong recoiled, arms up to shield himself, and looked in first alarm and then anger at Galen. "Call off your dog!"

Kayvin raised a hand, though Galen had already paused.

Galen shrugged. "I didn't hurt you. You made a threat, I made a threat. Now we all know where we stand."

Scallong dabbed at his chest through the torn fabric, checking for blood. "Empty void. You can't just set your guards on your courtiers."

Kayvin wrapped his fingers on the arms of the chair. "If you look at the histories of the Arch Potentate, you'll find I can." He drew a short breath, and it wasn't enough. "Thank you for your visit, Lord Scallong. I'll give your words the attention they deserve. May the rest of your day be as pleasant."

Scallong frowned. "Consider those words. You have little support and less experience."

"Thank you for your concern."

Scallong gave a small crooked smile, made a tiny mocking bow, and withdrew.

When he had gone, Kayvin turned to Galen. "What were you thinking?"

"I wasn't, not much," Galen admitted. "I just tried to imagine what Lisveth would do, and I thought she'd provoke him. And I supposed he was more interested in talking than fighting."

"He said he'd just killed Lord Fretton," Kayvin protested.

"Either he killed a severely injured man, recently bedridden, or he had someone else do it. And if he used magic, I still have the amulet."

Still, that had been brave, or foolhardy, or bolder than Kayvin had been in the same moment. "You skimmed his chest neatly enough. That got his attention."

"Yeah." Galen grinned sheepishly. "I didn't mean to get that close. I misstepped on the stairs. But I suppose it made the point."

"I doubt it put him off his intent, but I confess I was grateful for the intervention."

"I hate him," Dielo said numbly from Kayvin's other side. "He is—he came to order you to...like a..."

"Surely the worst is over, then?" Kayvin sighed and shifted in the chair, newly uncomfortable. "Send in the next. And let's hope there will be fewer threats."

CHAPTER 119

THE SKIN ON GALEN's chest was reddened and blistered, but he was fortunate. Raea, the Shining Gem, was learning to lean upon a new walking stick, and Yovela was still pale and weak from her time in the ice. After her sleep Lisveth was able to stand and speak normally, but Galen knew her well enough to know she was still recovering from whatever magical exertions had been necessary.

So he had not bothered the physicians sent to the Shining Gem's rooms with his own injury, and instead he had smeared some cold grease from a lunch plate over it when no one was looking, which was easy enough with so much distraction.

Raea insisted Kayvin be housed immediately in the Arch Potentate's royal quarters, nominally even if he had not moved in fully. The appearance of establishment was important, she said. Arad had been dispatched to order the other sera qadra out and to prepare for his prince's arrival.

Galen had gaped at the rooms, remembering belatedly to close his mouth. But he'd never been in a palace, much less a Mandoral palace, much less the Arch Potentate's innermost refuge. Whatever he might have imagined would have been less colorful, less ornate, and less splendid. There was a long, low table in front of Kayvin's couch, with benches and seats near should a meeting become friendly. Behind the couch was an inlaid table and a cabinet full of small figures. To one side, the room opened onto a balcony that overlooked what must be an expansive garden. Overhead, the ceiling was painted in exquisite jewel tones.

Galen had stood behind Kayvin's bull-headed chair for two hours or so, he thought. He kept the Poet's Eye outside his shirt, both to display it prominently (and perhaps discourage any magical attacks from other discontent courtiers) and to keep it from lying directly atop the burn mark. Fortunately, there had been no more menace of Scallong's ilk.

Galen could walk for miles and hours, but standing still was an entirely different challenge, and by midday he was ready to throw himself down on one of the pillows on the steps. He and Kayvin sighed together in relieved gratitude when Dielo excused himself after the final supplicant and then reappeared to report the sleeping room was ready, if His Illustrious Excellency would care for a rest.

"Empty void, I'm not ready for all that," Kayvin muttered in response. "'My lord' will do, if we're in private."

Dielo's eyes slid to Galen.

"He's not an outsider," Kayvin said firmly. "Not anymore, not after he's fought me and taunted me and blocked me and saved me. Not to mention he stood as my guard through all my first audiences, so he knows as much of my nascent rule as I do. You may speak before him as you would before Yovela."

Galen was not sure how to respond to this. *Thank you* seemed inappropriate, especially as he did not want a position in Kayvin's court. But he recognized the gesture of trust for what it was, and he gave a small bow, wondering if it was the right kind.

"The others will come soon," Dielo promised. "Yovela is escorting the Shining Gem to her own apartments to change. Then we'll go to the dining room and—"

"No," Kayvin said shortly. "I can't see straight, I can barely speak my name in proper order, and I'm far too tired to present myself yet again as a new ruler. Tonight I will eat a small, informal supper in my own rooms, with my mother and sera qadra and my human friends to explain what they've done. That is good enough."

Galen thought Kayvin was probably also afraid of making a visible mistake, especially in his fatigue. It would be difficult enough to claim a throne, but proving himself against popular opinion... Galen did not know much of court politics, and he was grateful for that, but he'd heard enough today ever after Scallong to know Kayvin's position was far from secure. Anyone with a promising alternative to the past usurper or the weak usurped might take the field.

Dielo nodded, bowed, and left the room.

Kayvin dropped into a low-backed lounge and propped his elbow upon the cushioned arm. Galen ventured, "I..."

"Yes?"

Galen was not a subject, but he thought it was impolite to sit in the presence of any royalty. On the other hand, he'd sat beside Kayvin many times, and he'd been awake through the night and this difficult day. Though it would be a strain to call their connection a friendship, this felt awkward, and he was so tired.

What would Lisveth do? She would probably sit, and chance the consequences or talk herself out of them. Galen looked around, found a bench, and went to it.

"Yes," Kayvin said simply. "Yes, of course." He rubbed his forehead. "I'm sure I'll be told I should start by strengthening my image and emphasizing my position, but as long as I'm failing in that, at least I'll fail where I can show my appreciation."

"You're not failing," Galen said automatically. Then he added, "You've been king through at least midday, and no revolution yet."

"Yet." Kayvin blew out his breath. "I am not ready to rule," he admitted. "Not now. Perhaps not ever. My father was far better prepared to be the Arch Potentate, and he was killed by his own courtesan."

Galen listened.

"I am a musician, at best a composer. Even the woman who killed my father mocked me. She called me an artist, not a ruler—and she is right."

Galen frowned. "Why can't one be both?"

Kayvin shook his head. "Art cannot rule; art is a pretty waste of time and energy, a distraction. It is imaginary purpose, a false picture for fools to believe in. If I had been a better prince instead of a distracted artist, I might have prevented my father's death, might have saved my mother sooner, might not have lost my servants to Pasiphae Jade's cruelty."

Galen shifted and looked away, uncomfortable with the prince's raw confession in his fatigue. "It's hard for me to say, as I'm just a runaway farm boy and I don't know much about princes or statecraft." He crossed his arms and looked across the balcony. "But the way I see it, Lisveth's art just prevented a war."

"What?"

"Her compelling picture saved you from Pasiphae Jade's coercion, saved your mother's life and Yovela's, kept your Rideis army from marching on our people." He shrugged. "It's a pretty waste of time, but it has its small uses."

Kayvin conceded a small, wistful smile. "You tell a good story, at least."

Galen grinned. "And did that additional small art serve its purpose?"

Now Kayvin laughed aloud, a full, appreciative sound and Galen realized the prince had a good laugh. "Yes," Kayvin admitted at last. "I am not sure I believe you, but I agree you've spun a nice tale to placate my conscience."

"Good. And now, if you can spare me, I'm going to take a nap." Galen lay back on the cushioned bench. "I was awake all last night, watching for patrols and planning a small revolution."

Kayvin looked startled and then nodded. "Oh, I suppose, yes, of course. Yes, get some sleep."

Galen hardly heard the end of the sentence.

It was not nearly long enough later that the others arrived. "We are here at last," announced a voice, and Galen turned his head to see the liberated queen limping into the room, supported by a walking stick and Yovela at her arm.

Galen stood and bowed. Kayvin hurried forward to take her other arm and ease her into one of the cushioned chairs.

She settled back and propped her stick under her hand. "Curse this foot. I'm going to need some time to work out how to use this."

Kayvin winced. "I'm sorry. I—"

She raised a hand to cut him off. "Don't apologize for what is not your fault," she said firmly. "The Arch Potentate should know better."

He stopped and smiled, but the smile did not reach his eyes, and even Galen could see he did not believe it.

"This is Lisveth, the Fire Brigand," Dielo said grandly from the door, and then he stepped aside to gesture Lisveth in.

Galen laughed aloud. "Couldn't you have given him another name?"

"Quit ruining my entrance." Lisveth, dressed in Mandoral silks, made an elegant curtsy to Prince Kayvin. "Your Highness."

"That was a prince's address," Raea said gently but emphatically. "Now he is to be—"

"Just now, I am entertaining my nearest friends and family in my closest room," Kayvin interrupted, "and I assure you, Lisveth has called me much worse." He smiled wearily. "Lisveth, please, come and sit down beside Galen there. Fire Brigand, you say? That was the bandit you killed, that first night. What do you want with her name?"

Lisveth scowled. "The Fire Brigand has more history than that whiny monster." She sat down beside Galen and gave a long, soft exhale.

Galen slid an arm behind her and leaned close. Perhaps she had another name she could claim, from before her Fire Brigand days, but he would not ask again. Instead he whispered, "How are you?"

"Still tired," she admitted. "I slept, hard, but I woke up tired. And most of my muscles think I carried an ox over a mountain pass."

Galen shifted his arm, opening it, and she slowly relaxed into him, letting him take her weight.

"So, your first audience is ended," Raea declared. "Now, in the privacy of our own rooms, before our meal is brought, I have a request."

Kayvin put on a brave smile. "Yes?"

"May I hear my birthday song now?" Raea asked with a better smile. "May we put aside politics and planning for a handful of minutes, to indulge me before we dine?"

Kayvin sagged with relief, and he looked from Dielo to Yovela. "I had originally hoped for a larger chorus, but we may be able to make do."

Dielo rose and went to a nearby room, returning almost immediately with a lyre. "I think three voices can carry it nicely, my lord."

Kayvin looked at the instrument and gave a small smile.

Dielo and Yovela joined Kayvin as he settled the lyre in place. He gave it a single strum, approving the tuning, and then he nodded to his sera qadra. He picked out a waterfall of notes, and the music began in earnest.

Galen listened in faint wonder. He had often heard music, of course, songs around fires and across tables and on roads. He had even heard Kayvin play, that first night they met. He had never imagined music like this, all tightly interlocking harmony and close rhythms and sweeping runs that seemed to carry him with the notes. This was no tavern song, no common melody to be shared on a road; this was a story worked in notes, a sculpture of rhythm, a portrait of sound.

Beside him, Lisveth was equally rapt. When at last the song ended, they both sat for a moment, caught in a disorientation like they had drunk too quickly.

Raea clapped her hands and beamed at them. "Such beautiful music."

Kayvin grinned, happy and proud, and he acknowledged the compliment with a nod. Then he turned and looked between Dielo and Yovela. "Thank you. That was well done."

Raea settled her hands in her lap and nodded. "If you order your kingdom as well as you order your scores, you will be a fine Arch Potentate."

Kayvin's grin tightened. "Thank you. I'm glad you enjoyed it."

"I'll see to the food," Dielo said quickly.

"The song was wonderful," Raea said, smoothly returning to the music. "Thank you, my son, for composing it for me, and thank you, Dielo and Yovela, for performing it tonight."

Dielo and Yovela gave gracious bows.

"I know you sent away the sera qadra that was here," Raea said to Kayvin. "That's understandable. But where is the rest of your own? I thought perhaps you wanted only your favorites tonight, but this place seems quite empty."

Kayvin's jaw tightened. "This is my sera qadra. I sent the others away after Pasiphae Jade killed Father. I wanted no one I did not fully trust."

Raea's lips thinned. "I understand that, of course. Very wise. But now that you've reclaimed your place, you must fill your sera qadra and demonstrate—"

Kayvin held up a hand and looked at his knees. "Not now, I—"

"It's good that you have a virilo, as that will help to show your new strength, but you—"

"Please!" Kayvin moderated his voice. "Let's not talk about it before we eat."

"But if you want to present the image of a strong Arch—"

"Not today," Kayvin repeated, his voice strained.

"There is another of us, my lady," Yovela intervened. "Lirin is younger and is—undoubtedly affected by the events of the day.

I'm sure His Highness has given her leave to take some time for herself."

But Kayvin looked confusedly at her. "No, I—I thought you had... You took Lisveth, and I assumed Lirin went with you."

The two of them looked at Dielo, who shook his head. "I haven't seen her. Not here, and not in the Amethyst Prince's rooms."

Galen didn't know who they were talking about; Yovela had mentioned only Dielo. "Who is she? What does she look like?"

Kayvin made an exasperated gesture. "Young woman, really a girl, dark hair... You wouldn't have seen her today."

"Was she the one to bull into you during the fight?" Lisveth suggested gently.

Kayvin looked at her sharply. "Yes, that's Lirin."

Lisveth nodded. "She went with the guards and Pasiphae Jade."

Kayvin's face lost color. "Empty..."

"What's happened?" Raea demanded. "Did they take her? Will she be held to coerce you, as Yovela was?"

"No." Kayvin's mouth drew tight. "She's there to protect her mother."

"Her—Kayvin!"

"It's a long story," he said preemptively.

"Let her go," Raea said firmly. "Whatever happened, whatever you may feel for her—if Pasiphae Jade thinks she can use her against you, so will others, and you cannot show any weakness now. You cut off your sera qadra for safety before, and that was wise. Do it again with this girl now."

"She is my sister." Kayvin's jaw tightened.

"In your sera qadra?" Raea spoke in disbelief, and then she shook her head. "No, Pasiphae Jade didn't come to your father until..." She began to count on her fingers.

"She is my sister!" Kayvin repeated. "Whether or not my father is also her father, her mother was courtesan to the Arch Potentate. And I have taken her into my household."

Raea's mouth settled in a thin line. "I can see it must have been a long story, indeed."

"I'll go," Yovela said quietly. "I can speak with her."

CHAPTER 120

YOVELA STOPPED, HOLDING BACK from the final spiral staircase. "Go and get her," she said to the guard. "Do not tell her who is waiting, only that she is to come."

As he climbed the twisting stairs to the room above, she retreated a little distance. She did not want Lirin to call her name; from what Yovela had heard, Pasiphae Jade believed her dead, and there was no reason yet to disillusion her. Not until things were settled and Kayvin's position was secure. Yovela didn't know what leverage Pasiphae Jade might still have, even here, but denying her full knowledge seemed wise in any case.

Indistinct voices filtered down to her, first Lirin's high protest against the guard's baritone and a quieter feminine remonstrance. At last Lirin subsided, and footsteps moved toward the stairs. Yovela folded her hands and waited.

Lirin did not see her at first, not until she was only a few paces away. Then she raised her head and gasped. "Yovela!" She rushed to embrace her. "I thought you were dead!"

"Not quite," Yovela whispered, hugging the girl in return.

"But—but then she didn't kill you!" Lirin drew back. "You can tell them to release her. She didn't kill you!" She started back toward the stairs.

Yovela caught her arm. "Lirin..."

Lirin let herself be pulled to a stop. She remained facing away. "But she didn't kill you."

"She killed the Arch Potentate," Yovela said simply.

Lirin dropped her head, and Yovela drew her back into another embrace.

"Did you stay with her all this time today?"

Lirin nodded into Yovela's shoulder. "I was—afraid for her."

"She won't be killed here."

"That's not what I'm afraid of."

Yovela nodded, understanding.

"If I stay there... I'm a member of the prince's sera qadra. They cannot touch me, not since they've heard about Lord Fretton. If I stay with her..."

That wouldn't be enough, Yovela thought, but she understood. She turned to the guard waiting a short distance away. "What's your name?"

"Piero."

"His Illustrious Excellency will want to see the prisoner himself soon. He will want her to be just as he left her in your care. He will not want the mother of his youngest sera qadra girl to be harmed. I am counting on you, Piero, to communicate this to your fellow guards."

Piero frowned. "I am just one of the many who serve here, and I'm afraid I cannot promise that."

Yovela tightened her grip on Lirin. "Then tell me your captain's name."

"That's Captain Falchen."

"Please communicate this to Captain Falchen, then, and His Illustrious Excellency will count on him to manage his own men. If keeping order is beyond him, then I'm sure someone more capable can be found."

Piero's scowl deepened. "Don't come down here and threaten us, whore."

"Then don't require threat merely to keep a prisoner secure." Yovela's heart was racing, but she kept her expression firm. "I'll tell His Illustrious Excellency of your service to him."

She stepped back, pulling Lirin with her, and turned to go up the passage. She didn't know if she was shaking; she couldn't feel her fingers. She had invoked Kayvin like a protective charm, underscoring her own powerlessness, but she knew Piero needed more than her words.

She put an arm around Lirin again. "We didn't know where you were."

"I came with her when they arrested her." Lirin was quiet for a moment, and then she asked, "Is he angry with me?"

"What?"

"For—stopping him. Is he angry with me?"

"He is not," Yovela answered readily.

"Are you sure?"

They passed into the proper area of the palace, fresh and spacious after the close tower. "He is angry with Pasiphae Jade, and with himself, and with his courtiers, and with a good number of other people and things. He does not have time to be angry with you."

"But I stopped him from killing her. He must have wanted to."

"Wasn't she trying to kill him at the same time?" Yovela squeezed Lirin's shoulders. "Do you think Kayvin would be happy if he killed someone?"

"No," Lirin answered immediately.

Yovela nodded. "He may not be able to admit it aloud, not yet, but he's a little grateful to you for stopping him." She gave Lirin a hard look. "But still, she is a murderer. She stole his throne. She put me into ice. She must answer for her crimes."

Lirin fell silent. She had been placed in an impossible position by Kayvin, whom she admired, and Yovela could empathize even while hating the woman Lirin felt sympathy toward.

If any doubt remained as to Kayvin's resentment, he crushed it with the hug he gave Lirin as she entered. "We didn't know you were there," he explained gruffly, rocking her in a tight embrace. "Are you all right?"

"Yes." Lirin sniffed. "But she—will she be safe there?"

Yovela tapped Kayvin's shoulder and gave him a warning look behind Lirin's back.

"I only want her held for her trial," Kayvin said carefully. He furrowed his eyebrows at Yovela, and then understanding came. "I'll send word that she is to be kept secure and comfortable until then, with reports and responsibility to me."

Lirin squeezed him again. "Thank you."

Kayvin drew back gently. "Of course. I'm glad you're here and safe. Now, I have some people I'd like you to meet. Are you ready?"

Lirin rubbed at her face. "I'm a mess. Not a very hospitable sera qadra member."

"You are here as my younger sister," Kayvin said firmly.

Lirin turned her face up to him in shock. "I—your sister—!"

"Yes."

"But if—"

He placed a finger on her lips. "There will be no counting. You are the daughter of an Arch Potentate, and of the woman who sat for a time on his throne, and you are a princess in my household."

Yovela smiled. This was the best he could give her, protection and status and freedom from both her mother's shadow and his sera qadra. It was messy, but it provided its own explanation, offering the dramatic and mostly true story of hiding a princess in an unlikely place to overwrite duller rumors of the disinterested prince and a courtesan's daughter.

"I don't look much like a princess, either," Lirin protested, pushing a hand through her tangled hair.

"Go and wash your face, then. But don't bother changing; one of my guests is still wearing his road clothes from Sayinia."

"Sayinia?" she gasped.

"Two from there, in fact. Hurry, and I'll introduce you." Kayvin held out a hand to Yovela, and as Lirin went off, he said in a low voice, "Thank you for fetching her."

"She's worried. I warned a guard called Piero and his captain Falchen that you would hold them responsible for keeping Pasiphae Jade unmolested."

Kayvin nodded. "Make a note of their names, please."

When Lirin slipped into the gathering a few moments later, she smiled shyly around as Kayvin beckoned her to join them. Her eyes went wide and she curtsied low to Raea, and she stared in open fascination at Galen and Lisveth. "So you are—human?"

"Very," Lisveth replied.

"But you—you don't look..." Lirin closed her mouth firmly.

Lisveth leaned forward and whispered, "Neither do you." She winked.

CHAPTER 121

"NOW THAT WE HAVE a moment," Kayvin said, selecting a berry from the overfull bowl, "without someone trying to kill me or courtiers shouting for precedence to appraise me, at last I want to know—how did you release them from the ice? How did you unwork that spell without harming them?"

Lisveth took a drink and set her partly gilded cup beside her cushion. "I am not nearly smart enough to understand this," she warned. "I am not a state mage, and I did not train to be anything near one. I am a barely adequate sorceress making my best guesses."

"Your guesses seem to have been plausible enough to work. Go on." Kayvin glanced at Dielo, settling beside Yovela and setting a newly filled plate before her, and gestured for Lisveth to continue.

Lisveth folded her hands. "The fountains are not merely fountains; they're reservoirs, but for arcane energy rather than water. They're very like the amulets, and I wouldn't be surprised to find an Eye or three if you tore one down to the base. Maybe they were put there to provide extra power when needed, in case something should happen in the throne room."

Kayvin nodded. "That would have been the place of negotiations, back when we conquered. A wise man might want extra assurance when bartering with a dragon."

Lisveth continued, "When I heard about the ice, I was astounded that anyone could hold a spell so powerful, but I thought I simply didn't understand Rideis magic. I don't, actually, but at least in this case I was right to question it. Pasiphae Jade did capture her prisoners in ice"—she gave an apologetic nod to Raea and Yovela—"but she did not maintain the spell constantly, all day without ceasing, while sleeping, and for weeks or months. That was sustained by the fountain, which drew energy for the spell from the body inside."

Kayvin stared. "Their own bodies were fueling the spell that kept them entrapped."

"In part. It's diabolical, but very practical." Lisveth reached for a honeyed roll. "It would not have lasted forever, of course; the fountains would need occasional maintenance, and the reservoirs would have at last been drained at some point. The prisoner could provide only the continuing impetus for the spell. But they enabled her to do magic that was otherwise impossible."

Kayvin shook his head. "I never dreamed of such a thing. Mother, did you know about the fountains?"

"I did not."

Dielo's expression had tightened, and his fingers flexed on the cushion beneath him. Yovela gave him a suspicious look. Kayvin, following her eyes, prompted, "Did you know something about this?"

Dielo shook his head quickly. "No."

Yovela frowned.

Dielo looked away from her, toward Lirin. "This maintenance, as you say—would it also have been drawn from a body?"

Lirin shrugged. "This is all far beyond me. I can tell you a fine horse needs to eat, but I don't know how best to feed it."

Kayvin tried to keep his question quiet. "What did you see?"

Dielo's eyes flicked around, touching none of them. "While you were away, after I returned, she had me taken into the throne room. I didn't know what was happening, but there was something—it was like the healing amulet, but so much more intense. It left me exhausted for days."

Lisveth nodded. "That could have been it. She found a way to fuel it with someone else, to avoid incapacitating herself." She gave a small huff of impressed disgust. "Clever, anyway."

Dielo was clearly uncomfortable, avoiding Yovela's concerned look, so Kayvin turned again to the magic of it. "I wonder how she knew," he mused. "Did she read about them, or did she discover them? Did she used to sit at night in the throne room, staring into the fountains and wondering?" He tightened his jaw. "Maybe Pasiphae Jade will be kind enough to write out the theory of it for us."

"She'll have to dictate," Raea said darkly, picking up a little roll of thinly sliced pork.

"What?"

Raea gave him a sharp look. "She can't write with her fingers broken, of course." She kept her eyes on him, and they all could read clearly enough the question she did not voice aloud before his tiny court.

Kayvin stared in a moment of quiet horror, and then he nodded. "Yes, I—I heard it done, when she was taken."

Raea nodded. "And you won't be able to let them heal, not while she lives. Or you will wake to find a trail of dead prison guards leading to your sleeping pit and an icicle in your heart."

Galen stared. Lirin kept her eyes on her knees. Kayvin looked at his plate and did not answer. Beside Galen, Lisveth gave a tiny shudder and closed her fists.

Raea thinned her lips and looked again to Lisveth. "But how did you break the spell itself, without Pasiphae Jade knowing what you did?"

Lisveth cleared her throat. "That was simple enough, once I knew what the fountains did. If I hold a flame"—she raised a small flicker in her palm—"I'd know immediately if Kayvin wicks it out. But if Kayvin lit a candle and left it on a table, he wouldn't know if someone later blew it out, not until he came back into the room hours later. As long as I worked between the times when she checked on the candle, so to speak, I could handle the magic however I wanted."

"But how?" Kayvin pressed, and Galen thought he looked strained.

"You had told us Pasiphae Jade wanted multiple amulets, and there must have been a reason beyond just completing a collection. Could they do something together that they couldn't do apart? So I began to try things, perhaps a little recklessly, and I found that an amulet that absorbs magic can pass that energy to one that expends it." She reached across and laid a finger on the Poet's Eye on Galen's shirt. "I drained Galen's amulet into the two I had, pushing the power of all three into the two fountains. That was enough new energy to disrupt the spell and the fountain's supporting magic, and I could drag the women out of the fountains." She turned to Raea and Yovela. "I beg your pardons." She nodded to Kayvin. "Then you helpfully recharged

Galen's amulet—thank you, Your Highness—and I drained it and the others again to break them safely out of the remaining ice."

"But she said she was the only one who could lift the spell without killing them."

"She lied." Lisveth shrugged. "That's no surprise. If she would murder and take hostages, why quibble in being strictly accurate about a spell? Especially the one that's keeping her safe?"

"She just—lied," Kayvin repeated in soft incredulity.

Yovela slid a hand about his arm and gave a sympathetic squeeze.

Raea had stopped pretending to eat, and she gazed at her son, her expression unreadable. Galen wondered if she was grateful to him, or angry with him, or disappointed, or proud.

"At least it's over," Raea said heavily. "Now we can get back to the way things should be."

Screams erupted from outside, carrying over the balcony. Galen jerked around with the others to stare toward the garden. "What is that?"

Kayvin went toward the balustrade, shaking his head. "I can't see. Just the garden."

The sounds were growing—shouts of alarm, and others of warning, and the sounds of spreading chaos as people abandoned their work or their colleagues. Kayvin rose on his toes, as if he could see further.

Yovela followed and put a hand about his upper arm without speaking. Dielo asked quietly from his place, "What do you think it is?"

"I'm afraid it may be a revolt." Kayvin's voice was steady but low. "Word has gotten out by now that I fought the Arch Potentate this morning. If Pasiphae Jade and the others thought I would be welcomed as a new ruler, I would not have been suffered to remain the Amethyst Prince all this time. I was safe only because I was unimportant."

"What has been going on?" Raea demanded. "What do you mean, you were unimportant?"

Kayvin shook his head. "Now is not the time, not if there is something at the gates."

Yovela shook her head. "No, that's within the walls. Listen."

He stepped back from the balustrade, frowning. "You may be right. It's coming from the west. I'm going to go look." He turned toward the door.

"I'll go with—"

"No, Yovela, stay here."

Galen followed, because he hadn't been told not to and because he'd been called a bodyguard and because the sounds were too disturbing to ignore. They recalled a time when Galen had seen an angry ox push into a market street, shouldering aside vendor carts and overturning a few tables. One man had been thrown into a wall and another trampled before the ox was herded into an alley. That, with the shouting and crashing and screaming, had sounded something like this.

Or maybe like a stampede of traffic to escape a rising fire...

He followed Kayvin at a jog through the corridors, some closed and some more like porches along the palace exterior. At last the prince turned and leaned out to look over a wide courtyard, walled and green in the golden evening light. Galen had no time to notice its other features, for within the courtyard two monsters were mauling a man while people fled in all directions, shouting for help or wailing in fear.

"Empty void," Kayvin breathed.

Galen had never seen anything like the beasts. They looked a bit like short snakes, if snakes were the height of a small donkey and had stubby outset legs like lizards. Their heads were enormous, long and flat and wide, and they bit the limp body with toothy jaws that tore flesh with each twist of their heads.

"Spawning." Kayvin stared, his body rigid.

Galen couldn't breathe. He wanted to run, to run simultaneously into the courtyard to pull someone to safety and back down the corridor away from the lizard-like beasts.

"What are they?" His voice was quiet against the shouting.

"It's the spawning." Kayvin looked behind them and then again to the courtyard. "They are basilisk hatchlings." He opened his mouth, hesitated, spoke. "I've never seen them, but they're worse than I imagined."

"This is the spawning? This is—isn't this what the..." Galen stopped. He couldn't ask if this was what Pasiphae Jade had meant to prevent, not mere hours after her defeat. Dethroning her hadn't brought the hatchlings—had it? Surely it was a terrible coincidence of timing.

The ground in the courtyard heaved, and a wide, flat head emerged, shaking soil away as the hatchling crawled into the open. It turned, looking after the fleeing people, and opened its gaping mouth.

Kayvin seized Galen's arm and drew him backward. "Don't look."

It would not have been worse than the sight they'd already seen, but Galen went with the prince.

"We have to get back." Kayvin turned and began to run.

Galen kept pace. What would they do? Yovela had described them as swarming, at least in the stories. What could be done against such creatures?

"How do we stop them?" he asked, running at Kayvin's elbow.

Kayvin didn't answer.

Chapter 122

WHEN THEY REACHED THE Arch Potentate's rooms, a half dozen guards stood at the door. Kayvin stiffened, and Galen stepped aside to give himself a little space—as if fighting a half dozen palace guards was a reasonable option to consider.

But the man in front gave a saluting bow. "I know you ordered most guards away until allegiances could be reviewed, but we could not stand aside while something is happening and our lord is unprotected." He went to one knee and bent his head. "I am willing to swear to you here, if you will have me."

Kayvin hesitated for only a breath. "Do you know what is happening outside?"

"No, my lord. But that is the duty of others. Our duty is to rush to the defense of the Arch Potentate in times of threat." He looked up. "The usurper is imprisoned, and the previous ruler is dead. Any assault on the palace can be only a pretender hoping to take advantage of instability. I do not need to know who it is to know I cannot aid them."

Kayvin nodded once. "But this is not a political assault—this is the spawning."

The man gaped for just a moment, and then he gave a firm jerk of his chin. "Then you'll need good guards."

Kayvin gestured down the hall. "If anyone wishes to go, now that you understand what we face, then go. If anyone wishes to stay with me, I will take your oaths now."

The men looked at one another, and then one put his eyes to the floor and separated from the group, walking quickly down the corridor. The others knelt before Kayvin. "I pledge to serve my Arch Potentate, to my very life."

"I thank you sincerely and pledge to honor your trust and service."

The first raised his head. "I'm Harrith, my lord."

"Thank you for coming. Follow me."

Inside, the others were grouped close together in their worry. "Is it a rebellion?" Raea asked before Kayvin could speak.

He shook his head. "It's the spawning."

"The spawning!"

"I've seen it. I don't know how it can be here already."

Her hand was bloodless on her walking stick. "I only know the stories."

"It looks like the stories are accurate," Kayvin admitted worriedly. "At least in terms of threat. People are already dying."

"But you have the amulets," Dielo protested. "You can stop them."

"What?" Raea looked back and forth between them.

"Pasiphae Jade wanted the amulets to stop the spawning," Kayvin explained briefly. "But I don't know..."

"What about the amulets?" Lisveth demanded. "And what's this spawning look like?"

"Monsters." Galen's voice scraped in his throat. "Like lizards trying to grow into horses. They were eating someone."

"Fair night," she breathed.

"She wanted the amulets to stop the spawning. But how can the spawning have come so quickly after Pasiphae Jade is gone?" Kayvin put his hands to his head as if he wanted to rip his dark red hair. "I—I wasn't sure... It was such a self-aggrandizing explanation, that she only wanted to save the nation. I believed her, yes, but also... Why now?"

"If it comes this year, it comes on some day of this year. This must be that day." Raea's tight expression belied her resigned words.

"They appear first near the mountains and in the palace," Lirin offered hurriedly. "Then they spread into the surrounding areas."

Kayvin looked at her. "What?"

"I was with her while you were in Sayinia. I know a little bit. They appear here first, and then they move outward from the palace into the city and through the countryside."

"A curse," Kayvin muttered. "A curse on the royal house or a judgment. What do we do with them? How do we stop them?"

Lirin shook her head frantically. "I don't know."

"But you were with her while she was preparing!"

"I don't know! I don't understand any of it. She had—she had notes! I can get the notes!"

Lirin rushed away, hair flying. Kayvin leaped up behind her. "Lirin!"

She didn't go far. Lirin dashed to the study where Raea had sat during Kayvin's audiences. She raced around the desk and began to paw through papers. "I saw them here. There were notes here. Calculations or something."

"And they were about the spawning?" Kayvin began to skim the pages, stacking them as he went. Galen's hands hovered over the desk; he wanted to help but was afraid to disturb anything. Beside him, Lisveth, Dielo, and Yovela watched and chewed their lips.

"I'm sure of it." Lirin shoved aside a pile that offered no help. "She said it was about the amulets."

"She needed the amulets... Here!" Kayvin pressed back the cover of a small bound book filled with handwritten notes, with numbers and arrows filling the margins. He pulled it close and bent to study it. "This has all the amulets listed and some sort of emission calculations." He ran his thumb over the pages, fanning them into a full finger's breadth of written notes. "Empty void, this is a couple years of work, at least. Give me a moment."

They all stood about the desk and watched Kayvin read.

Galen felt foolish, running after the prince only to watch him search the desk and read a notebook. This was worse than waiting for Lisveth to work some sort of magic, where at least something useful was being done while he stood by. Now there were five useless observers, and Kayvin was not even working magic but merely reading.

Lirin was the only one to keep shuffling through the desk. She did not disturb the papers before Kayvin, but she drew open the drawers around him, lifted and tipped a little vase, shook an elegant coffer. She turned to Galen with the coffer in her hands. "Can you break this open?"

He eyed it. While the decoration was worked in metal, it looked as if it were meant more for storing knickknacks than holding coin on a high road journey. He took it from her. "Stand back."

"Be careful."

He set it on the floor and swung a brazier's poker into the coffer's lid. The iron bar stuck, and he bashed the coffer against the tile with his second blow.

Lisveth put a hand on his arm. "That's enough. Pry it from here; you can't risk penetrating to what's inside."

He wrenched apart the broken wood and shook out two amulets. Red and violet—the Singer's Eye they had left with General Artextra, and the Player's Eye that had once frightened the boy Harold by blinking in the temple.

Lisveth took them eagerly. "Hello, my lambs. It's good to see you again."

Lirin eyed her suspiciously, and she edged nearer Dielo and Yovela.

But Yovela only gave Lisveth a quick glance and then squeezed Lirin's hand. Her eyes were fixed on Kayvin, and she put a hand on his shoulder, her expression shifting from watchful concern to resignation. Dielo sank to his knees beside the desk, hardly breathing, leaning close as if he could will the notebook to give up its secrets.

A moment later, Kayvin shook his head. "I don't—I don't understand. Almost all of it, I don't understand. Some of it is obvious, like the amulets themselves, but most of it... It's as if it's written in code. I don't think it truly is, I only mean that I can't make anything of it."

"Is there anything about using the amulets?" Lirin asked breathlessly, as if he needed prompting. She pulled the notebook toward herself and looked at it.

Kayvin shook his head. "Maybe if I had a week or two to take this apart and piece it together. But this—it might as well be in another language. I don't know what these numbers are; she hasn't labeled anything on this entire page. She did this for herself, and if it's from her courtesan days, then it probably was intentionally obtuse in case it was found." Kayvin groaned and propped his forehead in his hands. "I might be able to work out some of this, but never in time to help anyone today."

"Then we flee," Yovela said firmly. "We go through the mountains, as our people did before."

"Straight into the human lands and human armies," Kayvin said heavily, "with monsters picking off the slowest all the way."

"How can we stay?" Yovela's curt gesture encompassed the rising noise.

"How can we flee?" Kayvin jerked his head back to indicate the other room. "Can my mother run? We cannot fit wagons into the passage, even if we could get her safely there. If we run, we sacrifice the elderly, the young, the ill, the injured, and all those who love them too much to let them die alone."

"What else can we do?" Galen heard himself say, as if he were a part of this decision and as if he knew anything about it. "I'll do what I can, but I don't know how to fight those things."

He glanced at Lisveth, who raised her eyes from the notes with an apologetic expression. She'd made less of them than Kayvin.

Kayvin flattened his hand against the topmost page, as if he could absorb its secrets through sheer will. He squeezed his eyes tightly shut and shook his head. "I don't know. I don't know!"

"These rooms look more secure than others," Galen said, looking around. This was only partly true; the balcony was exposed over an open garden, though there was an extra corridor leading away from the study, which he supposed could be barricaded if necessary. But he thought having a suggested action would help Kayvin in this moment. "Let's keep your mother here, where she may be more protected while we make the next decisions."

"Why are you all speaking as if she's dead?" Lirin demanded. "Ask her what the notes mean. Ask her yourself!"

They turned to stare at Lirin. "But she's lost the throne," Yovela said. "Why would she help the one who overthrew her?"

"This was what she wanted—to stop the spawning!"

Galen didn't know much of Rideis politics, but he thought it unlikely that Pasiphae Jade had done all he had seen from pure altruism.

But Kayvin nodded. "Yes." He tucked the notebook into his long vest, securing it above his sash. "I'll go to Pasiphae Jade."

"Yes!" Lirin nodded enthusiastically. "She can help."

"Will she?" Yovela asked, with a worried look toward Lirin.

"If she refuses, we will have lost nothing except a moment of my pride," Kayvin replied tersely. "Lisveth, will you come with me? You've used these amulets; she might say something you'll understand."

"Of course."

"Yovela, Dielo, Lirin, stay with my mother."

Galen followed back to the main room, where Raea sat on her couch with her hands folded white on the head of the walking stick. "Didn't you find anything helpful?" she asked, looking from face to face.

"We must go to Pasiphae Jade," Kayvin said firmly. "In the meantime—Harrith! We need to know what's happening outside. Send someone to learn how many of these monsters are in the city, or what reports we have thus far. Everyone must plan to evacuate to the south gate. Orderly lines, supplies where they can—but everything must be in packs to be carried. There's no room for wagons or handcarts in the tunnel. Fighters at the front, to clear a way and protect from human interference, and at the rear to slow pursuit. But we don't want to rely on fighting, not if we can possibly avoid it."

Galen now knew what could frighten a powerful sorceress such as Pasiphae Jade, and he wished he had not learned. "We should wait here?"

"Keep my mother safe," Kayvin said. "And the others. Only Lisveth and I need to see Pasiphae Jade, and the rest of you should stay out of the open corridors unless necessary."

Yovela and Dielo looked as if they wanted to argue, but there was little for them to do if they went. They nodded.

"We'll move into the study, away from the balcony," Galen said. "Good luck."

CHAPTER 123

KAYVIN HAD NEVER BEEN in the prison.

This wasn't where common criminals would be incarcerated or await their corporal punishments; the Green Tower was for critical political prisoners who must be kept close or high-ranking offenders who could not be sent to a common cell.

Pasiphae Jade was on the topmost floor, accessed by a narrow spiraling stair to a circular door set in the floor of her cell. Two guards preceded Kayvin, in case the prisoner should rush him as he climbed through the door, but when he emerged into the room, she was sitting at a small desk, waiting.

Kayvin walked to her. "It's happening now. The spawning has begun."

She gave him a startled look. "And you've come to me?" Her voice was level but brittle. She was in the same clothing, charred and smoke-stained. Her hands were flat on the empty desktop.

"You said the coming spawning was the reason you killed my father, so you could prevent it. This is your time to act."

Her fingers were red and distorted, a jigsaw of short lines and knuckles. Kayvin's gut tightened. He had not thought to order her magic disabled, but they had known to do it. It may have saved the lives of a few guards. He was foolish to feel sympathy for a murderer. He hated her. But it felt wrong to look at her broken hands.

None of this should have happened. Things should have been different, and this would not have happened. But he could not spare time for those thoughts now, not while monsters rose from the earth outside the walls.

"My time to act?" She sat still, her eyes locked on him.

Kayvin felt bare, exposed. "Please. I've come to ask for your help."

"And I should help you?" She leaned over her ruined hands. "How many hours have passed since you tried to kill me? Since you threw me down from the place I had made to solve this very problem?" She shook her head, and one corner of her mouth pulled into a sneer. "And now you have taken that place, and you've found yourself even more woefully unprepared than you thought."

Kayvin flinched. "We have six amulets. I looked—"

"Six?"

"I looked at your research notes, and they are beyond me. But I know you've prepared for this day. You sent me for the amulets to use them to stop this. Pasiphae Jade, if you truly did everything you've done for the sake of saving lives, and not for power and acclaim, then you'll help me now."

She sat back in her chair, and the corner of her mouth lifted a little more. "There's nothing wrong with a little acclaim. It's nice to be appreciated. Yet you will make me a villain even as you use my knowledge and skills to make yourself a hero."

He did not want to barter with her. He did not want to pardon her, to promise his tormentor safety. But he had seen the thing crawl out of the earth, and there were countless more coming, and it was her life against hundreds or thousands. "What is it that you want? Tell me your price."

"My *price*?" She half-rose behind the desk, leaning on the heels of her palms. "Again, as always, you think you can buy me. Get out."

Panic twisted in Kayvin's chest. "No—no, I spoke of the price of your knowledge. I wish to hire a craftsman. I will purchase your research. Please, help us!"

"Your father had the chance to listen to me and act for himself, and he refused. You had the chance to listen and help me, and you resisted at every opportunity. You even held back amulets from me, it seems. And you've broken my fingers to curtail my magic. Now you want me to forget all of that and help you to take credit for my work?"

"It's not about the fame!" Kayvin snapped. "We are discussing lives. I will say to all that you were the one who knew what to do. Only, you must do it."

"I must do nothing." Her voice was chilling. "You have restored the world to your liking; now live in it. Take responsibility for the failures you chose."

For a moment they stared at one another, and Kayvin felt all the old desperation rising again. He was helpless to save those in danger, and he was not prepared, and he would watch them suffer while he did nothing...

"You're a monster," he snapped. "You'll sacrifice in spite all those you professed to save. You're heartless."

Her lip curled in open disgust. "You kill your own mother to excuse your attack on me, bare your nation to the disaster I warned was coming, and then blame me for the tragedy, and you dare to call me heartless."

Kayvin did not have time to explain the illusion he had also believed. "I want to save my people."

"And why do you think I did everything I've done?" she demanded. "If I'm heartless, then what is it that aches in this futility?"

"There's no time for this," Kayvin pressed. "The spawning is already here. People are dying."

She looked down at the desk. "Lirin is with you." The sentence was flat, but there was a question in the quiver of her lip.

Kayvin nodded. "Of course. She is with my mother. I have declared her my sister."

"Your...?"

"She is the daughter of my father's concubine, and so she is a princess. Who can contradict me?"

Pasiphae Jade's eyelids flickered, and then she gave a single nod. "That is a good place for her." She set her mouth firmly. "You deserve nothing. You should have begged me on your knees, and still I would have refused you. But if I help you, Lirin will be safe." She jerked her head to indicate the wall of the tower and all that lay beyond. "And I will have saved them all, and that is what I wanted."

Kayvin's heart leaped in his chest. "Thank you! Thank you. Now, we have six amulets. And I've brought someone else who can help." He turned and gestured, and a guard opened the door in the floor and waved Lisveth up the stairs.

She looked at Kayvin, then at Pasiphae Jade, and then she gave a quick curtsy that might have been meant for either or both of them. She looked at Pasiphae Jade's hands and then quickly away. She came to stand beside Kayvin, an arm's reach from the desk, and opened a cloth bag slung across her torso. "I have here five amulets."

Pasiphae Jade stared at them. "You have so many. Nearly all of them. And you did not tell me?"

"Lisveth brought several with her," Kayvin said briefly.

"And who is Lisveth?"

"I'm a free lance," she answered before Kayvin could. "I do magic for hire. I'd like to get paid, so tell me what I'm to do with these."

"The amulets can be used together to share power."

"Yes, I know. Some draw energy, and some expend it. They can fit together."

"That's right." Pasiphae Jade lifted a crooked hand and looked expectantly at the desk.

Kayvin glanced at Lisveth. She could probably make Pasiphae Jade think she was holding an amulet; she had once made Kayvin think the same. But Pasiphae Jade would not be able to assess an illusory amulet.

Lisveth placed the golden eye unblinking onto the desk, keeping the amulet's chain in her grip. A sharp tug would pull it from Pasiphae Jade's broken grasp.

Pasiphae Jade laid her left palm atop the golden eye, wincing a little. She half closed her eyes, drawing her eyebrows together. She frowned, and then she opened her eyes. "This amulet is exhausted. It's completely drained."

"Yes, that's right."

"Give me another."

"They're mostly drained. I used them to release the ice spells."

"You..." Pasiphae Jade stared.

Lisveth held up the violet and red eyes, without passing them over. "These have some power to them."

"We have this one, too." Kayvin drew out Dielo's orange-eyed amulet from its place hidden within his robe. He picked free the end of the linen strips that had buffered it from his skin and held it in place, and he let the amulet slide into Lisveth's waiting palm.

Pasiphae Jade did not miss the meaning of the additional amulet. "You held one back from me."

"I did not. I offered everything you asked for." Kayvin moderated his voice; he needed her cooperation. "Dielo carried this one back, for me to offer to you."

She raised an eyebrow. "Stubborn, that one." She held out a hand, palm up and fingers splayed.

"It's drained as well," Kayvin told her. "But they're—"

"Drained, again?" Pasiphae Jade stared open-mouthed. "You've drained them. You've drained so many of them. They're useless."

"They can be refilled," Lisveth said. "They must have been fed power in the beginning, and surely since they were first made. Tell us how to do it."

"It cannot be done quickly, not to the degree we need."

"They're recharged with contact," Kayvin offered. "This was completely dead when Dielo found it in Sayinia, but it recovered when he held it. He said it used his strength to heal someone."

"He is not enough! Or did you think that it takes only a man's strength to turn back a spawning? In that case, why would we need tools at all? No, I'm sure it only funneled some of his own vitality to someone with less, like balancing water in two basins. One thin virilo will not entirely refresh an amulet any more than he did my fountain. You'd need dozens or hundreds of lives."

"Lives?" Kayvin repeated. "As in—would they die to power the amulet?"

"My sweet boy, how do you think they were created?" Pasiphae Jade sat back in her chair, letting her palms trail across the polished wood. "I told you I needed six amulets. Practically speaking, you have two."

"But we have six, and you can—"

"I can do nothing with what you've brought me! There is nothing to be done. I offered you their lives in exchange for the amulets, and instead you spent the amulets to break them free. Now they're useless. Everything I've done, everything you've done, all of it is wasted in disaster." She fixed her eyes on Kayvin. "I hope you consider saving your sullen sera qadra girl worth the ruin of your people."

CHAPTER 124

GALEN COULD SEE, WHEN they returned, that they had not been successful. Kayvin did not meet their eyes, and Lisveth had a pale tightness to her mouth when she looked at him that Galen had never seen before.

Pasiphae Jade had refused, or she had been unable to help. The exact details did not matter.

Raea could see it as well. "What can we do, then? How do we get enough people out?"

Kayvin's voice came almost too quiet to hear. "How many is enough?"

Lisveth held her bag of amulets in both hands, looking down at it as if it were a dead bird.

The guard waiting to the side cleared his throat lightly. Kayvin looked at him. "What did you learn?"

"The creatures are in the city, but reports are scattered and the exact number is uncertain. Current estimates are fewer than ten so far. There are unconfirmed sightings further outside the city as well."

Kayvin's jaw tightened. "We need to know locations. We need a way to contain them while we evacuate. We—"

"What's that?" Raea asked, turning. "Did you hear something?"

Abruptly Kayvin ran to the balcony and seized the railing as if the room had pitched sideways. "They're here."

They followed him, and Galen watched as the earth in the twilight garden swelled and shifted, shaking bushes and the small trees. The upright carved stones shook and tipped over as the ground heaved beneath them.

Kayvin stepped backward and took his mother's arm. "We have to get you to safety."

"Go!" she retorted, trying to pull free. "You can be faster without me."

"No!"

And then the earth erupted, and a lizard's head broke free, shaking dirt as a dog might shake water.

"Turn away!" Raea ordered, shielding her eyes,. "Look away from it now!"

Galen could not. The pony-sized creature pulled itself from the hole, wriggling forward like a snake but with short, unimpressive limbs. A frill of loose skin hung behind its head, and its golden eyes—

Someone seized Galen and jerked him away, spinning him. "Do not look!" Kayvin ordered. "Do not meet their eyes! It is death!"

Fair night.

In his side vision, the monster swung its head back and forth, looking across the courtyard, opening its mouth and calling in—birdsong. Galen was startled by the sound and realized he had expected a squawk or a roar, like a dragon of story. But instead the creature sang in a beautiful lilting voice.

Caught in its song, Galen stared, watching the monster's profile. The teeth were large and yellow, when the lips lifted to bare them, and its eyes were unnaturally large and brightly colored.

Its eyes—they were the amulets' eyes, the amulets, they were eyes taken from these creatures, whatever they were, and their magic—

Kayvin struck Galen across the face. "Do not look at them!"

Galen could not spare the time or worry for offense at the blow. "What? Why not?" They were at the back of the balcony, and he could hear screams. He did not remember how they had come here.

"Paralysis," said Kayvin shortly, tearing his robe along the grain. "The stories say you stare into their eyes and you forget yourself, forget time, forget to run. I don't know what you think about, but it isn't self-preservation."

"And then?" Galen thought of the two monsters he'd seen before, tearing apart their victim.

"And then they eat you."

Galen gulped. "I was thinking about their eyes. About the magic."

"That magic would lead you straight to certain death."

Raea handed Galen a strip of ragged cloth, trailing threads. "Tie this around your face."

"To filter the air?"

"To filter your vision." She demonstrated, tying the strip like a blindfold about her eyes. "If you can see just a little, but not clearly, you may be able to withstand the effect."

Lisveth was standing on the balcony, looking out at the creatures. She stood utterly still, and Galen's heart sank. *She's already been transfixed.*

But as he took her arm to pull her away, she spoke. "That man is going to die."

He followed her eyes and saw a Rideis standing stupidly, watching a basilisk waddle toward him with a fixed gaze. Kayvin leaned over the balustrade and shouted. "What are you doing? Run! Get away!"

But the man kept his eyes on the basilisk, almost unblinking. As the creature neared him, he still watched, a faintly wondering look on his face. He lowered his gaze to keep steady contact with the monster as it closed the gap between them. Then it bit him in the thigh, pulling him forward and down. The man gasped but did not scream, caught between pain and the lingering fixation.

Kayvin stretched out a hand and shot fire at the monster. The flames rolled over it, and it swung its head like a horse shaking away a fly, tossing the unfortunate man to one side. Released from his trance, he drew a breath, looking about in confusion, and then screamed as he saw or felt his savaged leg. The basilisk swung back, took a step, and bit him again. The screams were muffled and then stopped.

The basilisk mouthed its prey, biting repeatedly and then nudging the body. Then it started to eat, and they flinched away.

"It didn't mind the fire," Lisveth observed unnecessarily, her voice strained. "It was a little startled, but only for a moment, and it wasn't harmed."

Galen nodded. "I think—I think that's where my eye came from."

"What?"

"I think my amulet has an eye from one of these things. Maybe they're resistant to magic." He pulled Lisveth away from the railing. "We have to go."

She shook her head. "There's nowhere to go. Look, they travel in the ground. They would feel our running. Burrowing creatures are almost certainly sensitive to vibrations. We would draw them to us."

Galen stepped close to Lisveth. "They're going to evacuate, so there must be a way. We can make it to the mountain passage, probably."

She shook her head, her face drawn tight.

"Then what do you intend to do? Stay here and wait for it to find us?"

She turned to face him, but she did not look up at him. "You can go—you've already done more than you needed to. You helped me with the landslide; now this is my dragon."

"What are you talking about?" Yovela asked impatiently.

"Dragons would be a sort of blessing right now," Lirin said in a voice that suggested she knew her words weren't really helpful. "My—she said she thought dragons used to eat the hatchlings. That's why there were so many hatched at once, so some would survive."

"Well, if we had any dragons left, that would be something," Kayvin said tersely. He turned to his mother. "Stay in the Arch Potentate's rooms. They're the most secure. Arad! Help the Shining Gem to the study. Harrith, set some men to guard her." He held out a hand to help her to stand. "You'll be safest here while we see what can be done."

She nodded soberly, understanding their limited options. When the servant came to take her arm, she kissed her son and turned silently away.

Kayvin turned. "Lirin, stay with her. Help her."

She shook her head. "Let me go with you! I want to help. I want to—"

He took her arms. "Lirin, I am asking you to keep my mother safe. If I can't trust in that, I cannot do anything else. Do you understand this *is* helping? Can you do that?"

She quieted and sucked in her lip, and then she nodded. "I'm sorry. I can do that."

"Thank you. Please. I need to know she's safe. After all we've done... Keep both of you safe."

It was an unfair request, because Lirin couldn't be expected to fight off a monster, but Galen knew she'd have less need to try in the Arch Potentate's rooms. He watched her hurry away after the servant and Shining Gem.

"He's still alive," Dielo said softly.

"What?" Kayvin turned to him.

Dielo pointed. "That man. He's moving."

The basilisk had taken flesh from his leg, but Dielo was right, and the victim was moving weakly as the basilisk chewed. They stared in horror, breathing shocked curses.

"We should bring him in," Dielo said shakily. "We could drag him to the steps, if someone distracted the basilisk. You could use fire again, just keep it occupied. I know enough not to look."

"No," Kayvin began. "My fire isn't enough."

Galen looked at Lisveth. "Could you distract it? With an illusion?"

She blinked at him in surprised alarm. "I don't know anything about how these things think. I'm only guessing at what senses they most rely on. I wouldn't trust any illusion to hold—certainly not enough to risk someone's life."

"What about the amulets?" Kayvin demanded.

"The Eye that hides is exhausted," Lisveth said unhappily. "Also the one that aids perception, though that seems more a liability in this—"

"No!" gasped Yovela.

They turned together to look over the balcony and saw Dielo creeping out from the base of the stairs, toward where the man lay among crushed flower stalks, reaching with one outstretched arm.

"Dielo!" Yovela and Kayvin called together.

The ground in the garden was heaving, and Dielo, slack-jawed, shook his head slightly. On either side monsters were wriggling free, burrowing upward into the twilight.

"Look." Lisveth pointed.

Two more creatures were sliding into view, pushing their way through dry shrubs. The first tugged at its victim and then turned its long head to look at Dielo.

Dielo was not transfixed, not yet, but he was not running. There was nowhere for him to run. There were snake-monsters all around him, on the grass, the patio, the beds of late blooms.

Dielo was trapped in a ring of basilisks.

CHAPTER 125

"No!" Kayvin gripped the railing, and for a moment Galen thought he would climb it and drop to the dangerous ground below.

But it was Yovela who tried. Lisveth caught her arm and held her. "Don't—you can't help him that way."

"How then?" Yovela demanded as she pulled free. "He is trapped there!"

"I know." Kayvin's voice caught. "Let me try fire."

Yovela turned on him. "It didn't work the last time!"

"Do you have a better idea?" He thrust his hands before him and spewed bright fire into the grassy courtyard, turning the dry plants to ash. Dielo flinched away, wrapping his head in his arms as he shrank from the flames.

The basilisk under Kayvin's targeted stream of flame turned its head from the fiery stream and hissed its annoyance—but only annoyance, as the fire flared over it and left it unharmed.

"It's like the amulet," Galen protested. "The eyes are what power the amulets, and the magic cannot hurt them."

"The root source," Lisveth agreed. "Fair night, it makes sense. The magic-absorbing amulet uses the natural magic of the eye. The others are turning the natural magic to another spell and so lose some of the innate power."

"This is all very interesting," Kayvin said sharply, "but it is doing nothing to help Dielo."

The man on the ground began to moan and drew one leg up slightly. The monster whipped back toward him and bit down across his torso, tearing his chest with a twist of its head. The man went silent, and he did not move again.

Dielo stood frozen, one hand raised to his eyes, the other splayed wide as if his fingers might find some lifeline or weapon. There would be none.

The answer struck Galen like a blow to the stomach. "If their eyes naturally stop magic, like the amulet," he said, gulping air, "then, like the amulet, their eyes do not naturally stop physical attacks."

"Galen, don't!" Lisveth cried as she turned from Yovela to him. "Don't do it!"

A display rack of ornate weapons stood in the sitting area, and he took a sword from it. "My amulet should protect me," he said, trying to convince himself. His stomach compressed as if he should vomit. He drew the sword—his fingers were thick and clumsy on the hilt—and discarded the beautiful sheath. The blade beneath was also ornamented, but it looked serviceable enough. "After all, they can't paralyze each other with their own gazes. They have to be immune to their own effects, and I have one of their eyes."

Before he could allow himself to think of all the reasons this was the worst idea he had ever had, he placed a hand on the cool stone railing and vaulted it, falling twenty paces to the back of a basilisk below.

He landed sword-first, putting his weight into the blow and trying to keep the blade straight. A glancing strike would only anger the monster.

But his strike was true, and the blade drove straight down into the creature's torso. It screamed, throwing its head up, and thrashed side to side. Galen was flung to one side, breaking his grip on the stuck sword.

Fair night, now he was unarmed and alone on a field of angry lizard-monsters with paralyzing vision and an indifference to fire. He was going to die.

Lisveth was shouting, but he couldn't understand her. Around him, monsters turned to stare, as the injured basilisk strained its neck to stretch around and bite at the sword. Its first grip slid off, and then it got another bite and tugged at the blade, wailing. The sword came free and fell to the ground, and the monster sang its misery.

Sang. Still it was birdsong, or something beyond birdsong, something nearer to Kayvin and Dielo's song of grief as the prince mourned the women he believed dead. It was a wordless cry, rising and falling with untethered notes, and despite everything it tore at Galen's heart.

The amulet lying against his chest trembled with the song.

Galen looked at Dielo, wide-eyed on the patio and staring as if he could not believe Galen's stupidity in jumping into death. Galen found it hard to argue with that apparent assessment, but they could have that conversation if they survived. "Sing," Galen urged.

"What?"

Galen had perhaps a modicum of protection with the Poet's Eye; Dielo had none. "That song! The one they keep calling? Sing it back to them!"

Dielo did not understand. The pressure of the amulet increased against Galen's heart, and he began to hum, his voice shaking with his breathless fear as he crept nearer Dielo. It was hard to hold the melody.

But the monster heard him. It whipped its head toward him, and for a moment Galen forgot the danger of the eyes, so taken by alarm at its sudden attention. And then it was not fear of the basilisk's interest that held him in place, but he was captivated by its golden gaze, with the vertical-slit pupils that had perplexed Lisveth, the great golden eyes too large for its lizard-like head, the eyes that held him and fascinated him—

He tore himself away, blinking, and realized with relief he could do so. It had nearly held him, but the magic that locked so firmly onto most people had a weaker hold on him and his amulet, and he could slip from its grasp if he remembered he had to struggle.

The remembering would be the most difficult part of it.

The song pulsed against his chest. Another basilisk was singing now, the same call. Again and again, the call came from around the palace. Galen could not tell if they were singing to each other or were merely all singing the same melody. But it was definitely a melody.

He began to sing.

Galen was only the most casual of singers, but he clung desperately to the song. He fixed his eyes slightly above the nearest lizard, able to perceive its movement in the rim of his vision without actually making contact with its eyes.

The monster stopped and looked at him. It did not seem to stare at him as prey, not like the one that had killed the man, but more with intense interest. Its golden eyes, just visible on the edge of Galen's perception, did not blink or swerve from him. It was unnerving.

Galen's breath caught, and the song failed, and the basilisk dropped its head and started toward him.

But Dielo's voice picked up the broken song and carried it high, louder and stronger than Galen had managed, and the great lizards paused again in place. Galen gulped and spun around, looking at the creatures as they shook their heads, tilted their skulls to one side, listened.

Listened.

Dielo kept singing as he turned toward Galen, his eyes wide with astonishment. *Do you see this?* he seemed to ask as he sang. *Do you see how they are not killing us as we stand?*

Galen turned and looked up at the balcony. Kayvin was hanging over the railing, his mouth agape. One hand was stretching out, waiting for something.

And then Galen realized Kayvin was not only staring in surprise, he was singing as well. He took the song in his own voice, quieter than Dielo's, testing it, probing it.

Yovela reappeared and pushed paper and pencil into Kayvin's outstretched hand. He flattened the paper on the railing and began to make furious marks upon it.

Lisveth hung over the rail beside him, her eyes on Galen. "Farm boy," she whispered, as if she did not dare to disturb the singers or the listeners, "keep up that song for yourself."

He nodded, resuming his humming.

"I don't know what's happening, but it's possible your amulet is pulling a bit of magic in the same way that the exhausted amulet pulled from Dielo. But it's not enough to count on, so please try to keep your eyes to yourself."

Galen reached a hand to his amulet, as if touching it could do anything more. He looked about for his lost sword and saw it lying beneath the monster's torso.

He was not sure he trusted the amulet so far. Not yet.

Dielo was still singing, rotating slowly and peeking through his fingers at the basilisks. Galen didn't know if that slight protection would be enough, if his eyes met theirs. Dielo pushed the song through his quivering voice and glanced up at the balcony, where Kayvin was looking from his notes to the scene below.

"That is a chromatic scale up to the tritone," the prince called softly. "Sing it again."

Dielo obeyed, repeating just the requested phrase.

The lizards lifted their heads, and Galen thought they were startled.

Dielo noted it too, and he turned and sang to them again.

Two of the lizards rocked back where they stood, and they sang the phrase back to Dielo, their inhuman voices blending with his.

Fair night, what was this?

Kayvin's pencil flew across his paper. "Add the diminished seventh at the end," he said. "Empty void, I think they are speaking."

Dielo sang as directed, and the lizards changed their own melody—this time not repeating, but altering, singing what Galen thought was a question.

A *question*.

Fair night, this was a conversation.

"They're singing to communicate," Lisveth said, her voice soft and wondrous. "They are speaking to us."

One of the lizards moved forward, and Dielo's voice shook, but somehow he held on to the song in the face of approaching death.

But the monster only moved around him, shoulder to shoulder, and began to nod its head alongside him.

"Is it going to sing a duet?" breathed Yovela.

Dielo's eyes were white-rimmed, but he clung to the song as if it were the rope holding him from falling into a golden-eyed chasm, and he did not break the melody. When the lizard sang the question, Dielo repeated the first phrase.

Galen wondered what the snake-monsters were asking, and what Dielo was answering. He clung to his first simple phrase, afraid to vary it. If this song was a language, and they were merely aping it without understanding what they said, they might be worsening the problem rather than solving it. Maybe they were declaring war on the monsters?

On the other hand, a moment ago the creatures had been swarming the palace and eating every person they encountered. Whatever Dielo might say, it could not make it worse than that. And since the creatures had stopped attacking since Dielo had begun singing, it seemed he was improving the situation, at least for a time.

If Dielo could bravely sing without breaking his song in the face of such danger, even as a basilisk stood beside him, then Galen could at least retrieve his sword. He would have to be cautious, and he would not be able to use it—surely stabbing a basilisk would counter whatever progress Dielo was making—but he would have it ready, and he would feel better for holding it instead of standing unarmed among man-eating magical monsters out of a nightmarish fairy tale.

Galen sucked in a great breath and started forward, keeping his eyes on the lizard-monster that stood over his sword. It was bleeding, and he thought its skin pouched a little beneath the stab wound. It might be bleeding internally, perhaps from a punctured organ. For a short moment Galen felt guilty for his attack from above—but it was too early to have those regrets, only a dozen paces from a dead man.

He took a breath and repeated the song, softly echoing Dielo's phrases. He crouched and reached forward—slowly, slowly. His fingers brushed the hilt, stretched over it, closed upon it. He would have to draw the sword back to him now, dragging the blade across the grass, and even the tiny hiss of that might be enough to betray him. What would he do if the creature turned on him? It could swing in place faster than he could retreat, could end him with a single bite as he crouched nearly helpless beside the wounded lizard. His struggling voice faded.

But the monster seemed intent wholly on Dielo and his song, and it did not turn as Galen lifted the sword. He drew it back toward him, pulled it close, held it to him as he crept backward.

Kayvin re-joined the song now, looking between his paper and the lizards assembled below his balcony. Galen looked around—while he had been concentrating on the single beast, moving as stealthily as possible around it, he had missed that the other basilisks had come together, forming in rough ranks about the patio with Dielo. The virilo was still singing, still looking wide-eyed up to his prince for encouragement and instruction.

Kayvin began to vary the melody, putting phrases of song together, echoes of the song the monsters had sung as they crawled over the palace but new. Words and sentences, Galen thought, fascinated by the process. How did the prince know how to do this? Did he know what his song meant? Was he mimicking sounds and phrases, like an infant pretending to converse with parents?

Galen stood in place, barely breathing, afraid to disrupt whatever fragile miracle was happening. Dielo sang, and Kayvin's harmony turned the basilisks toward the balcony with curiosity and maybe even a sense of astonishment. One of the lizards sang back, a new phrase, and Kayvin held a quivering note while he checked his paper, and then he sang back a phrase only vaguely familiar to Galen from the recent flurry of song, but which seemed to mean something to the creatures, who shuffled in their ranks and looked from Dielo to Kayvin without any sense of the hungry predation of mere minutes before.

They were no longer merely singing, Galen realized—they were communicating. Kayvin had struck upon the words they needed. They were almost certainly simple words, a baby-talk of babble and childish attempts, but they were enough to stop the basilisks from eating their way through the palace.

Yovela looked at Kayvin and then gestured to Dielo and Galen, waving them toward the steps below the balcony. The two of them hesitated, gulped, and then eased their way toward their retreat. Galen went up backwards, singing with his sword ready, feeling for notes as he felt for the steps, and Dielo kept a guiding hand on his arm.

Once on the balcony, which somehow felt safer despite the open stairs below, Galen and Dielo stopped singing. Galen's legs began to quiver, belatedly failing in the face of terror. Dielo sank to the floor, his back against a column, and clutched Yovela's hand.

"Are you all right?" Lisveth crouched close over Galen. "Nothing touched you? Not in that first scuffle?"

He shook his head. "Do they think? Or are they like animals?"

"Animals think."

Galen shook his head. "You know what I mean."

"No, I don't. Just because they're animals, it doesn't mean they don't think."

"Animals don't communicate."

Lisveth tipped her head to give him a flatly disapproving look. "Even I know an angry cow will tell you when she needs milking."

"That's not communication..." Galen protested, his conviction fading even as he said it. "That's just seeking relief. Everything does that."

"I think they're seeking something, too," Lisveth said seriously. "Even if it's just supper. I think they didn't expect their supper to answer them. They're probably as confused as if a farmer saw a chicken start making baby talk at him."

"Could the chicken ask the farmer to consider an alternate supper?" Galen looked worriedly toward Kayvin at the balustrade.

Kayvin let his song fade, and for a moment there was stillness. Then the great lizards began shuffling about the patio, and one put its head over the base of the stairs but did not climb. Galen held his breath until it turned away.

"Empty void." Kayvin's voice was barely audible. "We can bring them away from the palace."

"What?"

"We can sing them away." He turned, clutching his annotations. "I need an instrument."

THE PRINCE WHO SANG

CHAPTER 126

KAYVIN WAS AFRAID.

He had every reason to be afraid. He was going down to meet dangerous creatures out of legend, armed only with the vaguest guesses at musical phrases that seemed to give them pause. If he sang a wrong phrase or note, he would die.

If he did nothing, hundreds in the palace and city would die. After the chaos and deaths, the resulting collapse of farms and artisan markets would wreak more havoc and bring more suffering.

He'd seen only a dozen or so—as if they were not enough on their own!—but there would be more. Already there were more, in the fragmented reports. He had to go out and find them.

He had slept a little, but he had woken repeatedly, listening in the dark as more monsters burst into the palace grounds. He'd sent for a lamp and studied the notes he'd made of the creatures' songs. He'd hummed and waited for the dawn.

Kayvin's fingers were half-numb on the gittern, and that also frightened him. He could not afford mistakes.

He plucked his first notes and hummed to match; he did not trust his sense of pitch, not for this, and with his nerves strung this tightly he knew he would veer sharp. He adjusted and then opened his mouth, shifting from a hum to a long sung note.

Around the courtyard's disturbed plantings, large, flat heads swung toward him, swaying on thick necks, and golden eyes blinked at him.

Kayvin quickly looked up, setting his gaze just over the basilisks so they were only a dark blur. He was not brave enough to close his eyes, but if he looked directly at them, he would never sing again. He fixed his vision on a poet stone beyond the creatures, and he shifted to the augmented fifth. He left the final note hanging in the air, an invitation.

He held his breath.

One of the creatures tipped its head, like a puppy listening for a mouse in the wall, and then it grunted and sang the notes back. Kayvin sucked a breath of sweet relief.

But it was not enough. That was only an overture; it was not acceptance or commitment. He played the arpeggio again and hummed—the notes still hung in the air, fresh in his mind, but he would not risk an error—and then he sang the invitation once more.

Ta teee...

Another young basilisk returned the call, and then a third. Kayvin's heart leaped in his chest and for a moment he thought he would lose his breath control. No concert had ever been so gravely critical as this one.

Ta tee ta tee... He took a step backward, keeping the note alive on the string and drawing it out with his voice. *Ta tee ta tee...* He took another step back, and another.

Ta tee ta tee...

At last one of the creatures took a step forward. With its motion, several others followed. Kayvin had to fight to still himself; despite his intentions and hopes, the sight of them moving after him compelled him to run.

He drew a measured breath; he had to keep control of his diaphragm against the fear. He nodded to himself and to the monsters, and he sang a call.

They moved forward as a group, matching his pace.

Kayvin could have gasped with relief, but he had to keep the song. He walked backward, repeating the phrase, and tried to increase his pace.

It was terrifying. He wanted to look down and check his footing, walking backwards, but he couldn't take his eyes from that poet stone, now receding as they moved away. He couldn't let his eyes cross over the basilisks between the stone and his feet. He wanted to turn and lead them boldly away, but beneath his barely steady voice, in the dark void beneath his unsteady diaphragm, he knew he did not have the strength to turn his back on the monsters he had seen kill and devour.

So he walked backward, praying his voice would hold steady, praying he would not stumble and make himself easy, inviting prey.

The gateposts rose on either side of him, indicating he had moved far enough in the right direction. A wild joy rose at this tiny milestone, and he recalled how some humans had kissed their temple gateposts, and he nearly laughed aloud. He adjusted his angle, trying to glance over his shoulder without letting his eyes pass too closely over the basilisks, and then looked back. The poet stone vanished, slipping out of his line of sight, and he cast about for a new target to keep his eyes safely above the golden gaze of the monsters.

Something touched the back of his shoulder, and he jumped in place, breaking his musical phrase for an instant. But the touch resolved into hands on his shoulders. "It's all right," Dielo assured him. "I'll guide you. Walk with me."

Kayvin glanced sideways without meaning to, and he caught the briefest glimpse of Dielo's dark hair and a scarf tied over his face. He had given strict orders that he would go out alone. But he did not want to order the virilo back, not now.

Dielo's hand curved over Kayvin's upper arm, gently leading without interfering with the plucked notes Kayvin repeated to keep the pitch pure, and Kayvin relaxed into a surer pace.

"I'm going to cover your eyes." This was Yovela's voice, from the other side. Her hands slipped over his head and a dark fabric settled over his eyes. "Is that all right? Is it too tight?"

He started to nod while singing, then tried to shake his head, and then he realized he could do neither while she was trying to tie the scarf over his face. He hesitated, balanced between strides, and let her finish.

Dielo's fingers pressed him onward. "Sing. We'll watch for you."

With his eyes mostly obscured, and with trusted help to shake him free if he fell into trance, he risked a glance toward the group of hatchlings. They were closely grouped, only an arm's spread apart, and they kept even pace with him as he walked backwards.

More were coming. As they moved through the gate, other basilisks lifted their heads from fresh burrows or from victims to observe their passing. Kayvin raised his voice, sending the call further to invite them away with him.

Yovela began to sing with him, her voice harmonizing in an easy fourth over the awkward interval. The creatures raised their heads and called back, singing their matching replies, and the watching basilisks began to follow, singing along with their broodmates.

Kayvin was fascinated. The more he had, the more creatures singing, the easier it seemed to be to take them to one place.

Dielo had observed it, too. "Keep singing, my lord. They will come." He sounded nervous, but his steps continued unbroken and his fingers kept a steady light pressure on Kayvin's upper arm.

Kayvin could count them, if he didn't let his eyes linger too long on each. With the newly joined, he had nearly a dozen.

"Where shall we go?" Dielo asked in a carefully steady tone overlaying the freefall of giddy terror they surely all shared. "Away from the palace, to begin, and out of the city, and then where?"

Kayvin nodded slowly, continuing his odd song. The hatchlings wanted to feed; they could not lead them into the countryside and set them on a hapless village.

"Meat," Yovela said suddenly. "We take them to where there is meat. The grazing, in the north hills—there are hundreds of cattle there, thousands, all fattened with the summer grasses. We take them there."

Kayvin's mind whirled. He knew vaguely of the summer grazing grounds, but few details; it had not been key in a prince's tutelage. How far was that?

Dielo echoed his question aloud. "Where is that? How far?"

Yovela was the only one of them who had traveled before Pasiphae Jade sent Kayvin to Sayinia. She turned up the road, as if she might see a signpost, and her tone grew hesitant. "The foothills, to the northwest of here. It's not as far as to the passage, but it's a fair walk. Maybe—maybe eighteen miles. Maybe a little less, if the cattle have come lower in the late season."

Kayvin's chest tightened, and his note wavered. Eighteen miles! But what else could they do?

"All right." Dielo sounded afraid but resolute. "We've walked farther. And if we grow weary, we can always look over our shoulder to find new encouragement."

Yovela laughed, high and nervous but a laugh.

Kayvin nodded agreement, though they had made the decision without him. He glanced to the side as another young basilisk lumbered curiously toward the group, singing back his tune. That made twelve.

Chapter 127

Lisveth breathed hard as she descended the stairs, though from behind her Galen couldn't tell whether it was lingering exhaustion or worry as they neared where the monsters had been. She paused on the tile walkway and peered out through a decorated arch. "I don't see any."

Galen looked over her head. The courtyard looked empty. "I think it's clear."

"Fair night, I feel helpless." Lisveth licked her lips. "I wish I could use an illusion or three."

"You could try." Galen knew it sounded foolish and unhelpful, but he was also worried. His amulet helped, even weakened as it was, but it did not negate the eyes' effect, and it did nothing to protect Lisveth.

"I don't know how they perceive things, by vision or by sensation or by scent. I don't know what kind of magic they use. What if my magic draws it, rather than distracts it?"

Galen grimaced. "Then let's not risk it until absolutely necessary."

They started across the walled yard, scanning for fresh disturbances in the ground or for bulky shapes crawling in from a side garden. They covered a quarter of the distance, and then they were halfway across—farther, more than halfway...

In front of them a wide ornate gate opened onto a garden, part ornamental and part kitchen supply. Through the gate lay neat rows of herbs, alternating with mint and rosemary to repel pests. By this time of year most were trimmed short, and the garden looked austere with its straight lines and shorn plants.

They reached the gate, and Lisveth glanced behind them at the empty yard. "So far, so good."

Galen nodded. They had only to go through the remaining garden, and then they would find a stone path along the outer palace wall that would lead eventually to an external gate. Kayvin had insisted they could not lose their way.

Perhaps not the way, but Galen thought it was still possible to lose something else. They were to flush any basilisks along the way, toward Kayvin's gate if possible, and warn any outer servants into the central palace for protection. Once outside the palace, they were to warn anyone on the road to take shelter.

No one had spoken of what would come next. Galen wondered if Kayvin had quietly left them the chance to flee to the mountain passage. But Lisveth was strangely focused on staying to counter the spawning, and Galen knew he would not return alone.

A little pile of deadheaded flowers in faded yellow lay at one end of a planted row, ready to be spread again in the soil. Galen looked across the garden and then back at the gate. Should they have closed it? But the basilisks could burrow, and a gate would hardly inconvenience them.

The browning plantings alongside the path heaved, and Lisveth leaped back to stumble against Galen. He caught her and threw her behind him as the plants broke apart and a wide, flat head emerged. Its bright eyes fixed on Galen, and he was too close, too surprised, and he knew he should look away but he could not. He felt Lisveth's weight shift in his hands and he heard his name, and part of him noticed detachedly that with the amulet's help he could remain distantly aware of things outside of the golden gaze, even as he stared, but none of it could draw him away—

Then Galen was on the ground, knuckle-deep in leaf litter, gasping. Lisveth was staring into his eyes, her eyebrows drawn close, and she had a hand on his mouth to silence him.

He blinked and nodded once to indicate he was aware again. She removed her hand, and he whispered, "What happened?"

"I threw my bag and hit it in the face." Lisveth jerked her head toward the basilisk on the other side of the shrub row. "Shoved you over here. You're too heavy to move often, farm boy."

"I'll try to carry my own weight from here." He rocked onto his feet, staying low behind the sheltering plants. Through the shrubs, he could just make out a lizard's shape and Lisveth's abandoned bag. "Can we get past to the wall path?"

Lisveth did not answer directly. "There's another one. Behind us."

"Behind..." Galen trailed off. They could escape to the gate, but that would leave two monsters near the palace.

"We can't leave them crawling around the palace."

"What do you think we can do? Tempt them away?" Galen's heart pounded against his breath.

"I don't know... Fair night." Lisveth kept looking past the hedge. "There's another one."

Three. Galen did not have the courage to leap among them again, not without someone to save. But he was also uncomfortable with the idea of leaving them to wander in the palace grounds. It was only a matter of time before they breached the steps or climbed the walls, or simply found the doors and windows on the ground floor...

One of the creatures snorted and began to hum, and the others turned toward it. The first raised its head as if to sniff the air, and then it shuffled about to face the palace, looking through the gates.

"Don't," Lisveth said in a low voice. "Don't do it."

But the creature gave a little shake to shed loose dirt and started toward the courtyard.

"Stop it!" Lisveth clenched her fists. "Stop!"

Galen caught her arm, for a moment irrationally afraid that she would run after the monster. Far beyond, through the gates, he could see someone moving on the raised outer walkway of the palace.

"Go away," Lisveth hissed. "Get inside. Get away. Get out of sight!"

But the basilisks gave a few clicks of seeming agreement and moved together, crawling though the gates.

Galen tugged Lisveth's arm. "Can you stop them?"

She shook her head. "Kayvin's fire didn't bother them, and he's much better at it."

Galen stared uselessly. If they shouted warning at the Rideis on the walkway, they would draw the basilisks back to themselves. If they said nothing, he might unwittingly be caught in their gaze.

"They should be afraid of dragons," Lisveth said breathlessly. "The girl said dragons used to eat them. But I don't know how they perceive things, I don't know how they perceive magic."

There were several figures on the walkway. One was pushing another forward. What was happening? "I think—I think someone is trying to force someone down to them." Galen felt ill. "They're going to throw someone down."

"Transition politics, maybe," Lisveth growled.

Galen thought of the nobleman who had backed both Pasiphae Jade's supporter and Kayvin's. There surely were others who would be less forthcoming about their allegiance to the usurper. "Secrets to hide or scores to settle. We have to do something."

"I don't know how to make a convincing dragon." Lisveth's voice was tight, almost cracking. "I've never seen a dragon. Fair night, I feel so useless." She folded her arms across herself, squeezing tightly. "I didn't realize how much I've depended on being able to cheat. Oh, I'm so helpless, after all! But I can't cheat this, and I've never seen a dragon." Her breath rasped audibly. "I'm going to watch it again..."

Galen caught her by the shoulders and pulled her close. She didn't unfold her arms to embrace him back, but he held on anyway, her pulse pounding against him. He took a slow breath, hoping she could feel it. He bent his head to speak softly. "They've never seen a dragon, either."

She took a little breath.

"You don't have to create a perfect replica of a dragon. You create the feeling of a dragon, the impression of a dragon. You show them the memory of a dragon that never was."

They stood still for a moment, and then she nodded. "That makes sense."

Her arms slid apart and then around him, and she squeezed him wordlessly. Then she drew back and took a long breath. "Dragon."

Galen looked down at the three basilisks, now swaying their heads in consideration. There was nothing to hunt here, and they would start into the palace in a moment.

Lisveth reached out a hand and took Galen's. "It may take me a few tries to find what will reach them." She pressed his hand in hers. "Please keep me steady, if I need it, or for Fortuna's sake, pull me away if they come this way."

Galen nodded and folded her hand in both of his. There was nothing else he could do in this moment.

Lisveth closed her eyes, and for half a minute nothing happened. Then an enormous pair of wings unfurled above them with a crack like canvas in wind, and Galen ducked instinctively from the great beast that swept over them, long neck and tail weaving like a swimming snake.

It sailed away toward the basilisks, leaving Galen's heart pounding, and none of them seemed to react. No heads turned toward it, no hatchling shifted nervously away.

Lisveth shook her head, watching them group together. "They didn't see it. They didn't even see it." Her tone grew shrill. "They don't perceive magic like we do?"

"Can you try again?" Galen tried to keep his voice steady. She was pressuring herself enough already, and this was the second massacre she was living through. He had never seen cool, collected Lisveth so strained. "What can you change to maybe reach them?"

She shook her head. "I can—I can wiggle it around a little, maybe find what colors they see more of or something."

Galen nodded. "Think of it as a con. Let them take the bait, and you have some time before you have to set the hook."

She gave a little huff of a laugh. "You're not a good conman, farm boy."

"No, but I'm the best partner you've ever had, and I'm waiting here until you can do it."

She shook her head, but she closed her eyes again. This time the dragon did not appear in a sudden flash but drifted in and out of the sky, more and less real, a murmuration of a dragon. Galen tried to follow it, but it was as if the dragon wore the Painter's Eye, and his gaze kept slipping off it as it traced a wide circle overhead.

Then the dragon disappeared, and Lisveth made a sound somewhere between a groan and a sob. "I can—I can almost feel it. I can feel the edges of their minds, bumping against the illusion. I just can't..." She blew out her breath. "I'm sorry. I'm trying."

He squeezed her hand. "Start with something easier, if you think that would help? It doesn't have to be a dragon to begin."

She gave a little growl and closed her eyes again. Galen wondered what this meant; she often closed her eyes for difficult magic, "real" magic, as she called it, but he couldn't remember seeing her do it for even the most complex illusions.

He looked away from her to the basilisks. One had started crawling toward the palace, and another was looking after it as if considering joining. The third dropped its head to look at a sparrow on the ground, hopping in a short zigzag as it probed for bugs in the newly disturbed earth. Galen glanced at Lisveth, noting her eyes were now open, but still she said nothing.

The basilisk rotated its head, examining the bird with one eye. The sparrow slowed, its movements becoming hesitant, and then it stopped, its tiny eyes fixed on the basilisk's large ones. For a moment, neither moved. Then the basilisk lunged.

The bird vanished, and Lisveth gave a little jump beside him, catching her breath. "Fair night!"

But the bird had not vanished into the basilisk's mouth—it had simply vanished. The basilisk snapped its jaws twice and rolled its head as if perplexed. Galen turned. "Was that you?"

She nodded, drawing a deep breath. "I found the place where it could see me. It's not as easy as working with humans—or Rideis, I suppose—but then, I haven't had much practice." She forced an unsteady grin. "Yet."

The three beasts began together to move toward the palace, suddenly adopting a quick, steady pace. They all looked forward to where a Rideis was struggling against the two others pushing him against the railing. Lisveth tightened her hand on Galen's. "No, no, no!"

Galen looked from her to the basilisks to the palace, and then a dragon plunged from the sky to the earth, pulling up in the palace courtyard and striking with its long neck.

The basilisks wheeled and scrabbled away, awkward in their hurry. The dragon roared, frustrated by their escape, and then kicked again into the sky with wings extended. The basilisks fled in silence, pushing under the plantings.

At the palace, all the Rideis fled, racing inside. Galen tugged Lisveth close and embraced her tightly. "You did it! That was amazing!"

She nodded and hugged him back, hanging on him. "I know! They saw a dragon!"

"We all saw a dragon," Galen confirmed. "A good one. I think I soiled myself a little."

She laughed and drew away so she could elbow him. "Don't be disgusting. But I am very pleased with that. And now we chase them out to where Kayvin is collecting them."

Galen shook his head. "Don't chase them; we don't want them to scatter, or to burrow. Put another dragon where they can see it but with some distance, maybe out toward that stand of trees, and let that pressure them to turn."

She tipped her head. "Are you giving me herding advice, farm boy? Are we going to move these monsters like sheep?"

He chuckled nervously. "Probably more like goats. Or maybe the most ornery of young bulls. We'll see."

CHAPTER 128

AFTER HALF A MILE, Kayvin's legs were burning, and despite Dielo's steady hand he felt increasingly uncomfortable walking backward. So he played another arpeggio to verify his melody and to supplement his voice if this went poorly, and he began to edge around.

Some of the twenty or so basilisks following sent a few calls, and Kayvin's fingers clenched on the neck of the gittern. Now he sang away from them, instead of directly to them, and that was enough of a difference to matter.

But they seemed to settle with his repeated musical assurances, and he gradually looked ahead instead of over his shoulder. Dielo still guided him, a light touch on his arm, while Yovela moved away, beyond what he could sense.

He could do this. He could walk forward for miles, and he could play and he could sing. Dielo would not let him fall.

Yovela returned and gently tugged his hand away from the strings. "Take some water. I'll sing." She began to carry the melody, and she pressed something into his free hand.

She had filled a little water bag from somewhere, and it was still cool. He drank thirstily. He would have to care for his throat, if he wanted to make it to the grazing hills.

Dielo sang harmony with Yovela, his voice soft and clear. Kayvin gave a quick backward glance, worried as he paused his song, but the basilisks looked more curious than rebellious. Still, he could see a subtle change in them, so he picked up his song again.

For a moment the three sang together, Yovela leaving the melody for another harmony, and the basilisks behind them began to sing as well. Most kept the same phrase, but Kayvin heard a few variations. He wondered what those meant, and whether it signified trouble. How far would the basilisks follow his music?

Yovela slipped out of the song, and she leaned close to speak. "I'll go ahead and clear the road. Going around the villages, far enough to safely avoid them, would add too many miles, and we're only hoping we can keep them that long already." Then she was away, jogging up the road before them.

Now that he was facing forward on the road, Kayvin could see the upcoming village, if he peered hard through his scarf. It was still a good walk away, but he could imagine the open workshops, the marketplace, the traffic, the children in the roads. He wouldn't have to lead the hatchlings directly through the center of town to put everyone in danger, and yet he hadn't thought of how to navigate the villages.

"Another one." Dielo gestured, broadly enough to see through the obscuring cloth, toward another basilisk merging into their group, a snaking tributary joining a swelling river. Kayvin pushed aside a brief mental image of what might happen if his music stopped, and he improvised a little ripple across the key to hold their attention. One in the rear called loudly forward, and Kayvin smiled to himself, interpreting it as a kind of praise.

Yovela met them outside the village. She had water for them both, and two dumplings cooled from a food cart. "We'll sing while you eat."

Kayvin was too nervous to be hungry, but he ate half his dumpling. "Where is everyone?"

"Hiding. I told them what was coming. Come this way; it's the shortest through."

The village was deserted, eerily silent. Kayvin wondered briefly whether Yovela had lied to him, whether the basilisks had already come here and killed the villagers. He pushed away the thought and concentrated on his call to follow.

On the far side of the village, as they emerged, Kayvin heard the sound of hoofbeats and caught a blur of motion up the road. He nodded toward the sound, a question.

"I asked them to send word to the next town, so they'll have time to prepare and get everyone safely off the roads. I suppose he waited long enough to see if I was telling the truth." She chuckled. "I did sound more than a bit mad, explaining that you were singing the spawning up the road and everyone needed to hide."

"You did it all well," Dielo said. "The village felt deserted."

Kayvin nodded for Dielo to take the melody, and with the song safely started he said, "We'll have to feed them. They're hungry; that's the problem, and we'll lose them if we pull them along too far."

Yovela nodded. "I'm trying to think of something."

It had been a long time since Galen had brought in a herd of sheep, or goats, or ornery young bulls, and Lisveth's fictitious dragon was not nearly so experienced as a good stock dog. It actually felt a little like working with a new and unreliable dog, one who would run too close to the stock and push them in the wrong direction, or one who hesitated at a key moment.

But it was what they had, and they were learning. Galen was watching for basilisks, risking searching for them with the partial protection of his amulet. He'd found three more so far, and on his detailed instructions, Lisveth had placed an illusion of a dragon at an angle and distance that, more or less, moved each basilisk toward the little group.

They weren't herd animals, Galen thought, but they didn't seem to mind grouping up. They were broodmates, after all, and he supposed that while they were predators themselves, they might behave somewhat like prey when their own predator appeared. There was usually safety in numbers, and broods hatched together to maximize survival.

"Look. No, don't." It was easy to forget for a moment that he was the only one who could safely scan the area. "I see Kayvin's group, on the road ahead. And he's got quite a few now."

"Well done, him." Lisveth was a little breathless. For all her skill with illusions, these seemed to take a higher toll. "Let's hand these over, so I can take a break."

But joining up with Kayvin and the others would not be simple. Galen did not want to shout to them and risk disrupting the prince's fragile singing bond or drawing attention from either group of basilisks. Nor did he want to run to catch up with them, for the same reason. Anyway, they were a long way apart, as Galen and Lisveth had to guide their dangerous charges from a distance, and even a shout might not carry so far. The practical choice was to try to turn their monsters toward the prince's and hope they decided to swarm together.

"Keep the dragon well away from Kayvin's flock," he warned. "We don't want to alarm them."

"Flock, is it now?" Lisveth grinned wearily. "And what are we naming the dragon?"

"What?"

"The dragon. She's such a good worker, she deserves a name."

"I'll think on it," Galen promised, looking back up the road.

It was quite a different thing to look on Kayvin's basilisks. Unworried by glimpses of dragon, they were strung behind him in a loose crowd, occasionally sweeping their heads low to investigate a scent or probe a roadside bush for potential prey, ambling after the prince like curious dogs. Kayvin carried a long-necked instrument and wore a protective scarf over his eyes, and he looked back regularly over his shoulders as if doubting the creatures were still there—or perhaps that they were merely following instead of pursuing.

The other two also wore protective eye coverings, but they rarely looked back. Dielo kept a hand on Kayvin's arm, guiding him up the road, and Yovela moved back and forth, doing something Galen couldn't identify.

One of Galen's basilisks lifted a flat head and gave a curious trill, and the others mimicked the movement. A moment later they increased their shuffling pace, newly energized. Galen hoped they had caught the scent or sound of the prince's beasts and not some farmers resting in a meadow. He hoped the intermittent dragon had them wanting to hide in a group.

He and Lisveth couldn't pass the creatures to reach Kayvin and the others at the front; they had all survived thus far, but it was not yet time for taking unnecessary risks. They hung back behind the line of hatchlings, and when at last Kayvin noticed the increased number, he looked further and saw them at the back, and he nodded. Galen raised a hand and nodded in return.

"How are you holding up?" he asked Lisveth. She looked pale and tired.

But she only nodded. "I'll be all right."

They were approaching a town, and Galen wondered why they continued toward it. They could not take the monsters into a town! But Yovela went ahead, taking the main road directly into the heart of town, and—where was the traffic? It was afternoon, and the roads should have been busy.

"Look at them," Lisveth breathed. "Look at them all."

They were on the roofs. The upper balconies were crowded with townspeople, and windows each showed at least one face. As the road narrowed, Kayvin played his instrument and sang, and the spectators watched in perfect silence.

The basilisks began to sniff the air, and for a moment one considered turning aside into an alley. Galen pointed. "Lisveth." Even if the town had been cleared, there would be street cats and rats in the side streets, enticing a hungry predator.

Lisveth nodded and focused on the alley, and at its far end a dark shape shifted and rose from the mud, flexing its wings. The errant basilisk drew back with a little snort and continued past without turning again.

They were well inside the town now. Kayvin was walking backward, wholly focused on keeping his creatures together and focused. He poured little ripples of notes from his strings and repeated his wordless song, sweeping his hidden gaze through the air a little above the snake-lizards' heads. Dielo was as alert in the other direction, one hand still guiding his master safely through the plaza.

The watching townspeople stared in awe, almost as if transfixed by the uncanny eyes. Then one white-haired man, sharing a wide window with two others, raised his arms in silent salute.

The gesture spread, and men and women lifted their hands from windows, balconies, rooftops. Those with small children in their arms, kept close for immediate hushing, lifted one arm or nodded in appreciation. Children old enough to be trusted to follow directions stared open-mouthed. A few pointed and started to call for a parent's attention, but quick warning glances and gestures hushed them before they could call out.

The only sound was Kayvin's voice, rising above the scrape of toes and claws.

Yovela moved gracefully to one side, doing nothing to disturb the watching creatures, and collected a basket left by the street. She took out a loaf of bread and a small jug, and she nodded her thanks. She returned and passed a piece of the loaf to Dielo.

They passed through the town like a procession of ghosts. Lisveth leaned close and whispered, "You know we're the first humans these people have ever seen, and they're not going to even remember we were here."

Galen nodded. The parade of legendary terrors was much more compelling.

As they exited the town, an ordinary sound intruded, as Galen heard the honking of geese. Kayvin looked to Yovela, who nodded, and Kayvin changed his melody. The basilisks quickened their steps, and they crossed a small bridge beneath a spreading oak tree onto a green.

A large flock of geese spread over the green, tearing up grass and milling lazily. Kayvin turned to look at them, and his song jumped in excited intervals.

The basilisks split apart and waded into the geese, open mouthed and singing softly in their own tunes. Geese blared their indignation and scattered or else turned and watched gently as the hatchlings approached.

Then the killing began.

Yovela shielded her eyes, either disturbed by the sight or distrusting her protective scarf. Dielo stepped close to Kayvin, mouth slightly open as he turned in place, wary of the chaos around them.

"Galen, look." Lisveth's voice was full of warning.

There was a girl in the tree. She was maybe eight years old, dressed in plain, serviceable clothes. She had climbed, but Galen didn't know if it was enough to protect her. She looked terrified.

Galen put up a hand to warn her against moving. She nodded, eyes wide. And then she stared at the monsters, and one looked back at her.

Galen watched her eyes go glassy, saw her drawn expression soften and relax. He started to run. The girl swayed and tipped from her hiding place.

She hit the ground with a loud impact and gave a little yelp. The fall had broken her eye contact, and within a moment she tried to push herself upright. Her arm shifted beneath her, and she gave a wail of both fear and pain.

Galen skidded to the ground beside her, gathering her as carefully as he could. Her arm might be broken, but that was unimportant beside the need to get her out of reach. The basilisk that had looked at her in the tree was shuffling toward them, head fixed on its prey.

Galen put a hand over the girl's mouth. "Be quiet," he whispered, though he wasn't sure that would help. "Don't look." He wondered then if he should let her look, if she would be easier to move if unafraid and without pain.

The basilisk slowed, tipping its head as if listening for a mouse beneath snow. Galen held his breath. This was Lisveth's doing; she was fooling the creature into thinking they had gone, or had become something else.

Across the green, Kayvin began to play his instrument. The basilisks, still gulping down whole geese, swung their heads to look toward him. He played, taking a few steps as if to lure them away, and began to sing again.

"Keep still," Galen whispered. "They're going to leave." His hand was wet with the girl's tears.

The basilisks began to turn in one direction, gathering again. Kayvin moved backward, enticing them with song, coaxing them to come away from the feather-strewn green and follow. His eyes were hidden, but Galen thought he looked over the beasts toward the tree for a moment; he had seen them.

Lisveth dropped to her knees beside Galen. "Are you all right? Fair night, I thought I would watch—I don't think I took a breath in all that time." She cradled the girl's face, pushing back her sweat-slicked hair. "That was terrifying, no question! You were very brave, and I'm so impressed at how you stayed quiet with Galen. May I see your arm?"

Galen didn't remember Lisveth having a quiet manner with children, but she usually rose to a moment's need. He slumped to the ground, suddenly too tired to sit upright.

The girl was frantically trying to explain why she'd been in the tree. "The geese were supposed to be on the green, past the bridge," she sobbed. "I put the geese there like I was supposed to.

Then the geese were moving, and they wouldn't be on the green. So I stayed to keep them where they were supposed to be. And when the things came, I got scared, and I knew everyone was climbing on the roofs, and—"

"You did fine," Lisveth assured her. "The geese were right there, waiting for the prince when he needed them. You just fell out of the tree, and that's unfortunate, but it could have been much worse."

Galen nodded.

"Where's your—where were you supposed to go after you left the geese?"

Galen caught the correction, and he understood. A parent wouldn't have left a goose girl alone to find her own way back in such danger, even if she was supposed to return before the arrival of the hatchlings.

"I was supposed to go to Mistress Burlins," she answered, rubbing her nose across her arm. "She couldn't go because of the babies, they're both fever-sick, and she told me to hurry back but I couldn't because of the geese."

At least this Mistress Burlins seemed to be trying to help, Galen observed. He rocked onto his knees. "Do you think you can make it to Mistress Burlins now?"

The goose girl nodded wetly.

"Just hold your arm carefully, like that, and take your time. Go slowly, so you don't trip. We have to follow the prince."

The girl's expression transformed into awe. "Did you see him? Did you see him sing away the monsters?"

Lisveth nodded. "He did. He's magnificent. Now, can you make it to Mistress Burlins?"

"I have to help her with the babies. They're sick. And Jeri comes to help sometimes but he's the one who went to tell Norboford to prepare for the prince, because he has a fast horse named Klaud."

Ah, so they were passing word to the towns before the prince's arrival—that made sense. It was impressive how quickly they were adapting a process. Galen lifted the girl by her waist and set her gently on her feet. "All set?"

She nodded, and she started back to the town at the assigned careful pace.

"Poor Mistress Burlins is going to have another needy one with the babies," Lisveth mused. "I hope she's got kind neighbors."

They set off after the basilisks. One was lingering on the road, working on a goose that had strayed, and Lisveth put a distant dragon circling the town behind to pressure it forward with the others.

"I hope no one saw that," she said, half with regret and half with a chuckle. "The town can handle only one terrifying predator a day."

They fell into a sort of pattern. Kayvin sang the beasts down the road, joined at times by Dielo or Yovela, or rarely both. When the creatures tired or were distracted, Lisveth hung a dragon in the sky to warn them forward with the group. Galen kept first an eye and then a hand on Lisveth, as she began to stumble more frequently and her pace dragged.

Ahead of them, Kayvin's voice was growing thinner as the sun sank in the sky.

They passed through another town, waiting like the first. This time the silent salute of hands in the air began immediately, rippling through the streets as Kayvin passed. Again Yovela found an offering of food and drink, and she divided it among them. Kayvin gulped his down while the basilisks tore apart a few goat carcasses left in the road. Yovela took the long-necked instrument from him, and Dielo slipped his hand beneath Kayvin's arm to provide support as well as direction.

The sun slipped behind the first of the mountain peaks, turning shadows to twilight.

CHAPTER 129

KAYVIN WAS SO TIRED. His feet were blistered and bruised; he would never have chosen palace slippers for such a trek. He had torn two callouses from his fingertips. The scarf on his face was catching on the scabs forming after Pasiphae Jade's ice, and the tear across his ribs ached. His throat was growing raw, and he worried his hoarse voice would not carry to the hatchlings.

But they were growing more—well, not tractable, that wasn't the word. But they were becoming accustomed to the pattern of following him and his promise to feed them, of passing through the temptations of a town and finding meat on the far side. The instructions Yovela had given at the first town, and the shared innovations as they went on, were lifesaving.

Dielo kept an arm close to steady Kayvin when he slipped and stumbled. Kayvin had given up trying to calculate their progress; he followed the light pressure of Dielo's fingers and wished for the end.

He was so thirsty. They gave him water, but he had been singing for hours, and walking without stop, and he could drink only in quick breaks. Yovela occasionally sang, but her voice was not as compelling; Kayvin wondered if they did not hear the higher tones, or if her range was too different from the mountain's song. So she accompanied Kayvin at times, but she could not relieve him for long, and anyway she was frequently sweeping the road before them, warning away travelers or workers returning from fields.

The sun was sinking in the sky, and Kayvin did not know what would happen in the dark. The creatures might follow the music in just the same way, or they might scatter and hunt, or turn on their musician.

Dielo helped with the singing at times as well, but his voice seemed to agitate the creatures somewhat. They followed, but clacking their jaws and occasionally swinging their heads. Kayvin wondered if some of them recalled Dielo's voice from the previous night in the garden, uncertain and experimental, and if their reserve was somehow shared with the others. That might have been a wild supposition, but he did not have another idea yet to explain, and anyway, it did not matter in the moment more than his melody—all that mattered was that Kayvin keep singing them on.

Yovela was currently out of sight, clearing the road ahead of them. Kayvin reached for the waterbag, distressingly light again. He stopped singing and poured a few mouthfuls down his raw throat. "I don't know how much longer I can last," he whispered, wiping his face with the back of his arm.

"You can," Dielo said with more determination than conviction. After a short pause he added, "Taking these hatchlings to the grazing grounds to eat cattle was a brilliant idea. Saving your people is such a *mooving* purpose."

Had he...? Kayvin tried to give him a flat look, but the scarf over his eyes undercut his effort.

Dielo, however, seemed encouraged by the response. "Only a skilled musician could *steer* these creatures in the right direction."

Kayvin shook his head. He could not waste his voice on answering terrible puns.

"I'm only glad to aid in such a cow-culated effort."

Kayvin gave Dielo's arm a light punch, and the virilo grinned beneath his scarf. Kayvin took another drink, leaving some water on his cracked lips, and restarted his song.

The road became a steady slow incline. Kayvin tried to tell himself this was a promising sign, they must be nearing the grazing hills, but his feet and lungs ached. He reached for the waterbag, but it did not slosh when he shook it.

"I'll look for water," Dielo offered. He took the bag and started ahead.

Kayvin felt suddenly adrift, without a hand on his arm. But he had only to follow the road, feeling his way over the ruts, and if he went carefully, he should be all right.

He wondered where Dielo would find water. With luck, there would be a farm building near the road, with stored jars or a well. It was more likely they wouldn't find water until the next town, and he did not know how far that might be.

He sang a new phrase to his charges, and most called back in a sort of chorus. He'd found this could keep them with him when they had more miles between meat, and he worried about them tiring on the incline and leaving to find easier meals.

Galen and Lisveth were somewhere behind them. He'd seen their dragon—the first sight had given his heart a terrible wrench, before he realized it must be Lisveth's doing—and they could keep the basilisks from turning back to a past village, at least while the sun remained in the sky to show the dragon.

Abruptly he saw someone on the side of the road, and a moment later he recognized Dielo through the obscuring scarf. Dielo held two waterbags, dangling full from his left hand. His right hand held his scarf, floating in the light breeze. His gaze was fixed toward Kayvin and the basilisks, and he did not look toward Kayvin, and he did not blink.

Kayvin bolted toward him, or tried to. His blistered feet stumbled on the rutted road and he caught his breath. A basilisk in the lead was eying Dielo, head unwavering as its shuffling legs angled toward the edge of the road. The others roused at Kayvin's sudden movement, and one gave a little mewling growl.

Kayvin dropped the song and ran ahead to Dielo, catching him about the shoulders and turning him away from the oncoming beast, pulling his hand across his eyes. "Dielo!"

The virilo shuddered and seemed to wake. "My—my lord?"

But now the basilisk was nearly upon them, quickening its stride, and it did not mind whether Dielo was entranced or not as long as it could reach him.

Kayvin held Dielo tightly to him and began to sing. He let the song pour through him, almost shaking with the urgency of it. The creature was an arm's length away. Kayvin sang. It pressed at his leg with its blunt muzzle, jaws slightly agape. Kayvin sang.

He sang promise, he sang hope, he sang an impossible tunnel through the base of a mountain glowing with infinite subterranean stars. He sang loss, and grief, and the joy of a dance, and the ache of harmony, and the thirst for trust and love.

Dielo held his breath beneath Kayvin's shielding hand. Kayvin did not move, either, not daring to rupture the fragile connection he wove with his song.

At last the basilisk pulled back, chuffing irritably. Kayvin felt Dielo's shoulders drop. Together they turned, and Dielo lifted the cloth to tie over his eyes again.

"I'm so sorry," he offered breathlessly between phrases of Kayvin's song. "I had to take it off to manage the pump. I thought you would be farther. I'm so sorry."

Kayvin tightened his arm on Dielo's shoulders, pulling him close. He folded the new song into the original, leading the hatchlings on.

Dielo rubbed an arm over his newly covered face and started up the road, drawing Kayvin with him. He drew a long, shuddering breath. "I'm glad we can look out for one an-udder."

Kayvin coughed out a laugh mid-measure, and for a moment he struggled to find the note again. Behind him two of the basilisks sent a questioning trill. He fell back to the more familiar phrases and glanced over his shoulder to confirm the hatchlings were following reliably.

It was only a couple of minutes before Yovela crossed the road to join them. She took each of them by the hand and squeezed. "I saw it," she whispered. "I didn't want to disrupt the song, so I stayed where I was. But I saw it all." She squeezed again. "Be careful."

Dielo laughed, a high laugh of nervous relief. "It was all right in the end. His Highness has developed an extensive cow-talog of melodies."

Yovela did not understand. "What?"

"I'm only trying to lighten the *mood*."

Kayvin gave Dielo a one-armed hug and shook his head, grinning through his singing.

Yovela began to sing, and then she pushed a waterbag—forgotten in the urgent song to save them—toward Kayvin's hand. He gulped water down greedily, breathed, drank again.

Dielo harmonized with Yovela, and their voices blended well. Kayvin thought for a moment that he should write them a duet, when they were back home, and then he laughed internally at his ranging thoughts. He was tiring, and his mind was wavering.

When the basilisks began glancing around, considering the countryside, Kayvin began to sing again. His voice was cracking, but they still seemed to prefer it. He wondered how many miles remained.

Another hour or so passed. The sun sank, and the light grew more yellow. Kayvin's shadow trailed long behind him. And then suddenly Dielo's hand closed tightly on Kayvin's arm. "My lord! Do you hear that?"

Kayvin could hear little but his own voice. He paused, drew air, and hesitated just a moment before beginning again. What had Dielo heard? Was it a warning—or was this a preamble to another terrible pun?

And then, magnificent in its promise, he heard the long low call of a grazing cow.

Hope flooded him, and he felt his face crack into a smile as he restarted his song. Yovela caught his other hand, and then she withdrew to start playing the gittern once more.

"They sent riders ahead," Yovela explained. "Every cowherd, every crofter was to be warned and brought away. There should be no one here. Just up this hill, and we can release them into the hills and valleys."

Some part of Kayvin knew there would be consequences, that the sudden loss of so many cattle must affect markets and the price of milk and cheese and meat. The towns that had sacrificed their geese and their goats would feel the pinch this winter and next year. But they would not mourn their dead.

There were so many of the beasts now. Kayvin could not count them, he could only pass his eyes over them as if addressing a crowd at a banquet or festival. He turned, backing up the hill with Dielo's direction, scanning for Lisveth and Galen in the twilight.

Yes, there was the dragon executing a lazy wide turn and exhaling a flicker of fire. That had been clever—and the dragon itself invaluable. Lisveth and Galen were difficult to see in the distance and dark, but they were not too far behind.

He owed them all so much.

"The hill," Dielo said.

Kayvin turned and looked down over green slopes and more hills, rising gradually to the western mountains. Cattle were spread over the green shoulders, grazing in scattered groups, content in the peace of the evening.

Kayvin was about to destroy that peace.

He faced the basilisks and changed his song again, singing the melody of feast and flesh, making good on the promise they had faithfully followed. The foremost of the creatures crested the hill, passing only spears' lengths from them as they fixed on the plentiful slopes beyond.

Kayvin couldn't collapse, not yet. He had to stand and sing the rest of them into the hills, without letting any slip back toward the towns and the capital. He forced sound from his cracking throat, and he clenched his sore fingers into fists as he willed the last of them through.

He didn't know what would happen when he stopped. He had broken the song for only a moment at a time, and each time he had needed to coax them back. If he stopped singing altogether, would they turn on him?

He waved Dielo and Yovela away. They hesitated, and he gestured more fiercely, with the little strength he had left. He would sing this last crossing alone, and he would bear the risk of stopping.

They retreated unwillingly, going partway down the slope they'd just climbed. He supposed that was far enough, as the slowest hatchlings crested the hill. If they turned back on him, Dielo and Yovela would have time to observe and flee.

The first basilisks were reaching the outlying cattle in the shallow valley. There was some initial movement away from the strange beasts, but the cattle were not particularly flighty; they had few predators here. And then the chosen prey were entranced, and they did not run or bellow as the basilisks moved in.

There were thousands of cattle in these hills. They had successfully directed the hatchlings away from the cities and towns. And now he could rest.

Kayvin stopped singing and sank to the ground. He gulped air and slumped low, letting his head hang. Now he would learn if he would die.

He heard nothing. No basilisk turned to waddle up again toward him.

Then there was a soft flurry of footsteps in the grass. Dielo knelt beside him, hands on Kayvin's shoulders. Yovela came from the other side, catching the hand that lay limp in his lap. They were speaking, but Kayvin shook his head. He was fine. Just exhausted.

With the others here, he could let his weight fall back. He propped one leg before himself and leaned on it. He wasn't sure how much time passed—he might have fallen asleep with his elbow upon his knee—before he heard Galen's voice. "Are you hurt? Any of you?"

"We're all right," Yovela answered wearily above Kayvin. "Just glad that's done."

"Now we have to find a place to go back to," Dielo pointed out in near dejection. "We dare not stay here overnight."

"There's a hut at the base of the hill, to the south." Galen partially turned, probably pointing. "We can stay there tonight. It's stone."

Galen pulled Kayvin and Dielo to their feet, and they limped together down the slope. Lisveth was nearly to the hut already, moving slowly. The hut was stone, as Galen had described, and well-appointed for a herder's seasonal dwelling. It had probably been in use for generations.

The door was unlocked, and they tumbled inside. Dielo pushed Kayvin directly to the shallow nest of pillows on the floor. "Sleep, my lord."

"Drink first," Yovela interrupted. "You need water as much as sleep. Take both."

Galen spotted a bucket. "There's a water source nearby. I'll bring some."

CHAPTER 130

THERE WAS A SPRING just two dozen steps behind the hut, probably descending from the mountains and easily located by its happy burble. Galen liked the sound of it, but he was too tired to linger. A day of walking wasn't so unusual, but the strain of watching for terrifying monsters was.

When he returned to the hut, Kayvin was already leaning into the corner with the pillows. Lisveth was unrolling a matted fur into the opposite corner, having cleared the limited furniture out of the way.

They gave Kayvin the first dipper of water. Galen wasn't sure if it was because he was the prince, but regardless, the singer deserved it. He still had not spoken yet.

When everyone had drunk, they separated without discussion into two piles. Kayvin slumped into the corner, with Diego and Yovela on either side, and Galen looked at Lisveth, crawling into the opposite corner. "You might be warmer with more people. We don't have much in the way of blankets here."

"There's only one person I share a bed with, even if it's not a bed."

Galen joined her, wedging himself against the wall. He opened an arm and let her fall against his shoulder, sliding toward his collarbone. "I think you malign our poor friends."

"I think we'll talk about it tomorrow."

He expected more from her, but her breathing was already slowing, and she slept.

Galen had bolted the shutters and pushed a trunk against the door before sitting down, and he felt that someone should probably keep watch, just in case one of the basilisks came down this side of the hill. A bare minute after this consideration, he also slept.

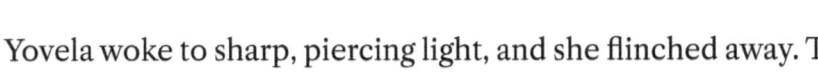

Yovela woke to sharp, piercing light, and she flinched away. There was a gap in the shutter, sending a narrow beam of dawn sunlight directly at her face. She shifted, careful not to jar Kayvin, and moved out of its path.

Her neck hurt; she had leaned at an awkward angle as she slept, too tired to adjust. She thought of rubbing it, but her arm was still too heavy to lift.

"Yovela?"

The whisper was so slight, she wasn't sure if she'd actually heard it. She turned her head, and Dielo was looking at her.

"I'm sorry. I thought you were awake."

She nodded and winced. Between them, Kayvin slept heavily, lips slightly parted and face slack.

Dielo glanced across the room to the two humans, also still sleeping. "Couldn't you sleep?"

She indicated the window. "The light did it. Weren't you tired?"

"I wish I could sleep again." He looked down. "But I woke this morning, thinking of...everything."

There was much to think about. The last day had been a year's fill of events. She nodded, and then made a face as her neck seized.

Dielo slid carefully away from Kayvin and walked around to her other side. He crouched beside her and lifted a hand. "May I?"

"I suppose."

His hand rested gently on her neck, a moment of calm before he began softly kneading up the muscle along her spine. The touch was so accurate, so specific to her pain, and she rested against the wall heavily, realizing she'd been holding herself more upright than she'd known.

His low whisper hid much of his tone. "She's—gone. The Arch Potentate is imprisoned and now Prince Kayvin holds the throne."

She nodded, moving more freely now.

"Is the spawning really done? What if they come out of the hills? What if there are more of them?"

She was too tired for these questions. "We'll face it when it comes. I'm happy to have survived this long."

"I'm happy you survived." He glanced at her and then away again. "I didn't know when—when you were taken. His Excellency told me she'd put you into the fountain, and... I'm so sorry."

Sorry he hadn't been there when Pasiphae Jade's guards came for her? She shook her head. "There was nothing you could have done."

He blew out a soft breath and drew back his hand to gesture at Kayvin's leg. "You can lie flat now. Pillow your head just above his knee there."

Lying down would feel heavenly. Kayvin would welcome her and want her to be comfortable. But the distance was still too far. She gave a small grunt of denial.

Dielo pushed himself against the wall. "Use my shoulder, if you prefer."

His shoulder was at exactly the right height, a feat that impressed her. She let her head roll the slight distance.

Dielo folded his hands in his lap. "I went to Sayinia."

"What?"

"When the two of you went, this last time, I followed you. I knew Lirin would be all right in the Arch Potentate's care, and I wanted to help." He gave an embarrassed smile. "I lost you on the far side of the passage. But I traveled on my own."

She thought she understood the unspoken accomplishment. "Alone? Being someone else?"

"Being myself, when I am not in the palace." He said the words quickly, as if afraid they would stick. "I brushed oxen. I listened to stories. I did not dance. I like to dance, but it would have felt like... I can't explain it."

"You didn't know how to do it as that self without being another self." She remembered the sensation.

"Yes, that's it." He drew one knee up, bracing himself.

Yovela was tired, but she knew now this was a confession of sorts, and he needed to tell someone who might understand.

"I took a girl to a hospital. She was having trouble with a baby. I was there for the birth."

"The live birth?" She was curious.

"It was a little fascinating." He chuckled nervously. "And so horrific. But it was bad even for a live birth and she nearly died, and I was there with her, and I was able to help her."

She sensed this was the important part, what he'd built up to say.

"I'd never done anything like that. She needed me—not to tickle her fancy or flatter her, but to really help her. They said I saved her life, and I held her hand while her child was born." He swallowed. "She named her baby Dielo."

Yovela put a hand atop his. She didn't know what to say to that. What an experience...

"I don't know what it means, now that I'm here again. But to know that I could do something like that—it was incredible."

She nodded against his shoulder.

"And I wanted...I wanted someone to know that I could. That I was able to do something really useful, and even if I come back to..." He stopped, chewed his lip, tried again. "I wanted you to know. I know you think I am worthless for anything else, but—"

She pulled away, ignoring the twinge in her neck, and put a hand on his mouth. He froze, eyes alarmed.

Yovela took a breath to moderate her voice, keeping it a whisper. "I meant you believed you were worthless for anything else. You'd been told your only purpose was your master." She shook her head. "But if I believed that, I wouldn't have been upset by the lie."

Beneath her hand, he drew a quick breath. For three heartbeats he stared at her, wide-eyed, and then he looked down at his folded hands, his face sliding from her quieting fingers.

Yovela moved back, and she did not rest her head on his shoulder again. "I'm glad you told me. Even if you didn't need to."

He didn't answer. She thought, listening to his breathing, that he was struggling with something he could not say.

Beside them, Kayvin sighed in his sleep. Yovela glanced across the room, but Galen and Lisveth were both still deeply asleep.

"Thank you." The words were so quick and so quiet that she nearly missed them. Then Dielo stood and returned to his more traditional place beside the prince.

She felt there was some gulf that she had missed and perhaps stumbled into. What else should she have said? She should apologize for what she said when he first came, when she was angry and hurt and reminded of all the things she was and was not... She had turned that anger on him, for not fighting back in the way she could not. She had been unfair and cruel.

But he had found a way to be more than his upbringing, and she was pleased for him. He didn't need to tell her—a virilo could have little use for the approbation of a sera qadra dancer—but it had been thoughtful of him to include her.

The spot of sun was sliding slowly across the wall, but she couldn't guess the time. She was thirsty. The others were still asleep; she should rest again. She closed her eyes and thought hard of nothing.

CHAPTER 131

WHEN THE SUN WAS too high to pretend otherwise any longer, they dragged themselves from their various positions and stared at one another.

"Someone should look," Lisveth said practically. "We should see what's happening, if they're still in the valley."

"If they hunted in the same way, if they were well fed here, they should still be here?" Yovela suggested hopefully. "We didn't hear any cattle panicking."

"We wouldn't have heard a chorus of brass horns," Kayvin croaked heavily. "I'll go and look."

"I'll go," Lisveth said. "I can be less visible, now that I know how to pitch an illusion for them."

"And if they can't see you, then you can't see them?" Galen interrupted. "I'll go. I have the most resistance."

"And that's been so reliable for you?"

"We can go together," Kayvin decided. "Galen, Lisveth, and me. Dielo and Yovela can wait here; they have the fewest protections."

Dielo and Yovela predictably protested, of course, and in the end they all climbed the hill above the hut, legs aching and feet dragging with both lingering fatigue and reluctance to see what awaited them.

But the carnage was not what they expected. There were a dozen carcasses spread across the valley, and a few hatchlings lingered near to worry scraps of meat from the bones. The remaining cattle were grazing within sight, and they had not fled. None were close to the dead, but the herd looked calm enough.

"It's not the danger that alarms them," Kayvin observed wonderingly. "It's the others' fear. If they don't see the fear, they don't perceive the danger."

"I think there's a sort of moral in there somewhere, if I'd had another six hours of sleep and could think on it." Lisveth gathered her hair and scratched her scalp. "Do you mean to leave them here?"

"I don't know where else to take them." Kayvin took a breath. "The stories say they kill and eat for several weeks, and then they sort of disappear. Back into the mountain, I suppose? Usually the chronicler has been across the mountains and is recording the words of survivors, so it's not a terribly detailed account, but that seems to be consistent."

"Do they stay in one place?" Galen asked. "Will they stay here?"

Kayvin looked over the valley. "As long as the cattle hold out, probably."

"That's long enough for us to think about it," Yovela said quickly. "We don't have to know the complete action yet. You've solved the immediate crisis, and we'll warn everyone to stay away from the grazing."

They looked at one another and nodded. "I suppose we walk back," Kayvin said.

Lisveth had her hands over her forehead, shielding her eyes. "You start first, and Galen and I will meet you in the capital."

"You're not walking with us?"

"I have a murderous headache, and this sunlight is making it worse. I'm going back to the hut, and I'll see if I'm up to walking this evening or tomorrow."

Dielo frowned. "What about—are you comfortable sleeping another night so close..."

"If they leave the mountains and cattle, it's only a matter of time between the hut and a village," Lisveth said with dark practicality. "We trust them to stay in the valley, or we don't." She folded her hands over her eyes and screwed up her face. "And I'm barring all the doors and windows."

Galen slid an arm around her shoulders, partly protective and partly ready to guide her. "Too much magic yesterday. She'll sleep it off and then she'll be all right. You go on."

"If you're sure..." Kayvin sounded uncertain, as if he wanted to protest more.

"You have to get back; you're the prince. Potentate. We're less important."

Kayvin hesitated and then gave a single nod. "Be safe. We'll start back now." He looked down the slope. "How I wish I'd thought to bring another pair of shoes."

There was no reason to hurry, and they were all exhausted and sore. A pleasant breeze caressed their faces, free now of protective blindfolds, and hunger began to set in. They had not thought to bring rations yesterday, and the villages' offerings had not lasted.

They were nearly to the first town on their return path when it happened.

Kayvin was taking shallow steps, but it was not difficult to avoid limping, as both feet hurt equally. He was sure his skin was open and bleeding, but there was little to be done for it and he didn't want the others to fuss over it. They matched his reduced pace, and maybe Dielo and Yovela were glad of that as well.

The village came into sight at the end of the long decline, with vendors hawking along the road and a few laborers in the nearby fields. When they called to one another and went into the village, Kayvin did not think much of it; it was midday and time for a meal, and if they hurried a little more than strictly necessary, what did he know of villager schedules?

But when, as they reached the outermost ring of buildings, a group burst from one of the larger buildings, cheering and singing and beating copper pots, Kayvin flinched back, and Yovela caught Kayvin's arm. But Dielo only began to laugh joyously. "A welcome!"

It was. They were singing and cheering for Kayvin and his coterie. A woman approached him with a braid of colorful scarves twisted together and shyly crowned him with it, leaving gauzy green, teal, and gold tails to fall down his back.

Kayvin looked around at them, aware he was grinning stupidly in his surprise and unable to stop. "What's this?" he asked, feeling foolish.

"We are the first to welcome you again!" A man stepped forward and bowed. "Your lady told us yesterday that you were coming and why. No prince has ever visited us before, and we have never heard of something so brave as you did. We wanted to thank you, in our poor way."

Kayvin looked at Dielo and Yovela on either side of him. They looked disheveled and filthy, and he must look worse.

"What can we do for you, my lord prince?" a woman asked. She had a bottle in her hand, and an empty clay cup.

"Do you—do you have anything to eat?" Kayvin asked. "We walked a long way yesterday, and we had no supper."

"A meal!" the man shouted, and the woman beamed and began to fill her cup. Arms beckoned Kayvin to a large round table back inside the building, and cups and bottles and bowls and baskets began to appear on the scuffed wooden surface.

He gestured for Dielo to sit beside him. "Don't leave me alone. I don't know what to say."

"Thank them," Dielo said while smiling around. "Let them feel your appreciation. They want to know they've reached you."

"Reached me? If they just bring us a meal, I'll—"

"Kiss a baby?" Dielo grinned and indicated a child being borne toward them.

Kayvin was startled by the presentation of the toddler, who stared at him in solemn curiosity. "Who is this?" he managed.

"Dulf," the child's mother said. "Please greet him, so that he may have met the prince who sang."

It was a country name, but Kayvin had heard stranger in the human land. "It is good to meet you, Dulf," he said seriously. "I look forward to receiving your pledge one day."

"Of course!" the mother agreed.

Dulf reached out to feel Kayvin's crown of scarves.

Kayvin stretched his legs out under the table and felt the ache and pull up through his hips. His feet began to throb as he took the weight from them.

"Eat, eat!" urged the woman who set another steaming bowl before him. "You need broth to recover your voice."

That might be true. Kayvin nodded his thanks and picked up a spoon.

"Georgie! Get your horse!" She turned back. "He's riding ahead so each town will know you're coming and can have refreshment ready."

"That's very thoughtful," Yovela said. "Thank you."

"Of course, of course!" The woman smiled and nodded. "We are all speaking of the prince who sang."

Dielo gave a tiny cough. "Since yesterday morning—"

Yovela touched his arm. "Yesterday was long. Thank you for thinking to care for us."

Kayvin nodded. "Indeed, thank you."

They thought he was still the prince, not the new Arch Potentate—indeed, how would they know otherwise? He had not thought to send proclaimers, and no court had formally acknowledged him, and there had been no coronation.

And he liked that. He liked being the prince who sang. Later, he would have to be the Arch Potentate. Today, here, he was the Amethyst Prince, purger of poisons, who sang to save his people.

The soup was made of broth, root vegetables, and cream, and it was one of the best things he'd ever tasted.

Galen waved a hopeful farewell to the prince's group, turning Lisveth slightly so that she waved in the correct direction while her other hand remained over her eyes, her face tipped down.

The sun already blazed on the eastern hills, making Galen squint. His hat was in his bag, which he hadn't carried up to look over the valley. He blinked against the light and steered Lisveth down to the hut, and then he looked to the east where

Kayvin, Dielo, and Yovela were disappearing down into the bright horizon. "Okay, they're off."

"Good for them."

"You can uncover your eyes now."

"Aw, you knew?"

"I've seen you with real headaches. You make a different face."

"What's the difference?"

"Oh, no, I'm not giving away my advantage. I like knowing a tell." He pulled open the door. "So why are we going back separately?"

Lisveth sobered. "He left the palace. It was the right thing, a good thing, but... He's only a contender for the throne, and not a popular or strong one."

Galen, reaching for his pack, stiffened and looked at her. "You think... But then shouldn't we be with them?"

She shook her head. "See, I knew you would say that. But you aren't his bodyguard, not really, and even if you were, do you think you and your sword could protect him from a bank of archers? Ones you never saw in the trees or town until after they'd loosed a few dozen shafts at you?"

Galen's gut seemed to hollow out and grow cold. "Then we're just going to let them die? After coming all this way to help?"

"We came to deal with a fountain, not to retake a country," Lisveth said sharply. Then she jerked her head toward the road. "But no, I'm not a complete monster. I think we'll do better if we're not with them, if we can see things for ourselves and look ahead."

"They're a bit far ahead for us to be watching their road."

She snorted. "Do you think the three of them will be making any kind of time? Poor things in their pretty slippers, while we've got years of callouses. Too bad we don't have the Golden Eye to stay unnoticed, but we'll do what we can."

Galen passed her pack to her. "As long as we get to stop by a food stall."

"Fried bread and cheese?"

"Don't say such things until we're in sight, or I'll start drooling right now down this scruffy chin."

CHAPTER 132

THERE WAS A DELEGATION of sorts waiting at the next village. It was not like the commoners' delegations Kayvin had seen occasionally in the palace, stiff and formal and serious. This one drowned its own inaudible speech in music, as villagers beat drums and played plain stringed instruments and blew one horn that even most of the grinning gathering seemed to find too much.

Kayvin hobbled to the tables waiting in the street, with a brightly striped awning spread overhead, and eased gratefully to a bench. "Thank you," he said, raising his hands and hoping that looked appreciative even as he sat down to address them. "Your kindness and welcome are very much appreciated."

A child with hair tails stared at him, open-mouthed, and he felt the sudden, ridiculous urge to make a silly face at her. He was too tired and too giddy with relief to conduct himself appropriately, and too tired and too giddy to worry enough about that.

Dielo sat on another bench, and the little girl turned to stare at him. Dielo grinned at her. "Did you come to help, too?"

The girl did not answer aloud, but after a moment she gave a solemn nod.

"Thank you," he answered as seriously, nodding in return.

Kayvin extended his legs again and drew a breath against the pain in his feet. "I don't suppose," he said to the young woman who set a bowl of cut fruits before him, "there might be a cobbler near here?"

"A cobbler? Yes, my husband, though I don't think our wares will be up to palace standards."

"My standards are quite practical, I assure you."

Puzzled, she stepped to the side and bent to peer under the table. "What length—oh! Oh, my lord, we can get you some proper shoes. Empty void."

Kayvin squinted down at the torn slippers, stained with dirt and blood. "Thank you."

By the time he finished the fruit, a young man, nearly too young to be a merchant of his own shop, pushed breathlessly to the royal group and knelt by Kayvin's bench. "Your Highness, my lord, my wife—she said I could bring you shoes, my lord, and I have." He took a large sack from his shoulder and opened it, showing a tumble of shoes and boots. "I will find something in your size, my lord, and I hope to your liking."

"If it has a proper sole, it will be to my liking." Kayvin rotated on the bench. "And if anyone can offer a pair of—"

"I have some woolens!" someone called. "Do you have a favorite color?"

Kayvin looked at the little girl still standing near Dielo. "What color should I say?"

She stared at him expressionlessly for a moment, and he thought he'd just made a fool of himself, and then at last she said, "Green."

He nodded. "Green. If you have them."

They brought more than just the woolen stockings and shoes; there was warm water and rags and a soothing salve to cover the raw sections where the skin had sloughed away. A chatty man had also applied a salve to his scabbed face and the wound in his side. When at last all was finished and it was time to leave, Kayvin got tentatively to his feet and smiled his approval. His feet hurt, but at least there would be less new damage.

"My lord! If you please!"

He turned to a grey-haired man bowing in the street.

"My lord, we have prepared transportation for you, if you will accept it." He rose and made a grand gesture down the empty street.

But someone had been watching for the sign, and an oxcart came around the corner of the weaver's store. They needn't have waited for a moment of quiet to introduce it; the two oxen were painted with purple across shoulders and horns, with small bits of crystal dangling from each horn tip. Cloth had been draped over their hips and along the sides of the cart, newly furnished with fresh straw and blankets.

Kayvin stared at it, and he had to suppress a sudden laugh that bubbled up, lest they think he was mocking their effort. Still, he felt a grin break through his efforts.

There was an ancient tradition of oxcarts for royal conveyance, if one looked back far enough, but no Arch Potentate had used one since the old wars. Certainly no Arch Potentate had ever used oxen conscripted from the day's threshing and a cart decorated with household linen. It was ridiculous, and sweetly thoughtful.

"It's the most wonderful thing I could imagine," he said, spreading his arms. "I am delighted. Thank you."

The villagers beamed and gestured him and his attendants into the cart.

Yovela tapped his arm. "My lord, you have a dispute."

He followed her eyes and saw two people holding back a girl a little older than Lirin, as she protested and tried to move toward the oxcart. It was a markedly different tone than the rest of the happy town gathering in the street, and he pointed. "What's the trouble there?"

Everyone turned, and the three froze in sudden self-consciousness. The girl recovered first. "They're mine!"

Immediately one of the men near her made a hushing sound and a gesture to be quiet. Kayvin frowned and beckoned her forward. "Do you mean the oxen? I'll return them, of course."

She compressed her lips, and he realized she was fighting tears. "But I'm the better driver, and he"—she pointed at the young man at the front of the cart—"tries to make up by using the goad and nose rings instead of just handling them like they're trained, and—"

"That is training!" he retorted, forgetting they were in front of a prince.

"I'm the better driver, and they're my oxen, and I trained them, and you all took them because they're the best but you took them from me and won't let me drive them!"

Her tears, Kayvin now understood, were ones of frustration rather than grief. Around them many people began to speak, some pointing at the man or the oxen or down the street, and she tightened her jaw and refused to retract her accusation even as it was clear they thought she was embarrassing them before the prince.

Kayvin held up a hand. "Are these indeed her oxen?"

"They're our family's," a man said.

"I raised and trained them!"

"That doesn't make you the sole owner of them."

Kayvin exhaled and addressed the young woman. "And do you drive them for most of their work?"

"Nearly all of it, my lord."

Kayvin looked to the two men—probably a father and uncle, or other relatives—and waited, but neither denied what she said.

"It's different out here, my lord," the older man said after a moment. "Everyone has to pull together in a village like this, and we all do our share. But for a prince, the traditions must be observed, and we wouldn't send a girl to serve in a man's post."

Kayvin nodded as if appreciating their reasoning, and then he said, "You have all offered such wonderful hospitality and taken such good care of me, and why should you not provide me with your most skilled driver?"

There was a strained moment, and then Yovela sat forward in the cart. "You'd better bring your hat."

The young woman's face broke into a fierce smile, and she moved to the front of the cart to replace the other driver.

Kayvin moved quickly to relieve the tension. "Again, I thank you all for your splendid welcome, and we are grateful for your care. I will remember your kindness."

The cart started forward, facing north as it had been brought out, and the young woman called instructions to the two oxen and executed a surprisingly tight reversal in the street. Whatever else had happened, her skill as a driver was unquestionable.

They were waved and cheered out of the village and onto the road, and Kayvin sat down on the covered straw. "I could fall asleep right here."

"Not for long," Yovela warned. "We'll have another town, and you'll need to greet them just the same."

"A few minutes, at least," Kayvin begged. He rotated to face their new driver. "Thank you for the use of your oxen. I am truly appreciative."

"Of course, my lord!" She gave an awkward bow. "I began to paint them as soon as we had word you were returning. I was so hoping to—thank you for letting me come."

"Letting you? I believe it is you who are letting us come along." Kayvin smiled, and then he slid down the pile of straw, wrinkling the blanket. "And if you began painting them, it sounds like the oxcart was your idea in the first place."

She bobbed her head with shy pride. "Yes."

"What's your name?"

"Minera. And this is Arrow and Bow."

"Lovely to meet each of you. Minera, please alert us when we're within eyesight of the next town. Or if anything urgent comes." Kayvin did not want to think of another basilisk appearing, but it was possible. "I'm going to sleep while I can."

"Of course, my lord! We'll go as quietly as possible."

CHAPTER 133

KAYVIN WAS AWAKENED WITH a gentle shake to his shoulder, which was probably not within the protocol of addressing a sleeping Arch Potentate but likely necessary in the rocking oxcart. "Where are we?"

"Another village. They've turned out as well." Yovela nodded toward the road ahead. "You should be prepared to greet them, and without straw in your hair."

Kayvin ran a hand through his hair and felt a few pieces snag. "Did I get them all?"

Yovela made a small despairing scowl and turned to Dielo. "You'll be more efficient."

Kayvin sat for Dielo's reach. The virilo's hands moved efficiently, without lingering, just as he had served Kayvin at his homecoming. "Thank you," Kayvin attempted, and the words felt brittle.

Dielo heard what Kayvin meant, and his reply was nearly too quiet to hear. "It's only setting your hair."

Kayvin cleared his throat. "You sat by my first audience."

"As furniture in your reception hall. No more. I'll help how I can, and there are many ways to serve."

Guilt gnawed at Kayvin, though he couldn't exactly explain why... Yes, he could. He owed nothing; he could kindly reject any village woman who might smile and bat eyelashes at him today, and he would have done no wrong. But Dielo had been raised entirely for a purpose that was, Kayvin could see now, isolating and minimizing and exploitative, and he could empathize with the tragedy of it.

Now, though, he said only, "I hope you find better joy." And it was a stupid, feeble thing to say, and he regretted speaking so plainly and without offering more hope, and so he turned to face the road.

As Dielo pulled Kayvin's hair into place, the cart rumbled down to the village, and welcoming townspeople began to appear on the roadside. Kayvin smiled and nodded and waved, feeling awkward though in a sense this was what he'd been born for. People moved alongside the cart, following and cheering, and the crowd swelled as they entered the main street of the village.

"My lord!"

The voice caught Kayvin's ear through the others, and he turned to see a slender, veiled woman waving to him. The face and voice made no sense in the crowd, and then he realized, "Nala!"

She smiled broadly beneath the veil, still swept over one eye as Dielo had first styled it. "Your Highness!"

Kayvin eased a leg over the oxcart's side and slid stiffly into the street. The crowd drew back a step and seemed to hold its breath for a moment, unsure of what this meant. Kayvin caught Nala's outstretched hand. "It's good to see you! Are you well?"

"I am well," she answered, beaming. "Would my lord honor my house with a visit?"

"Gladly." Kayvin gestured. "Lead on."

The spectators gave a hesitant cheer, uncertain of this departure from the route but pleased that one of their own had drawn royal attention.

Nala led Kayvin to a shop. Rugs hung on every wall, two or three in a row, and more layered the floor in uneven piles. Kayvin turned in place, looking at the rugs, and saw that Yovela and Dielo had followed him.

Nala hurriedly placed several stools into a circle. "Please, my lord, be seated. I'll make tea."

"Is this your shop?"

"Yes, with my husband." Her voice warmed as she spoke.

"Your husband?" Kayvin felt a smile break onto his face. "I'm glad to hear it."

"Who is he?" Yovela prompted. "Will he be here as well?"

"He went down the street for a better place to watch,' Nala admitted with a chuckle. "He did not think you would stop here."

"I'm glad you had more confidence in me," Kayvin said, "and gladder still I was able to hear you and bear that confidence out."

"How did you come to marry him?" Dielo leaned forward, eyes bright.

Kayvin gave him a sharp look; the tale might not be kind to Nala and her damaged face, if the man had been convinced with a large dowry or if she was a second or third wife brought in to manage the others' children—or did commoners take multiple wives? But Dielo's expression was happily expectant, and already Nala's smile had broadened and her eyes crinkled in embarrassed pleasure.

She set out tea cups. "He approached my father, about two weeks after I went home. He said he had loved me since childhood but knew he could not provide a serious offer for me." She gave a shy smile. "He told me later he'd cried when I went into the palace. I think he was only being kind, but it was nice of him to say so, anyway."

Kayvin thought some part of her wanted to believe it. He thought she probably should. "And when you went home?"

"By then, he was starting to see returns on his shop, opened in this town away from family competition. He came to see me a few times, and I was glad to see him, too. Then he told my father he was prepared to propose marriage." She lowered her voice. "My father said my bride price was reduced."

Kayvin gave a single nod and clenched his fist out of sight. That was Pasiphae Jade's cruelty, forever following poor Nala.

"But Terro said it was not my face he wanted, and my heart must only have grown in value, and so he insisted upon paying one and a half times what the bride price would have been before I went into the palace." Nala could not suppress her warm, proud smile. "He made me the most expensive bride in my family."

An odd warmth spread through Kayvin's torso. "As you should be," he murmured.

"It was foolish of him," Nala continued quickly. "It used most of his profits here, and now he's nearly back to his start."

But he had purchased the pride of his wife, now a figure of renown instead of scathing disgust and pity. That had been well worth the price.

At that moment a young man came in a rear door, stopping abruptly upon seeing the little group. Kayvin could nearly observe the realization working through his initial disbelief. At last he managed, "Your Highness?"

"His Illustrious Excellency," Dielo corrected quietly.

Terro's face grew more tense. "Nala, we..."

"Nala was kind enough to invite us for some refreshment," Kayvin said, "and I am glad to see her settled so well."

Terro managed a surprised grin. "We're honored by your visit."

"These are lovely rugs," Yovela said, running her hand over one. "The workmanship is very fine."

"Er, thank you. Our workshop is very skilled, and I am fortunate to have such craftspeople."

Yovela looked at Kayvin. "They're beautiful."

He nodded. "Indeed."

Yovela continued to look at him, as Dielo agreed and admired the intense indigo of a particular pattern.

Slowly Kayvin grasped their message. He pursed his lips and made a show of thoughtful consideration. "They are very fine rugs. I think I would like one of these."

Terro's face went still.

Kayvin was not securely in place as Arch Potentate, and he had little idea of what kind of purse was open to him; he'd had an allowance as Amethyst Prince, but his habits of sheet music and an occasional instrument had not stretched it to the point of discussion. But surely his reduced sera qadra would compensate for one large and beautiful rug, the finest from their workshop, and if a steward or accountant complained, he would economize in wines or flower petals for the next banquet.

Empty void, a banquet. He would need to arrange for his own coronation and then feasting to impress and secure the courtiers. His stomach lurched.

But Yovela was nodding. "A wonderful idea! Nala, you and Terro could see it delivered to the palace, yes? And of course there must be a mark to authorize your entrance, as purveyors to the palace."

Terro's eyes were growing dangerously wide, and his words seemed to require unusual effort. "I...we could..."

Nala reached for his hand, her smile too brilliant to suppress. "Thank you, my lord."

Kayvin nodded, and the warmth in his chest flared again. Nala's status would be secured, and her husband established. He could make a difference for them with just a few words.

Nala knelt, and Terro followed her example. "Thank you, Your Highness," she said. "That was not my intent in bringing you here, and—"

"I know," Kayvin said. "But they are exquisite, and once I had seen them, I could not leave without my own. Please, stand. I'd love to try that tea."

"Of course! I am so sorry—I started a berry sweetcake, but there wasn't time to finish it before you arrived."

As Nala poured, Dielo slipped from his seat and went around the chairs to stand beside Terro, and the two removed themselves a few steps from the group. Kayvin was grateful; a virilo could handle the inconvenient details of payment without troubling his master, who in this case was unsure of the protocol. He knew how to pay his own way only when he was a nameless nobody in the human lands. There was a good jest in that, if he had time to think on it.

Once the payment was agreed and promised, and the tea finished, Kayvin took his leave. The oxcart waiting outside had been additionally furnished with more pigment for the two oxen and more ribbons for both oxen and cart. As Kayvin mounted the cart, the crowd gathered around, and someone began playing a drum. When the cart started, many moved with it, calling encouragement or praise. Nala and Terro, arm in arm, waved and shouted with the others.

They had not gone far beyond the village when a dark line appeared on the road before them. Yovela put a worried hand on Kayvin's arm, and he straightened to squint through the distance.

Armed men. Dozens, or perhaps hundreds, he wasn't good at estimating. Too many.

If Lord Scallong had determined to dispose of Kayvin and seize the Bull Throne for himself, this was where it would happen.

CHAPTER 134

THE VILLAGERS BEGAN TO slow and fall away, their laughter fading. Minera looked over her shoulder. "My lord, what shall I do?"

He did not want to put her at risk, but turning back might trigger a rushed attack on all the villagers. "Keep going. When we're nearer, I'll go ahead."

The opposing line was formed of armored soldiers, with a scattering of officers in colored sashes and then three courtiers in stylized war costume, with gilded armor and brightly colored capes. Kayvin felt pitifully under-dressed. "Stop here."

He got out of the cart, unsure of what to say. He should stride confidently forward, suggesting he was master even on foot against their horses, but his legs were too stiff for such an attempt.

But then one figure saluted, and Kayvin's heart warmed as he recognized Harrith, so lately sworn to him. "My lord," Harrith said firmly, "we have come to meet you and escort you home."

Even with Harrith's presence, Kayvin was not so foolish as to believe he was being welcomed. The soldiers could be equally an honor guard or an attacking force, and the courtiers gave the encounter an air of interrogation. Kayvin thought he had met all three two days before—could it be only two days? How was that possible?—but he recalled the greetings as merely ceremonial, without real allegiance or affection.

He straightened as if his joints were not watery with exhaustion and fear, and he said, "I thank you. It has been a long day and a longer one before that."

The nearest lord nudged his horse forward and approached Kayvin without dismounting. Kayvin frowned and lifted his chin, giving himself time to scan his memory for a name. "Lord Malvin."

Lord Malvin glanced over his shoulder to the other nobles. "We came to see if you conduct yourself as an Arch Potentate," he said bluntly.

Kayvin tried to suppress the curling of his fingers, as if the challenge did not concern him. "That is simple. As I am the Arch Potentate, then however I conduct myself must be the manner of the Arch Potentate." This was a weak argument in the face of the responsibilities and ethics that had long been ignored, but it was the first response he could think of.

Lord Malvin did not seem to think much of the argument, either. "Will you be returning to the palace?"

No honorific was used, Kayvin noted. This was a direct test—no, not a test, for Lord Malvin was not his tutor or father to administer a test. This was a challenge, a bid to exclude Kayvin from the throne he had inherited and the palace he had saved.

Kayvin's mind spun. What should he do? What *could* he do?

"Are you his escort?"

Kayvin half whirled at the sound, and Minera gave him a shy smile before looking back at Lord Malvin. "If you've come to parade him in, I can promise my team will be steady. They may be country oxen, but they've seen a few harvest festivals, and I'll speak for them. Where do you want me to put them?"

Bless her. She did not fully understand the gravity and fragility of the situation, but she was there to offer her oxcart, and she had bought him enough time to remember who he was.

He did not have to scrabble for an immediate answer to placate Lord Malvin. He was the Amethyst Prince. He was the Arch Potentate.

Lord Malvin was staring at Minera, his expression somewhere between amusement and indignation. Kayvin turned and crossed his arms, drawing Malvin's attention back. "How do you propose to escort us in, then?"

Malvin's face tightened as he faced the definitive question of whether he would escort or impede. "Are you sure you wish to return at this time?" he asked. "You left so suddenly, and with such little preparation, and I'm sure the journey has been exhausting."

The other riders drew closer, watching keenly. Kayvin fixed his eyes on Malvin's, clenching his muscles against the panic rising in him. "I am on my way to the palace now."

"You might be more comfortable if you spend the night near here," Malvin said. "I will ride ahead and announce you."

It was his condescending smile that undid Kayvin.

Kayvin reached for the reins, grasping them together about a hand-span behind the heavy bit. "I'd prefer you travel with us, my lord."

Lord Malvin drew his rein hand back, pulling against Kayvin's grip. Then he leaned forward from the saddle, his face set in a sneer. "Do you really think you have control here?" he asked quietly. Then he spurred his horse hard.

The horse squealed and jumped, startled by pain, and lunged out of Kayvin's hold. Malvin jerked the reins to his chest to bring the horse back to a halt—and the leather snapped, charred ends slapping back against him. The horse bolted and Malvin fell backward, snatching at the useless reins for balance in an open display of inferior horsemanship. Three strides later he was grasping desperately at the saddle as he slid to one side, accidentally raking the horse again with his spurs as he clutched for safety. The horse gave a small buck as it ran, and that was enough to dump the lord unceremoniously on the road.

Kayvin turned from the fallen noble to the others, staring in surprise. Before they could speak he opened, "I may not be fully master of this situation, no, and I admit that. But be careful in your assumption that you are."

They looked at him, resentful but without an immediate retort.

"Which of you is reporting for Scallong?" Kayvin demanded.

They each frowned, pursed lips, started to answer, and then looked suddenly at the other with irritated surprise.

Kayvin nodded as if he'd expected this. "Each of you thought he was a particular trusted favorite, and see how trustworthy that was." He hoped he was reading those expressions correctly. He hoped at least they were as suspicious as he was becoming. "You may think about your allegiances on our way."

He turned and walked, head up, to the oxcart. "Let's go, Minera, if you please. Send Arrow and Bow on our way."

"Are you sure you wouldn't prefer a horse, my lord?" Minera asked in a low voice.

Kayvin looked at Lord Malvin's mount, trotting riderless up the road with head high as a man jogged after it. "I don't think so. That one lacks a complete bridle, for one thing."

She laughed. "Thank you for letting us carry you."

"Thank you for being a trustworthy driver."

The cart drew near the soldiers. "They'll make way for us, won't they?" Minera asked.

Yovela put her hand into Kayvin's and squeezed it.

Dielo stood in the cart, swaying a little, and faced forward. He began an old song, a song of planting in expectation of summer, his face to the sky. He had sung only a few bars before voices joined him as the villagers moved about the cart. Those nearest put a hand on the cart, and those who could not reach put a hand on those who could, and the movement and song rippled outward.

Kayvin did not think they were prepared to fight for him. He wasn't sure they understood the precariousness of his position or even that he was not assuredly a prince. The soldiers had made no open signs of deterrence. Still, the movement and song filled him with a curiously uncomfortable warmth, and his chest was tight around his breath.

The soldiers stood in place. Minera spoke to the oxen, and they moved forward steadily. Bow gave a little irritated shake of his head.

Kayvin held his breath. The oxen could push though a line of men, until the men used their spears. Or, if physical obstruction became violence, the villagers would be harmed, and Minera... He should never have left Scallong in the palace while he went out into the countryside alone. But what else could he have done?

The song rose. Bow tossed his head, rippling the streamers on his horns. The soldiers shuffled and then moved back, parting before the cart. Then one stretched a hand toward the villagers, fingers reaching for a shoulder or arm, and he began to sing with them.

Kayvin's heart leaped and for a moment he couldn't inhale. More soldiers fell into place around the cart, and Kayvin saw a captain's plumed helmet at the outer edge, walking near the front of the line.

The two nobles still mounted nudged their horses into place, moving with the throng. Behind them, Lord Malvin walked on foot, scowling.

The two nobles on horseback tried to move near the cart, but the common crowd was too close and too thick, and they could not get nearer than a dozen paces. Kayvin glanced at them—did they mean to reach him to speak further with him? Be seen with him? Warn him? Strike him?—and then faced forward, keeping his chin level and his eyes to the light, grateful for the singing around him.

They would reach the palace, and he would make the next decision there.

Chapter 135

They approached the city gates with cheers and song and waving scarves. Arrow and Bow plodded steadily forward, trailing streaming cloth from horns and harness, and the accompanying soldiers—an escort now, even if unplanned—pressed into formation to pass through the narrower gate. Inside, citizens turned and gathered at the curious noise and then the curious sight, and they began to follow, questioning the villagers and joining in the excitement, eager to see the prince's triumphant return.

"What happened? Where had he gone?"

"He sang the beasts out! He led them out of the cities and towns, and he sang them away!"

The crowd grew, and Arrow and Bow lifted their heads and snorted as the singing and dancing closed about them. Soon the soldiers were pushing through the clinging throng, so that they were opening a path for the oxcart as well as themselves.

Kayvin's chest closed, making his breath difficult. He had never had so many people acknowledge him—cheer him—and he knew this was a decisive moment. Without intending to, he had entered the city in a display of popular power. He might almost be a conquering Arch Potentate returning to his adoring capital.

Long ago, the Arch Potentates had ridden oxcarts in parades to display their captives and trophies en route to their palaces...

One of the accompanying nobles leaped off his nervously jigging horse and pushed fiercely through the crowd, jabbing elbows to force a path to the cart. Kayvin watched warily as he swung up into the bed, and Yovela stepped forward as if to block his path.

But the man bowed. "My lord, please let me speak."

Kayvin did not know if he was wise or fearful to watch warily for a sudden knife. "If it is to speak, yes."

"I am Insmel, vassal-sworn to Lord Brennit."

"And eyes for Lord Scallong," Kayvin suggested.

He had the grace to look slightly abashed. "Yes, that too. But even Lord Brennit knows to pay honor to Lord Scallong, and it is not outside my allegiance to tell another lord what I have seen."

"Perhaps not. What is it you wish to tell me?"

"To ask you, my lord." He lowered his head in another half-bow. "To ask if you mean to take your father's throne, or—even if it is contested."

This was it, then. But it was too plainly spoken even for Kayvin's dull expectations. Surely court intrigue would be traded in more sophisticated words.

"It is my throne by inheritance," he said. "And I have fought to reclaim it. Finally, I have received the greetings and pledges of my court."

"You know there are...there are some who would..."

"If you're trying to tell me there are some who would rather sit on my throne than see me on it, yes, I'd already gathered as much."

"That's not what I meant." Insmel glanced to the side, as if looking for an escape though he had brought himself here. "Many were dissatisfied with a woman as Arch Potentate. They tolerated it only through Lord Fretton's insistence and Lord Scallong's forbearance. There is unrest, and most will be glad of any man who—"

"Stop there." Kayvin spoke almost before realizing it, and then he struggled for words to illuminate what he could only just barely explain. He looked forward, across Minera and the oxen and the noisy street. "Do not follow me because I am not a woman," he warned firmly. "Have you not seen men deceive and fawn, falling upon themselves for favor? They were not more reliable, more loyal, more measured in their decisions than the women who have aided me. No, I will not fix my career on so slight a foundation as form." Kayvin straightened his shoulders and turned to face Insmel. "Follow me if you believe me competent and dedicated, and if you wish to serve me. Follow me if you share my vision for a better Mandoral, not merely restored to our fond legends but newly sculpted for greater service. I mean to improve our land for our people, and you should come with me only if you wish to be a part of that."

Insmel regarded him with a curiously still face. "I am not free to declare allegiance to you, my—"

"Your loyalty to Lord Brennit does not supersede your loyalty to your Arch Potentate."

Insmel caught his breath. "That is so, my lord. Of course."

This was a delicate moment. If Kayvin pressed too hard, he would frighten Insmel back to the safety of his high lord and the established court. If he did not draw him out, he could miss an ally, and he needed all he could get.

They turned, and now the palace gates stood before the oxen's heads. Insmel lifted his hand as if to shade his eyes, but the sight was clear enough in the bright sun.

Arrow and Bow came to a halt, snorting. Beyond their heads Kayvin saw a row of lancers, pikes extended, helmet guards down. Behind them, just visible through the pikes, stood Lord Scallong.

Empty void. Kayvin had thought he might at least make it inside the palace. But now, challenged in the street by Scallong himself, about to be shamed and humiliated in front of even the peasants who had cheered him...

They watched one another, gazes crackling with malice. Kayvin knew he should move first, try to seize some advantage of momentum, but he could not. There would be no advantage, no matter when he struck. Scallong was older, stronger, more practiced, more trained, more skilled, more ruthless. Kayvin had a shelf of books and a handful of useless idealism.

Scallong read all this in Kayvin's eyes, and he grinned.

Minera twisted to look at Kayvin, anxious for instruction, and he shook his head. These guards would not give way before farm oxen, and there would be blood, first animal and then Rideis.

Someone touched his forearm—Yovela or Dielo, but he did not turn his head to see. Whichever it was, they did not embarrass him by holding him back when he moved to the side of the oxcart and stepped over the bars to the ground.

"I thought you'd gone for good," Scallong called as Kayvin walked forward, loud enough for the nearest of the surrounding crowd to hear. "I thought you'd fled the palace with your tail between your legs."

"A curious conclusion, after you'd come to make your obeisance to me," Kayvin retorted just as loudly.

Around them the street quieted, with only the rustling murmur of spectators passing the words backward to those behind them, as if this were a public announcement or a speech. Everything said would be shared. Kayvin wished he'd practiced in rhetoric—or if he couldn't be brilliant and convincing, at least he might have studied the flavor of old theater with rapid witty barbs.

But Scallong had not read the old plays, either. "No, I didn't," he said bluntly. "Why would I pledge to a prince who has hardly been seen in the court since his father died?"

"Because I bested the usurper on my throne and took it back." Kayvin kept his chin level and his eyes fixed on Scallong. Let the onlookers repeat his words for the rest of the crowd; that at least would be known.

"Oh, you fought a woman, well done," Scallong drawled with sarcasm thick enough to taste. "You didn't even kill her. And you fought with magic, didn't you? A coward's weapon, thrown from a distance."

The painful marks on his torso and arms were proof enough of close combat, but that could not easily be explained before their bated-breath audience. Instead Kayvin countered, "I won with my hands on her neck."

This was a mistake, he sensed. This was playing to Scallong's standards, their measures of validity and virility and strength. This was how Kayvin would lose. Yet he did not know what else to do.

"You defeated a woman. How bold." Scallong drew his mouth into a sneer.

"I never saw you fight a sorceress," Kayvin tried desperately. "Not after she killed the Arch Potentate."

"He died of his own carelessness," Scallong said dismissively. "He did not keep his household well-ordered, and he fell to that weakness. A tragedy, but without glory to his murderer."

"Then there should have been nothing to hold your loyal hand from avenging your lord, if you had no fear of her."

Scallong lifted his chin, his expression twisting in derision. "How boldly you speak of your own failures."

Scallong had been uncertain, Kayvin realized. All the politicking and bartering had been real, trading power for influence and future power, but there had been fear, too—fear of the sorceress who had killed the Arch Potentate, and fear of mockery if they killed a woman from a distance, proving their cowardice. They had used her for their own intrigues, and they had despised her, but they had feared her as well.

"Why have you come here, Lord Scallong? Do you mean to put yourself on the throne now?"

"It has not borne a true Arch Potentate since Gromgest's death, and it remains empty now." Scallong's level threat was clear, and Kayvin's gut shivered at the overtness of it. They were beyond intrigue. The removal of Pasiphae Jade had left a gaping opportunity, and Kayvin had left the palace.

"Then if—" Kayvin began.

But Scallong shouted over him. "Come on, if you are so brave and so strong, and show your worth. We have weapons of all forms to hand. Fight me, here and before all, and we will see what crystal the Amethyst Prince is made of."

Empty void, Kayvin thought, and then he could think of nothing. This was impossible; he did not have the training or experience to fight a man like Scallong, who had fully embraced the need to hone his strength and his dueling skills.

It seemed as though all the crowd held their breath along with Kayvin. But they were anxious for him to accept; they believed him capable. They thought he was a true prince, a worthy heir to the Bull Throne, a warrior. They were delighted with his songs for the basilisks, but that was only a trick to save them; the throne required a true champion.

Kayvin gulped for air, and he wanted to protest, but he could not explain. No one in the streets cared that he had wandered through cold Sayinia searching for an amulet to save them; no one murmuring in the crowd had quickened to the tale of his pleading with Pasiphae Jade for the secret to turning back the basilisks. They rose now on their toes, anticipating a bloody duel, and he would fall and disappoint them for the last time.

"All right," he said finally, and it was a concession not only to Scallong but to everything he had been told, all the ways he fell short.

For a moment, for a day, he'd thought it might be different. He had used his magic to fight Pasiphae Jade, and he had used his music to lead away the monsters, and he had used his words to embrace and engage the villagers, Nala, Minera. He had seen Dielo and Yovela smile with pride, more than a sera qadra's due, and he had thought things might be different.

Nothing was ever different.

"Give the boy a sword!" Scallong ordered, wasting no time, and one of the guards ran forward to present his weapon. To the side, nearly behind Kayvin's vision, Yovela shouted something and tried to rush forward, restrained by Dielo's arms about her. Around them all, the sound of the excited crowd grew strangely muted, as Kayvin's hearing began to blur.

"This will do, don't you think?" Scallong gestured to the stretch of grass and flowers along the gate. He walked into the opening between his guards and Kayvin's oxcart.

Kayvin's chest seized and he couldn't breathe—frozen not with fear, or humiliation, but with grief. To have done so much, and at last cared so deeply, and to know in the end he would fail, unable to protect his country from itself... It was all he could do to keep from keening where he stood, hand wrapped about an unfamiliar hilt and waiting to die.

Scallong bared his teeth in a contemptuous grin. "This shouldn't take long, if that's some comfort to you."

It was not. Kayvin lifted the sword and took the first stance he recalled. It was probably wrong.

The ground heaved. A dozen paces to the left and nearly evenly spaced from the combatants, as if to watch the ridiculous duel, a basilisk burst through the surface and reared up—and up. It was larger than the others, much larger, and its eyes glowed with firelit orange. It opened its mouth and screeched in place of song, a harsh, rising note that tore at Kayvin's ears.

He drew back without thinking, unable to look away from the terrible gaze even as the screams began around him. Scallong bolted, rushing into the encircling guards and crowd as if to hide himself among living shields. Kayvin flinched away from the crescendo screech and staggered back, covering his eyes and blindly feeling for shelter.

Something swept his rear leg, and he stumbled backward. Galen—Galen was here?—Galen caught him, steadying him with one arm while extending a sword before them as if to ward off the monster. With his mouth close to Kayvin's ear, pressing him upright, he murmured, "Go and sing to it. Don't be afraid."

"What—"

"Sing to it, like the others. Push me away and go boldly forward to save everyone here. Show them your power."

Galen was mad, clearly. But he was right that Kayvin was the only one here who might at all slow the attack. Kayvin sucked in his breath and shoved Galen, who fell back with greater force than Kayvin had meant to use, windmilling an arm for balance. Kayvin stepped forward.

The creature looked down at him and snarled, teeth bared. This was unlike the others—so much larger, at least twice the size. Was it one of the singers in the mountain?

Kayvin had been prepared to die when he led the hatchlings away from the city. He'd been prepared to die at Scallong's hand. It was silly to hesitate now before a different form of death. He took a long breath to steady his diaphragm, and he began to sing.

He had no instrument, and his mind was wildly unsettled; his pitch was probably wrong. But he sang, and he stepped forward, and he prayed.

The snarl faded, and lips lowered over the pointed teeth. The great basilisk tipped its muzzle down to regard him with curious disdain, and Kayvin jerked his eyes away from it. But he had felt no pull, and his focus had not wavered. Was it somehow not employing its magic?

He kept walking. There was cacophony all around him, cries of warning and terror as the crowd drew back, but he sang. He took another step. The creature lowered its head with a little shake. Kayvin sang, and he raised a hand as if in supplication or invitation. The basilisk tipped its head, a fox listening for a mouse, and then it began to sing along, matching his melody.

For a moment they stood still, their duet rising above the muffled crowd. Kayvin's voice poured through him, more a river of its own destiny than any instrument of his, and the basilisk's followed it spiraling into the sky.

And then the basilisk bent its neck—not a bow, but an acknowledgment—and its song stopped. It turned, long tail threshing the air dangerously over Kayvin's head, and nosed into its hole. With a kick it wriggled down, too quick and lithe for such a massive creature, and its waving tail vanished into the ground.

Kayvin stared at the empty hole. What had... What had happened? He had sung his best, but that should not have been enough to turn back the creature. The hatchlings had followed his song, not been driven away by it.

But behind him, the crowd was beginning to cheer.

Kayvin turned, and they rushed forward. Yovela flung her arms about him, nearly knocking him back, and Dielo embraced them both with wild glee. Around them guards were leaping into the air, pumping their fists with the exhilaration of relief, and townspeople clutched children or each other.

Kayvin looked up and his eyes met Scallong's. The lord stood behind a row of armed men who were now cheering the Amethyst Prince. Scallong wore an expression of baleful resignation. He knew he had lost this duel that had not been fought; Kayvin had truly seized the hearts of all those present with his bold display, and they would spread the word.

Kayvin drew back from Yovela and Dielo, taking their hands instead. He did not care what spectators might think; he needed their support. He raised his voice and said the terrifying words, "Take me to my throne."

The crowd cheered, the armed men formed a path, and his friends drew him along toward the palace.

CHAPTER 136

"WHAT WAS THAT?"

Galen and Lisveth, who had somehow followed Kayvin's oxcart into the palace with Dielo and Yovela, listened to Kayvin's question with perfectly flat expressions. Far too flat for sincerity. "What was what, my lord?" Lisveth asked, nearly curious.

Kayvin did not roll his eyes, but it was a near thing. "At the duel. That basilisk. It wasn't like the others, and Galen knocked my foot out to keep me from backing away from it." He had needed time to realize what had truly transpired, and why Galen had fallen so hard from Kayvin's slight push.

Lisveth shrugged. "Perhaps it was a hatchling from a different brood, or something else entirely."

"I suspect it's something else entirely." Kayvin pointed. "You have made me a liar to my people and a pretender to this—"

"That's not so," Lisveth snapped with sudden ferocity.

"If there was no basilisk, then my performance was a lie."

"Scallong chose a situation for his advantage, where he could use his skill to humiliate and kill you publicly. You bravely met him there. You did not choose the second situation with your advantage, but you showed your own skill anyway, while he fled. Your actions were true in each case."

"But it wasn't real. It was a lie."

Galen shook his head. "Scallong, presenting himself as a superior warrior, could have fought to give the crowd time to flee, but he did not. That was his lie. While he ran to save himself, you stepped forward and sang to protect everyone there, despite your fear. That was no lie."

Kayvin scowled. "I'm not sure anyone else will see it that way."

"It was only partly for them." Lisveth gave Kayvin a hard look.

He looked back at her, seeking something to say. "Empty void," he managed at last.

She chuckled. "A sound argument, that. Well said."

He decided to change the subject. "I don't suppose you two will stay. I have a new court and much that needs to be done."

"Every ruler needs a court sorceress," Lisveth said lightly, "but I want only my ridiculous amount of money, thank you."

"We didn't come here to become courtiers in a foreign nation," Galen added. "We came to prevent an incursion into our own land. And I hope that's what we've done."

"We won't need to flee the hatchlings, anyway, at least not this year. And I intend to put a dozen scholars on those notes to learn what more we can do with those songs. I almost feel there's a new diplomacy to be opened there." That diplomacy was too great to think about yet, but he would assign the scholars first thing in the morning. "I'm sorry to lose you, but I understand. We will wish you safe travels home."

"If you could write us a letter," Lisveth suggested slowly, "from the Rideis head of state to the Octovirate and General Artextra, we may have a warmer welcome, with fewer remonstrances about the borrowing of certain amulets."

Kayvin took on a sober expression. "Those amulets... They were ours."

"That's a conversation I'm not authorized to have, my lord," Lisveth said in a warning tone. "Put an extra line in your letter regarding them."

Kayvin forced a smile. "They are drained now, anyway." He stood and went to his new desk. "How much did Yovela promise you?"

"The coronet of her station."

Kayvin whistled. "That is a grand prize." He took a pen, wet it, and began to write. "But I suppose she will not need it in her new position as people's adviser."

"Adviser? Good for her!" Lisveth grinned.

Kayvin, glad to see they were pleased, lifted the pen. "She backed me into a wall and began to lecture on what she expected of me, and I thought it more expedient to put her in a place to make some of those decisions." He smiled and returned to writing. "It's a start, now that I need an administration."

"What?" Galen asked. "With new courtiers, you mean?"

"The court is not just noble courtiers, and the Arch Potentate cannot personally oversee every part of a complex bureaucracy. Surely there were fractures, both inadvertent and deliberate, since my father's death and during the uneasy interim. I need to know what ministers are reliable and how to restore a functional administration."

Galen frowned. "Can't you...ask them?"

Now it was Kayvin's turn. "What?" He chuckled grimly. "No one will report their own deficiencies."

"No, that's not it, of course. I mean... Well, why don't you call in your new advisers, and we'll work out the wording?"

Dielo was tired.

That wasn't the right word for it. Yes, the last three days had been both exhausting and terrifying, and he wanted to curl into a sleeping pit for three days more to recover. And he'd hardly rested well in the days before, living beneath Pasiphae Jade's anger and hiding the amulet.

Now that they had survived—survived Pasiphae Jade, survived the basilisks, survived Lord Scallong—now he wanted only to sink into his pillows and furs and dream a peaceful court of the Arch Potentate. But they did not have that luxury, not yet. Kayvin was still a new ruler, on tenuous footing, and Dielo knew more of the presentation of an Arch Potentate.

Still, he would take a moment to rest.

Dielo lowered himself to the step beside Kayvin's empty chair, where he had sat as Kayvin received his new lords, and rested his head on his forearms, braced across his knees. Muscles pulled taut across his neck and back, reaching down toward his hips. He needed to stretch, but it seemed too much effort just then.

"I understand the feeling."

He looked up as Yovela slid into a low guest seat. She wore one of her sera qadra gowns, but she'd re-pinned it with two jeweled brooches so that it draped luxuriously rather than tantalizingly. The result was effective and flattering.

"You've done well with that," he said. "I'll need to go to the market to find something more suitable for myself."

"Doesn't it feel odd, still needing to dress for the right court position?" She shook her head. "The prince also had to present himself appropriately, even then. And the lords. I just didn't think I would need to adjust my own wardrobe to match theirs."

Dielo looked at her in faint recollected awe. "Did you really ask the humans to come and free the Shining Gem?"

"I did." Yovela's voice was tighter than it should have been for such a simple answer.

Dielo looked at her. Had she asked them to falsify the death of the Shining Gem? Had she—asked them to free Kayvin however possible?

"Kayvin is trying to change things," Yovela said abruptly. "He doesn't want to be Arch Potentate. He had to be forced onto the throne, and that will help to make him an empathetic ruler."

"It's a fair start, with the bureaucrats."

"He'll do more. I think he liked the idea of the Octovirate. And he's setting up new advisers... He'll make something new."

"But first, he has to fit into the role enough that the court will follow him."

"They'll have to, now. He's the Prince Who Sang." Yovela smiled, small and satisfied.

He watched as she closed her eyes and tipped back her head, an odd pull in his chest. He had been anxious to explain his experience across the mountains to her, and so he had pressed it upon her in the herder's cabin despite their exhaustion. He hadn't understood why it was so important to him that she know, not until she had told him how she had not actually believed he was useless. That whiplash, believing first in her disdain and then in her frustrated faith in him, had gnawed at him all the way back to the capital.

You believed you were worthless for anything else. But if I had believed that, I wouldn't have been upset by the lie.

She had not hated him for his worthlessness; she had been angry at the lies that had manipulated him. He still was grappling with this new revelation.

He rotated on the step and slid toward her chair, reaching to the twisted sash about his waist. "Yovela?" he said softly, almost hoping she would not hear him.

She did. She sat up and opened her eyes. "Yes?"

He held out the small figure of dusky gold in a kilt. "Would you keep this?"

Her eyebrows drew together as she focused on it and recognized it. "Your chit?" Her hand started toward it, and then she arrested the movement and looked at him. "Why me?"

He looked forward and gently chewed his inner lip. "The mistress who brought me into the palace is fallen and imprisoned. I could serve her no longer, even if I wished even had I not stolen my chit."

She nodded, agreeing with the obvious.

"His Illustrious Excellency is giving us new roles. He calls us advisers"—the word was heady, like thick incense—"and there's no need of a chit for that. And—I have an idea."

"Yes?"

"I want to start a clinic. A hospital for those without physicians. I don't think I could learn medicine myself; I haven't much education in that sort of thing, and I'm not sure I have the stomach for it." He chuckled nervously. "But I'm very good at talking to rich men, and I'm close to the new Arch Potentate in an uneasy succession, and I think I could flatter some nervous courtiers into funding a hospital."

She bent her head to look at him, smiling in slight awe. "That's an excellent idea."

He had almost been afraid to say it aloud, in case it was too grand a purpose for him, but now fresh warmth spread through him. "Thank you. I hope it will be helpful."

She nodded again toward the chit. "So why me?" she repeated.

He didn't know how to explain it. "I want you to hold me to what you believe of me."

Her confusion softened, and for a moment she looked sad. And then she nodded, and she turned her palm upward. He dropped the figurine into it, and she closed her fingers over it, hiding it.

He gave a long sigh and closed his eyes. There was an odd relief in consciously releasing the chit, letting its original meaning fade and dedicating himself instead to a different standard, and he almost felt his breath come more easily now. He let his neck relax, and a moment later his shoulder bumped the chair's side. He stayed there. He could rest a few moments.

Something brushed his head, and then again, settling into fingertips against his skin. Yovela's hand drew lightly through his hair and then stroked his head again, releasing little rivulets of ease that ran down him like water and left him leaning more heavily against the chair. He lifted his head slightly, and her fingers passed gently over his forehead and back to his neck, not teasing but affectionate.

Warmth bubbled within him, and for a moment he could not think of any words that could answer her.

He lifted his own hand so that it met hers—not blocking it, not taking it, just brushing in passing. Her hand stilled, and he thought he had destroyed the fragile gleaming moment. Then at last she curled her fingers into his and he breathed again, content.

"We have much to do," she said quietly.

He nodded against her fingers.

She withdrew her hand. "But there will be tomorrow, and the next day."

"Are you looking forward to them?"

When he looked at her, she nodded. "Yes."

CHAPTER 137

THE ARCH POTENTATE'S ORDER went out the next morning. The first five levels of ministry bureaucracy—the court ministers themselves, their immediate subordinates, the overseers beneath them, the managers, the chief bookkeepers—were summoned to the greatest courtyard in the palace, softly lit in the slanting morning sun. They were each provided with a writing desk, paper, pen and ink, and a cushion for the courtyard's tiles.

Kayvin faced them once they were arranged, with the court ministers in the front and center, comfortable upon fine tasseled pillows, and the ranks of bureaucrats arrayed behind and around them. They had worn their robes of office, appropriate for a royal summons, and so together they looked like a colorful design in fabric over the tessellated tiles.

"Thank you for coming, and thank you for your service to this land. Today I ask you to help me restore the often-unseen underpinnings to the Bull Throne, the essential foundation of our administration. I rely upon you as our land relies upon this administration.

"Please write the names of one or more public servants who has held steady to their duty and performed their role steadily despite all, with a short description of their exemplary work. No one may submit their own name; I ask each of you to speak for each other, as you know your own colleagues' work best. These responses will be collated, and the most deserving will be rewarded appropriately.

"If you raise your hand, a servant will come to provide water or juice, fruit or nuts, more ink or paper. As needed, you will be escorted to a privy, and escorted in return. If you remain working through the day, meals will be brought to you, as I expect the most senior of you will know which of your staff have been the most dedicated, and it may take some time to list all the deserving. These lists will be reviewed and tabulated by those without any connection to your ministries, without prejudice as we learn which names are mentioned most frequently." And, he left in the unspoken breath, with little fear of retribution for a name unlisted.

There was a ripple in the lines of seated men, none quite looking at one another. Kayvin nodded and continued, gesturing to a new influx of servants, "These maids are distributing hats against the rising sun, for your comfort, and you will notice also the light fabric draping on sides and back. This will ensure your privacy as you work, preventing anyone from attempting to influence or threaten you with a warning glance. Your writing is your own."

It was not a perfect system, but it was a good one. Without a chance for prior collusion, clerics could not easily barter or blackmail names into placement. Without the ability to put oneself forward, there was no temptation to belittle the work of others to advance one's own record.

"Thank you all for your efforts on behalf of the nation and your service to the Bull Throne. I look forward to seeing your recommendations." This was true; he knew an autocrat could not manage an entire country, and he would be glad of competent help.

He turned back to the portico opening upon the courtyard and went into the palace. Inside, Yovela and Dielo were sharing a scroll on a table. He was in loose sleeves and billowing trousers, and she wore an elegant sheath of fabric and a wrapped scarf that trailed down her back. Kayvin liked the change, he thought. Dielo must have been a whirlwind through the textile market, to have dressed them both in their new stations so quickly.

They did not have the expertise he needed—but they knew this, and they were anxious to learn. What they had, at least as valuable, was commitment to repairing and improving the damaged edifice of their history, now a propped-up facade but ready for renovation.

"Where are Galen and Lisveth?" he asked.

Dielo straightened. "They said they would go this morning, after you'd begun the assessments. They may be packing."

"They don't have much to pack," Yovela pointed out.

"Only coins and jewels," Kayvin offered with a laugh. He turned. "Arad! Could you find Lisveth and Galen for me, please?"

He wouldn't mind if the two humans stayed, human as they were. Their support had been invaluable, impossible to overstate—and it was nice to have someone who argued he was capable.

"My lord." This was Galen, entering with an awkward bow, as if the motion were still new to him. Beside him, Lisveth swept a more practiced curtsy.

Kayvin faced them. "I have much to do, and a very tenuous seat from which to do it. Are you sure I cannot induce you to stay? I'm doing my best to freshen the court, and I could find a place for you."

Lisveth shook her head. "This was your objective, prince, not ours. We're happy to have helped you to it, but that was all we ever wanted of it."

Kayvin crossed his arms. "And what is your objective, then?"

Lisveth's eyes flickered down and returned. "I didn't know it, but apparently I wanted to stop an avalanche. And now I have."

Kayvin raised an eyebrow. "And are you satisfied?"

"I'll need some time to think on it." She turned to Galen, clearly shifting the conversation to him. "What about you, farm boy?"

Galen compressed his lips and then said, "I'll think about it. But I don't think it was to join a foreign court."

"Not foreign," Kayvin said. "You may return to the capital at any time, and I hope you do. I've ordered letters to make you honorary citizens of Mandoral."

"Without tax obligations, I hope?" Lisveth asked, and they all laughed.

"Not on your current reward, at least. But I'd appreciate it if you also would carry my letter to the Octovirate, informing them of the new Arch Potentate and requesting an established relation between our courts." Kayvin held out his hands. "I cannot thank you enough. You have been my favorite adversaries, and I have respected you even when we were opposed—all but for the time when Lisveth made me believe a chicken bone was the amulet I needed."

Lisveth shook her head. "It was the amulet all the while, and you only thought it was a chicken bone."

"You—" Kayvin clamped his jaw and scowled. "Get out, then."

Yovela embraced them, whispering thanks of her own, and they bowed, and they left, two humans on foot with worn boots and a fortune in jewels.

It was an odd leavetaking; Kayvin did not know them well as friends—did not know what they preferred for a soup or a sweet treat, or how the two had met, or what their favorite songs were—but he felt for them as he imagined surviving soldiers must feel for their surviving comrades.

But they were going back to Sayinia, and he had a kingdom to rebuild. He turned and joined Dielo and Yovela at the table.

CHAPTER 139

IT FELT A LITTLE strange to be walking toward the mountains again. But this time there were no monsters with piercing gazes, and this time there was no dragon in the sky, and this time they could go as slowly as they liked. Galen let his head fall back and closed his eyes against the warm sun.

Lisveth had said, rightly, that Kayvin's wish had been fulfilled when they diverted the hatchlings, and it had earned him the throne at the same time. Kayvin had asked what their wishes were, and Lisveth had answered that she had been glad of the opportunity to help both nations—and to accept the promised payment, even delivered in coins rather than the coronet.

Galen had put off the question for himself, and now, no longer shielded by the bustle of the palace and warm under the bright sun, he faced it again.

What was it he wanted?

Rather—dared he admit what he wanted?

He was glad to wander with Lisveth, picking up jobs where they could. Some of the jobs were merely work that paid, and some felt as if they were really helping others. Was that enough?

"What are you thinking?"

He glanced down at Lisveth, who scooped breeze-blown hair from her eye and continued, "You are thinking, don't deny it. I can hear the wooden cogs creaking."

He gave a single nod. "I was reflecting how nice it was for Kayvin to have his purpose laid out so clearly. He never had to wonder what he should be doing."

"Nice?" Lisveth snorted. "I'm sure he would have preferred a duller life with a less-clear purpose. When the house is on fire, it's clear you should be running inside to rescue the baby, but you might prefer overall to have a garden, a book, and the mild question of whether to plant more potatoes or paint the shed."

"Plant more potatoes," Galen answered readily. "More potatoes is nearly always the answer."

"You're probably right, and yet you miss the point entirely."

He sighed. "I see your point. Kayvin's purpose was clear because of crisis." He rolled his head back again. "But then I think with a little crisis, which I feel we've had, I should have at least some purpose, yes?"

"Purpose is a very grand word. Maybe it's better suited for princes than for farm boys."

"That's fine talk from someone who just risked her life in several ways for people who will never know her and whom she doesn't even much like."

"It's good to keep one's circle of friends small. Helps to keep secrets safe and tables cozy." But Lisveth gave him a concerned look. "You did good here, too. Is that what you wanted?"

He wasn't sure of what he wanted. That was the problem. He'd thought he'd been content to drift, waiting for something to change, and now that he had watched others achieve their changes, he worried for his own.

But did he want something more enough to risk what he had?

"Maybe we can't always get what we want." Lisveth examined a cloud, her tone neutral. "But I can live with some of these successes." She glanced back at him. "I didn't have the chance to ask you what you did to the prince."

"What?"

"To make him angry enough to use the fire. What did you do?"

A malicious glee rose in Galen. "I told him a story."

"You what? You mean he got to hear one of your stories, and I never have?"

"Well, it was more of a lie," Galen amended. "Not much for narrative."

"Still." Lisveth shook her head. "What did I miss?"

"You were dead, for one thing. Killed in your sleep by Rideis bandits."

"What a dreadful story. Unbelievable. It's a wonder he fell for it."

Galen laughed, but it didn't reach his core.

He walked up the road, and he thought about what he had confessed to Kayvin in his lies.

He clenched his jaw, tightened his fists, bit his lip. Finally he sighed, stretched his arms overhead, and then settled into his stride. "Once upon a time," he began slowly.

"Oh?" Lisveth's eyes shone. "Are you finally going to tell me a story?"

"Hush, or you'll talk right through it. Once upon a time, there was a beautiful young sorceress. She wielded magic in ways most could not even dream of, and she was kind, and clever, and usually hungry."

Lisveth screwed her mouth into a wary look. "I'm not sure this is a good story."

"Don't be so disparaging of my first sharing. So this young woman, clever and beautiful and hungry, kept a secret for many years. I cannot tell you what it was—it was a secret, after all—but it made her believe that she needed to fight dragons just to walk among society. And she never let anyone tell her otherwise."

Lisveth was no longer smiling, and Galen's gut contracted. But he kept going.

"She had someone to tell her otherwise, but she didn't listen to him. He was a farm boy, mostly good at pushing heavy things or reaching objects on a high shelf."

"I think you're selling him a little short."

"I've just said he was tall, reaching the high shelves. Anyway, she was wrong, because she'd never needed to fight the dragon. She belonged in a temple each time she kissed a gatepost."

Lisveth stared at him, her face hard. To keep speaking under her gaze felt like facing Kayvin's fire.

"Anyway, this tall farm boy hadn't had many hopes or plans when he was at home, and he just took what lessons he could and didn't think he'd have many options when the lessons were done. After he fell in with the sorceress, he still didn't have many hopes or plans, and he just took what jobs he could and punched what needed punching along the way."

Lisveth crossed her arms and nodded. "I see."

"But even the farm boy knew he couldn't do this forever. And when he thought about it, which he didn't do often, he knew in his heart he wanted a home."

"Roots," Lisveth observed, more quietly. "Makes sense for a farm boy, I suppose."

"So when they came into some money, he started to look around, and—"

"Stop." The word came fast and hard. Lisveth drew her mouth into a tight little circle, and then she continued, "You were right, that was a terrible little story."

Galen shrank a little.

"The obvious stories are the very worst, and they aren't even stories. Just lectures dressed up. No one wants to be lectured—well, maybe a farm boy trying to get extra classes at a temple school." She shook her head, avoiding his eyes. "If you're a storyteller, don't you have anything better?"

"Are you going to blow some glass for me?"

"Do I have a glass furnace? No. Do you have bellows for lungs? Yes."

"You can't tell me my first story for you is terrible and then demand another one." Galen sniffed ostentatiously, trying to push banter into the dark void that had opened between them "You tell a story, then, if you know so much about it."

"Fine." She sucked in a breath and squeezed her folded arms against her chest. "Once there was a farm boy, who very stupidly fell in with an outlaw girl who didn't deserve him. They wandered together over high roads and hills and even through a mountain tunnel. And in all that, he kept a secret until she demanded one of him, in the dark of night. And when at last he confessed, it was not a secret to be addressed in the midst of saving their country from an invading horde and sneaking into another country to assist a coup."

They had said nothing at all of it since that night. Galen had, somewhere deep within, decided Lisveth was pretending it had never happened, thinking it kinder than rejection as they continued together. But if she brought it up now, only after stopping his gentle query about a home...

He quickly deflected. "Is it a coup if it's the prince?"

"Princes can lead coups, sure. A coup is about how it's done."

"You mean, putting himself in mortal danger to save his people without wanting to take the throne?"

"All right, you may have a point about this particular case. But let me tell my story."

Galen fell silent and waited, his breath tight in his throat.

"The girl had been sure that no one... She had to fight a dragon or stop a landslide. In this job that wasn't a coup, she managed to do those things, and then...she didn't feel very different. She was glad to have done them, of course, very glad—but they didn't make her feel wiser or cleaner."

Galen couldn't decide whether to shake his head or nod. He stared at the road.

Lisveth kept walking, but her pace slowed. "She'd accomplished her dreams of wealth and heroism, and she no longer had the excuse to put off the farm boy in case they died. She had only her own mind to judge."

"In case they died?" Galen echoed. "Shouldn't they have made the most of their time, if that was going to happen?"

"All right, if you know so much about it, you tell the next part." Lisveth looked straight ahead as she walked. "What would the farm boy do?"

Galen's heart sank. *He would spend some time sad, mostly out of her sight, and then he would go on with her for all the same reasons he had done so far. He would trust her not to shame him about it, because she wouldn't, because he wouldn't have wanted someone with that kind of character.*

But aloud he said, his voice a little shaky with honesty, "He'd want a home."

Lisveth hugged her arms to her chest. "Go on with your story, then."

Galen would have held his breath if he could have done so while speaking. "So when they came into money, he thought he might want to buy one. A house, anyway, which could be made into a home."

Lisveth's pace had slowed to nearly a crawl. "And did he go alone to this house?"

This was the moment. Galen pushed the words through his tight throat. "Do you want to go with me?"

She stopped, and he saw the weight of his words strike her. She would not be an itinerant any longer; she would live in one place, fixed for the first time in years. She might be known by shopkeepers in town, neighbors, temple congregants.

She might be known.

She said in a low voice, "I won't go back to Atalasu City."

He nodded. "There are a lot of cities. Or towns. Or villages."

"A town, at least. I do like a few luxuries." She chewed her lip. "I can't use my own name, either. Not the full one."

"I could share." Galen held out a hand, palm up, and did not breathe. He thought he might not hear her reply over the pulse in his ears.

Lisveth gnawed her lip a moment longer, and then she said quietly, "I want to be more than a day or two out from all this, to know—to trust that I'm not speaking from giddiness at having survived." She looked worriedly at him. "I trust you more than I trust myself, if that makes sense."

"It mostly does," Galen answered. It hurt—but he did not want her to come only because he had asked too soon. He wanted her to be sure.

And she had not said no.

His hand was still hanging in the air, waiting, and with an embarrassed start he drew it back. Lisveth looked down at it. "You shouldn't keep Heelsbottom either. I won't have any ugly cousins knocking on my door at farmers' hours."

He hadn't thought about it, but she was right; using his own name in a settled place wasn't wise. "What do you suggest for me?"

She frowned. "We'll think of something. No need to settle on it before we cross the mountains."

"That's true." He wondered why the thought of giving up his name felt so slight. He supposed he hadn't been using it much lately; it wasn't a part of him as it had been. He was no longer the anxious boy from the Heel.

"Wait a moment." Lisveth's voice was low and tight as she abruptly tugged his sleeve and drew them both to a stop. "I want to understand you properly."

He looked down at her. "Yes?"

Her face was tight. "Are you saying you want to use your share of the payment to buy a house in a village somewhere?"

"A town, you suggested, but yes." The specificity of *your share* stung a little, suggesting he would be on his own, but he did not address that.

"And you want me to come with you."

"Yes." He thought he'd made that clear. She had seemed to understand.

"And you—and you want me with you."

He stared at her. "Isn't that what I said?"

"Just say it again."

"I want you to come with me, if you will. If you won't, then I'll keep on the road with you."

Her eyes shone, and her voice thickened. "You want me to settle with you—even after everything."

"Fair night, mage girl, especially after everything." Suddenly he understood, and he took her face gently in his hands. "I want to be with you. I want to give you a home, or I want to live on the road with you. But I want to be with my dearest friend, however that must happen."

Tears began to seep down her cheeks, but she was smiling. "I want that, too. Fair night, I want that."

"Even if—"

She seized his head, fingers weaving through his hair, and drew him down to her. The kiss pierced him like lightning, burning his lips and reaching through all of him, calling him to a place he'd never imagined.

She drew back, crying and laughing. "I'm sorry for doubting you. I thought—I thought you were trying to tell me gently that you were leaving."

He shook his head, amazed and a little incredulous. "Haven't I made that clear?"

"It wasn't that I didn't trust you. Just—please believe that." She sniffed.

He pulled her close, their bodies pressed together, arms tight around each other, melding in the center of the empty road. Her hair rose in the breeze to tickle his cheek. She clung to him, breathing hard, fingers wrapped about his torso like grappling hooks, and he pressed his face into her hair, holding her more tightly than ever before.

She trusted him. She trusted him entirely. Of all the spoils of their palace adventure, it was the most precious gem he carried.

"I don't know how to live a normal life," Lisveth said softly, chuckling. "This might be a disaster."

"I wouldn't ask you to change," Galen said, "and it's been a long time since I was a farm boy by trade. But we'll figure something out."

"We can live on our riches for a while, anyway."

"While we set up new lives as elegant diplomats between nations."

They laughed together and slid apart, letting their hands stay linked. Then they turned up the road toward the mountains.

THE EYES OF MANDORAL

The Poet's Eye—*provides protection from magical attack, blue*
The Painter's Eye—*obfuscates, gold*
The Dancer's Eye—*provides protection from physical attack, green*
The Singer's Eye—*enhances perception, red*
The Storyteller's Eye—*aids in healing, orange*
The Player's Eye—*enhances magic, violet*
The Sculptor's Eye—*increases physical strength, opalescent*

Author's Appreciation

I must thank the experts who lent realism and plausibility to particular scenes, including Kristina Smith for her comments on shoulder dystocia during childbirth and Joe Larson for aid with music theory. Any errors are of course my own.

Did you enjoy this book?

If you've enjoyed this story, whether you purchased or borrowed this copy, please leave a review at your favorite retailers or review site. This is really helpful to support a book, and I read every one. Then, please tell a friend who might also like this story!

Next, go to **https://go.lauravab.com/news** to receive free stories immediately as well as sneak peeks, special discounts, advance offers, and more. Enjoy your new books!